D1462171

BOOKS BY TIM MCBAIN & L.T. VARGUS
Casting Shadows Everywhere
The Awake in the Dark series
The Scattered and the Dead series
The Clowns
The Violet Darger series
The Victor Loshak series

THE GIRL IN THE SAND

THE GIRL IN THE SAND

a Violet Darger novel

LT VARGUS & TIM MCBAIN

THE GIRL
IN THE
SAND

PROLOGUE

The city throbs around her. Burning bright all night long.

Emily walks the bustling Strip, thinks about getting home to the kids, tastes that faintest touch of yeast clinging to the place where her tongue meets her throat.

Neon signs shimmer above as always, flashing like strobe lights. The casinos make it plain enough that the party never ends — not in Las Vegas. The lights speak a pulsing language even the drunkest tourist could understand.

And they do.

Mobs of them clutter the sidewalks. Hawaiian shirts. Fanny packs. Fresh faces adorned with gentle expressions. Soft eyes like a cow's, she thinks.

Not like the locals she deals with. The wolves.

She navigates her way through the mob, turning sideways at times to squeeze through gaps in the wall of humanity. Twisting. Weaving. Darting.

Music blares everywhere, and the chatter of the crowd rises to match its volume. Loud enough to make her brain quiver and chime like a rung bell, but she keeps going, keeps going.

And before long the harsh glow falls behind her. The crowd thins. The sound fades.

She checks her phone.

She had told the babysitter, Vanessa, that it'd be an early night, that she'd be home before Austin's bedtime. It's going to be close.

And then it hits.

A block and a half away from the Strip, away from the bustle

1

and the lights and the streams of tourists and degenerates, it hits her how tired she really is. Almost drunk with it.

It always works this way. The stimulation of downtown Vegas provides that little extra sizzle in her head, that drip feed of adrenaline to keep the full brunt of the exhaustion at arm's length. As soon as the sizzle fades, the fatigue washes over her, pulls her under, mutes her tongue and makes her legs shaky beneath her.

The few drinks she had at the end of the night surely didn't help matters. Gabriela would be so pissed if she knew. *Drinking on the job, Emily?*

On the other hand, it was Coors Light. Did the thimbleful of alcohol in that fizzy rocky mountain water even count as a real drink?

In any case, the beers seem to be helping her exhaustion along, feeding the sleepy feeling now that she's away from the crowd. The depressant finally depressing. She thinks of all possible depressions, alcohol is the great depression, no?

Her head grows heavy, eyelids sag, and her motor skills diminish rapidly. Still, she won't be sick tonight, she thinks. That's something. Five silver bullets aren't enough for that.

And, anyway, it could be worse. The girls who work down here tend to get hooked on a variety of pills and powders. She's proud that it's only the drink for her. Same as it was before she got here.

The thought tumbles in her head as it often does during this walk home from work: How did she get here? A Stanford graduate living in the slums of Las Vegas, doing what she does? How did her life lead to this?

She waits at the corner, her neck struggling to hold her head up, eyelids drooping and smudging her vision, refracting everything so it snaps in and out of double.

So she doesn't entirely trust the blurred image of the Don't Walk sign across the street, the one that won't quite hold still, but it's OK. She can watch the cars, watch the other pedestrians.

The light changes, and she falls in with the trickle of foot traffic crossing the way. No problem. She stumbles a little, but it's all good. For now.

Alas, the crowd seems hell-bent on dispersing. The fledgling mob splinters further at each intersection. Within two and a half blocks, she's on her own.

She banks to the right and moves into a residential zone, little adobe houses packed as tightly as possible. Quiet and dark and dead at this hour. Strange that just minutes ago she was encased in a throng of writhing human bodies, fanny packs touching like bumper to bumper traffic, and now she's alone.

The faintest chill in the air grips her around the waist, slides its cold hand past her hip to touch the small of her back. She adjusts her shirt, but it's no help. Cold night. Crisp.

And then she hears it.

The car engine grinds, slowing as it creeps up behind her.

Her skin crawls along the nape of her neck. This doesn't feel right.

The car glides up beside her, engine growling out threats. She can see it out of the corner of her eye. A lurking darkness that matches her pace.

She hears the window retract into the door, the faintest whine and friction, but she keeps her eyes straight ahead, picks up her pace a little.

The driver is going to say something. Something sexual, maybe. Or something menacing, something suggesting violence. Any second now. Isn't he?

Now the engine revs, the guttural whir hitting some higher note, and the car speeds up, passing her.

Not a car, she sees now. A truck. Either way, it moves on.

She takes a deep breath, watches the red of the taillights tint the world with their crimson glow.

Thank Christ.

She feels her abdominal muscles relax, her teeth unclench, her fingernails retract from her palms.

The truck jerks into a driveway four houses up, however, and she stops walking. Waits. Holds her breath.

The machine's movements are somehow aggressive, she thinks. Savage.

She sways a little, some detached part of her finding her fear humorous — the part that tells everyone that of course they're safe, of course nothing bad will happen, that it's childish to be scared.

The driver's side door opens, the truck's cab shielding most of the rising figure from her view and the shadows swirling around what little she could see.

He was looking at her. She could tell that much.

A man. Tall.

And the rest unfolds in slow motion.

He walks around the truck, hands raised in front of him in a disarming gesture that seems odd and out of place in this after-dark scenario. He speaks, but she has retracted into some simpler version of consciousness that is entirely incapable of comprehending language.

Watching. Waiting.

Without thought, her fingers dig in her pocket until they find her phone. She grips it a moment, sweaty fingers clenching the cool plastic shell, but it squirts out of her hand like a fish.

4

The figure draws closer. Closer. Closer.

She blinks. Looks again.

Yes.

The face is familiar. Smiling.

She can't quite place him, but once more the context clues are enough. This is someone she knows. Someone she can trust.

It must be. It must be.

He's close now. Smiling, like he's glad to see her. She knows him, has seen him before.

She never sees the punch. The looping hook that catches her on the side of the jaw and tilts not just her skull but all of reality, snaps the whole world hard to the right.

To her, it's a twitch of his shoulders. A white flash.

And pain.

And she slides along with the tilt, a violent lurch of gravity that pulls the ground right up to meet her. Someone's front yard, or what serves for one here in the desert. A bed of mulch surrounding a feathery mesquite tree.

Her fingers claw at the wood chips. And she's moving. Running. Before she really knows what's happening.

The reality settles in slowly: It was him. He hit her. It had to be him. But why?

Her mind leaps to place him. So many faces in her line of work. They all blend together after a while, become one face, one mask. Featureless and unknowable.

Or maybe she just didn't want to know them anymore.

She veers off to her right as the panicked thoughts gush through her head, stumbling over the curb and spilling onto the asphalt, her steps going choppy as she loses her balance. Again the ground jerks up toward her, smashing into her knees and elbows hard enough to rattle her bones, rough blacktop scraping away swaths of flesh.

And she hears him. Footsteps clattering toward her. Echoes ringing out everywhere.

She scrambles like a panicking squirrel, little jittery gallops that skitter her over the ground and get her to her feet. Her gait wobbles, stutters, sends her on a careening path.

But she's upright, gaining speed, climbing the curb on the other side of the street.

Moving. Moving. Moving.

And then he's on her.

His arms loop around her waist as his chest collides with her back. Her shoulders pitch forward, lifting her feet off the ground, and they float together, weightless and out of control.

He pulls up, rocking back onto his knees, rolling to his left and driving her shoulder-first to the ground with incredible force. Hugging her against him as their hurled bodies swish through a display bed of exotic grass, drifting over another Vegas lawn, wood chips flung everywhere.

They stop at last, her face down with his bulk resting on her legs, and the inertia is overwhelming. Jarring and violent. Like she was just in a car crash.

All is still for a beat. Her chest heaves, breath rushing into the void in her torso.

She feels his body slide up her back, cold and hard and reptilian.

A vicious punch cracks the back of her head, a *thock* sound filling her skull, reverberating, her cranium vibrating like a struck tuning fork. The sound overwhelms reality.

Her consciousness cinches up into something small, all of existence squeezed into a tiny box, a little compartment separated from the rest of the world. Tunnel vision. She looks out of the tiny opening, can just make out a patch of wood chips.

And the ground before her recedes. Wilts into darkness.

CHAPTER 1

The palm trees lining the boulevard whipped in the wind. Violet Darger had seen the massive thunderhead looming in the distance from the plane, and now the storm was closing in on the city. From the air, the mass of clouds had looked as solid as stone. A strange roiling mountain that flashed like a strobe.

She thought she'd feel better once the plane touched down — that the gnawing anticipating in her gut would calm itself — but that wasn't the case. And she knew it wouldn't go away until the question was answered: What was she doing here? Loshak had called and told her she needed to be on the next flight to Las Vegas, but he'd refused to say more than that over the phone.

Her partner was always being cryptic like that, and just now she didn't find it to be the most endearing trait of his. What she couldn't decide was whether Loshak's evasiveness was business as usual, or if he hadn't wanted to say what was going on for a reason.

Her gut had been telling her all along that Loshak had been keeping something from her. Something big. All that crap about coming out to Vegas for some criminology conference she'd never heard of. A pile of horse shit.

And the more she wondered, the louder a single name echoed in her mind, no matter how fiercely she tried to quiet it.

Leonard Stump.

The name of the most-feared serial killer in Darger's lifetime had rooted itself deep in her thoughts, putting out new creeping shoots like some kind of carnivorous plant.

Of course, 5-7 adults were reported missing every day in Las

Vegas — over 200 a month. And that was a number that didn't include potentially double that in unreported cases from marginalized communities, mostly prostitutes. That left a lot of possibilities for their case here, didn't it? It could be anything from a serial murder case *à la* Stump to something on the scale of human trafficking. But thanks to Loshak, she had no idea what she was heading into.

She reached a traffic light at the northern edge of the city, and the land opened up before her. There were no trees here, just low desert scrub and dusty-looking foothills in the distance. After the colored lights and rows of palmettos along the Strip, the landscape here felt barren. Vast and empty. The steel-blue sky cast a grayish light over everything. It leached the color from the world, leaving it pale and bloodless.

Thunder boomed and crackled, sounding like the mountains around her were being cloven by a great hammer. On average, there were only about a dozen rainy days per year in Las Vegas, and naturally she'd arrived to find they were getting hit with their biggest thunderstorm in years. What luck.

The first few drops of rain splatted on the windshield as she steered onto the highway. The cars heading the opposite direction were drenched, wipers on full blast. A bolt of lightning forked against the dark stain of the clouds, and then the storm was on her. A full driving rain that battered against the roof of the car and splashed onto the road.

The downpour itself and the extra wet kicked up by the tires of the cars in front of her made visibility on the road absolute hell. If not for the glow of taillights, she wouldn't have been sure she was still on the road. As it was, the lights looked like glowing orbs hovering over the concrete.

Darger considered pulling onto the shoulder until the storm

had passed. Aside from the fact that she could barely see past the hood of her own car, the amount of water on the road made hydroplaning a real concern. She'd already gone by half a dozen other drivers who'd decided to wait it out. But no. She didn't want even five minutes delay. She was already behind. As if driving through this monsoon wasn't stressful enough.

She wrapped her fingers a little tighter around the steering wheel and fixed her eyes ahead.

The mountains to the west had disappeared behind a veil of mist and clouds and rain. The barren feeling of the desert closed in on her, making her feel cut off from the rest of the world.

Rocketing along at 70 mph, she figured she might as well be the only person left on the planet, but then she changed her mind. She might not be alone at all.

Her eyes shifted to her purse, to the little box within, waiting to be used.

A pregnancy test.

CHAPTER 2

Emily drifts in the black nothing of unconsciousness. Numb. Peaceful. Removed from the reality of her abduction.

Random dream images flit and bob up from the blackness in pulses, painted on the surface of her psyche and erased almost as quickly, gone before they can coalesce into any kind of narrative.

No story. No sound. Just a flicker of pictures fading in and out.

She sinks deeper into the nowhere, into the big nothing. Finds it tranquil. Almost totally still. Not unpleasant.

A woman's voice speaks from somewhere beyond the darkness, interrupts her slumber.

"Probably ought to wake up, you know."

The voice is harsh. A little bitter. Familiar. Emily knows right away that it's Gabriela, even if it takes the conscious part of her mind a moment to grasp this fact.

"Emily. Open your eyes."

Gabby sounds serious. A hard edge to her tone.

Emily tries to obey the order, but her eyelids won't oblige her. She can feel them. The thin flaps of skin that shield her from the real world, the tiny muscles she can't quite command, the lashes all mashed together and unwilling to budge.

Now the smallest quiver of panic worms its way into the nowhere place, breaking up the stillness that seemed so peaceful a moment ago. This is not good.

The first layer of reality invades her brain.

She is sleeping, to some degree dreaming, and she needs to

11

wake up. The realization flares in her head, brightens, and finally settles over her.

Just like that, the nothing shifts from a peaceful void to something hostile. Something holding her against her will. Trapping her in the dark.

Paralyzed.

And her mind focuses on the blackness. The nothingness. Really seeing it instead of drifting in it without thought.

She hears the little snick of Gabriela lighting a cigarette. Can hear the tube of tobacco impeding her friend's words as she speaks again.

"Jesus, Emily. He's going to kill you. Seems like the least you could do is peel open those peepers."

Wait. Why is Gabriela even here? Does that make sense?

She stares into the darkness, but it offers no answers.

She hears the smack of Gabby's lips touching the butt of the cigarette again, the sizzle of the cherry as she inhales, the snuffle of smoke spiraling into her friend's lungs, hesitating for a beat, and then venting like exhaust during a long exhale.

Gabby speaks again:

"Yeah, you're pretty much fucked."

Emily jerks awake, breath rushing to fill her mouth and throat with a ragged gasp.

Pain pulses in her head, little tendrils of current that jolt through the rounded bone at her temple. It makes her eye twitch on that side.

She blinks a few times. Fighting off the hurt. Eyes swiveling in their sockets, trying and failing to make sense of her surroundings.

All she can discern is black with green smears in it. The scent of stale cigarette smoke mixed with some indefinable masculine smell that she can only relate to the odor of a leather belt.

Her chest and shoulders heave, the rhythm of her lungs unsteady. Lurching and jerky like a drummer who can't keep time.

She catches herself at the apex of an inhale. Holds her breath for just a moment to try to help things even out.

Calm down. She needs to calm down.

After another flurry of blinks, the blur of her surroundings slowly sharpens around her. Dark. Foreign.

She sits in the passenger seat of a truck. The glowing dash lights tint the interior pale green.

Rain pelts the windshield. The water beads and drains down the slope.

Looking through the glass, she can only make out shadows. Dark shapes that don't make much sense.

And now the sound of the radio seeps into her consciousness. Deep, compressed voices murmuring on and on. Corporate rock radio based on the cadence and tone of the deejay, but in her panic she can't make out the words. An endless babble. Meaningless.

The truck. The dark. The pain in her skull. None of this makes sense. Some crucial piece of this puzzle is missing.

At last, her head rotates 90 degrees to the left.

The driver's seat next to her is empty. And that's when it all snaps back for her.

The man. The chase. That final blow to her brain stem and everything fading to black.

Her heart lurches in her chest, trying to match the wildness of her breathing.

A fresh wave of panic whittles her thoughts down to primal

urges. Feelings. Smeared images. Simple phrases.

Run. She needs to run.

But somehow she knows she can't.

Why?

She looks down at herself. Sees the ring of plastic circling her ankles. Pinning them together and pulling them taut.

Her wrists are stuck together just the same, fastened behind her back.

Zip ties. Yes. Her hands and feet are bound. Cinched tight. Some part of her knew this. She could feel the ties even before she saw.

She pumps her legs a few times. Tests the strength of the plastic fastening her ankles. Strains muscle and flesh against it, but it's no use. It's secure.

Light glitters in the rearview mirror just then.

Wheeling, gazing through the back windshield.

The glow of the gas station shimmers on the other side of what feels like a narrow sea of asphalt. The building appears small and distant — the pumps even farther — all lit up in the lot on the opposite side.

All that light. So close but out of reach.

The paltry ring of illumination spilling out of the windows and crawling over the ground cannot reach her. The light doesn't even make it halfway over the parking lot.

She takes a breath. Her chest shaking on the inhale.

She knows she doesn't stand a chance.

Even if she manages to get the truck door open with her hands secured the way they are, she'd never make it into the light. Tied up like this, feet bound? Wriggling over the ground like a worm?

Never.

The Girl in the Sand

But she has to try.

She watches for movement in the gas station windows for just a moment. Looking for any signs of life. But there are none. Just static scenes of a beer cooler and a rack of magazines, all those colorful heads and torsos of celebrities on the covers staring back at her.

She skids her shoulders over the back of the seat. Wobbling. Arms poking around behind her like clumsy crab legs.

Fingertips and the heels of her hands skim over the door. Cold and textured. The plastic transitions to a rubbery handle. The joints of her fingers flex over these surfaces, seeking out the small metal door handle, finding it.

Air gulps into her all at once as she grips the handle. It makes her cough twice.

She pulls.

Nothing.

It's locked.

Fuck.

She wrenches her arms up, arcing her elbows out to the sides of her back, but it's no use. She can't reach the lock. Maybe if she dislocated her shoulders, but no.

And he's there. A dark shape on the opposite side of the driver's side window.

The door latch pops as he opens it, and she gasps once more.

It's too late to play dead. Too late to move. Too late to pray.

His torso jerks into the car. A shadow stooping low. Almost touching the floor.

Through the tears she watches him jam an arm under the seat and root around. His hand comes back with a length of metal in it. A pipe or a club of some kind. Metal that seems to just keep spilling out from under the seat.

He speaks, his voice gruff but without malice.

"It's going to be a long drive. Better keep still."

He doesn't hesitate.

His arm raises, draws taut like the string of a bow, snaps the pipe into the side of her head.

It's heavy. Harder than his fist. The momentum rocks her face first into the dashboard.

The pain is enormous, a jolt of white current flowing through all of her.

Hurt. Everywhere.

It surges deep into her eye sockets, the wet of her lungs, the bones of her fingers, the squish of her guts, but just for a second, and then everything gets farther away. Numbed. Confused.

That familiar *thock* sound fills her skull, and all of her consciousness sucks back into that black hole all at once.

CHAPTER 3

The rain was still coming down when Darger turned off the highway. The tires almost sounded resentful as they rolled through a pool of water collecting in a low spot on the road.

She leaned forward, trying to squint through the sheets of rain. The GPS said she was close, but she couldn't see a damn thing out here.

And then she saw the first pulse of red and blue through the mist. Police lights.

She crawled up behind a fire engine and tugged the key from the ignition. The steady beat of the wipers cut out all at once, leaving her in the drowning white noise of pattering rain. It dribbled down on her arm when she opened the door, and she watched the water soak into the sleeve of her jacket. She hadn't brought an umbrella. Who would on a trip to the desert?

Two open-sided police tents had been erected farther up the road. As she approached, Darger could see that a blackened car took up most of the space at one end. A cluster of police and other first responders stood out of the rain at the other. But it was the car that caught Darger's attention.

Her heart started beating a little harder.

Quickening her pace, she veered only slightly from her path to avoid a large puddle of murky water. She was wet enough as it was, the last thing she needed was soggy boots and socks.

She stepped under the shelter of the canopy and flashed her ID at the group of men and women huddled inside, eyes never straying from the burned-out car.

A toxic perfume of scorched plastic, rubber, and automotive

paint hung in the air. It was a sedan, but most of the exterior was so marred and blackened she couldn't place the make or model. Where the paint hadn't been consumed, it was bubbled or flaking off. Anything plastic or glass had melted or broken away — taillights, bumper, logo decals.

She could see where the flames had inched toward the front half of the car, igniting the paint before dying out. It was evident from this detail that the fire had started at the rear of the car. This more or less confirmed what she'd known as soon as she laid eyes on it: the fire had been set intentionally.

A strand of hair clung to the moistness near Darger's temple, and she reached up to brush it away. She wondered where she'd find the courage to step around to the trunk.

The hatch was open, and likely it was practically welded that way now from the heat of the fire. She had a feeling what she'd find inside, but she wasn't ready. No one was ever truly ready to see such things.

Another few seconds ticked by while she pulled on a pair of gloves, and then it was time. She couldn't put it off any longer.

She took a deep breath through her mouth, trying to avoid the lingering smell of smoke and char. Instead, she tasted notes of scorched upholstery on her tongue. So much for that idea.

Careful to keep her boots out of the blackened bits of debris all over, she crept toward the rear end of the car.

A new odor joined the mix as she moved closer to the trunk — something that somehow registered as sweet, sour, and savory all at once.

When Darger was in middle school, she'd once forgotten a pan of Chef Boyardee ravioli heating on the stove. By the time the smoke filtered into her bedroom, there was a good one-inch-thick layer of pasta and sauce burned onto the bottom of the pan. The smell was awful, with a bitter note that reminded her of vomit.

The memory of that stink came to her now, as she leaned forward to gaze into the gaping maw of the trunk.

There were two bodies, small and shriveled. Both were curled into a fetal position, hands together as if in prayer, though she knew it was more than likely that their wrists had been bound. The flesh of the lips had burned away, leaving the teeth exposed in a permanent grimace. One mouth stretched open, frozen in a silent scream.

Darger swallowed, feeling hot and sick. She took a few steps back, eager to put even a small distance between her and the car and the burned up young women inside. The fact that the victims were female was another detail she didn't need anyone to tell her.

The nitrile gloves clung to the moistness on her palms, snapping like rubber bands when they finally came free. She stuffed them in her pocket and dragged the back of her knuckles through the perspiration on her forehead.

Closing her eyes, photographs from the old Leonard Stump crime scenes flashed in her mind. The scene here was nearly identical. Two bodies curled in the trunk, burned beyond recognition. Could it really be him?

When her eyelids rolled open, she caught sight of her partner crossing the tent to meet her.

Loshak stopped when he drew even with her and took in the rain-spattered jacket and stringy hair.

"No umbrella?"

Darger met his eyes. "What tipped you off?"

He smirked, but there was a tension in the line of his mouth that didn't quite go away.

"What the hell is this, Loshak?"

Loshak glanced over his shoulder, ensuring no one was within earshot.

"I know you have a million questions, and I promise I'll explain everything. But right now, I need you to do me a favor and not mention Leonard Stump."

Darger blinked, trying to make sense of the words. After all this, he wanted her to *not* talk about Stump?

"Fuck that, Loshak. I want to know what's going on."

"I told you—"

Before he could say more, one of the uniformed men broke off from the nearby huddle.

"You must be Agent Darger," the man said, thrusting a hand at her. "Assistant Sheriff Wayne Corby. Pleased to meet you."

He had big, fleshy sausage fingers, and Darger watched her own hand disappear in his fist when they shook.

"I've seen a lot of shit in my time, but never anything quite as grisly as this." He paused to adjust his belt, hiking it a little higher on his waist. "I imagine you two are privy to some things in your travels. Ever seen anything like it?"

Darger's gaze flicked over to Loshak, who gave an almost imperceptible head shake. Again, warning her off mentioning Stump. Why the hell was he being so cagey?

"Only in pictures," she said, not willing to lie outright. Her eyes fell back on the blackened remains in the trunk. "And I'd say they didn't quite do the horror of it justice."

"It's the smell I can't get over," Corby said. "I'm the grill master in the family. Come Saturday afternoon, I'm on the back patio with an ice cold beer in one hand and a pair of kitchen tongs in the other."

He pantomimed clutching each item in his meaty digits.

"But after this…" the man paused and shook his head. "Well, it's gonna be a while before I can stomach firing up the grill. Let alone eating the, uh, meat."

Not wanting to linger on the topic of chargrilled animal flesh, Darger pushed on.

"Do we know who the victims are? Or who the car belongs to?"

"Nothing on the car, yet. VIN numbers are obliterated, but the lab guys tell me they have some tricks. We're gonna have a hell of a time IDing the bodies with the state they're in, but we'll do our damnedest. Figure it'll come down to dental records, most likely. The medical examiner is waiting on the bodies as we speak. As soon as I give the word, they'll start packing things up here. I think we're set on our end, but if you need more time with the scene…"

With a wordless exchange, she and Loshak agreed that they were finished.

"We're good," Loshak said.

Corby nodded once. "Myself and the lead investigators are meeting back at my office in a few hours. We'd appreciate any insight you could bring to the table."

"We'll be there," Loshak said.

With that, they turned to leave. Even though the rain had slowed to a sprinkle, Loshak produced an umbrella and insisted on walking Darger to her car. When they reached her rented Taurus, she rounded on him.

"What the fuck was that? If this is Stump, then they have a right to know who they're dealing with," she said.

Loshak glanced back at the tent.

"Not here."

With a growl, Darger slammed the door and started the car.

CHAPTER 4

Darger spent the entire drive back to the city stewing in damp clothes and a sense of righteous indignation. He'd done it again. Loshak — the man who was supposed to be her partner — had left her out again.

And not just her. He hadn't wanted her to mention Leonard Stump near the local cops. Why? She went over it again, trying to give him the benefit of the doubt. He'd waited until she'd taken in the crime scene before mentioning Stump. Maybe he hadn't wanted to cloud her objectivity. But after one look at that car, her objectivity had flown out the window.

So he could have been trying to keep her from jumping to conclusions. That was fair, she supposed. She wasn't being clear-headed about this. Stump had entered her mind as soon as she stepped foot on that scene.

But then why had Loshak run out here on his own? What had he been up to before this double murder landed in his lap? He'd known something.

The radio was on in the background, two DJs arguing about the college football playoff selections. Darger jabbed at the volume knob, thrusting the car into silence.

Whatever was going on here, the fact remained that Loshak obviously didn't trust her.

Her mind flashed to Ohio, back to their first case together. Loshak had been sick, but refused to see a doctor, lied to her about just how ill he was. He'd almost died because of it.

She'd thought things had changed since then. That they'd grown to trust one another. But now here they were, back at square one with Loshak keeping secrets. Running off to do things on his own.

By the time she changed into dry clothes and went downstairs to meet Loshak in the lounge of their hotel, she was practically steaming with fury.

He must have seen it on her face. Before she even sat down, he was trying to smooth things over. He pulled a manila folder from his lap.

"I've got something for you. Fresh out of the hotel office laser printer. Still warm, even."

This was classic Loshak. Holding back key information. Keeping her in the dark until he decided it was time to let her in. Then he'd wave some juicy bit of info in front of her, knowing her innate curiosity always got the better of her. Well, not this time.

"Oh no, you don't. I've got something for *you*." She tossed her phone down on the table in front of him.

"What's this?"

"That," she said, pointing at the text on the screen, "is the Merriam-Webster's Dictionary definition of the word *partner*. I thought you might need a refresher. Would you care to read it aloud?"

As usual, he seemed unruffled by her outburst. He only sniffed and looked away from the phone.

"No, thanks."

This only irritated her more. She snatched the phone from the table and started reading.

"*Partner: one that shares. One associated with another, especially in action.* Oh, here. I like this one. *One of two or more persons who play together in a game against an opposing side.*"

"Enough," Loshak interrupted. "You're pissed. I get it."

He picked up the manila folder again and waved it at her.

"That's why I'm trying to give you this. To bring you up to speed."

"See, I don't think you actually do get it. You lied to me about why you were coming out here. And it's not just about this case. It's about all of them. Ohio, Washington, Georgia. This isn't an isolated incident. This is a pattern where you keep all the cards to yourself. And then, when you've decided you'll let me play, you parcel out what you're willing to give. And that's usually only because you have some errand you want me to run. I'm not your fucking assistant."

He was still wearing the mask of nonchalance, but underneath it, Darger thought she could see something else. A fierceness in his gaze.

"Are you done?"

She stared back at him, gritting her molars together. She knew what he meant, but just now she had an urge to be melodramatic. Anything to rattle that unflappable expression he was wearing.

"Maybe I am."

His eyebrows finally twitched.

"What does that mean?"

She shrugged.

"You're gonna quit, then? Go back to teaching deep breathing exercises in OVA? If the Bureau would even let you, that is."

She shook her head, not quite able to believe he could be such an asshole. At least not to her.

"Best of luck to you," she said, scooping her phone from the table and rising to her feet.

When she reached the doorway of the lounge, she didn't

look back.

CHAPTER 5

Darger flopped onto the hard hotel mattress and glared up at the ceiling. Loshak's words repeated in her head.

Go back to teaching deep breathing exercises, if they'll even let you.

Dickhead.

But he wasn't wrong. She didn't know where she'd go at this point if she left her current position. She seemed to have a knack for losing the few friends she had in the FBI.

And leaving was the last thing she really wanted. Darger had never been the quitting type.

Her eyes wandered over to her purse, and she remembered the rectangular package inside. She sighed. Might as well get it over with.

But just as her fingers wrapped around the pregnancy test and slid it free, a musical jingle spurted out of her phone. She glanced at the screen, saw it was Owen, and winced.

"Hey," she answered.

"You never called me back."

"I know," she said, staring at the fuchsia box still clutched in her hand.

She hadn't told him about her missed period yet. Figured she might as well be certain before she dragged someone else into the mess. Still, she felt guilty about it. Like she was keeping secrets.

"I had to rush to make a flight, and then I forgot. I'm sorry."

"So I'm assuming you're now in some exotic locale?"

Darger's eyes flitted to the window, catching a glimpse of the glittering lights of the Strip in the distance.

"Does Las Vegas count as exotic?"

"What's in Vegas?"

Darger sat up, eyes roaming the flowered wallpaper border while she considered how she should answer. Owen would worry if he knew this was about Stump. He'd been there when she opened the letter and hadn't stopped worrying since.

But he must have made the connection on his own.

"Does this have to do with Stump?"

"I don't know. It might."

No one had seen or heard from Leonard Stump since he'd escaped from a Carson City courthouse twenty years ago, after his first string of murders. It was one of the biggest unsolved mysteries of the last century, right up there with D.B. Cooper and Jimmy Hoffa.

True crime message boards on the internet were rife with theories: He lived in a remote cabin somewhere in the wilderness of Canada or Alaska. He'd gone to Mexico for radical plastic surgery and now sold life insurance in Fort Lauderdale. Many were convinced he was dead.

Even Darger might have entertained this last hypothesis up until a few months ago, when she received a letter signed by Leonard Stump. The FBI document lab analyzed the handwriting — comparing it to Stump's jailhouse diary — and told her what she already knew: the letter was either authentic or an expert-level forgery.

I get the feeling, just now, that our paths may cross again. Perhaps soon, he'd written.

And now it looked like he was making good on his promise. Two female victims found burned in a car was textbook Stump.

Owen's voice was tense. "I don't like this, Violet."

"No? I love it. Popping a trunk and finding two burned up bodies inside? Good times."

"Jesus."

"Yeah," she said, dropping the sarcastic tone. "Have you ever seen pictures of Pompeii? The plaster casts of the bodies?"

"That's the volcano in Italy, right? I've seen photos, yeah."

"That's what the bodies reminded me of. The way they were huddled in that trunk. All curled up."

Darger shook her head, trying to shake the images loose. When that didn't work, she let herself fall backward until she was lying flat again.

"Anyway, it's probably all moot at this point. I think I'm off the case."

"What happened?"

"Loshak and I got into an argument. I may or may not have been a little overly dramatic."

"How so?"

"Threatened to quit and then stormed out."

"He knows you don't mean it. It'll blow over."

She pressed a fist against her forehead. "Maybe I did mean it."

"Seriously?" Owen asked. "You'd leave the FBI?"

"I don't know. He lied to me about why he was coming out here in the first place. I'm sick of getting jerked around. "

"I'm sure he has his reasons."

"He always does," she said. "Know anyone looking to hire a loose cannon criminal psychologist?"

"As a matter of fact, I know of a very talented PI firm that might be able to make use of your skills."

She scoffed. "Yeah, I know the kind of skills you have in mind."

"You make it sound as if I'm suggesting something untoward, Miss Darger."

She smiled at the old nickname.

"That's because I know you. There'd be fine print in the job description that requires me to work in the nude."

"Please. This is a legitimate operation I'm running here. I'd provide a uniform."

"What kind of uniform?"

"Well, I was thinking one of those little French maid outfits."

She rolled her eyes but couldn't keep herself from grinning.

"Pass."

Over the line, she heard the clack of lightning fast drums and a heavy distorted guitar.

"What are you working on right now?"

"How do you know I'm working?"

"Because I can hear the music in the background. You always listen to metal when you're on surveillance."

"Then you answered your own question right there, didn't you? I'm on surveillance."

"Well, what's happening?"

"Nothing at the moment. I'm just sitting in my car waiting for the subject to come out of the house."

"Who's the subject?"

"I can't really talk about it."

Darger chuckled. "Cheating husband?"

"No."

"Cheating wife?"

"No."

"Trying to catch someone claiming a workman's comp injury doing cartwheels through their front yard?"

"No."

"Something more illicit? Does it involve our favorite biker gang, the Nameless Brotherhood?"

"No."

"OK, I give up."

Only silence answered her on the other line.

"Hello?"

"I'm still here."

"But you're not going to tell me what you're up to, is that it?"

"Hard as this might be for you to believe, Violet, I am a professional."

She snorted. "Says the guy suggesting a prospective employee wear a French maid outfit."

"Hey, I'm not really supposed to discuss these things. There's a certain level of discretion and privacy inherent to the job."

"Discretion and privacy… What about the girl that ran off to join the alien sex cult? Or the landlord that was convinced one of his tenants was a Russian spy?"

"That was different."

"Why?"

"It just was."

"You're being shady."

"I'm not discussing an ongoing investigation with you. How does that make me shady?"

"Because it's not about being professional. You obviously have something to hide."

"You're being ridiculous."

"No, I'm not. I can hear it in your voice. You're all tense and defensive and, like, nervous. You never get nervous. You're like… the Fonz."

"The Fonz? Huh. I always thought of myself as more of a Han Solo."

"Don't try to change the subject. Are you doing something mildly illegal? Is that why you don't want to tell me?"

He sighed.

"No."

Darger twirled a lock of hair around her finger.

"Alright, well then I'll have to assume the reason you don't want to tell me is that you've been rethinking our relationship and—"

She heard an irritated grunt over the line and then Owen said, "Oh, for crying out loud. It's a cat, OK?"

"A cat? What's a cat?"

"The client is apparently just dying to know what her cat does when she's away from the house. Not for any particular reason, mind you. She's just curious."

"About her cat?"

"Lady's a higher-up at Delta. One of those corporate jobs that sound so boring they have to give you the big bucks just so you won't off yourself. So she's bored and loaded, and now she's paying me to follow her cat."

"Tail."

"Pardon?"

"In this situation, you'd be remiss not to use the term tail. She paid you to *tail* the cat."

"You know, I wouldn't normally take on something this absurd. But it's been a slow couple of weeks, and when I turned her down, she offered to pay double my usual fee."

"What is the going rate for spying on a household pet these days?"

"I'm glad you're so tickled by this."

"Oh, I'm sorry. I didn't realize how serious this was." She cleared her throat. "Maybe she's worried that Muffin has been cheating on her with the cat lady down the street?"

"And you wondered why I didn't want to tell you."

"So what kind of cat is it? I'm picturing one of those overly inbred Siamese cats with the crossed eyes, because who else pays to have a cat followed around?"

"It's gray and white."

"And?"

"How else can I describe a cat? He's got four legs, two eyes—"

"No, I want to know if he's done anything that's going to get him in trouble with your client."

"He's a cat. He walks around and licks himself. Yesterday he chased a bird, and earlier today he used a neighbor kid's sandbox as a toilet."

"Scandalous."

"Hold on… he just came out through the cat door. I have to go. One thing I'll say about following a cat is that he's forced me to hone my shadow skills. Any little noise or sudden movement tips him off. I'll be a ninja by the time I'm through with this job."

Darger squeezed her eyes together, thinking.

"Violet?"

"Sorry, I was trying to come up with a cat-related pun that would work as a goodbye, but I can't think of anything."

"Goodnight, Violet," he said, only sounding a little annoyed. And she could tell he was smiling when he said it.

"Goodnight, Owen."

She'd been able to forget her fight with Loshak during the

phone call, but as soon as the line went dead, it all came flooding back. Muffled voices passed by the door on the way to the elevator, and Darger realized the thing that bothered her most about the argument was how much Loshak hadn't seemed to care. He'd shrugged her off like it was nothing.

Her hands clenched into fists, and it was then that she realized she still held the pregnancy test box in one hand.

She'd put it off long enough. It was time.

((

Three minutes the box said, but it felt more like three hours.

Darger paced the length of her hotel room, back and forth, trying to keep her mind clear.

What if it was positive?

The question forced itself to the churning surface of her thoughts no matter how much she tried to push it away.

It wasn't that she didn't want kids. She liked them well enough. Thought it might be nice to one day have a family. But now? She tried to imagine cooking up a stack of pancakes for the kids in the morning and then running out to the latest grisly crime scene.

And what would Owen think? They'd never discussed it. Hell, they'd only been together for a few months.

She checked the timer on her phone. There was still a whole minute left and then some.

The ability to create life, to produce a fully formed human being — a body and a soul — that was the real magic of the universe. It made every woman a potential Goddess. But what an incredible responsibility. Too much for her, perhaps.

And now she waited. Waited to find out if she would wield

that power. Watched from her place on the edge of the threshold of life and death — stared down the well to see if any light flared in its depths.

Her phone screeched. Time was up.

She inhaled long and deep and then stalked over to the bathroom.

Darger paused just inside the threshold, not quite having the courage to look yet. The stick rested on the sink with the business end hanging over the edge of the basin. Two lines meant the test was positive. One line was negative.

She counted to three and took the last few steps across the tile floor. Her eyes scanned along the white stick, coming to rest on the small window.

One line.

A sigh filled her chest, relief mixed with a bit of sadness. She was glad, of course, for all the reasons she'd recounted a hundred times over the last day or so. But a very small part of her worried that she may never have a family of her own, whether by fate or by choice.

Knuckles rapped lightly at her door, interrupting her thoughts.

She tossed the test into the trash bin and dragged herself to the peephole.

It was Loshak, of course. Who else?

The latch clicked as she turned the handle and opened the door. Loshak met her eyes from across the threshold. She stared back. Neither of them spoke for a moment. She sure as hell wasn't going to be the first one to talk.

Finally, he sighed.

"Can I come in?"

He lifted his arm then, and she saw that he had a brown

paper bag in his hand.

"I brought beer."

Darger stepped back to let him through.

"First, I owe you an apology," he said. "This whole thing has me a little rattled. And you're right. I haven't been a very good partner these last few weeks. I've kept things from you. Lied about why I was coming out here. I hope you know that it isn't an issue of trust."

"Then why? Explain it to me," she said, closing the door behind her.

Loshak set the beer down and slumped into the chair by the desk.

"It got to me. The Stump case, I mean. It was my first big one. I was young and ambitious, and when he got away, I took it personally. This is a wrong I've been waiting to right for almost twenty years, and I know it's dangerous to be that far in, but I can't help it."

Darger didn't speak. She wanted to hear him out from beginning to end.

"Not to mention, I made promises the first time around. Promises that are still hanging over my head."

"But why not just tell me?"

"Because of the letter. When he sent you that letter, I knew it was as much for my benefit as it was for yours. He's messing with me. It's a test. He wants to know if he's gotten so far in my head that I'd use my partner as bait. But I won't. I won't do that to you, Violet."

"Letting me do my job isn't using me as bait."

"Are you sure about that?"

She threw her hands in the air.

"So what am I supposed to do? Not work the case?"

Loshak snorted.

"Like you'd ever agree to that."

Darger smiled.

"Besides that, when all is said and done, you're still my partner. I need your help. Why else do you think I called you out here?"

"I don't know, I figured you might have a hot gambling tip. A sure bet."

Loshak raised his head finally and looked her square in the eye. "There's no such thing as a sure bet."

And Darger didn't think he was talking about gambling anymore.

CHAPTER 6

The house creaks. The timber breathing.

Shifting a little in her seat, the pain flares again. Makes everything go dark for a few seconds.

Emily takes deep breaths as reality fades back in.

She can only picture her skull as a broken eggshell. All spider-webbed like a shattered mirror. Shards of bone missing. Scalp flaking off at the edges like peeling wallpaper.

It's probably not that bad. Almost surely not. She knows this. It hurts worse than it is. Like all those times as a kid she was sure she was bleeding but the fingers checking the point of impact came away clean.

Not today. This time there's blood.

She tastes it at the corner of her lip. It's caked there along the left side of her mouth. Crusty and dry.

She probes with her tongue. Investigates. No wounds that she can find.

The red must have drained down from the dome of her skull. The point where the steel made impact. Blinking a few times she can feel where the dried blood pulls her eyelid taut as well.

She opens her eyes wide. Sits up a little. Another stab of hurt jabs at her temple as soon as she moves. Pain so sharp it wobbles her reality. Shuts her eyes for her. Almost pulls her back into unconsciousness.

She takes deep breaths. Endures it. Watches everything go darker and fade back to bright again. Conscious of little but her breathing and the awful throb in her skull.

The pain makes it hard to think. Hard to open her eyes. Hard to exist at all.

She waits a time like that. Just breathing. Chin tucked almost to her sternum. And then she opens her eyes again. Careful not to move at all.

At first, she is only conscious that she is alone, at least in terms of her immediate surroundings.

This room is empty of other life. He isn't here.

With that settled, the details of her surroundings begin to filter into her awareness.

A new feeling at her wrists has replaced the bite of the plastic zip ties.

Handcuffs.

They attach her to what looks like a typical school desk, the kind with the desktop and chair built as one piece. The chain of the cuffs is looped around one of the steel support bars under the laminated wood tabletop.

She jerks her arms a few times, metal rattling against metal, before all of this fully registers.

She's trapped.

She takes a few breaths. Concentrates to keep the churning panic from taking over.

She needs to focus on the room around her. Needs to learn it. Needs to find a way out.

She finds herself in a great room almost barren of furniture. Almost. There are four more desks similar to hers, the others shoved into the corner behind her.

A cast iron stove mans the center of the wall across the room. Between that and all the wood showing, all the rustic details, she knows it must be a cabin.

Probably in the middle of nowhere. Somewhere up in the

mountains, away from the city.

Thick bands of what looks like stucco surround the dark planks of wood that comprise the structure, striping the wall in light and dark. The messy edges where the white touches the lumber looks like foamy toothpaste in the half-light.

It's dark. Is it still night? She's not sure.

Gray shadows fall over the floors, climb up the walls, collect into clouds of black in every corner.

A single burning bulb in a track lighting fixture provides what little light there is, all of it angled away from her. A circle glowing on the far wall.

Boards block out every window. Heavy wood. Nailed or screwed in tightly. She couldn't remove it without tools and time.

That leaves the heavy steel door off to her right as the only way out. A blue-gray thing that offers little hope of escape. The metal looks out of place among all the wood. Probably added by him. The finishing touch to complete his dream torture chamber. Really ties the room together.

A silent laugh emits from her nostrils, more injured than joyous. The sardonic thought is too scary to be funny. She cuts it off so she won't start crying.

She stirs a little then, the pang of pain in her head not so bad as it was last time. Moving her feet, it occurs to her how cold they are.

Tiles the color of brick etch a grid into the floor. The little gray seams of grout dividing everything up into boxes. Into cells.

Appropriate, she thinks. This is her cell.

Again she rattles her cuffs against the bar. Makes the desk hop up and down a little, metal feet scratching at the tile with angry squawks.

But her headache flares back into blinding territory, and she gives it up.

Rest. For now, she will rest.

She will save her strength for the fight ahead.

☾

Emily thinks of Gabby as she drifts, her thoughts half-conscious and half-dream. Somewhere in between and both at once.

Images of her friend flicker in her head. Silent movies. Slices of life where little happens.

Coils of dark hair bunch at each side of Gabby's face. The cigarette perpetually dangles from her lip. She smiles. She smokes. She looks bored. The background shifts and morphs along with her expressions — rooms and cityscapes taking shape behind her in pulses.

Some other part of Emily's mind works at the knot of how to get out of this room, prodding at the tangle of information in hopes of finding something workable, some detail she has overlooked, some way to progress.

Gabby would know what to do about this, how to get out of this. She always knew what to do.

When Emily first arrived in Vegas, she had nothing but kids' mouths to feed and trouble to hide from. That's how she wound up on the street so quickly.

She still remembers that first night. Waiting around outside one of the casinos. Leaning against a brick facade. Trying to look natural but unable to keep from fidgeting.

She had wondered how anyone would know what she was selling since she was wearing jeans and a t-shirt, her hair still greasy from driving all day to get there.

But they knew.

Like it was a wave in the air, they knew. And they approached. Circled like vultures. Hungry for fresh meat.

She made $90 that night.

The details of the acts themselves are no longer sharp in her mind. Hazy. Distant. No longer quite real. The money was real, though. It helped pay for their room and a couple days' worth of food. Kept them alive. Kept them safe.

On the second night, she met Gabriela.

Most of the other girls kept their distance, not that Emily blamed them. Gabby was different.

She introduced herself. Offered advice.

No. More than advice.

She took Emily under her wing. Taught her. Nurtured her. Saved her.

It was Gabby who made all of the connections she needed to get by for a while. Safe rooms she could use on the cheap. Amiable bouncers she might turn to if there was trouble. Clearance with the thugs who ran the area, though she had to pay for that privilege.

Gabby had rules she lived by. A code. A way to stay safe even with danger swirling on all sides. And she'd passed all of her nuggets of wisdom onto Emily, whether she wanted them or not.

For a little over a year they were close to inseparable. Traveling in packs was one of Gabby's rules. One girl being the lookout while the other was with a john was another.

But no code could keep them safe forever. Nothing could.

Six weeks earlier, Gabby had gone missing. She'd walked Emily home late on a Thursday night. Not a trace since.

The city reacted not at all. Nobody cared.

It wasn't uncommon for one of the girls to go missing in the area. Hookers vanished every day in Las Vegas with little fanfare.

No headlines. Little if any help from the police.

Still, Emily had now dreamed of Gabby every night for 23 straight nights, and in that way, they were still together.

Having her friend back at night felt like a resurrection — somehow shocking and completely inevitable at the same time. Like she couldn't believe it and yet she'd been waiting for just that all the while. Of course she'd come back. She had to, didn't she?

And every morning, she had to re-accept that Gabby really was gone.

Maybe for good.

Probably for good.

Sometimes, usually in those last few moments just before she fell asleep, it felt like Gabby was there with her. In the room. Somehow.

CHAPTER 7

Neither Darger nor Loshak was in the mood to go out for food, so they ordered in. While they waited for the pizza to arrive, they went over it.

"You seem pretty certain it's him."

Loshak blinked at her. "You're not?"

"It's not that. Especially not after the letter. But you usually hesitate to jump to conclusions like this. It just surprises me is all. And I worry about getting tunnel vision. Confirmation bias and all that."

"That's why I wanted you out here. I need your objectivity."

Wrinkles formed over Darger's brow. "I'm the objective one now?"

"Sure," Loshak said with one of his wry smiles.

"What about the cops?"

"What about them?"

"Aren't you worried they're going to freak when you tell them that their personal nightmare from twenty years ago is back?"

"You mean when *we* tell them."

She gestured with the neck of her beer bottle.

"So you are worried."

"Of course I'm worried. I have sense, don't I?"

"You think they'll push back?"

"Probably at first. But at some point, they'll have to come around. There's too much evidence."

"So take me through it. Convince me," she said.

Now it was her turn to smile. This was usually Loshak's

move. The master making the apprentice prove their knowledge.

"We have two female victims. Hands and feet bound. Coroner's report will show they were dead before the fire was set. Found in the trunk of a car, abandoned on a remote part of the highway outside a major city where Stump committed part of his initial series of murders. The only part that doesn't fit is the fact that he took twenty-odd years off. Aside from that, it's his M.O., one-hundred percent."

There was a scratchy sound like sandpaper on rough wood as he pawed at the stubble along his jawline.

"I've considered the alternatives. That it's someone else. A coincidental set of similarities. But there's too much going against that. I could buy the idea that some other psycho likes the idea of torching the bodies to get rid of evidence. But two female victims? In the Vegas area?"

Loshak shook his head, and Darger waited for him to go on.

"So then the devil's advocate part of me says: OK, how about a copycat? Someone imitating Stump intentionally. I don't hate that theory until I consider the little love note he sent you."

Darger nodded, having already considered the possibility herself.

"It would have to be someone with enough inside information and skill to forge his handwriting," she said.

"Exactly. Either that or I have to accept that Leonard Stump *did* send you the letter but isn't involved in the current murders. I'm afraid I can't suspend my disbelief that far. Too complicated. Too messy. I like my explanations clean and simple."

Darger toyed with the cap to her beer bottle, running her thumb over the bumpy metal circumference.

"The local guys have to have some idea," she said. "Some inkling. That crime scene was a carbon copy of the original Stump murders."

"Yeah, but it was twenty years ago. Most of these guys weren't on the force yet. I'm sure they know the name, but I doubt they know the file. It's more likely that Stump is the starring villain in all the urban legends around here. More myth than fact."

"What about Corby or even the Sheriff?"

"What about them?"

"They're older. Could've been around back then."

"Could have. But it doesn't change the fact that no one knows it like we do. We see a burned-out car with two girls in the back, and we don't have to do any mental gymnastics to get to Stump. It's automatic."

Knuckles thudded against the door.

"Mancino's Pizza."

They both stood.

"I got it," Darger said, reaching for her wallet.

"After my idiotic performance earlier? I think not. Sit."

Darger dropped back into her chair and watched Loshak exchange a handful of bills for the box of pizza.

They didn't have plates, so they ate the pizza straight from the box — a slice in one hand and a beer in the other.

Darger chewed, swallowed, and washed it all down with a drink.

"OK, so it's Stump. Why send the letter? Just to fuck with us? As a distraction?"

Paper rustled as Loshak wiped his greasy fingers on a napkin.

"I think it was his way of dropping a breadcrumb for us to

find. From the letter and then the car, it's obvious he's playing games with us. Because this is personal. He wants us paying attention. He'll draw us into his web if he can. We have to be careful. And by *we* I mean *you*, especially."

Darger kept eating and watched a bead of condensation roll down the side of her beer. She felt Loshak's eyes on her but didn't look up.

"You're being uncharacteristically quiet," he said after a moment. "Usually when I warn you to be careful, you get salty."

"Just thinking."

"About?"

"If I hadn't mentioned him in that *Vanity Fair* interview…"

She didn't finish the sentence. She didn't need to. Loshak could fill in the blank: *If I hadn't mentioned Stump in that interview, then maybe he wouldn't have started killing again.*

Loshak made a chopping motion with his hand.

"That's a bunch of hooey. Guys like Stump don't just quit."

"BTK quit."

"Yeah, but he'd never really given it up. Dennis Rader may have played the family man and kept his real self all bottled up for a few decades, but eventually something set him off. It wasn't like he suddenly grew a conscience and decided what he'd done was wrong. I guarantee he fantasized about the murders every day. Still played little games in his head, how he'd do the next one. He never actually started killing again before he got himself caught, but he wanted to."

Loshak paused and took a long pull from the bottle in his fist. He swallowed then shook his head.

"He didn't change. He just managed to sustain a little more impulse control than most of these guys usually can."

"But there was still something… the proverbial straw that

broke the serial killing camel's back," Darger insisted. "Something that made him want to start up again. Maybe that's what my *Vanity Fair* interview was for Stump. A catalyst."

"Look, you can sit there and feel culpable all you want, but it doesn't change the fact that Leonard Stump was a serial killer long before you'd ever heard of him."

Darger knew he was right, but that didn't make the guilt any easier to swallow. She tipped back her beer in an effort to wash it down a little more quickly.

"So what's in the folder?" Darger gestured to the manila file Loshak had set on the floor.

"Right. I almost forgot."

He nudged it with the toe of his shoe, sending it sliding over the carpet to her. Darger found a pinkie finger unstained by cheese grease or pizza sauce and used the fingernail to flick the folder open.

The mouthful of half-chewed food caught in her throat when she saw what was inside. She coughed twice, tears springing to her eyes.

"Sorry, I should have prepared you for that," Loshak said.

With her airway finally clear, Darger took a shaky breath and let it out.

"Where did you get this?"

"Had a couple of the composite artists at Quantico put it together."

Darger stared down at the artist's rendition of Leonard Stump. Even in a drawing, the cold, calculating eyes were recognizable. The angular cheekbones. The square chin. It was a face some had dared to call handsome, though Darger couldn't agree. If anything, she'd always considered Leonard Stump plain. Maybe it was the assumption that someone capable of such hideous crimes should have the literal appearance of a monster that made people mistake his normalcy for good looks. But Violet Darger knew that monsters came in all shapes and sizes: tall and short, fat and skinny, beautiful and ugly.

As familiar as the face was, there were details in the sketch Darger hadn't noticed in any of the photographs or video footage she'd seen of Leonard Stump over the years: crow's feet around his eyes, frown lines on either side of his mouth. Stump was young in all the known pictures of him, but this version was middle-aged.

"I had them do a full composite and then run it through the aging software," Loshak explained.

She stared at it a while longer. There were variations around the main sketch. One with glasses, another with a full beard, and a third depicting Stump with male pattern baldness.

"What do you think?"

"It's… freaky," she said, finally closing the folder. "And it makes it seem more real, him being out there."

A chill ran down her spine, and she shook it off.

If he was out there, they needed to find him. Soon.

CHAPTER 8

The Clark County Sheriff's Office was located in a large complex a few miles off the Strip. The drive up to the building was lined with rows of date palms dramatically lit from below.

"Pretty swanky for a police department," Darger said.

Loshak slid the gearshift into park and turned off the ignition.

"That's Vegas, baby."

It was late, and the parking lot was mostly empty. Their footsteps echoed over the blacktop as they made for the front entrance, lonely claps ringing out in the night.

Something Darger had forgotten after the other events of the evening suddenly surfaced.

"So how did you know?"

"Know what?"

"That it could be Stump. You were out here days before they found that car."

Loshak nodded.

"Right. It was Malenchok."

"Malenchok? He was the tech nerd we worked with in Atlanta, right? The tip line guy."

"The very same. One of his other pet projects at the Bureau is the use of machine learning to track and analyze violent crime statistics across the country. The idea is that we can use it to identify potential hot spots: gang and organized crime activity, threats to homeland security, but also serial killers. It's still in the beginning stages, but I wanted to see how it worked. So I had him run the serial killer data."

They pushed through the first set of double doors into the LVMPD building.

"Half a dozen locations lit up as having homicides and missing persons cases that would suggest possible serial killer activity in the past five years."

"And Vegas was one of those locations."

"Bingo."

"Naturally your mind went directly to Leonard Stump," Darger continued, finishing the thought. "Which explains why you immediately jumped on a plane. And just so you know, that pizza and beer from earlier doesn't mean we're even. I'm still pissed that you lied to me."

"Oh, I know. I figured it'd take at least three pizzas."

The inside of the building was just as luxe as the outside, with marble floors and potted plants. Signs for the various bureaus and sections of the building featured casino-themed clip art: a royal flush or a pair of dice. It was as if the entire city was focused on keeping their branding consistent.

"This place is something else," Darger muttered.

"It's not a town that's shy about which side of their bread is buttered."

A secretary at the front desk directed them to a small meeting room on the second floor. As they entered, a dark-haired woman got up from her seat and approached.

"I didn't get a chance to introduce myself at the scene," she said, reaching for Darger's hand. "Detective Castellano. Daniella. I'm the lead on this investigation."

She wore a pair of gray dress pants and a black shirt, and her raven-black hair was pulled back into a twisted bun at the nape of her neck. Castellano didn't smile during their greeting, but Darger didn't interpret it as an unfriendly gesture. There was something about the firmness of her grip during the handshake and the hard look in her eye that told Darger this was the detective she'd want on her case if she were ever a victim.

"Violet Darger. Nice to meet you."

Corby was in the back corner of the room, talking to another woman and a man. Both were impeccably dressed in expensive suits, the woman in red, the man in gray. Darger wondered if they were also detectives assigned to the case, but before introductions could be made, Corby spun around and clapped his hands together.

"We're all here," the Assistant Sheriff said. "Wonderful."

The points of the star-shaped badge on his chest caught the light as he moved to the front of the room, almost seeming to glitter.

"Just a quick summary of events to get everyone up to speed: at just after 1800 hours, a burning vehicle was reported on Kyle Canyon Road. Police and fire were dispatched, and the fire was extinguished. No passengers found in the cabin of the vehicle, but the trunk revealed two victims, deceased. The medical examiner was able to give me a very preliminary report, enough to determine that both victims were indeed female, both between the ages of 20-35. We will most likely have to rely on dental records for official identification, but we have possibilities from the area Missing Persons database. The process will take time."

Corby shuffled some papers and Darger spoke up.

"Would it be possible to prioritize abductions that happened in tandem? Two girls taken at the same time?"

Detective Castellano took a step away from the bulletin board that had been propping her up.

"Is that important?"

Darger glanced at Loshak and then back at the detective. "It could be."

What Darger left unsaid was that Stump had always abducted his victims in pairs. If that wasn't the case here, she wondered if she and Loshak were leaping to conclusions on his involvement.

Castellano held up a finger to indicate she wasn't finished.

"Sorry, but I have to speak my mind. I know it's what everyone's thinking," she said, glancing from Corby to the two FBI agents. "You think it's a serial killer. That's why you're here, isn't it? The FBI doesn't send agents out to assist in routine homicide investigations."

The two suits in the back eyeballed each other. Darger still hadn't figured out what their deal was. She'd dismissed her earlier idea that they might be detectives. They didn't feel like cops.

Whoever they were, the way they sat in back and a little off to one side gave Darger the feeling that she was being judged or... *observed.*

Finally Loshak spoke up.

"There are patterns in both your missing persons statistics and particular details of this crime that suggest a serial killer, yes."

Mr. Fancypants in the gray suit raised his hand.

"I apologize for interrupting, but we only have the one crime scene, is that correct?"

"It is. But the odds of this being a first-time killer are slim, and I'll explain why. First is the fact that we have two victims. Your average crime of passion — when some Average Joe goes off and kills his wife or girlfriend — there's only one victim."

Corby cleared his throat.

"What about that guy… the one in northern California that killed his girlfriend, and while he was in the middle of rolling her up in the living room rug, his cousin's wife walks in, so he kills her, too?"

"Harold Visser," Loshak said with a nod. "Well the circumstances in that case resulted in something that deviated from the norm, obviously."

"So why can't this be the same kind of deal?"

"Because the victims were bound. You don't tie someone up after they're dead. So that probably means a few things: it means he held them captive. Kidnapping scenarios usually involve premeditation. He spent some time planning this out. Unless we're talking about a rampage killer — and we're not — killing multiple victims simultaneously is too risky for most people to even consider. One guy might be absolutely confident in his ability to overpower one woman. But two women? Too many ways for things to go wrong."

"What about the drug cartels?" It was the man in the gray suit again.

Loshak shook his head slowly.

"If this were related to organized crime of some sort, I would expect a completely different crime scene. Either bodies dumped way out in the middle of nowhere, or the car would have been torched right off the Strip. In the former case, the murders are about covering something up. Keeping someone quiet. The bodies need to disappear. The latter is about intimidation. Leaving the car somewhere a lot of people will see it to send a message: this is what happens if you blab the wrong things to the wrong people."

"And why can't it be that?"

"Because the car was too far out. It was on a main road,

which says the killer wanted it to be found, but it wasn't in the middle of the city. It still needed to be found by the right people — us. Organized crime doesn't taunt police like this. Serial killers do."

"But you said most killers wouldn't have two simultaneous victims," the suit said. "Isn't that arguing against your point?"

"Not in this case. We're talking about someone abnormally confident in his abilities. Someone who's done this before and gotten away with it."

"Sounds like you already have an idea of who this guy is," Detective Castellano said.

"I do."

They waited.

"Leonard Stump."

Darger let her eyes flit around the room, wanting to gauge the reaction. Castellano looked baffled, Corby seemed mildly amused. But the two suits were grim. The woman leaned over and murmured something to Corby that Darger couldn't hear. She didn't like how this was going.

Loshak flipped open his folder and began leafing through the profile.

"We've put together a summarized version of the original file along with a sketch—"

Corby stopped Loshak with an outstretched palm.

"Is this some kind of a joke?"

"I wish it was."

"Leonard Stump disappeared over twenty years ago. What makes you think there's any connection?"

Darger took this one.

"You mean other than the M.O. and the location of the murders being exactly the same?"

Corby stared her down, his plump fingers balled into fists and propped on his hips. He didn't seem as amused now.

"The guy'd have to be, what, forty-something years old? A little old for this kind of thing."

"Not really. Albert Fish killed in his 50s. Ed Gein and Dennis Rader into their forties."

"So I'm supposed to believe that Leonard Stump escapes, goes into hiding for twenty years, and for all intents and purposes has gotten away with his crimes. And then what? He gets bored doing the daily crossword puzzle and decides, *Hell, I think I'll start killing again?*"

"Just look at the file." Darger pointed at one of the photocopied pages. "The crime scene photos are an exact match for what we saw today. Identical."

"Has it occurred to either of you that we may have a copycat on our hands? Either a serial killer or someone trying to cover up a run-of-the-mill murder by making it look like the Stump murders?"

Darger's fingernails pressed into the meat of her palms. He wasn't listening. No one was listening. But before she could say more, Loshak interjected.

Taking a step forward, he raised one of the composites in front of him like a shield.

"All we want to do right now is circulate this sketch around the local news stations and papers."

The sheet of paper rattled as Corby plucked it from Loshak's grasp.

"What's this?"

Out of the corner of her eye, Darger noticed the two suits shifting in their seats.

"It's an artist's rendering of what we think Leonard Stump

55

might look like now. He's been digitally aged, but other things might have changed as well — facial hair, glasses, maybe some extra weight. It's even possible that he would have gone to such lengths as to get plastic surgery, but we can only speculate on what we have. Anyway, I can have digital copies forwarded to the—"

"We'll take it under consideration," Corby said. "I appreciate you leaving it to local law enforcement to make the call on this matter."

The interruption was assertive enough on its own, but the way he bit off his words spoke volumes.

Nobody moved for a beat, and then Darger spoke up.

"Is that a fancy way of saying *no*?" she said.

He stared at her.

"It's a fancy way of saying that we'll take it under consideration."

Darger really wanted to let him have it then, but Loshak clapped a hand on her shoulder.

"I think it's time for us to go, Darger. This is a local investigation, and it's obvious they're taking things in another direction. We've said our part."

He kept a hand on her elbow, like she might try to escape his grip and lunge at somebody. It was a tempting thought, but she let herself be led out into the hallway.

☾

As they walked to the car, Darger blew off steam leftover from the argument.

"Wanting to downplay the serial killer angle — it's got to be about the headlines hurting tourism, right?" Darger said.

"I figure so," Loshak said. "There were members of the tourist board sitting in on the meeting, so…."

"Guy in gray? Lady in red?"

Loshak nodded, and Darger rolled her eyes.

"God forbid this puts a damper on their precious slot machine industry," she said with a sneer. "Who cares if a few more girls get barbecued, right? As long as it's business as usual, funneling the rubes into town so the casinos can dangle them upside-down until every last penny's fallen out of their pocket."

Loshak's eyes looked glassy and far away. Her brow furrowed.

"Are you even listening?"

He blinked a few times before he focused on her, as if clearing his vision of a daydream.

"I heard you. Dangling rubes upside-down."

She squinted.

"You're not feeling sick again, are you? You're being weird."

"Weird?"

"Yeah. It's like you're somewhere else. Up in your head, I mean. Distracted."

He shrugged.

"Just… thinking. Catching Stump is too damn important to waste time on these pissing contests with the locals."

"This is really your Moby Dick scenario, huh?"

"Come again?"

"Stump is the whale that bit off your leg, and you're Captain Ahab, tottering around on a stick, pissed as hell and determined to get vengeance."

"Cute," Loshak said, but the way his mouth puckered like he'd eaten something sour said he found it anything but.

"How is it that you ended up dragging me out of there,

anyway? Shouldn't it have been the other way around? You were the one that wanted to lay out the Stump theory in all its glory."

"I can't help it if you get carried away," he said, ignoring the withering look she gave him. "And if you're wondering why I pulled you out of there, it's because I had an idea."

Loshak's eyes sparkled with something like triumph.

"You have a plan."

He nodded.

CHAPTER 9

They sat in the hotel, waiting. Loshak was glued to the TV.
Darger had her phone out and swiped at the screen to make it
refresh every minute or so. She bounced her leg up and down in
a fit of agitation.

Eventually she slammed the phone down with a grunt.
Loshak turned at her outburst, saw the frustrated expression on
her face.

"Patience, grasshopper," he said.

"I've never counted that as one of my strengths, honestly."

"No kidding." He stood and turned the TV off. "Grab your
jacket."

"Where are we going?"

"To take in the sights."

She raised an eyebrow.

"I sort of forgot you spent the day on the plane. You're
gonna lose it if you stay cooped up in this room any longer. And
we don't really need the TV if you have your phone."

"All true," she said, sliding the phone into her pocket.

They took the elevator down to the lobby and walked
toward the Strip. It was only a block away, and the lights stood
out like a beacon.

Traffic was light, but there were still people everywhere.
Laughter and raucous voices combined with the music blasting
from the storefronts to create a deafening mélange of noise.

Everything was lit up: the buildings, the trees, the fountains.
A man rode by on a bike with blue lights threaded through the
spokes of his tires. Another passed them carrying a large

beverage in a plastic cup with blinking red LEDs. Cameras flashed as people snapped photos.

With the noise and the lights, it was a circus-like atmosphere. It would be easy to hide in a crowd like this.

They moved with the mob, not having a particular destination in mind. There was a chill in the air, and Darger's fingers started to feel the cold. Eventually they ducked inside a food court and ordered two coffees.

While they sipped the hot brew, Darger flicked at her phone. She took a drink and almost choked.

"Oh crap," she said, half-coughing. "It's happening."

She held out her phone so Loshak could see the headline. His eyes flitted over the screen.

"That was fast."

She nodded and blew over the top of her cup. Tiny ghosts made of steam danced over the black liquid.

"Now what?"

Loshak shrugged.

"More waiting."

She drank and stared at the sketch of Stump pasted front and center on the Daily Gawk website.

"I still can't believe you leaked the story to the tabloids on purpose."

"Technically, I didn't leak anything directly. I was discreet."

"If that's your idea of discreet, remind me not to tell you any of my secrets," Darger said.

Loshak watched through slitted eyes while she dumped coffee down her throat.

"What?"

"I didn't say anything."

"You didn't have to with that face you're making. Spit it

out."

Darger shrugged.

"Just that usually you're the one accusing *me* of stirring the pot."

"Jealous that I'm taking all the heat for once?"

She snorted. "Oh yeah. That's exactly it."

"I have full authorization from Washington, so if these local hacks don't like it, they can screw," he said, and then the corner of his mouth twitched into a funny little smirk.

"You know, you can be kind of a bastard sometimes," Darger said and lifted her cup. "Here's to you."

CHAPTER 10

Emily fades back in to a repeated syllable. The voice is close. Right on top of her. And yet her groggy mind cannot understand.

The blur around her sharpens to reveal the cabin in half-light. Everything still. Everything quiet.

The dark figure sits within an arm's length. He blocks out most of the light so a darkness falls between them. A shade that shrouds his features in wispy black.

Still, she can make out his silhouette clearly. He seems bigger this close up. Shoulders broad. Arms and legs both oddly thick. Substantial.

She blinks. Tries to force her eyes to focus.

Something glitters in the shadow between them. A rippling surface floating toward her face, drawing closer in slow motion.

He holds a cup to her lips. A glass of water.

"Drink."

She drinks. Feels the wet soften the dried out places on her tongue and throat. It feels good.

Her head sags again. So heavy. Her neck can't hold it up.

She should be terrified. Shaking. Thrashing and clawing and biting. But she's too tired for any of that.

Her chin rests on her sternum again, and she watches him stand and leave the little section of the floor that comprises her field of vision. Hears his footsteps trail away.

She doesn't feel in immediate danger, though she doesn't know why.

She pumps her hands in and out of fists to try to wake up,

but it's no good. The motion slows, slows, stops.

Within a few seconds her eyelids bob closed. The warmth of slumber swells in her face again.

And she drifts. Drifts. Sails toward that stillness once more. The emptiness.

The deep swallows her. No dreams. No stirring. Just the endless numb.

CHAPTER 11

The technicolored lights of the Strip swiped by in a blur. Loshak manned the wheel, driving north again, away from the city.

"Tell me again what Corby said on the phone," Darger said.

"I can repeat it ten more times, and you're not going to wring any more information from it. A gas station attendant called in, says he saw the guy from our sketch."

"I just can't believe we got a tip so fast. What time did the kid see him?"

"I already told you: I don't know. Geez, you really aren't good with anticipation, are you?"

Darger tugged at her seatbelt and brushed her hair from her eyes. She couldn't seem to stop fidgeting.

"I just like knowing the details."

"I bet you were one of those kids who tried to sneak peeks at your Christmas gifts before the big day, weren't you?"

Darger waited a few moments before responding, "The Fifth Amendment protects me from being compelled to incriminate myself."

"Yeah, OK."

"So on a scale from one to Flamin' Hot Cheetos, how red do you think Corby's face was when he turned on the TV and saw the Stump sketch on the evening news?"

Loshak chuckled his distinctive silent laugh and drove on through the night.

Two police cruisers and one SUV were parked near the entrance of the service station when they arrived. A sign hung over the building with glowing letters that read: Marco's Travel

Stop. Loshak pulled in next to the white Chevy Tahoe and cut the ignition. Before they were out of the car, Assistant Sheriff Corby was pushing through the glass front door to meet them. He tipped his hat.

"Evening, agents."

"We appreciate you calling us down here," Loshak said.

"Well, considering it was your handiwork that brought the tip in, I figured it was only right." Corby's tone was wry, but not altogether unfriendly.

Darger had been expecting worse. After all, Loshak had specifically gone behind his back when he released the composite to the news outlets. She hadn't thought the locals would react kindly to that. The two suits from their earlier meeting probably had their overpriced underpants in a real twist by now.

"Can we talk to the witness?" she asked. "The one who called it in?"

"Knock yourself out. You'll want to after five minutes with him."

"Why's that?"

"See for yourself."

They followed Corby inside, past rows of chips, gum, and beef jerky. Behind the register and beyond a door marked *OFFICE - EMPLOYEES ONLY*, one of the patrolmen sat in a molded plastic chair, typing up a witness statement. The witness in this case was a young man, maybe twenty-five at the oldest. He wore a black polo shirt, and the name badge pinned to chest read *Ty*.

Ty had a long-boned, scrawny build. Coupled with his mop of hair and sparse goatee, he reminded Darger of Shaggy from *Scooby-Doo*.

"I mean, I didn't really get a super good look at his face. Dude had his hood up. And he was wearing glasses."

"Then how was it that you recognized him?" the officer asked.

Ty frowned and wiggled his lip ring with the tip of his tongue.

"I don't know. I guess it was just the dude's vibe, man."

"His *vibe*?"

"You know, there was just something funny about this hombre."

The officer stopped typing, and he fixed the kid with a dead stare. "I'm going to need you to be a little more specific."

Ty blinked a few times, mouth hanging slightly open. It was evident that the policeman and Ty were not on the same wavelength, communication-wise, and Darger took a step into the room.

"I don't mean to interrupt, but I think what Ty here is trying to say is that it *felt* like the right guy. In his gut. Is that right?"

"Well, yeah."

Darger tried to think how she could coax more information out of the kid.

"So maybe think back to before you saw him. When did you notice that you had a customer? Did you see him pull up?"

"Naw, I was watching South Park. When he came to prepay, that's when I first noticed the dude. The door chime made that like… dinging sound."

"And then what?"

"He came up to the counter. Said he wanted $10 in gas. I looked out and didn't see a car at the pumps, so I was a little confused, but he had one of them gas cans. The big metal ones."

"Did you know right away that something felt off?"

Ty nodded.

"How?"

"I mean, dude had his hood up around his face. Made me think of that other dude. The one that lived in a shack and blew a bunch of people up."

"The Unabomber?" Loshak offered.

Ty's face lit up. "Yeah, that's it! This dude looked just like the Unabomber."

Corby cleared his throat, and Darger took that as a sign that her time with the witness was over.

"We'll let you finish up your report, Schneider. I'd like to have a chat with our *guests* here."

He emphasized the word guests, and Darger braced herself.

As they moved away from the office, she heard Officer Schneider get back to the interview.

"OK, Ty. Did the *dude* say anything?"

"Oh yeah," Ty answered. "After he handed me his money, the dude said, *Nice night for a drive.* Or something like that."

Back amongst the Slim Jims and Funyuns, Corby took a standard cop stance with his legs spread shoulder-width apart and his hands clasped over his belt buckle. His lips pouted out in an exaggerated frown, and Darger started to wonder if he was going to try to kill them with a disapproving look.

"I'm not one to cry over spilt milk, but I don't like to beat around the bush about things," he said finally.

Two clichés crammed into a single sentence, she thought. *Impressive.*

"So I'll be honest. The Sheriff's office is not pleased about how you've gone about things thus far."

Darger wanted to ask if it was really the Sheriff's office that was upset or the tourism board. But she kept her mouth shut for the time being.

Corby continued.

"I felt I was quite clear about not releasing that composite to the news outlets, but you saw fit to do it anyway."

"Actually, it wasn't—" Loshak started to say, but Corby held up his hand to stop him.

"I'm not interested in hearing your rationale, Agent Loshak. The FBI has its own purview, separate from our office. I understand that I am not in a position to be giving you orders of any kind."

Loshak shrugged.

"That being said," Corby continued, "We would appreciate a heads up if the FBI decides to employ any further creative tactics like this in the future. It's one thing to disagree about the particulars of an investigation. But I sure hate to be caught with my pants down."

"Understood," Loshak said.

Eager to move on to more pressing matters, Darger changed the subject.

"I assume this place has security cameras?"

Corby adjusted the brim of his hat and then gestured at a black dome mounted on the ceiling.

"Inside and out, but Jeffrey Lebowski in there doesn't have access to the archived footage. Store manager's on his way down here right now, though I don't mind telling you I think this is all a waste of time."

"How so?" Darger asked. "The kid says he saw Stump."

"Of course he did. That's what happens when you tell people there's a boogeyman about. They all *think* they see him. It's that — what do you call it — subliminal messaging or whatever. Especially a perma-bake like that." Corby tipped his head in the

68

general direction of the office.

"A what?"

"That's what we used to call it back in school when a kid smoked too much pot too early on. A drug counselor explained to me once that the brain is like Jell-o. In childhood it's still liquid, not set. It's only in the teen years that it begins to congeal into something resembling a solid. But if you interrupt that setting period with too many illicit substances, it won't set right. Stays partially liquid." He glanced back where Ty was giving his witness statement to Deputy Schneider.

"I don't think—" Darger paused, mid-sentence. She'd been on the verge of arguing that she doubted the Jell-o comparison was meant literally, but decided it was a fruitless effort. "Nevermind."

"My point is, he'd believe that Puff the Magic Dragon had come through for a fill-up if you put the idea in his head."

Through the bank of windows at the front of the gas station, the three of them watched as a silver SUV glided into the lot. It rolled to a stop in one of the parking spaces near the door, and a man climbed down from the driver's seat. He was shaped like a walrus, all sloped shoulders and barrel chest supported somewhat preposterously on tiny flipper-like feet.

"I think this is our illustrious store manager," Corby said. "If you'll excuse me for a moment."

Darger milled about under the harsh fluorescent lighting of the convenience store. She spun through a rack of postcards and then moved closer to a shelf filled with low-dollar souvenirs: shot glasses, ashtrays, sand art. One of the hooks held rabbit's foot keychains in a range of cotton candy colors.

Darger poked at one of the feet. It swayed like a pendulum from its chain.

"I had one of those. When I was a kid, of course," Loshak said from over her shoulder.

"Same here. Bright pink. I loved how soft it was." She ran her finger over the silky fur. "And just the idea of having a 'good luck charm' was fun, you know? When you're a kid, you actually believe it."

She released the trinket and spun away from it.

"And then one day, I asked my mom why they called it a rabbit's foot."

"Uh-oh."

"Yeah. She said, *Because that's what it is.*"

"What'd you do then?"

"I didn't get it at first. I thought she didn't understand my question. Or she was giving one of those stereotypical mom responses, like, *Because I said so.*"

An old home movie played in her mind's eye: Darger as a scrawny little girl, nine or ten years old, staring down at a furry lump clutched in her sweat-moist hand, trying to make sense of what her mother has said.

"And right before I started to pester her again, it clicked. I said, *You mean... from a real rabbit?* My mother nodded, I shrieked and dropped the thing, and then had a total hysterical meltdown. I made her promise to get rid of it, but I still spent weeks feeling guilty about the poor bunny that had met its untimely demise. All so I could have one of its limbs dangling from my school bag."

She shook her head.

"I want to know what sick fuck decided that a dismembered animal part was any kind of good luck?"

Loshak uttered one of his silent laughs, and Darger eyed the souvenirs warily.

"And people must still buy them, or they wouldn't give it shelf space."

She turned and watched Corby and the store manager talking in the parking lot.

"So what do you think?"

"About what?"

"The whatchamacallit subliminal messaging or whatever." Loshak sniffed.

"I'm not going to stand here and deny the existence of the power of suggestion. Can an idea — once planted in someone's subconscious — take root and make them see or believe things they wouldn't have otherwise? Sure. And maybe this particular incident could even fall into that category, but we both know that Stump is here somewhere."

She mulled that over for a moment.

"Yeah. Maybe everyone knows it."

"Why do you say that?"

"I expected Corby to be a lot more pissed off about the tabloid story, for one. When I pull that kind of crap, it never goes over quite this well."

"You're a woman."

"What does that mean?"

"It means that law enforcement isn't exactly known as a haven of feminist ideals. Loudmouthed, uppity girl like you pushes all the wrong buttons for a lot of these guys."

"Uppity?"

"I thought *loudmouthed* would have been the one that irked you."

"That too."

Darger blinked a few times, thought about Loshak's comment again.

"You really think it's because I'm a woman?"

Loshak shrugged. "In part. Probably doesn't help any that you're young, too. Us old fogeys don't like being told what to do by anyone younger than us, male or female."

Darger watched the Assistant Sheriff through the window. Corby smiled, nodded, spoke to the manager, hopefully getting access to the surveillance footage any second now.

"Even if you're right, I wonder if Corby has been chewing on the Stump theory all along. You'd have to be an idiot not to, and he doesn't quite strike me as one."

CHAPTER 12

The store manager's name was Marty Beck. He was an oily-looking man with slicked back hair and an unlit cigar in his mouth that he removed periodically to roll between his fingers. There was a gold chain clasped around his neck, and it lay nestled in a bed of graying chest hair, something he showed off intentionally by leaving the buttons of his polo shirt undone.

Ty had returned to his post at the register, and now Darger, Loshak, Corby, and Beck were crammed into the tiny office, huddled around a flat screen computer monitor. Beck was drenched in some ghastly aftershave or cologne, or maybe he just emitted the odor as a matter of course. Whatever it was, Darger wished she'd gotten the spot next to the door so she could at least poke her head out for some fresh air now and then.

"We got video but no sound, OK? What time are we lookin' for?" Beck asked.

"Around eleven is what the kid said. Maybe a little before."

Beck poked at the keyboard on the desk, using only the first fingers on either hand. The cigar wiggled in his lips.

Shapes flitted across the screen as the footage rewound. There was feed from four cameras: two showing the inside of the store and two fixed on the gas pumps and the parking lot outside. In one of the frames, Ty the clerk spent most of his time hunched over his phone, chuckling to himself.

When the timestamp reached their mark, Beck's finger jabbed the keyboard and the video went back to normal speed.

Darger tried to focus on the footage of the parking lot but

kept finding herself drawn back to watching Ty, giggling while he watched his TV show. Because he was alone, and because the angle of the video didn't show his phone, he seemed to be laughing at thin air. A solitary weirdo, staring into space and finding something amusing there.

Then they saw it. A huge old pickup truck lumbered into frame, pulling through to the parking lot on the far side of the building.

"Look at that old tank," Corby said. "Gotta be 1970s."

"Or early 80s. And domestic by the profile. Ford or Chevy, maybe Dodge," Loshak added.

Corby pointed at a corner of the screen, nearest to the entrance of the service station. It was just a patch of grainy blackness at the moment.

"Looks like he came in from the west."

The truck jolted to a stop in one of the parking spaces. A man climbed out.

A collective hush fell over the group. The loudest sound for the next several seconds was the buzzing overhead from the fluorescent lights.

After closing the door of his truck, the man stalked over the cement to the gas station entrance. Darger squinted and leaned a little closer to the monitor, but it did nothing to improve the quality of the video.

As the man crossed the lot, the first camera lost him. After a moment, another picked him up. With the monitor split into four panels, it gave the appearance of him jumping from one quadrant to the next, like a magic trick.

He pushed through the glass door, approached the counter. The size looked right for Stump, but that meant nothing on its own.

The Girl in the Sand

Darger tried to read his body language, size him up by the way he walked, the way he moved. He seemed confident, fairly nonchalant, but there was a touch of aggression to him somehow, an intensity she couldn't pin down to a feature or gesture.

His clothes seemed purposely nondescript — a plain hoodie, blue jeans, a pair of Adidas — but Darger had to agree with Ty: the hood and sunglasses felt wrong. Looked like a celebrity trying to escape the paparazzi. Trying too hard, even, like maybe he *wanted* to be noticed.

The man's mouth moved, but there was no voice to match, of course. A silent movie, though Darger wasn't sure of the genre yet. If it was Stump in the video, it was surely horror. If it wasn't him, a farce.

The mystery man handed a bill over to Ty. After punching a few buttons on the register, the drawer opened, and Ty deposited the cash. Meanwhile, the hooded man plucked something from one of the shelves, glanced at it for a moment, and then put it back.

"What was that?" Darger asked.

"One of our novelty beer koozies," the manager said. "Popular impulse buy."

From her vantage point, she could just make out the row of foam can covers printed with phrases like *In dog beers, I've only had one* and *Drinks well with others.*

"Could try for prints on that," Loshak said. "Same with the door handle and the counter area. Gas pump, too."

Darger studied Corby from the corner of her eye, waiting for him to protest, to talk about wasted manpower and lab costs on a wild goose chase.

Instead, he nodded.

"Worth a shot. I'll call in our crime scene techs."

Maybe he really was coming around.

She refocused her attention back on the video. The man was at one of the pumps now, filling the metal jerry can with his ten dollars in gasoline. When he finished, he sauntered back to his truck and stowed the gas in the rear bed. He opened the door, paused to reach for something, and climbed in. Several seconds passed before the truck's taillights came to life. As soon as the truck exited the lot and out of the camera's range, Loshak had Beck rewind so they could watch from the beginning.

Corby stepped away from the computer monitor, and Darger could hear him issuing orders to someone at his office.

"Bring Rita, she gets the best prints. We've got a door handle, a foam beer koozie, and some cash that might have latents."

In the meantime, Loshak and Beck tried to get a clearer picture of the man's face from the video.

"Just after he comes inside, when he goes past this camera," Loshak said, tapping the screen. "Can you pause there and go frame-by-frame?"

Beck obeyed, jabbing his short fingers at the keyboard.

"OK, stop there. Can we zoom in on this?"

The man's face grew in size until it filled the screen. She knew what Loshak was thinking, because it was the same question on her mind: Is it him? Were they looking at Leonard Stump?

They repeated this process with each of the cameras, trying to get a best possible picture of the mystery man from the various angles. Darger stared at the grainy footage until the picture devolved into individual pixels. A meaningless dot matrix. She squeezed her eyelids together and sighed. It was pointless. She could gaze into the screen until her eyes bled. The camera footage alone would never be enough evidence to prove it was Stump. But fingerprints would.

Her eyes strayed to the beer koozies. *Please God, let there be usable prints.*

"I think I'm going to take a break," she said. "Try to come back and look at it with fresh—"

She cut herself off mid-sentence. Something new in the video had caught her eye this time. Movement in the top left quadrant, from the camera mounted closest to the parking lot. "Go back. Back to when he starts pumping the gas."

Beck let out an annoyed puff of air and adjusted his hold on his cigar before typing a command. The video reversed in fast speed. When he let it play again, Darger held her breath and watched.

Yes.

In the moment just after the man removed the cap from the gas can, a car sped past the gas station. The headlights of the passing car illuminated a silhouette in the cab of the truck.

With a fingertip, she gestured at the screen.

"Rewind again and watch the feed from this camera."

Loshak's mouth took on a hard, straight line. His focus sharpened.

When he saw it, he sucked in a breath.

"Someone else was in the truck?"

"A girl," Darger said. "He had a girl in the truck."

☾

By the time Corby's crime scene tech arrived, they were all eager to give their eyes a rest from staring at the CCTV footage.

They'd zoomed in on the figure inside the truck, the same way they had on the mystery man. Frame by frame they advanced through the brief moment when she was illuminated by the lights of the passing car. It was definitely a woman. Young, with dark hair and an average build. And scared. There was an unmistakable panic in her movements.

Darger watched the tech examine the door handle using an alternative-light-emitting LED, but couldn't keep her mind from straying to the girl in the truck. Who was she? Was she still alive, or had she already become yet another of Leonard Stump's countless victims?

Then again, they still hadn't proven it was Stump in the video. She had to be careful about that. If they were wrong, and it wasn't him, they'd have wasted valuable time chasing ghosts.

Was Loshak giving himself similar internal warnings? She glanced at her partner and thought not. And that only made it more important that she keep her assumptions in check. Her feet needed to stay firmly on factual ground.

She played the video over in her head. By now she'd seen it enough times to have it memorized. The man hadn't been wearing gloves, despite knowing he'd touch the door handle, the money, the gas pump. Would Stump take that risk? He had to know his prints were on record from his previous arrest.

Then again, both the money and the door handle would have loads of prints from other people. Perhaps he figured they'd never get a usable print off either surface. But then he'd gone and picked up that koozie. Was he that brazen?

Suddenly Beck was shouting and waving his cigar in the air.

"They're getting this-this-this powder over my entire cash drawer! I can't give this as change now, it's ruined!"

Corby sniffed and said, "Oh, you don't need to worry about

that. We'll be taking that into evidence."

"Evidence! But this is my money! You're... you're stealing! That's legal tender, you can't just—"

"You'll receive itemized documentation of everything taken today, for which you will be reimbursed by the county once you submit the proper paperwork."

"Paperwork! I'm trying to run a business here!"

Corby's phone trilled. He reached for it while simultaneously trying to appease Beck.

"I do apologize for the inconvenience, but this is an official investigation by the Sheriff's department."

The manager's tone took on a harder, mocking edge. "The *inconvenience*, he says! Well, we'll just see what the Small Business Coalition has to say about this. I'm a citizen, you know. It's my hard-earned tax dollars that pay your salary."

Darger had to bite her lip to keep from smirking.

She glanced over to see if Loshak was enjoying the show as well, but he'd stepped back into the office to watch the video again.

Corby was on his cell now, holding one hand out and asking Beck to quiet down for a minute. The store manager was still reading him the riot act, arms swinging, face turning purple.

Leaning into the office, Darger nudged Loshak with her elbow.

"We might need to mediate soon."

Loshak's eyes never left the screen.

"Hm?"

Corby barged into the office then. Beck — still ranting — made to follow, but Corby closed the door in his face and engaged the lock.

Finally tearing himself from the video footage, Loshak raised an eyebrow at his partner. She shrugged.

"Sorry about that. Go ahead," Corby said into his phone.

Beck pounded at the door, shouting about property rights and eminent domain, but Corby barely seemed to notice. His face was grave. When he hung up, he made eye contact with Loshak and then Darger.

"We got something."

"What is it?"

"Car fire about a mile down the road."

"The truck from the video?"

He shook his head. "Honda Accord."

"Let's go."

CHAPTER 13

Corby led the way with his siren and flashers on, but the road was desolate this time of night. They didn't pass a single vehicle on their way to the scene.

Darger caught sight of the fire from some distance. The bright orange glow was like a beacon in the night. Three squad cars were already on the scene, with one deputy standing in the road to direct any potential traffic away from the burning car and two others setting down a line of emergency flares on the pavement.

Corby pulled to the shoulder and parked. Loshak followed suit.

The first thing Darger noticed when she climbed out of the car was the sound: a rumbling, hissing roar.

The second thing she noticed was the smell.

It was the acrid, chemical stench of burning plastic, upholstery, and enamel. It stung her nostrils and brought tears to her eyes. She covered her mouth and nose with her hand, more out of instinct than because she actually thought it would protect her from the smoke.

Corby hailed the deputy standing in the road for traffic control. He had to shout to be heard over the crackle and pop of combustibles igniting.

"You call Fire and Rescue?"

"Station 56 and 48 are on their way, sir."

Every inch of the car was consumed by flame and smoke. Darger's eyes followed the dancing, twisting, billowing vapor for a time before coming to rest on the back end of the vehicle.

What would they find in the trunk this time? The mystery girl from the gas station footage? Would there be another girl with her?

The heat of the fire prickled at her skin, even at a distance. Melted plastic sizzled as it hit the ground, so hot it stayed a glowing red, like the car was leaking magma. Then came a loud *pop*. Darger flinched, and her first thought was that it was a gunshot.

But Loshak pointed at the car and said, "Tires."

He gave her a reassuring half-nod, but the orange glow wavering against his face turned it into something demonic.

"The air inside expands from the heat and eventually they explode."

She studied the car. He was right. The left rear tire was gone, popped like an overfilled party balloon. A second mini-explosion followed and then another.

Each time, the group took a few steps back.

Just after the last tire exploded, flashing lights approached from down the road, and then the whine of the fire engine's siren. The truck came to a halt, and Corby crossed the pavement to meet the two firemen who hopped down from the cab.

Loshak tapped her on the shoulder.

"Things are about to get real messy," Loshak said. "I'd recommend sitting in the car for this part. Gets pretty nasty out here with all the steam and smoke mixing into a big toxic cloud. Not to mention the smell. Jesus."

She gave the flames one final glance, then followed Loshak back to their car. They climbed in and closed the doors. Loshak turned the key and the dash lit up.

"Stood right out in the open last time," he said, hitting a button to set the vents to recycle the air in the cabin. "Probably took a year or two off my life doing that. Like smoking three dozen cartons of Newports in the span of ninety seconds."

Through the windshield, they watched the firemen get into position. A second truck had arrived by then, and the crews hustled around, uncoiling hoses, checking pumps and gauges. While one of the men let loose the first blast of water, the others stood by with the second hose.

It was faster than she imagined, only taking the single hose and a few minutes to extinguish the flames. Even after the fire's glow had died, both of the men manning the hoses went around the vehicle spraying inside and out. At times, the steam and smoke were so heavy the car was completely obscured.

Again Darger's eyes fixed on the trunk, and her stomach churned at the knowledge of what probably lay inside.

A knock at her window startled her from these macabre thoughts. She lowered the glass and Corby bent down so his head was level with hers.

"It'll be another few minutes before they're ready for us. But the cabin of the car is clear."

"The trunk?"

"Welded shut, more or less. Probably they'll have to resort to cutting it open."

Indeed, it was only a few minutes later that one of the firemen emerged from behind the fire engine lugging a chop saw in his gloved hands.

The saw whined like a dentist's drill as it bit into the frame of the car, bucking in the man's grip and spraying the air with sparks. The other men shouted instructions and encouragement over the noise. And all around them, a haze of steam and smoke still hung in the air.

Neither Darger nor Loshak had spoken for some time when

he broke the silence.

"I feel like I should get my lighter out."

"What?"

He gestured at the men gathered around the destroyed car.

"We've got smoke, pyrotechnics, flashing lights," Loshak said. "Remind you of anything?"

Her eyes slid over to her partner.

"Warn me if you're going to start screaming out requests for 'Freebird.'"

He smirked but kept his eyes on the show. She continued to ponder the idea in a more serious light.

"That's why he does it, don't you think? The spectacle?"

Loshak nodded and then said, "That and the all-consuming, destructive power of fire. He loves that, I'm sure. The elemental nature of it. Fire was early man's first step toward shaping the modern world."

The man wielding the saw stepped away from the car, setting the tool at his feet, and shrugging out of his heavy jacket.

"I think they're in," Darger said, springing out of the car without waiting for Loshak.

Her feet skimmed over the blacktop, bringing her closer to the grimy shell of the car. The ruined vehicle reminded her of the desiccated husk left behind by a molting cicada.

Two of the firemen gripped the rectangle of sheet metal cut from the top of the trunk and lifted, but one of the corners stuck, and it was another several seconds before they could pry the piece free.

Darger bounced on her feet in anticipation, then remembered Loshak's comment about her sneaking peeks at her Christmas presents. The bouncing stopped. She shouldn't be so eager, knowing what was likely to be inside that trunk. Still, the

84

suspense of it caused her fingers to clench into fists.

Finally the men tore the top of the trunk away. Darger stepped closer, holding her breath as she peered inside.

It was empty.

She exchanged a baffled glance with Loshak, who had come up to stand beside her, along with Corby.

Staring back into the empty black pit of the trunk, she couldn't help but feel lost.

It was a moment before anyone spoke, each of them privately mulling it over before they could form words.

"I don't get it."

Loshak stroked his hair. "Me neither."

"It's like... he wanted to get us out here to see the spectacle and then—"

Darger threw her empty hands in the air to finish the thought.

"Don't get me wrong," Loshak said. "I'm glad there's no body. Obviously. But it does feel like a bit of an anticlimax."

Corby frowned and hooked his thumbs in his belt.

"You think the gas station kid is being funny? Playing some kind of prank for media attention or something?"

Loshak scoffed.

"No way. You saw that kid. I'd be surprised if he could muster enough attention span to saran wrap a toilet seat."

They stood and studied the car for a while before Corby spoke up again.

"What if..." he started but then trailed off.

"Say it," Loshak said.

Corby sighed and crossed his arms over his chest.

"What if the girl was in the car when he started the fire, and she... what if she was still alive, and she ran off into the desert?"

He gestured to the rocky landscape surrounding them. Beyond the lights from the vehicles and the flares, it was pitch black.

"But the trunk was closed," Darger said. "And all the doors, too."

"I know. I just don't have any better ideas."

They stood at the edge of the road and stared off into the night, wondering what secrets might lay in the desert.

CHAPTER 14

As soon as Emily wakes, she can feel his presence in the room. Something off. Something aggressive.

She opens her eyes. Scans for him.

There.

He sits in the dark at the edge of the room, tucked back in the shadows. Motionless.

When he speaks, it sounds like he's continuing a thought, like he's been talking for a while now, whether she could hear him or not.

"In that way, it's like all of this was meant to be. It couldn't have happened any other way. Not for you. Not for me. Not for any of us."

He swallows, and his throat clicks.

"The first time, I was so drunk, I don't think I really knew what I was doing. Didn't know why, that's for sure. It was like a dream, I guess.

"But there was a moment that somehow made it make sense. Sobered me up. I had the two girls — mother and daughter — in this cottage they'd rented. Way up in the San Juan mountains."

His tone is conversational. Relaxed, even.

"I was working maintenance up there at one of the resorts. Mostly cutting the grass in the picnic area, whacking weeds along the trails. And every evening I'd watch all of these girls disappear behind these cabin doors. Beautiful, mysterious creatures going into some other world. Apart from me. And I knew for a long time that I wanted to disappear there, too. I wanted to walk through one of those portals, wanted to be in

87

one of those cabins in the worst way. On the inside."

Emily shudders a little, a gesture she doesn't even notice until the handcuffs tinkle against the steel bar of her desk.

The noise jars her out of her daze. Startles her.

She goes motionless. Drops her gaze to the floor. Watches the man's face out of the corner of her eye.

The dark figure licks his lips. Blinks a couple times. But if he noticed the sound of her rattling chain, it doesn't show on his face. After a beat of silence, his tale goes on.

"They were these weird little buildings nestled in the forest. Vacation spots for rich people, I guess. Wide wooden planks on the exterior the color of dark chocolate, and these gauzy curtains hung over the windows. Semi-sheer like pantyhose or something. You could almost see through them. Feminine silhouettes moving inside and stuff."

He trails off for a moment. His eyes drifting up to the ceiling.

"I didn't know what would happen inside there, but I knew that whatever it was, it had to happen. It wasn't my choice, you understand. It was destiny. It was a mist in the air that seeped into my pores. Wormed its way under my skin. Pulled me along.

"Even after I'd kept the two of them tied up in there for three days, I didn't know I was going to do the first girl until it was done, you know? The daughter. Maybe seventeen. She bled out in the bathtub. All the color leaching out of her so fast, like the drain sucked that down, too."

He inhales.

"And I remember she was so cold almost right away. Her skin was like touching raw chicken in the meat department."

Emily's shoulders jerk a little, and she remembers to

breathe. Is he talking to her? Talking to himself? She doesn't know. He seems far away.

"Her mama had watched the whole thing, you know. And she'd been sniffling a long time through the gag I had on her, whimpering and whatever, but then she got real quiet."

He lets a stillness fall. Perhaps it is intentional. Or maybe he's only recalling the moment in his mind, reliving it.

"She'd been the fighter of the two of them. Wouldn't keep still, so we'd been fighting and everything. She bit the heel of my hand. Drew blood. I'd choked her out a couple different times just to make her stop thrashing. And I'd put a plastic bag over her head for a while there. One of those crinkly white bags from the grocery store, you know. I took it off her at some point. Didn't know why when I did it. Guess I wanted her to see. To see what was going to happen in the tub, I mean."

Emily stares down at the desktop, not wanting to hear any more. But he goes on.

"When it's done, I walk out of the bathroom, and she's sitting there on the bed, and she's looking at me. I'm covered in her daughter's blood. Just drenched in red. And she's blinking up at me. Tied up. Hands and feet. A sock wadded up and duct taped into her mouth to shut her up. And she's different. I can see that she's different now. Changed. And I guess I want to know what that's about."

The man adjusts a little in his seat. Continues.

"So I peel the tape away from her cheeks. I'm careful and all, but she doesn't try to bite. She barely moves at all except to breathe."

The wood pattern of the laminate goes blurry in Emily's eyes, but she doesn't dare blink.

"When I finally get the sock out of her mouth, she looks at

me, and she says…"

He pauses a moment. Licks his lips again. When he speaks her words, his voice is just louder than a whisper. Gritty and reverent.

"God forgive you. God have mercy on your soul."

He's quiet for a long time. His chest rises and falls with his breathing. Eyes still tracing invisible lines on the ceiling.

"That was it. That was the moment. For the first time, it kind of hit me. The weight of it. All of it. All of what was happening in that little cabin. It became real. What a fucking thing for her to say."

He leaned back. Let his head thump against one of those logs veining dark lines in the white wall.

"But nothing happened. I killed her daughter, and I killed her, and nothing happened. The sky didn't open up. No hand reached down from the heavens to stop me. No spirit of kindness or mercy possessed me to change my course. No divine force swelled in the vicinity. Nothing."

The man lets out a long sigh.

"When they were both gone, I went outside and smoked a cigarette. Looked up through the pines at the moon and the stars hung up there. Heavenly bodies so far away. They held no sway here from what I could tell."

He shakes his head a little, almost seeming disappointed.

"And whatever I was doing, it was what I had to do. It was fate.

"All of it could only happen that one way."

CHAPTER 15

Darger, along with Loshak, Corby, and three other LVMPD officers, armed themselves with flashlights and began a sweep of the terrain along the desert road.

"Watch out for gopher burrows," Corby said. "And rattlers."

Darger turned to Loshak, who was only a shaft of light in the blackness to her right.

"Rattlers? As in snakes?"

"What's the matter, Darger? You afraid of snakes?"

"Only the ones that bite," she said.

A wheeze of laughter filtered through the darkness.

The beam from Darger's own flashlight skimmed over the dusty ground and through the dry spines of prairie grass and tumbleweed, illuminating a single column for her to walk through.

They moved away from the constant diesel growl of the two fire engines. Aside from the chirping of the crickets and the swish of sand under her feet, the desert was as quiet as a graveyard.

One of the men coughed, interrupting the eerie peace, but eventually the desert closed in on them once again. Swallowed whole by the darkness, Darger felt like she was walking alone on a distant planet. When the light from her flashlight hit just right, she could see her breath fog in the cool, dry air.

There was a skittering sound like someone had kicked a stone over the hard ground and then a muttered curse.

Corby's voice cut through the night.

"We should call it off for now, come back out once it's

daylight. Maybe call in the K-9 cadaver team if it seems necessary, but if we keep this up, someone's liable to snap an ankle. "

Darger just stood and stared up at the stars for a moment, frustrated. He was right. It was too dark out here for any kind of search on foot, but she hated giving up. There had to be something out here. The burning car was left for a reason. It was a breadcrumb. They were meant to find more. But what? It was a clear night, and the stars shone like shards of glass on black velvet. She waited, but they had no answer.

She pivoted on her heel and started back toward the road.

Skirting around a clump of prickly pear, she felt the skeletal branches of desert shrubs clawing at the legs of her pants.

Her flashlight flicked off.

Darger gave the end a forceful tap. It flickered on and off again.

"Stupid piece of…," she hissed, whacking it with the heel of her hand.

The light came back, and she was momentarily satisfied, but she took another step and tipped forward, the bottom of her boot finding nothingness where the ground should be.

Falling.

A panicked thrill ran through her belly at the sensation of not knowing where she was in space. She lurched into the abyss, arms flinging out to her side.

The ground slammed hard into her right knee, and the flashlight flew from her grip, tumbling end over end.

"Shit!"

A different flashlight — held by someone off to her left — sliced through the night like a glowing sword and came to rest on her half-crumpled form.

The Girl in the Sand

"You OK?"

It was Loshak. He jogged a little closer, but she held up a hand to stop him.

"I just lost my footing. I'm fine."

Her light had skittered ahead of her about a yard. The wedge of illumination still glowed at one end, lighting up an oddly-shaped rock lying in the sand. Darger crawled forward on her hands and knees, grasping for the cylinder of metal with her fingers. It was still warm from where she'd held it before.

As the beam of light shifted, new features of the strange rock became discernible. Her breath caught in her throat, but it was still a few moments before her brain caught up with her eyes.

"Hey, Corby?" Her voice sounded odd in her own ears. Deadened and distant. "I think maybe you should call the cadaver dog in right now."

"Why's that?"

Darger stayed on her knees, not trusting her legs to hold her weight at the moment.

"Because I found something."

The footsteps of the other men drew closer, but Darger's eyes never left the place where her flashlight shone.

The strange rock wasn't a rock at all.

It was a human skull.

CHAPTER 16

The K-9 cadaver search team arrived just before dawn. The hills in the distance — normally a rusty red — were tinted blue and purple in the morning twilight. On the horizon, a soft pink haze announced the coming of the day, but the air still held a chill.

Detective Castellano became the savior of the morning when she showed up with coffee and donuts. They gathered around the food with the lid of the bakery box flapping in the cool breeze blowing in off the mountains.

It was chilly. Darger sipped at her coffee and danced from foot to foot, trying to keep her blood warm. She found herself glancing back into the wilderness every few seconds, trying to find the place where she'd discovered the skull. They agreed that it was best to leave it where it was found, with the hope that the rest of the skeleton would be nearby. And now she couldn't stop looking for it, as if it would disappear — roll away — when she wasn't paying attention.

Corby's phone blipped, and he stepped away to take the call. The rest of their party remained clustered around the donuts and coffee, shivering and waiting for the search team to say they were ready to start.

After a few moments, Corby rejoined the group, fastening the phone to a clip on his belt.

"That was your fingerprint lab back at Quantico," he said.

Loshak perked up. "Yeah?"

"No usable prints from the Travel Stop."

"Damn."

"Yeah," Corby agreed, pawing at the stubble along his fleshy

94

jawline. "Must be nice to get forensics back so quickly, though. I usually have to wait at least 48 hours for prints."

"This was a special circumstance. Had to call in a favor."

"Well, we appreciate it all the same. Even if this does end up to be a waste of time."

Darger ground her back teeth together. How could he possibly think they were still wasting their time after she'd found the skull?

But it wouldn't help things to get into a spat with him before the search had even started. She glared down at the gentle swirl of steam coiling above her coffee. Besides, the lot of them had been up all night. She probably wasn't the only one feeling irritable. Maybe he was just venting a little.

To ensure her mouth stayed shut, she grabbed a second donut and tore off a piece of fried dough with her incisors.

Her partner sniffed and squinted into the distance.

"Can't be total waste," he said, managing to keep his voice cool. "What are the odds of finding a lone skull in the desert? The rest of the skeleton is probably somewhere close-by."

She sipped her coffee to cover a smile and silently cheered Loshak on.

"Not necessarily. The carrion birds can do a hell of a job scattering bones over a good bit of land," Corby explained.

Castellano nodded her head in agreement. "And then once the coyotes get into it, you can have a skeleton spread miles in every direction."

Now Darger was the one scanning the endless desolation. Miles? How could they hope to find what they were looking for if that was true?

She dusted powdered sugar from her fingers and watched as the first sliver of sun peeked over the mountains off to the east.

The golden rays hit the line of clouds above, changing them from puffs of cotton candy to strands of sticky caramel. Instantly she felt a little warmer. She couldn't tell if it was an actual shift in temperature or some kind of placebo effect from seeing the sun rise.

Tara, the search dog's handler, approached. She was a small, muscular woman, built like an Olympic gymnast. Her black Labrador retriever, Hiro, followed just behind. When Tara stopped in front of the group, Hiro sat without command.

"We're ready when you are, sir," Tara said. "Just give the word."

Corby popped the remainder of his half-eaten donut in his mouth and tossed back enough coffee to wash it all down in a single swallow. Then he wadded the paper coffee cup into his fist and tossed it through the open window of his vehicle.

"Let's get this show on the road, then."

Tara kept Hiro on a leash as they trudged out into the desert, back to the place where Darger had found the skull.

The dog gave two short barks when Tara let him sniff the skull.

"Good boy."

Tara bent to unleash the dog, held up one hand, and gave the signal.

"OK, Hiro. Find it."

Hiro loped away, tail whipping to and fro.

Now the rising sun cast a flaming light on the land, turning the already orange hued rocks a bloody shade of crimson.

"Do you get a lot of false positives?" Darger asked. "Finding animals instead of people, I mean."

"No, ma'am. Hiro's trained to only find human remains."

Darger noted the *ma'am* and remembered that she'd called

Corby *sir* earlier. Military background, most likely.

"Really?"

"That's right."

"Impressive."

Tara didn't exactly smile, but something about the short nod she gave in response told Darger she was appreciative of the compliment.

Instead of a straight line, Hiro took a weaving, zigzag path through the scrub, pausing here and there to smell a rock or shrub more intensely. He kept his nose to the ground, better to inhale whatever trace scents his Sherlock of a nose was capable of detecting. She didn't know how the dog could sense anything over the fragrance of sagebrush that permeated the air.

Darger peered back at the cluster of parked cars they'd left behind. They were entirely surrounded by the vast emptiness of the desert, and it was difficult to fathom that they'd find anything out here but dust and stones and scratchy-looking plants. The starkness was overwhelming.

And already the heat of the day was making itself known. Darger slid off her jacket and pulled her hair up to keep it off her neck.

They crossed back and forth over the same ridge twice before Hiro stopped and pawed the sandy ground next to a lone Joshua tree. The dog barked once and laid down.

"He's got something," Tara said.

The two-legged members of their group picked their way through the brush slowly, gravel crunching underfoot. No one wanted to disturb a potential crime scene. Darger brushed at the little patch of sweat forming at her temple with the back of her hand.

They approached from behind, Hiro's body blocking their

view of what he'd found. Overhead, the twisting limbs of the Joshua tree looked like spined serpents. It cast a tangled shadow over the ground where the dog still lay, panting happily.

Tara closed in on Hiro and gave him his reward: some kind of purple ball with a tail. She tossed the toy, and Hiro bounded after it.

The rest of them fanned out around the spot in a lopsided circle, keeping a short distance.

No one spoke.

All eyes were on the jumble of bleach white bones partially buried in the sand.

CHAPTER 17

They heard the helicopter before they saw it. Corby scowled up at the news chopper as it came into view.

"Someone must have tipped off the media already. Damn it to hell."

From up there, Darger figured the forensic anthropologist and her team of graduate assistants looked like ants crawling over the dig site. It couldn't make for very intriguing news footage.

Even down at ground level, it was an agonizingly slow process. Dr. Siskin's world was one that utilized tweezers and brushes over shovels and pickaxes. She hovered over the bones with one of her students, using a brush to loosen the sandy earth. Another assistant fastened rows and columns of twine in a grid pattern to keep track of where each bone was found, while a third sifted through the loose dirt removed from the makeshift grave to make sure not so much as a stray tooth was missed.

Corby dabbed the leathery skin at the back of his neck with a handkerchief and tugged at the brim of his hat. He was getting antsy now that he knew the story would be hitting the news sometime today.

He waved a thick hand at Dr. Siskin, who indicated with a raised index finger that she'd be over in a moment.

Darger heard him mutter under his breath.

"Goddamned eggheads."

Dr. Siskin issued a few instructions to her student before brushing the dust from her fingers and rising to her feet.

"I know it's early, but can you tell us anything about it?"

Corby asked. "Age? Sex? How long it's been out here? I mean, how do we know we didn't stumble upon some ancient Indian burial site?"

Dr. Siskin signaled to a student cleaning the skull Darger had stumbled upon the previous night. Watching the white, bony orb change hands made Darger think of a macabre game of bowling.

With the skull in hand, Dr. Siskin flipped it upside-down, revealing an upper jaw with most of the teeth intact. She prodded at one of the molars.

"Well, to begin with, the skeletons found in a Native American burial ground wouldn't have had fillings."

Darger smiled a little at that. She wasn't sure if Dr. Siskin was being wry or just matter-of-fact, but she liked her either way.

"The only other thing I can tell you without a full examination is that this skull belonged to a female."

"You can know that this early? Just by the skull?" Castellano asked.

"Once I have the full skeleton, I can be certain, but there are several clues in a skull that can tell me whether it's male or female. The size, to begin with. Male skulls tend to be larger and thicker than female skulls. Also, the temporal line here."

She traced a gloved finger along a curving arc just above where the victim's ear should have been.

"It's not as thickly ridged as it would be on a male skull. And then there are the eyes."

She rotated the skull in her hands until the empty, black eye sockets were staring up at them. A latex fingertip tapped the lower edge of one of the sockets.

"The lower orbit here has that sort of sharp ridge to it, see?

That edge is much blunter on a male skull. The opposite is true with the superciliary arches here."

Dr. Siskin gestured at the forehead area.

"Male skulls have a little of that heavy, Neanderthal brow line left over from our archaic human ancestors. This one has no ridging. A few other signs are apparent: the less pronounced mastoid process, the zygomatic arch when compared to the external auditory meatus. All of these factors lead me to believe this skull is most definitely female."

Darger and Loshak had exchanged a few meaningful glances during Dr. Siskin's explanation. The skeleton was female. And while they had no proof at the moment that she'd been a victim of Leonard Stump, the fact that the remains were the correct gender didn't rule it out, either.

The local police and forensics team had set up several folding tables and some tents near the excavation site. One of the tables was dedicated to laying out the skeleton piece by piece. After a bone was cleaned, logged, and labeled, one of Dr. Siskin's students set it in a semi-anatomically correct position.

Darger scooted closer to the table and studied the bones of this girl in the sand. They'd assembled most of the right arm and a few of the ribs and vertebrae, but without the skull, Darger might have walked past the table and thought the collection nothing more than a jumble of ugly rocks. It was hard to reconcile that this was how every living person ended up.

Dust to dust, indeed, she thought.

She stared at the bones for some time, wanting to ask them questions and wishing they could answer.

Who are you?

How long have you been out here, alone underneath the fierce desert sun?

And lastly: *Who put you here?*

It was a sad fact that they'd spend more time on that question than any other. If they could match these remains to a missing person through dental records, the first two questions could be answered quickly. But after that was known, the *who* and the *why* of how the bones ended up here would become the primary focus. This girl would become just another victim.

Everyone knew Dahmer and Bundy and Stump by name, but how many could list the names of even one of their victims? There was something unfair about that. And unavoidable, she supposed.

A commotion near the partially excavated grave startled Darger from her reflections. She crept out from beneath the tent, abandoning the lonely bones and moving closer to the dig site.

The freshly churned dirt left a dark gash in the sand, a gaping mouth etched into the ground.

"Hand me the big square brush, would you?" Dr. Siskin was saying to one of her students.

It was only when the man moved aside that Darger saw what had caused the excitement.

Nestled in the crook of the first skeleton's knee was a second skull.

CHAPTER 18

Just before noon, when the two skeletons had been almost completely excavated, Dr. Siskin called out to Corby.

He glanced at the rest of their group, as if they needed encouragement to follow along. When they reached the edge of the pit, Siskin gestured at one wall of the broken earth.

"Is that..." Corby didn't — or couldn't — finish the sentence.

"A third skull," Dr. Siskin said. "Yes."

Corby swiped a palm across his brow.

"Holy hell."

"Can you tell if it's female, like the other two?" Castellano asked.

Siskin nodded. "From what I can see right now, I believe it is. It's been here longer, as well. The first two skeletons still have some skin attached. A few scraps of clothing. This one is pretty clean."

Corby sucked his teeth. His mouth quirked like he wanted to speak, but no words came.

"Our hands are more than full as it is," Siskin said. "I'd like your permission to call in some volunteers to help with the excavation. All people with experience, naturally. People I trust."

Corby blinked a few times before he answered.

"Right. Of course. Whatever you need."

He took a few steps away before he spoke again, Loshak and Darger following.

"I don't mind admitting this," Corby said. "I'm at a bit of a

103

loss. We've never dealt with something like this. Not in my time on the force."

"I think you should call the cadaver search team back in," Loshak said.

Darger nodded in agreement.

"There could be graves scattered all over this area if he was using it as a consistent dump site. He probably dumped them in twos. I'm guessing we'll find a fourth skeleton in this group, and more clusters of two in the surrounding area."

It didn't take long to confirm her hypothesis. Twenty minutes later they found the fourth skull.

This slab of desert had become a mass grave.

☾

Castellano strode up around 1:30 pm with a bag of Mexican food and big news. While they huddled in the shade of one of the tents to eat lunch, she shared a break in the case.

"We lucked out. One of the girls in the trunk broke her leg when she was a kid," she said, handing out burritos in foil sleeves. "It was bad. A compound fracture. Anyway, the coroner ran a serial number check on a surgical screw. Made a few calls this morning, and we've got our first positive ID."

Loshak stopped shy of biting his burrito to talk.

"Yeah?"

"Karli Reyes. Born in Bakersfield and new to town, according to the friend that reported her missing."

"When was she reported missing?" Darger asked. "Was she taken with someone else?"

"Missing Persons got the call five days ago. She was alone, but there's something else." Castellano took a sip of cola from a

Styrofoam cup before she went on. "She'd been working as an escort for the past couple years."

"A prostitute?" Darger said.

Castellano nodded.

A prostitute. Abducted alone. That didn't fit with Stump's body of work.

"I had a feeling this might be the case," Loshak said. "Leonard Stump has changed with the times. Evolved. He had to."

"What does that mean?" Castellano said.

"He started killing at a time when some people would still pick up a hitchhiker or pull over to help someone with a flat tire. People are too paranoid now, on top of the fact that if he kidnapped a suburban mom and her cheerleader daughter at four o'clock, it'd be national headlines by five, with a Nancy Grace special at seven."

Darger shook her head. She felt stupid for not considering this possibility before. Loshak obviously had.

"He's right," she said. "Working girls are low-hanging fruit for serial killers. They live and work under the radar, for the most part. A lot of sex workers go missing, and no one ever reports it. If you do end up with a body, then it's *No Human Involved* as far as a lot of law enforcement is concerned."

Loshak nodded, his jaw working up and down as he chewed. He wiped at the corners of his mouth with a napkin and went on.

"He's gone on killing all this time, picking off the people no one cares about. Burying them in the desert to go undetected. He burned those girls in the trunk the other night to raise his hand. To take credit. To let the world know that Leonard Stump is still in the game. But this?"

He gestured at the digging operation in the distance.

"These are his trophies. He wanted us to find them. Needed us to find them. It's an act of aggression. Territorial. What he'd been doing before was no longer enough. He needed to escalate the behavior, the spectacle."

Darger stared out at the horizon, barely tasting her mouthful of burrito.

"So what are you saying?" Castellano said.

"I think he knows we're out here, knows we're close, and I think that makes him more dangerous than ever."

(☾

Now the afternoon sun beat down, a sky so clear and blue and bright it almost seemed electric.

Corby stared at the group of volunteers busy in their assigned tasks. Digging, brushing, sifting, logging. A cloud of dust hung in the air.

"Two more vertebrae," one of the volunteers said.

A tech standing nearby photographed the bones and logged them on her clipboard.

A woman digging a few feet away stood then.

"I've got a femur."

Corby shook his head, lips pursed in disgust.

"Christ almighty," he said under his breath.

Detective Castellano folded her arms over her chest and turned to face Darger.

"So you really think it's him?"

Darger didn't need clarification on which *him* she was referring to.

"I do," Darger said, then nodded at her partner. "We do."

"What about the race issue? I'm no expert at the profiling business, but I know enough to understand that most serial killers choose victims from their own race. According to Siskin, we seem to have a whole mix of races here. And we know Karli Reyes was Latina."

Loshak shrugged and looked out at the horizon before he answered.

"Serial killing has changed along with society. It used to be lust murders happened almost exclusively within the same race as the perpetrator, but not anymore. There's some debate as to why that is. Some psychologists argue that it's because our culture has changed. We don't see race as a dividing line as much as we used to. We're less segregated as a society. Others believe that it's more about the availability of victims. People don't hitchhike anymore or let door-to-door salesmen into their homes. We're more paranoid as a society. Serial killers can't be choosy, so they take what they can get."

Corby squinted.

"Which do you think it is, if you don't mind my asking?"

"Me? I think it's probably a little of both, but I fall a little heavier on the side of opportunity. Same reason he's switched over to sex workers."

"Uh-huh."

One of the uniformed cops on site approached Corby. He was a younger officer with sandy hair and narrow lips that pressed into a frown.

"Can I talk to you, sir?" he said, before clarifying after a second. "Alone."

Corby nodded, and the two of them wandered out of earshot of the agents. Darger turned to look back on the digging, and Loshak followed her lead.

"Feel any better?" he said.

Darger crossed her arms. "Better?"

"Well, I think this will turn out to be pretty undeniable evidence that Leonard Stump has been killing all along. Dr. Siskin has already guessed that some of the remains have been here for a decade or more. All your *Vanity Fair* interview did was rekindle his desire for attention. You're off the hook."

Darger's eyes scanned from one excavated gravesite to the next. A cluster of finger bones. A femur and pelvis. And the skulls. So many skulls. They were up to twelve now and still hadn't started digging at some of the places marked by the cadaver dog.

She felt a touch nauseous from standing in the sun and the lack of sleep and the horror of what they'd discovered.

"Oh yeah. *Better* is exactly the word I'd use to describe finding a mass grave," she said with a scoff. "It's a real relief."

Loshak clapped her on the shoulder.

"That's the spirit."

Corby returned, hustling over the sand to rejoin Darger and Loshak.

"Just wanted to give you a heads up. We got a call about a possible ID from last night."

Loshak stood up a little straighter.

"The other girl in the trunk?" he said.

"Better. The girl in the gas station surveillance footage. The girl in the truck."

CHAPTER 19

A heavy thump jolts Emily awake. Solid objects colliding. Scraping.

Again, she can feel his presence in the room. A restless stirring somewhere nearby.

Her head snaps up.

It's darker now. Like the shadows have encroached. The creeping blackness swallowing the floor entirely, claiming more and more of the walls.

The light is gone. The lone bulb extinguished.

But one small square glows on the far wall. Orange flickers that don't make sense at first.

A fire.

Her mind leaps to an image of burned girls. Naked bodies shoved into car trunks. Torched. Reduced to charred meat and bone. Puddles of melted upholstery fused with the flesh.

That's who he is. His story about the cabins. She recognizes him at last. It's Leonard Stump.

She blinks. Frightened. Confused.

What's burning?

It's the stove. The little wood burning stove. Cast iron. The black tube of the chimney reaching up through the ceiling.

And then he comes into focus. His silhouette shifting. A flutter of darkness next to the flames.

Stump throws another wedge of wood into the stove, and the source of the thump that woke her is revealed.

He pokes at the fire with a stick a few times. Shifting branches scrape and thud.

Somehow this is a relief. Seeing him there before her. Knowing what he's doing. She doesn't know why, but it eases the tension.

Maybe knowing what's going on is always better, even when it's bad.

"Nah. It's called Stockholm syndrome," Gabby says in her head.

Maybe she's right. But Emily feels like there's something she's forgetting. Something important.

A deep breath inflates her torso, pulls her upright. She lets it out slowly. Sinking, sinking, sinking until her chin rests on her chest again.

The jolt of pain that accompanies her movements is distant now. More of a dull ache in her temple than the throbbing stab of an ice pick from before. It's the exhaustion she can't quite shake. The weakness in her arms, neck, eyelids.

She forces her head up, though. Forces herself to watch the dark figure who seems to float over the black nothing where the floor should be.

The flame flutters in the little metal chamber next to him. Orange wisps licking around the edges of split spruce and pinyon boughs. The haggard look of the wood makes her think that he has gathered this himself.

He sets his poking stick down. She thinks he'll close the stove door, shut out the light, wrap the darkness around both of them, but he doesn't.

Instead he starts talking again, his face angled toward the floor.

"That first time was the only spiritual experience I've ever had. In some ways I think I've been trying to recreate it ever since. Over and over. Trying to set up the circumstances that led

110

to that woman asking God to forgive me. Trying to catch that passing feeling so I could hold onto it this time. Keep it."

His voice grinds out of him. Gravelly. Hushed. It sounds a little hollow now that he's so far away, speaking into the tile floor.

"It always happens the same way. One drains out from the neck. Stains the bathtub bright red. Then I take the gag out of the other's mouth and see what she has to say. And it's this quiet moment. This reverent moment. We're right on the edge of something huge, and we can both feel it."

He lifts his head, but he still doesn't look at Emily. His eyes stare off into space.

"Not much, as it turns out. That's what they have to say, I mean. Maybe once you see that up close — that kind of brutality, naked violence without purpose, a human being killed for no good reason — it takes something out of most people. Changes them. Breaks them. That's what I figure anyhow."

The silence holds for a beat, and Emily feels the way her chest has gone taut, reminds herself to breathe.

"I suppose I can understand it. It brings the meaninglessness right up to your face. Presses your nose in it so you can't look any other way. Can't pretend it's not real. And that sucks some kind of feeling out of you. Some softness is gone for good. It changes who you are."

He scratches at his jaw.

"I tried it with a gun once, but it wasn't right. Too quick, I think. Don't get me wrong, guns are great for protection, but something like this… it has to feel right, has to evoke something, and that takes time."

She's certain now that this speech is more for himself than for her. It has the feeling of a monologue. Something he's said before. To other girls, maybe. Other girls he's killed. Emily feels a prickle of fear run up her spine.

"It's like I was starting to say before: We're all products of our culture. We're all whatever the world makes of us. For better or worse."

He stays crouched next to the stove while he talks, sitting on his haunches like some kind of beast.

"Just look at the story of humanity over the past 50 or 60 years. The picture painted in our culture. In the 60s, there was this big rejection of the way things had been. The hippies led this charge to change the rules, to change the world. We didn't need the old rules. Didn't need conformity and repression and, *Gee Wally, that's swell.* And for a little while it seemed like anything was possible. But look what we made of it."

His hands float before him, palms upturned.

"All that love and freedom and idealism turned into horror. Riots. Assassinations. Drug overdoses. Mass suicide in Jonestown. We had sensed that the materialistic, 1950s world we'd received had been empty, and we rejected it, but we still had nothing to put in its place. No meaning. Just more emptiness. New kinds of emptiness."

He smiles a little at this. Amused with his observations.

"All that free love got aborted. All the hippie couples grew up and got divorced."

She can see the white of his teeth reflecting the fire's light, the shine of it, but the grin fades as another flood of words pours out of him.

"Spirituality used to be the church. These traditions and rituals that kept us safe from evil, but they were empty like all the rest. No longer to be trusted. And now that anything was possible, spirituality's meaning was up for grabs. It morphed from the simplest protection, our safety net, into this terrifying unknowable chasm that could swallow reality out from under us. You can see these anxieties looking at the culture from that time. The horror genre was booming. We wanted answers about the supernatural, about the spiritual, wanted to know how to deal with the new darkness."

He pauses to swallow and then goes on.

"And then some time in the 80s, all of that died off almost overnight. Instead of fearing the afterlife, we simply rejected it as well. We'd somehow circled back to that original materialism we'd refused. No more dreams of peace and love. Everyone wanted to be wealthy, vying for some spot in a big corporation, snorting Tony Montana's mountain of cocaine. Greedy. Selfish. Painless. Like if you could just get rich enough, your life could become a blissful dream. You didn't have to worry about any of this other junk, didn't have to be scared or confused or feel pain at all. Disney World and commercials and all those blockbuster movies where the good guy wins, they were selling us this new vision. They were building a material dream world, and you could live there forever so long as you had the cash to pay for it."

Stump's tongue snaked out of his mouth to moisten his lips.

"Our collective idea of horror shifted from ghosts and vampires to slasher movies. We weren't scared of what might lurk in the great beyond so much as we were scared of really big knives, scared of the killer creeping in our window at night, the one who might take us out of this material dream world once and for all."

Again, a half-smile curls the corners of his lips as he stokes the fire.

"The one like me, I guess."

113

He falls quiet after that. Staring at the wall. His jaw churning some.

The warmth of the fire seems to swell then, and tranquility accompanies the silence this time. A stillness that spreads over the room like a puddle.

The firewood pops now and again. Little snaps like breaking twigs.

And the smell of the burning spruce fills the space. A pine odor reminiscent of Christmas. It is not unpleasant.

Sleepiness heavies her eyelids, and the heat flushes her face. She is nodding off as he speaks again.

"Wait."

He clears his throat, though he still doesn't look at her.

"You should eat."

Again she isn't sure if he's talking to her or himself. The words seem to be about her, but his tone sounds more like he's thinking out loud.

He stands. Moves to that big steel door. Fiddles with the lock.

The color leaches out of him now that he's away from the fire's glow, turning him gray and indistinct. More shadow than man.

Emily squints to try to see through the gloom. She can't make out the key in his hand, but she hears the snick of the deadbolt pulling out of the strike box, sliding out of the way.

He turns his wrist, and the door creaks a little as it peels free of the door frame, and it's open.

Emily can't help but gasp a little at the sight of it. The open door. The escape route laid bare.

His torso fills the door frame for just a second, and then he disappears into the dark on the other side.

The Girl in the Sand

His footsteps are light. More soft scuffing sounds than the pounding footfalls she might expect based on the size of him. She listens as their sound trails away to nothing.

The silence holds for three heartbeats, and then the panic is on her. Eyes locked on that open door.

She strains at the handcuffs. Rocks the desk up onto two legs and braces herself as it thumps back down a second later.

Her heart batters away at the walls of her chest. Awake. Alive.

The way free hangs open. So close.

She lurches toward it like an idiot dog at the end of its chain. Making almost no progress. The desk thrashing around. Scooting a couple of inches toward its destination.

The steel edges of the cuffs groove red circles into her wrists.

So close. It's all she can think. Wide eyes staring into the dark rectangular opening.

But no. Not now. Not yet. She can't be stupid.

It would never work like this. Attached to a desk. Him out there waiting.

She needs to think all of this through. Needs to be patient.

She stops flailing. Takes a breath.

The footsteps fade back in somewhere out there. The volume swelling as he draws near.

The shadow figure appears in the doorway. Something solid taking shape in the gloom. Blacker than the rest.

He pads toward her, walking on the balls of his feet, his movements somehow catlike. Lithe. Graceful. He passes into the fire's light, and color blooms once more on his body. The dark blue of his jeans. The brown of his button-down shirt.

The shadows still swirl about his face, though. Shifting pockets of blackness that obscure his features, shrouding most completely at his brow and jaw.

A bowl hovers before him, cupped there in both hands, the stem of a spoon rising out at an angle.

So he had been talking about feeding her.

He squats just in front of her desk, blocking out the fire's light.

This space seems very dark now. The nothingness along the floor lurching upward to swallow more of the room.

"Eat," he says, his voice going harder than it had been.

It takes a second, but she sees the spoon floating in front of her face, a scoop of something dark loaded on it. She obeys his command, mouth closing around the piece of cutlery, around some bit of food she can't quite see.

The foreign substance reveals itself to her in stages. Cold. Mushy. Sweet. The faintest bitterness in the aftertaste.

After the first bite, she's pretty sure it's pudding. The sweetness and the texture tell her that much. After the third, she believes it to be chocolate. That touch of bitterness leads her to this conclusion, though it's so subtle she's not certain. It could be butterscotch.

Her eyes adjust to the new level of light between them, and the features of his face start to become clear.

At first, he is all big eyes in the dark. Cold eyes that blink slowly, a motion that reminds her of some intelligent creature she can't place.

Then the vague shape of his nose fades into view. Straight and bony. The angular cheekbones and brow. The strong jaw.

His lips twitch twice. A pair of false starts before he begins to speak.

"Bodies and souls. That's the thing, right? That's what our culture can't make up its mind about. Our explanations of them

116

morph into something new every decade, and the shared dreams follow suit. All of our desires. All of our ideologies. They never stop shifting."

He offers another scoop, gently pushes it past her lips and into her mouth.

"That's the paradox that we'll probably never figure out. We are flesh. We are skin and bone and blood. A wrinkled up brain. All of our experiences filter through our bodies. And yet our bodies alone are not us. We are some kind of consciousness. We are ideas, dreams, a personality. Things that exist beyond the physical plane, at least in some sense. Something that exists in the abstract. Some people think there's a soul, but more people than ever don't. And maybe we're getting to some kind of crisis on that front."

The spoon tinkles against the side of the bowl, chimes out a shrill note, and the sound interrupts his thought.

He blinks a few times. Gathers another spoonful and feeds her.

"With the pervading point of view in the world today, life is mostly meaningless and yet it's the only thing with any purpose, which makes it deeply meaningful. It is both. It's everything and nothing. Positive and negative. Both things are equally true. It's a miracle and an abomination. The beginning and the end. The best of times and the worst of times."

He smiles, large teeth glowing purple among the shadows like strange hunks of porcelain.

"And sometimes I think that makes every experience a religious one. We look for some spiritual meaning everywhere, some way to make existence make sense. And that's what we're doing here. Both of us. We're right on the edge of it. Sitting on the lip of the thing, looking down into the well."

117

The tiredness hits her all at once as he jabbers on. Some emptiness spun into her head. Some weakness rendered in her neck and eyes.

Her internal world seems to deepen, to suck her further into her own skull. The outside world suddenly so far away.

Awareness of what's happening washes over her in waves. An explanation seeping into her consciousness. Slowly, slowly.

The pudding. He's drugged her. Of course.

"Sleep now. I have to head out for a bit. We'll have company soon, and uh…"

For the first time, he almost seems to be searching for words. Unrehearsed.

"See, you'll go second. You'll see everything. And something about you makes me think maybe you could be… I don't know. I don't want to jinx it. I've been disappointed so many times before."

Her head dips. Eyes droop. She catches a glimpse of the darkness before she bobs back to the surface. The black nothing waits just on the other side of her swoon.

She fights it just long enough to see him pass through the doorway again.

And reality is gone.

CHAPTER 20

Loshak navigated the rental car through the bustle of Las Vegas, though from the passenger seat Darger noticed the sights and sounds of the city not at all.

Instead she stared at the photograph on her phone, all other stimulus blocked out apart from that image. Sad eyes. Dark hair. There was an intelligence in the girl's features, Darger thought. A vulnerability balanced with a sense of humor, a sense of knowing.

It was the profile picture of a seemingly dormant Twitter account. The girl hadn't tweeted since late 2016. Her last tweet had been about her daughter's birthday cake.

Emily Kessler. That was the girl's name.

Technically, she was Emily Whitlock by marriage, but according to the babysitter who called in the Missing Persons report, the couple had separated some months earlier, and Emily had reverted to using her maiden name.

Darger compared Emily's photo to the grainy surveillance screenshot of the girl in the pickup truck, just faintly visible in those few moments when the lights of a passing car washed over her. It had to be Emily. The resemblance was there, and the timing was right. Emily had disappeared only hours before the truck was sighted at Marco's Travel Stop.

And now Leonard Stump had her somewhere, still alive most likely.

The next break came when Castellano found Emily listed on a local escort website called Sin City Bliss. Karli Reyes, the first girl they'd identified from the burned-out car, also had a profile on the site. A coincidental connection, perhaps. But for now, it was something to go on. A possibility.

Castellano and her team were busy running down more leads from the site. Pulling dental records of any missing girls who had a listing, hoping to match them to the other body they'd found in the trunk with Karli.

"Too bad the fingerprints at the gas station didn't pan out," Loshak said, shaking her from her thoughts. "Would have made things easier. As far as confirming once and for all that it's Stump, I mean."

Darger set the phone in her lap, the picture of Emily guttering to a black screen.

"Maybe today will be what we need."

"I hope so. Her house is just up here."

So this was it. Claire Garcia's house. Darger had heard a lot about Claire over the years, both in the media reports about Stump but also from Loshak.

Twenty years ago, Stump abducted Claire and her best friend, Tammy Podolak, outside of a bar in downtown Vegas. Somehow, despite being bound and drugged, Claire escaped, and it was this turn of fate that led to Stump's capture and arrest. Claire's friend was not so lucky.

And that's why they were here today. There was a chance Tammy lay among those skeletons buried in the sand. It was a long shot, perhaps, but if Claire could verify that, it'd be another break in the case. Finally they'd be able to get local law enforcement on board for a full-on Leonard Stump manhunt.

The car seemed to slow as they got closer to Claire's place. Loshak opened his mouth as if to speak, worked his jaw like he was chewing on something.

"What?" Darger said.

"Nothing, I just…"

He sighed.

"Spit it out. I can tell something's bugging you."

"OK, just don't take this the wrong way."

"You know, that's my second-favorite way to start a conversation. My favorite is, *You know what your problem is?*"

Loshak struggled against a smile.

"It's serious."

"I'm listening."

"Claire's been through a lot. She's… sensitive, I guess you could say. And she values her privacy. There's a reason she's never done interviews, never written a book. But there's something else, too."

Darger squinted into the sun and waited for him to go on.

"She blames herself, which isn't a surprise. Survivor's guilt and all that."

"Expected. I still don't know what you're getting at, though."

"Just don't push her too hard, OK? We might not get anything from her. She might not even want to talk to us. And we have to respect that."

Darger narrowed her eyes at him.

"What do you think I'm going to do? Bust out the waterboarding gear?"

"No. I didn't mean it like that. Just… you can be a little tenacious, you know?"

"Tenacious?"

"I mean, ferocious, maybe. You get that shark look in your eyes."

"Jesus, Loshak. You make me sound half-feral."

Loshak wheeled the rental into the driveway, and their attention shifted from the conversation to the house before them.

It was a small home — a stucco box with a tile roof like all the rest in the neighborhood. The front yard was a mostly barren swath of sand and rock.

Claire sat on the porch, if you could call it that. It was a simple slab of concrete with two steps down to the sidewalk, a small rectangle of shade provided by the overhang above the door.

The woman's face looked blank at first, but when Loshak stepped out of the car, she had a small smile for him.

"This is my partner, Violet Darger," he said.

"It's a pleasure to meet you," Darger said, reaching out to shake Claire's hand.

It was a small hand, delicate and girlish. Timid.

Up close, Darger could make out the scar — the puckered place extending from the corner of Claire's mouth where Leonard Stump's blade had left its mark, written something into her flesh forever.

"Maybe we could go inside if you have a minute," Loshak said. "So we could talk."

Claire stood and reached to open the door, but she stopped with her hand on the knob and turned back to face Loshak.

"Wait. I just have to know. It's her, isn't it? You found Tammy."

"We don't know yet," Loshak said. "That's why we're here. We need you to take a look at some things."

☾

Police photographs lay on the kitchen table — shots of the various incidentals found among the bodies in the desert grave.

122

The Girl in the Sand

Trinkets. Bracelets. Necklaces. Keychains. The objects looked strange — almost sinister — when isolated like this, each framed alone in the rectangle of glossy photo paper. The stark effect granted them an eerie quality, like talismans from a horror movie. Curios of the cursed, of the damned. When Darger really thought about it, it wasn't so far off from the truth.

Claire leaned over the pile Loshak had laid out on the tabletop, her eyes squinted. She took her time, studying one for several moments before moving on to the next. When she spoke, her voice came out just louder than a whisper.

"Is each one of these from a different girl?"

Darger answered in a measured tone.

"We're not sure. The identification process can be very slow…" Darger stopped talking and finished the thought in her head: *When we've only got bones to work with.*

"But you found a lot of bodies, right? They kept calling it a mass grave on the news."

Darger glanced at Loshak, not sure if he wanted to answer. He took a sip of lemonade. Stalling.

"Yes, there are quite a few."

"How many?"

Again Darger waited, deferring to Loshak's judgment.

"Nineteen confirmed, so far. But there are more."

Claire's hand flew up to cover her mouth, an involuntary movement that reminded Darger of a fleeing bird.

"Take your time, Claire," Loshak said. "I know it's hard."

After a second, the girl nodded and went back to examining the ghoulish photos, that serious look forming again on her face, replacing the frightened one.

Darger couldn't help but observe her as she worked. Long lashes. Heart-shaped face. Small, elfin features. Dark eyes. She still looked like a girl in most ways, though she had to be in her 40s by now. A wounded child. She'd been through so much already, and now she was tasked with looking through all these remnants of the dead.

In time, Loshak and Darger stood, obeying some unspoken instinct to give Claire space. They lingered a few paces away, sweaty glasses of lemonade clutched in their hands.

Out of the corner of her eye, Darger sensed a man's figure forming in the kitchen doorway, a dark shape that Darger took as hostile at first. Then some part of her remembered that Claire lived with someone. Mark Morgan, if she was remembering the name right.

"Good afternoon," Loshak said, holding his hand out to shake.

The man made no move to take it. His eyes had fallen on the photographs on the table.

"What's all this?" he said, his voice loud and a little piercing.

When no one answered, he took a step toward Claire.

"I thought we agreed you were done with this crap."

Claire answered him.

"I'm handling it, Mark. Just go watch TV, baby."

He just stood there, glaring, eyes swiveling from Darger to Loshak and back.

"Go on, Mark."

At last, he turned. Disappeared into the hall.

"I'm sorry," Claire said, eyes locked on Loshak. "He just…."

"No need to apologize, Claire. We're the ones intruding in your life."

She nodded, turned back to the pictures.

Within a few seconds, Claire blinked rapidly against a line of tears collecting at the corners of her eyes. At first, Darger took this as a sign, but when she peeked over at Loshak, he gave the tiniest shake of his head. And Claire kept sifting through.

Sensitive was how Loshak had described her, and Darger thought that seemed pretty spot on just now. What did it cost Claire — the only known survivor of Leonard Stump — to look through these mementos of all the girls who hadn't gotten away?

When Claire had shuffled through nearly the whole stack, Darger felt her hope dwindle. This was going to be another dead end.

She flexed her back muscles, trying to stifle the itch of frustration building between her shoulder blades. It wasn't Claire's fault if nothing looked familiar. It wasn't anyone's fault. But Darger had so wanted this to pan out.

Abruptly, Claire got to her feet, dropping the photographs onto the table in front of her. Before they could ask what was wrong, Claire had rushed out of the room.

Darger looked at her partner.

"Maybe this wasn't the best idea."

"It's not like we had a choice," Loshak answered, but his tone said it plainly. He was regretting the decision to come here.

There was a connection between Loshak and Claire. Darger felt it. Both were haunted by the same ghost.

Padded footsteps and a creaking floorboard announced Claire's return. Darger stood.

"I'm sorry if we've upset you. We shouldn't have pushed you to look at this stuff."

Claire swept past without acknowledging the words, one hand balled into a fist.

Darger questioned Loshak with her eyes, but he only shrugged.

Claire took her seat again, and began spreading the pictures out on the coffee table. She slid them around into piles, searching for something. Finally she stopped, with one of the photos separated from the rest.

It showed an oblong piece of metal, oddly shaped with one flat side and one rounded side. Darger remembered noticing it in one of the evidence baggies. She'd studied it for a long time, trying to determine what it might have been.

Claire's fingers unfolded. There was a necklace nestled in the cup of her palm: a silver ball chain with a charm on the end. The charm was similar in shape to the mystery item in the photograph, only this one hadn't been buried in the desert for twenty years.

Hand shaking, Claire set the necklace down on top of the photo. Together, the two pieces formed an egg-shaped oval.

Leaning closer, Darger made out a pattern in green and black enamel in the part Claire had brought. If the other piece hadn't been worn down by sand and time, the two halves would have formed a cartoonish alien face.

Her heart broke a little as the solution to the mystery came to her. The necklaces were the kind you bought as a set: one half for you to keep, the other to give to your best friend.

Claire fixed Loshak with her wet eyes.

"It's Tammy."

CHAPTER 21

The white sun bore down hard as they stepped out of the shade of Claire Garcia's house. Darger had almost forgotten it was the middle of the day while she sat in that dim little house with all the blinds drawn. It was like Claire's world was permanently twilight. Shut away from the world.

Darger's shadow stretched out before her on the dusty path that led to the car. Two kids wheeled around in circles on a driveway across the narrow lane, one on a scooter, the other on a Big Wheel tricycle. Overhead, the fronds of a date palm fluttered in the warm breeze.

Neither she nor Loshak uttered a word until they were inside the car. He fired up the engine and turned the air conditioning on full blast.

"So," Darger said, breaking the silence. "Now we know for sure."

"Yeah."

This was it. They finally had proof that the man they were hunting was indeed Leonard Stump. And yet instead of the excitement or vindication she thought they'd feel, the atmosphere in the car was somber.

Part of it was that Darger couldn't stop thinking about what Claire said before they left. How she'd told them about the necklaces.

"It was a Christmas present. There was that whole alien craze back then, and Tammy was obsessed. I saw these ridiculous Best Friends alien face necklaces, and I knew it was the kind of thing Tammy would love. She liked things like that.

127

Sort of intentionally tacky or whatever."

Two best friends, torn apart by bizarre circumstance. Tammy died, Claire lived. And every day Claire shouldered the weight of it. All the nostalgia and good memories of her youth tainted by guilt and regret.

How must it feel to blame yourself for your own survival? To feel guilty for merely being alive?

Loshak's voice interrupted her train of thought.

"You gonna make that call?"

"Huh?"

"To let Corby know we got a preliminary ID on Tammy?"

"Oh. Right," Darger murmured.

She reached for her phone. She must have been sitting there in contemplation for some time, because they were already on the highway.

Darger flipped through her contacts and dialed the Sheriff's office. A secretary answered but put Darger through immediately. Corby answered after the first ring.

"Agent Darger. I hope you're having a pleasant afternoon."

"Well, I don't know if *pleasant* is the right word for it. We talked to Claire Garcia. She recognized one of the objects from the grave site and confirmed it was a necklace that belonged to Tammy Podolak."

There was silence on the other end of the line.

"Are you still there?"

Darger heard a heavy sigh, and then the man spoke up.

"Sorry. I copy. Just thinking of the media circus this is going to stir up. The LVCVA is going to be all over my ass, pardon my French."

"Those were the people at the meeting, right?"

"Yes, ma'am. They oversee all the marketing for tourism and

conventions in town. That's where all our catchy slogans come from: *Only in Vegas. What happens here, stays here.* All that crap. They've got a lot of clout," Corby explained. "But it can't be helped now. And I suppose I owe you and your partner an apology. I was wrong. To dismiss your theory like that, I mean. I was wrong."

"No apology necessary. And now that we're all on the same page, perhaps we could put together some kind of task force. Start figuring out how we're going to find him."

"Took the words right out of my mouth. Though I have a development of my own, actually."

When he finished filling her in and suggested a rendezvous, Darger agreed.

"We'll be there."

She ended the call and felt a prickle of excitement run down her spine. Things were snowballing now, gaining momentum.

"Are you going to share, partner? Or are you just gonna sit there looking like a cat with a mouthful of canary?"

"They verified the second girl from the burned out car. Dental records."

"And?"

"Camila Newell. Local girl, born and raised. 22 years old."

"Escort?"

Darger nodded.

"Arrested last year, but the charges were dropped, so she doesn't technically have a record. But it's enough for our purposes. That makes two prostitute victims. If Emily Kessler is the girl in the gas station footage, it makes it three. And Loshak?"

"Yeah?"

"We have an address for this one."

Loshak turned his head. Their eyes met.

"Let's go."

CHAPTER 22

Camila Newell's home was a two-story stucco townhouse in North Las Vegas. It was clean and neat inside. Meticulous. Houses this tidy always made Darger feel acutely aware of her own slovenliness.

She let her gaze wander the room, touching on the Keurig machine with a selection of flavored pods, a stack of rainbow-colored mugs on the granite countertop, a hand-lettered wood sign hung on the wall that read, *But first... wine.*

Nearby, Corby and Detective Castellano sat at a small dining room table with Camila's roommate, Joshua Pierson. He was large in height and girth and just as well-groomed as the rest of the house, with dark, impeccably shaped eyebrows and carefully trimmed facial hair. He was also very tan, which seemed to be a recurring theme out here in Vegas.

Darger and Loshak stood off to the side and let the locals do their thing, though she was a little dismayed at Corby's interview technique. He launched straight into the tough questions with no warm-up.

"Did you know about Miss Newell's activities?"

Joshua crossed his arms.

"You mean, did I know she was an escort?" he asked. "Yes, I knew what she did for a living. But she was a nice girl. Really. If you walked past her on the street, you wouldn't have known. She was always very put together."

"And what is it you do for work, Mr. Pierson?"

"I'm a bartender. Weekdays I work at Beachlife." His eyes flicked over to Darger, who had raised a confused eyebrow. "It's the pool and cabana area of the Hard Rock Hotel."

"Gotcha."

"And on weekends, I work at Red Lotus. It's a… gentleman's club." Joshua gave a sheepish shrug. "That's how we met. Camila worked there for a while."

"Stripping?"

Joshua nodded.

"Is that how she got into her current line of business?"

Joshua brought his thumb to his lips as though to chew the nail but seemed to catch himself. He retracted the hand, picking at the nail instead.

"I don't really know."

"You don't know?" Corby repeated, his voice hard and almost mocking.

Darger stepped closer to the dining table and slid into the chair next to Joshua.

"If you're worried about telling us things that could get you in trouble at work, don't. That's not what we're here about, OK?"

She stared at Joshua until he made eye contact with her and nodded. He stopped fidgeting with his fingernails and clasped his hands together.

"Some of the girls — and geez, some of the guys — they offer *extras*, if you know what I mean. They'll offer to meet customers after hours. Usually it's the men that come in and throw a lot of money around in the private rooms. It's assumed that's what they're looking for, to be honest. And because it's not done on the premises, and it's up to the individual arranging the date, management tends to look the other way."

"And Camila was one of the girls that would go on these… after hours dates?"

Joshua bobbed his head once.

"Why did she leave Red Lotus?"

"She said she made better money on dates, and the hours were more flexible. Plus she hated the strip club atmosphere — I mean, I do too. Some of the girls can get kind of competitive and catty. The managers are almost all scumbags. And when she made her own dates, she didn't have to deal with the big groups of entitled frat douches that leave bad tips."

Corby, apparently bored with Darger's more subtle line of questioning, yanked the interview back into the fast lane.

"Were you two involved? Romantically, I mean?"

Darger glanced at Loshak and rolled her eyes.

"Uh, no," Joshua answered, blinking slowly. "I'm gay."

Corby's mouth puckered, a pink hue flushing his cheeks. Darger was glad when Castellano stepped in to take the reins. Detectives usually had more finesse when it came to questioning witnesses.

"Did Camila work through an agency?" she asked.

Loshak's voice came from the other end of the room. He'd been silent until now.

"An escort agency? I thought prostitution was illegal in Vegas."

"It is," Castellano said. "But there's nothing illegal about arranging for *companionship.* That's what the agencies call it, anyway."

When the focus was back on Joshua, he shook his head.

"No agency. She worked freelance."

"Did she ever bring dates back here?"

Joshua's hand cut through the air.

"Never. She said she needed to keep the two halves of her life completely separate."

Darger wasn't surprised. For a lot of these girls, it really was like living a double life.

"Did she have a boyfriend?" Castellano asked.

"No."

"When was the last time she had a boyfriend?"

"It's been a while. Over a year, at least. When she first started… the escort thing… she tried to keep dating for real. But I don't think it worked out."

"Did any of her previous boyfriends or dates cause trouble that you know of? Getting violent? Stalking her?"

"If they did, she never mentioned it to me."

Something about his phrasing caught Darger's attention.

"It sounds like you two were pretty close. Would that be the kind of thing she wouldn't tell you for some reason?"

Joshua looked down at his hands, and when he answered, his voice sounded thick from holding back tears.

"Probably not. I never judged her, but that doesn't mean I liked what she was doing. It was dangerous."

He exhaled a long and shaky breath.

"I begged her to stop. Not relentlessly, but a couple times. Tried to teach her how to mix drinks. She could have made a killing in tips at some of the bars around town. It's not hard, but you've got to memorize some stuff, and the other way was just… too easy."

Joshua picked at his cuticles in silence for a moment before continuing.

"She'd let me know when she was going out, but that was it."

"Did she tell you she was going out on Thursday?"

"Yes."

"But you don't know where?"

"At some hotel, but I don't know which one."

Darger sat up a little straighter but kept her voice cool.

"How do you know she was going to a hotel?"

"She always checked to make sure they had a room first. Because one time this guy wanted to… conduct their business… in his car instead of getting a room. He drove them out to one of the old gravel pits, and then he got a little rough with her. She was scared after that, always made sure she'd be around people when she was on a job."

Darger's gaze fell to the circle of light reflecting off the table. Somehow even being in a public place hadn't saved her from Leonard Stump.

Detective Castellano swiped at her phone and then held it out to Joshua. It was Karli Newell's Facebook profile.

"Have you ever seen this woman?"

Joshua frowned, taking some time to study the screen.

"No."

She swiped the screen again, and it now switched to Emily Kessler's sad Twitter photo.

"And her?"

Joshua shook his head.

"Are the names familiar at all? Maybe Camila had mentioned one of them before?"

"I don't think so. Sorry." His Adam's apple bobbed as he swallowed. "Is one of them… I mean, I saw on the news that there were two… bodies… in the trunk."

Castellano's eyes wandered over to Corby, who gave a small nod of approval.

"Yes, Karli and Camila were found together. We'd appreciate if you kept that to yourself for the time being."

"Sure. I just… I wish I could tell you more. I don't think she knew any other girls in the trade, if that helps. I mean, she never brought any over. I never heard her talking to anyone I didn't know… I mean, aside from when she was setting up dates. I guess she could have set up dates with other girls, if someone wanted more than one. Like a bachelor party or something? But I didn't really ask for details about her appointments. It was… unspoken. So much was unspoken between us."

Paper rustled as Castellano flipped through her notepad.

"What about a website called Sin City Bliss? Does that ring any bells?"

Joshua's eyes went wide, showing too much of the whites.

"We watched movies on her laptop sometimes," he said, swallowing loudly. "And I saw a tab open that caught my eye once. I didn't mean to click it. I was just curious. And when I did, it was a listing for her… services. I'm pretty sure that was the name of it. SinCityBliss.com"

"Do you know how long she'd been using it?"

Joshua's shoulders pulled into a shrug.

"I never asked. I didn't want her to think I'd been snooping or something." He paused, and his face flushed a little. "Even if I sort of was."

Fresh tears formed in the man's eyes.

"And now I wish I'd insisted on knowing more. Where she was going. Who she was with. I could have ridden along with her, made sure she was safe. Or at least had her leave the name of the hotel she'd be at for the night. But in a way, I think I didn't want to know. I didn't like to think of her that way. And maybe she wouldn't have wanted me knowing those things."

"Keeping the two lives separate," Darger repeated.

Joshua glanced up and met her eyes, nodding.

"But I could have tried."

CHAPTER 23

Three hours. That's how long they had to come up with a plan before the task force meeting. And they had jack squat, which was what Darger was telling Loshak over a cup of mediocre coffee.

"We have a little more than that," he said. "We know it's Stump. We know he's sticking to his pattern of killing in pairs. He has one already that we know of. That means he'll probably take another in the next day or two."

Darger poked at her half-eaten donut, which was worse than mediocre.

"You're really selling it. I'm getting all tingly thinking about the next girl he abducts."

Her sarcasm elicited a stony stare from her partner.

"Well, Malenchok said it shouldn't take long to get the site ownership information. That could give us something."

Darger shook her head. Loshak's pet geek was working on figuring out whatever he could about sincitybliss.com, but Darger knew it wouldn't matter. Whatever enterprising digital pimp or madam had conceived of Sin City Bliss, it wasn't who they were looking for. And yet she couldn't stop herself from checking the site every few minutes. There had to be a clue there somewhere, something they could use… they just hadn't found it yet.

Camila's profile was still open on her phone. She stared down at the screen before hitting the back button to return to the main listing page.

Scrolling through the seemingly endless listings filled her

with a sense of dread. So many potential victims to choose from for a monster like Leonard Stump. Who would be next?

If he was using this site — or another one like it — how did he choose? Was it random, or did he trawl through the list until he found a girl willing to meet?

Darger tapped a photo with her thumb. Each listing consisted of a name, age, description, photograph, and phone number. About half of the profiles featured photographs primarily focused on body parts. Teensy bikini tops stretched over large breasts. Barely-there thongs framing bare buttocks. The girls' faces were often cropped out or turned away from the camera. Darger wondered if that was more about anonymity or because the men interested in their services only cared about their bodies.

But they weren't all that way. Some of the girls provided headshots as well.

The current profile Darger was perusing was for Sapphire, age 29. Her pictures were surprisingly tame, barely more suggestive than your average Instagram selfie.

Sapphire described herself as a "BBW Seeking A Respectful Gentleman. Flirty, Fun, Exotic, And DRAMA FREE!!! Serious Calls Only."

Darger hoped Sapphire didn't get any *serious calls* from Leonard Stump.

She clicked back to the main listing page and scrolled through the listings once, twice, three times. She sat up taller in her seat.

"It's gone."

Loshak polished off the dregs in his cup.

"What's gone?"

"Camila's listing. It isn't here anymore," she said, refreshing the page and then turning her phone around to show him the screen. "How is that possible? Did someone delete it?"

While Darger refreshed the page a dozen more times, Loshak got back on the phone with Malenchok and relayed the new development. No matter how many times she reloaded the page, Camila Newell's profile did not reappear.

She heard the crackle of Malenchok's voice murmuring tech-babble into Loshak's ear. Her partner angled the receiver away from his mouth to repeat it back to her.

"He says the website is set up to automatically purge old listings. Anything older than seven days has to be resubmitted by the listing owner. It's pretty standard for a Classifieds-style website, apparently. But it's not gone. Not yet, anyway. He's emailing an archived version of the page to you now."

Darger's phone blipped, notifying her of new mail. She opened her inbox and clicked the link Malenchok sent for the archived page. It looked the same as she remembered. Her panic subsided.

Loshak was thanking Malenchok, preparing to hang up. Darger snapped her fingers and held up her hand to stop him.

"What?" he asked.

"Ask him if he can find other expired listings."

Malenchok must have heard her voice over the line, because without repeating the question, Loshak nodded.

"He says he can. It'll take a few minutes."

A rush of adrenaline flooded her system. She felt giddy.

Loshak had it, too. She could tell by the sharp look in his eye. Like a hawk that's spotted a shrew in the grass.

"You think we might be able to use old listings to identify bodies from the mass grave."

Darger nodded.

"It's a good starting point for pulling dental records, in any case. And the more victims we match to the website, the more certain we can be that he's finding them there."

Loshak hung up to allow Malenchok some time to do the work. He eyed her half-finished donut.

"Let's get some real food and head back to the hotel. Maybe we'll get lucky, and Malenchok will have something for us by then. And in the meantime, we can think about the next step."

CHAPTER 24

Electricity thrums in Emily's head. Cold current coursing through her veins. It stings. Pulses on and off. Makes pins prick along the flesh of her scalp, every follicle alive and writhing.

But she's awake. Or on her way there, in any case. Surfacing slowly from the nowhere place.

The medicated feeling still occupies her skull. Wooziness. Confusion.

Right away she knows he's not here, at least not in this room. She can feel his absence. That little disturbance in the atmosphere he creates when he's around. Something masculine and restless and threatening. It's not there.

Weird how that works. How his being near casts a pall over the room, changes the feel of everything. She tumbles the notion and starts to drift a little. Sinking a little instead of rising.

No. She can't.

She fights the sleepiness. Lifts her head on a wobbly neck. Forces her eyes open, even if it kills.

The tile floor bobs before her. Swimmy along the edges. Disappearing whenever her eyelids droop into a slow blink.

The fire has burned low on the other side of the room. Reduced to glowing chunks of orange that swell and wane rhythmically as though the coals are breathing.

But it hasn't burned all the way out. Time has passed since he drugged her, but not as much as he might have hoped. She is certain of this, somehow.

It's darker than it was, but her eyes have adjusted better than before. Her pupils open wide. Gaping. Finally able to see

141

through the charcoal smears of shadow layered over everything. She can even make out the grout lines carving the tile floor into a grid once more, but only if she doesn't look straight at them.

She takes a few breaths. Rolls her neck from shoulder to shoulder, stretches, some gristly popping sound emitting from the flesh along her spine.

Time to get out of here or die trying.

Pushing off with her legs, she rocks the desk back and forth. Not an easy feat with her arms chained to it the way they are. Her movements are awkward. Uneven.

Still, she gains momentum, the tabletop tipping a little further with every sway.

The steel legs stab at the tile each time she lands. Cracking like gunshots on impact. Pounding out a jerky drum beat on the ceramic.

The final push shifts her to her right. Rising. Rising. She hovers at the top. Weightless. Motionless like a cresting wave about to break. Her butt lifting out of the seat. A tingle crawling over the exposed flesh along her neck and arms and ankles.

And then she crashes to the ground, desk thudding onto its side.

This final drumbeat echoes about the room, louder than the rest. A tremendous thump.

The collision throttles her. Jolts her head around on her neck and rattles her torso. So much force.

Again she gets that sensation of reverberation in her head, like her skull itself screams out a high-pitched tone.

And then everything is quiet, and the room feels different. So still.

She holds her breath. Listens.

The new silence offers no relief to her worries. Just more

quiet that makes her skin crawl.

The cabin's emptiness grows uncomfortable. Creepy. Hollow. And the stillness somehow seems disturbing after all of that violent crashing about.

Her senses seem to heighten as she holds still. That Christmas odor of burning pine, all bright and sharp and almost minty, has vanished, turned to an earthy smell. It's not even a smoke scent so much as the smell of ash, somehow reminiscent of rich black soil in this moment.

And it strikes her for the first time how a chill has crept into the room now that the fire is mostly gone. She feels the coolness touch the flesh of her cheeks, the bare skin along the lengths of her arms, now sheening with sweat from her efforts.

At last, she summons the willpower to move. She lifts a hand, stretches out her fingers. A simple gesture to test this new atmosphere, to convince herself that she still can. The act sends a fresh wave of goose bumps rippling over most of her body, but it brings her back to the task at hand.

She tugs at her restraints, and the steel bar she's cuffed to wiggles like a loose tooth.

The weld must have cracked upon landing, and her fingers verify this by finding the wounded spot and tracing along its jagged edge. It's just barely hanging on to the underside of the desk. This is better than she could have hoped.

She works the bar back and forth, straining at the end of each swing. The smudged bead of solder creaks a little, but holds.

Damn. She stops working at it. Takes a breath. Needs to change tactics, maybe.

She climbs up onto her knees, the short leash of the handcuffs making this much trickier than it should be.

143

Now she leans back as she pulls on the bar, lets her body weight do some of the work. The bar bends further than it did before, a weird angle like a broken limb. It trembles in her hands, shaking, shaking, and then it pops and all the tension dies right away.

She flops onto her back, the slap a little wet from the sweat, the tiles so cold against her, and she's free.

She is free.

CHAPTER 25

The key members of the task force sat in the meeting room once more, the oblong expanse of table laid out before them. They all agreed that the Sin City Bliss site was the common thread between victims they'd been looking for. Now they only needed to figure out how to weave that thread into the net that would snare Leonard Stump.

After a little conversational throat-clearing, the room settled into a thoughtful quiet that reminded Darger of a hospital waiting room. Tense. Everyone fidgeting, compulsively reviewing files and legal pads with notes from interviews. Every mind drifted out into the abstract, pondering what their next move might be.

Castellano bounced a racquet ball on the floor, a mindless exercise she said helped her think. The carpet muffled the beat some, kept it from getting too obnoxious, but the steady rhythm pounded away nonetheless. A metronome for their brainstorming session. While the beat droned on, the detective threw out a thought.

"OK. How about this? I've been thinking about something the Newell girl's roommate said… that she only took dates in hotel rooms. How does that work when it comes to the abduction? He knocks them out in the room and carries them out to his vehicle?"

Loshak frowned.

"I don't know. The old Stump would never take that risk. Too many potential witnesses that way. Even if he had the means and the confidence to take them down quickly and

145

quietly, something could go wrong. Just one of these girls starts screaming her head off, or someone sees him in the hallway? He's fucked."

"That was my instinct as well," Castellano said. "Even so, we could ask around at the hotels. See if guests have reported anything suspicious that might fit an abduction scenario. If we get any hits, we could check security footage. Keep an eye on the place."

"Yeah but how many hotels are there in this town?" Loshak asked. "Three hundred? Four? He could pick a different one every night without hitting the same place twice for months."

"He'd favor places off the Strip. Less security. Less foot traffic."

Loshak shook his head.

"That's still a shitload of hotels. Too many to surveil all at once, and then it's just a crapshoot."

The group chewed on this idea for a while, eyeballing each other while they considered their options.

"What about using the website?" Corby said.

"Please don't suggest we bait the website," Darger said.

Without missing a beat, he said, "What if we bait the website?"

Darger scoffed.

"What? Makes sense to me. There's a high probability he's picking girls from these listings. We plant a few profiles of our own, undercover cops or whatever."

"And then we cross our fingers and hope he takes the bait, right? Meanwhile he kills again and again."

"It's better than doing nothing, isn't it?"

Loshak sighed.

"I think we can do better, but if we don't come up with

anything else… it's better than nothing."

Darger's thoughts got ahead of her, not fully revealing themselves until they were already out of her mouth.

"Maybe we don't need to bait the website or surveil the hotels."

"OK…"

She hesitated for a moment, and Loshak rotated his hand, gesturing for her to continue.

"Maybe we surveil the girls."

"How do you propose we do that?"

"Reverse ride-alongs. Instead of girls riding with cops, the cops ride with the girls."

Castellano, still bouncing away, chimed in.

"That's not going to work."

"Why not?"

"Because no hooker is going to willingly let a cop ride around with her while she works. It's like a wolf asking a sheep if it would mind sharing a cab."

"These girls know each other," Darger said. "Some would have known victims or girls who went missing. I think they'll want to help their own. Some of them, anyway. And I'm sure you have plenty of working girls you use as informants. This isn't so different."

Corby tilted his head to the side as he spoke.

"With Leonard Stump stalking through their territory, having police around might be more welcome than usual. We may need to convince the girls of that, but Stump makes our case pretty compelling, you ask me."

The regular beat kept by Castellano's ball cut out suddenly.

"I think I know a way we can convince them."

The intensity Darger noted when they first met was back in

the detective's eye. They all waited in silence while she laid it out.

"There's this community outreach group in town. It's called The Iris Project, run by former sex workers. They offer stuff like free condoms, access to low cost STD screening, and employment opportunities for girls that want to get out of the trade. They also monitor the community for signs of sex trafficking."

Castellano put up a hand, interrupting herself.

"I'm getting off track, though. My point is, I know one of the women that runs it, back from when I was on patrol. Maybe if the call came from someone these girls know, someone they trust, they'd be more receptive."

"And you think she'd be willing to help us contact some of them?" Darger asked.

"I do."

Darger's gaze fell on her partner. She raised an eyebrow.

"What do you think?"

"Hell. Let's do it," he said, leaning back in his chair. "We've got nothing to lose."

CHAPTER 26

With a few phone calls, the plan lurched into motion. While Castellano spoke with her friend at The Iris Project and assembled a list of girls they might reach out to, Darger, Loshak, and Corby started recruiting volunteers for the law enforcement side of the plan.

From there, it expanded exponentially.

The LVMPD vice squad reached out to contacts and informants. The local FBI office made similar calls on a smaller scale. Each new link in the chain offered what information they could, made suggestions, reached out to others.

Every possible resource was contacted. Leverage was applied where necessary. Favors were called in.

Castellano's initial doubts were proven correct. At first, most of the girls were spooked by the prospect of working with the police, and it took some convincing by the liaisons at The Iris Project. Assurances that the girls weren't walking into a trap. Promises that they'd all be safer when Leonard Stump was off the streets.

Soon, some of the girls were engaging their own networks — making calls within the community. And while some weren't comfortable accepting rides from law enforcement, they at least agreed to take the night off — to stay out of the operation's way.

Many girls turned them down, of course. Some politely declined. Some evaded. Many hung up before even hearing them out.

Corby headed home for a shower and some rest, but Darger, Loshak, and Castellano sat in the meeting room while this burst of networking took place all over the city — fielding the occasional call, fidgeting, scratching out names and figures on the whiteboard as the plan's possibilities turned into logistics.

All told, the task force managed to cobble together 27 girls willing to accept police escorts for the next evening or two. Not great, compared to the hundreds of listings on the Sin City Bliss site, but it was better than nothing.

The LVMPD authorized ten officers to do the driving, and the other seventeen would come by way of off-duty volunteers from a mix of local and federal agencies — Darger and Loshak among them.

All told, it was a whirlwind effort, and Darger's head felt tingly as she and Loshak walked out of the meeting room, their organizing complete for the day. She cast one final glance at the list of names they'd compiled on the whiteboard.

"Do you actually think this could work?"

"It seems like a long shot," Loshak said. "But that's better than no shot."

CHAPTER 27

Emily stands on wobbly legs. The weight of her torso teeters forward and then back, like a boat at risk of capsizing.

She steadies herself and brings her hands to her face. Rubs her eyes. Chest inflating and deflating with stuttering breaths that slowly even themselves out. The handcuffs still bind her wrists together, but it feels good to be able to lift her arms like this, to be free.

With her breathing under control, she gets moving. Staggers to the door. She leans and reaches for it with such eagerness she loses her balance, almost falls face-first into it, but her hand finds the knob, clutches it, hesitates a beat. Her heart hammers away in her core.

At last her wrist comes unfrozen. It rotates. Twists the knob. Locked. The deadbolt, of course.

Turning the knob the other way and yanking also does nothing, so her hands move to the steel itself. Fingers trace along the seam where the door butts up against the frame. Palms glide over the tapered cylinder protruding from the flat surface, brushing at the keyhole etched into the brass.

So close.

Freedom sprawls just on the other side of this steel. How far away could it be? A couple of inches?

But it is no good. Without the key, it is impossible.

She leans forward. Lets her head rest on the door for a moment and breathes. Breathes. Eyes closed.

A lump lifts higher in her throat, and no amount of swallowing seems to help.

It's hard to keep the feeling of defeat away, the feeling that all hope is lost.

All of the soreness in her head and shoulders seems to return as she stands there. Her forehead absorbs the metal's chill.

She opens her eyes. Stares at the tiny crack between the door and the frame. Even as minuscule as the opening is, she can see it. The darker place where the bolt extends into its hole. This is what keeps her here: a piece of metal about the size of a baby carrot.

Gabby's voice speaks from somewhere behind her.

"Windows."

It's different now. Not just in her head.

"Check the windows."

She wheels around to face the rest of the room. Empty. Of course.

Auditory hallucinations? Nice.

She hesitates a moment, eyes squinted to look for any subtle movement in the stillness even if she knows no one is there. She listens. Hears the faint snuffle of the coals breathing in the stove. Nothing more.

Well, hallucination or not, checking the windows is a good idea.

She walks to the nearest boarded up rectangle, runs her hands over the lumber. It's nailed down pretty good. She'd need tools and a lot of time to make any progress toward exiting via a window. Not really an option in her circumstances.

She steps back. Contemplates the windows one last time. Hoping to see any potential there at all. Even up close, there's no hint of light, nothing shining through. Of course, it could be night now. She has no clue.

The Girl in the Sand

Time has lost most of its meaning. Days. Hours. Minutes. They lack any context, any use.

The only time that matters is when he'll come back, and she has no way to even make a guess at that. It could be two minutes or two days from now.

Gabby's voice speaks up again.

"So get ready."

Emily doesn't look around this time. Doesn't even turn her head. She answers the disembodied voice.

"Get ready?"

"You can't get out, but you know he's coming back. So get ready for it."

Emily squirms a little. Feet fidgeting beneath her. She still doesn't understand.

"How?"

"You need a weapon."

A weapon? Yes. A weapon.

Right away her eyes fall on the upturned desk. Those steel legs sticking straight out of it.

CHAPTER 28

Darger's hands fidgeted at the steering wheel. She felt the vibration of the road in her seat, shimmying faintly in the small of her back. She licked her lips, tried to think of something to say, but nothing came.

Her eyes snapped to the rearview mirror, to the girl in the back seat reflected there.

Nicole. That was the girl's name, the escort Darger had been paired with. She had full lips and pale green eyes the color of an old glass Coke bottle.

Right now, tonight, Leonard Stump was out there setting up his next abduction. The odds that Nicole would be the one he called upon were slim, Darger knew, and yet it remained possible. It would happen to one of them, after all — a real live girl would be plucked from her life if their efforts failed.

It was hard for Darger to fathom what was happening here, to fully digest the sequence of unfolding events. When they arrived at their next destination, this girl sitting in the back seat would get out of the car and head into a hotel room to have sex for money. Darger would await her return, and then they'd repeat the process.

Nothing about this scenario seemed real, seemed like something possible in the world Darger lived in, and yet, for Nicole, this would be a routine evening of work. Apart from the FBI escort, anyway. It was a lot to try to process.

Again, Darger grasped after something — anything — to say, but her mind remained blank, void of content apart from self-consciousness.

The Girl in the Sand

She'd been chauffeuring Nicole for twenty minutes now, and after greeting each other, they'd barely spoken. The uncomfortable silence had only gained strength in that time. Awkward. Tense.

To her credit, Nicole seemed undisturbed by the quiet. She hunched over her phone, thumbs twiddling away at the screen.

Still, Darger felt bad about the stiffness of the scene, felt responsible in some vague way. She should be making this girl comfortable, chattering out small talk to put her at ease. She'd be happy to do just that, but no breezy dialogue sprang to mind. *Nothing* did, and the harder she tried to think of something to say, the deeper she sank into an awkward panic.

Just then Nicole's eyes met hers in the mirror, and Darger jumped a little. Startled.

"So... what do I call you? Agent or miss or—"

"How about just Violet?"

The corner of Nicole's mouth quirked up, amused.

"OK, Just Violet."

"Right. Should have seen that coming."

Nicole leaned forward, her head jutting into the front seat area.

"Can I ask you something kind of personal?"

Darger smiled, felt the muscles in her shoulders release a little, the tension dying back now that they'd broken the silence.

"Go ahead."

The girl's green eyes fell to the gun holstered at Darger's hip.

"Have you ever killed anyone?"

The smile slid from Darger's face, her gut twisting in knots the way it always did when James Joseph Clegg became a topic of conversation.

"Yes. Once."

Nicole watched her intently.

"Who was it?"

Instead of meeting Nicole's eyes, Darger stared out the windshield at the line of palm trees rushing past. "Someone a lot like the guy we're looking for right now."

"So he murdered people?"

Darger blinked a few times and finally glanced at Nicole when she answered.

"Yes. He kidnapped five girls in Ohio, killed them, and then dismembered the bodies. Dumped them right out in the open for the police to find."

Darger hadn't planned on getting so graphic with the description, but she didn't really know how to sugarcoat someone like Clegg.

"Jesus. That's pretty sick."

"Yes, it is."

"Who's sicker? The guy in Ohio, or the guy you're looking for now?"

There was no hesitation for Darger. "The guy we're looking for now."

"Really? I read he only burns the bodies. Seems like cutting them up is worse."

"I can see why you'd think that. But part of it is the scale. James Clegg — that was the man's name in Ohio — only killed five girls. And don't get me wrong, that's a lot, no matter what. But Leonard Stump has killed over 30, and those are just the ones we know about so far."

"But if you hadn't caught James Clegg, do you think he would have killed that many?"

"Hard to say. Probably. My partner always says they don't stop. They get caught, or they die. So yeah, he would have killed

156

more girls. But that's not the only thing that makes Leonard Stump worse."

Darger stopped then, not really wanting to go further with the discussion. But Nicole's interest hadn't been sated.

"Well? What is it?"

A long sigh preceded Darger's response.

"When James Clegg dismembered those girls, they were already dead. As odd as it sounds, his primary goal wasn't to hurt them."

Nicole stared at her for a few moments, and when she spoke, her voice was barely above a whisper.

"And what does *he* do to them?"

Darger didn't need her to clarify that she was talking about Stump now. She gazed out at the orange-red desert in the distance.

"We don't know for sure."

They fell quiet for a while, the rumble of the car churning out indifference.

"My turn," Darger said.

"What?"

"To ask you a personal question."

Nicole rolled her eyes, but her lips held a trace of a smile.

"You want to know why a nice girl like me has sex for money?"

"Well… yeah. But I was going to try to make it sound less judgmental than that."

Her shoulders pulled up into a shrug.

"I don't know. Maybe there's not a good answer. I guess it's a paycheck like any other. Pays better than some things."

"Right."

"And it's not like…. I mean, despite what people probably

think, I never have to do anything I don't want to do."

"Never?"

Nicole shook her head before she went on.

"If they want me to do something really crazy, I quote them such an insane amount of money that it makes it worth it. I mean, I have my limits. There are things I won't do, no matter how much money they offer. But a lot of the fetishes sound kinda weird, but they're pretty harmless."

"Have you ever had one of them get violent?"

"A few times, yeah. Some guys mistakenly think the rough stuff comes included with the usual fee," she said and then went quiet for a while.

Again the engine's hum rose to fill the quiet.

"Had one guy choke me so hard that I blacked out."

As Nicole spoke, one of her hands went to her neck, a subconscious gesture, Darger thought. The girl ran her knuckles over the vulnerable flesh there, remembering the old hurt.

"Christ. What did you do?"

Nicole shrugged.

"He was pretty freaked out. Kept apologizing. When I first passed out, I'm pretty sure he thought he'd killed me."

"He could have."

"Yeah, well. Got an extra hundred out of him, so... Besides, now I have this." She pulled a pink and black zebra print rectangle out of her purse.

Darger had seen something like it before.

"A stun gun?"

Nicole nodded and pushed the device back into the depths of her bag.

"Never had to use it — knock on wood. Just knowing it's there makes me feel better, though."

The practical part of Darger's mind couldn't help but wonder if the weapon would be enough against someone like Stump, but she kept her mouth shut.

"Anyway, you get pretty good at spotting the wackos. I think you have to. If anything feels off, I'm out."

The car thudded over patches in the asphalt, rhythmic thuds underlying Nicole's monologue.

"It's not all about the money, anyway. I mean, it is. But it's not for me. It's for my son."

"You have a son?"

Nicole nodded, a proud gleam in her eye.

"Hunter. He's eight. They've got him in the advanced math and science courses in school."

She paused a beat, eyelashes fluttering.

"He's on the spectrum, so his speech is a little delayed. But doing this means I can afford the best speech therapists. The best cognitive psychologist. Without the money, I don't know what I'd do."

She held out a hand and stared down at her purple stiletto nails.

"What about Hunter's dad?"

Nicole snorted. "He's a deadbeat. Haven't heard from him at all in…. I don't know. It's been years."

"You know you can take him to court."

"For what? He's a loser. Works at a liquor store where his uncle pays him under the table. What little he gets he spends on beer and scratch-offs. Not like that's going to change just because a court says he owes me. Owes us."

She looked out the window.

"It's better this way. I'm better off knowing it's all on me. Under my control. It keeps me grounded. I gotta be smart."

There was a pack of cigarettes partially protruding from the zippered mouth of Nicole's purse. She nudged the cellophane-wrapped package.

"I'm trying to quit smoking because of my son. Because he needs me to be here. Always. Used to smoke a pack a day. Now I just need one or two after work. To wind down, you know? I figure clients prefer that I don't smell like smoke, anyway, so it's a win-win."

Darger nodded, and the quiet nestled over them for a stretch, but now she wasn't so conversationally blocked.

"Let's say you could have any job… what would you do?"

Nicole tilted her head to the right before she answered.

"I'm pretty good at baking, I guess."

"Baking?"

"Yeah, like, I want to be in one of those baking contests someday. The ones where you make really elaborate sculptures and shit. I've done a little chocolate work. Just at home, I mean. Everything has to be just the right temp. If you're off by even a degree, the chocolate won't set right. Loses its shine and turns all dull. Doesn't snap the way it should, either."

"Would you go to culinary school, do you think?"

Again Nicole paused, and when she did answer, she looked far away.

"Yeah, I could do that. Go to school for baking. Yeah."

This time, when the silence descended upon them, it wasn't uncomfortable. Darger let it stay.

The city pulsed around them — a spastic thing flailing and blinking out the windows. Totally senseless, tasteless, and somehow stimulating nonetheless.

A few turns later, they pulled up to the hotel. It was a dated looking building a few blocks off the Strip.

The Girl in the Sand

"Thanks," Nicole said as she got out of the car, though Darger didn't know what she was thanking her for. The ride, maybe.

The girl slipped into the night, growing smaller as she trailed away over the parking lot. The automatic doors whooshed open, two sheets of glass sliding out of her path, and Nicole disappeared into the building.

CHAPTER 29

Darger saw the image again every time she closed her eyes — the girl crossing the parking lot, passing through those open doors into the hotel lobby. Vanishing. If she focused on the memory long enough, it made the hair on her arms stand up.

Darger's chest had tightened when Nicole crossed that threshold, and now, ten minutes later, it remained stiff, her breathing shallow and strange. She wanted to swallow, to maybe help those muscles in her torso loosen up, but her mouth was dry.

She squirmed a little in the car seat, trying to adjust so her holster would stop digging into her side, eyes never leaving that plate glass door across the lot. It was insane to sit in the car knowing what was about to happen just inside those walls. Uncomfortable. A violation. A case of too much information.

She wanted to let her mind drift away, to think of something else, but she couldn't do that. She had to stay alert. Vigilant. That was the whole point. If Nicole needed help, Darger had to be ready.

She checked her phone. Nothing, of course. Nicole had told her that half an hour was the usual, and they weren't even halfway there yet. It was going to feel like a year.

At last, she managed to swallow, a little sluice of saliva in a dry throat. It didn't help.

Why did this scenario bother her so much? She wasn't sure.

Of course, everyone working the Stump case was on edge tonight. He was out there right now, more than likely plotting his next abduction. If not tonight, he'd do it tomorrow, the way

162

Loshak figured it.

But it wasn't just the immediate danger of Stump. Something else here felt wrong to Darger. A sex thing, maybe.

Was she a prude? They were consenting adults. No one was forcing Nicole to do anything, at least not in any direct sense — she said so herself. Still, this concept of two strangers arranging to have sex the way you might hire someone to remodel your kitchen didn't sit right.

It was sex without intimacy. The encounter reduced to the physical act. Yet that was how most animals reproduced, wasn't it? But then maybe that was part of why it felt wrong. We were supposed to be different than our four-legged counterparts. More evolved. More civilized.

Of course, the other extreme of society would insist you should be married first — a legally binding contract before coitus can occur. That was pretty weird in its own way, she decided.

Movement fluttered in the distance, shaking her from her thoughts.

The glass door jerked and opened, and Darger's pulse quickened, pupils dilated, but no. It wasn't Nicole.

A janitor exited the front door, a frail older man pushing his cart. He emptied the ashtray and trash can near the entrance and wheeled his gear back inside.

The intrusion brought Darger back to the moment, in any case, and she started a little when she realized how lost she'd gotten in her thoughts. She couldn't do that. Had to stay focused.

Again, she fidgeted in her seat, leaning to the left and then the right, raging against the gun and sheath digging into her hip. Nothing helped. She'd never had a holster bother her like this, but this bordered on unbearable. Maybe it was the car or the fact that the leather was new, not broken in yet. Regardless of the explanation, she should remember to bring her thigh holster tomorrow — avoid the misery.

Thirty-four minutes had passed. Where was she? Surely these things didn't run on a set schedule, but still. What could be taking so long?

Darger stared at the door, willing Nicole to walk through it. There was movement behind the glass, and Darger leaned forward as if being a few inches closer might make a difference. A large man in an orange polo shirt came through, followed by two other men. They were all young, mid-to-late twenties, and they all had sunglasses tucked into the neckline of their shirts. There was no sign of Nicole.

She should have asked more questions. She hadn't thought to ask Nicole if she was meeting a regular or someone new. How could she be such an idiot?

Her anxiety level rose with each passing moment.

She counted out another thirty seconds. The sunglass trio was long gone. She couldn't wait here any longer, doing nothing.

Darger opened the car door and stepped out of the vehicle.

The cool evening air swirled around her. It wasn't all the way dark yet, but it was working its way there, and the chill had already descended upon the city.

Her boots clapped against the asphalt, a strident clatter that echoed in the emptiness. The walk across the lot felt slow. Tedious. She wanted to pick up the pace, to jog, to run, to sprint, but she kept her cool. She walked. Put one foot in front of the other.

She would go inside, ask the clerk for help, ask him or her if they'd seen Nicole. Surely a girl like her would stick out. And then maybe she'd be able to pry the room number out of them, flash her badge or something. Whatever it took.

Then what? Would she bust into the room? Just bang on the door? Call up to see if things were OK? She didn't know. She'd worry about that when she got there.

The streetlights buzzed overhead, still dim for the moment, their yellow glow slowly gaining strength as the night darkened around them.

With a mechanical whir, the automatic front door slid open, revealing Nicole about to exit the lobby. She froze, looking a bit stunned when she saw Darger on the other side of the threshold.

She's OK, Darger thought. Relief loosened the knot in her gut.

Everything's fine. Thank Christ.

Nicole opened her mouth to speak, then seemed to decide against it and brushed past the agent on her way to the car. That was when Darger realized she'd messed up big time.

The points of Nicole's heels rang out against the pavement as they crossed the parking lot. Each percussive click sounded like a reprimand.

Tsk, tsk, tsk, Agent Darger.

She didn't speak until they were back in the car with the doors closed.

"What the actual hell?"

"I know, I'm sorry." Darger felt her face redden, heat flushing her cheeks.

"Someone could have seen you! If any of my clients find out I'm riding around with a cop…" Nicole shook her head, pulling her phone from her purse. "I should have known this wouldn't work. I'm calling an Uber to come pick me up."

"No. Please, wait," Darger begged.

She closed her eyes and took a long breath.

"I screwed up. I got worried something went wrong, and I panicked. Please give me another chance."

Nicole's cheeks sucked in while she thought it over.

"I won't leave the car again. I swear."

The girl bobbed her head once.

"OK."

Darger drove on to the next hotel in almost total silence. The awkwardness she'd felt earlier in the evening had returned tenfold. The quiet after the engine cut out only heightened things.

Nicole slid out of the car, then turned back, pausing with her hand on the door.

"It'll be about an hour this time."

The pointed look that accompanied this statement almost made Darger squirm.

"My ass is glued to the driver's seat," she said, trying to joke, but Nicole didn't laugh.

The door thumped shut, and Darger was left alone to stew in her own self-reproach.

CHAPTER 30

No light came from the crack under Loshak's hotel room door, so Darger moved on to her own room without knocking.

The door closed behind her with a whoosh and a click. She kicked off her boots and went into the bathroom to wash her face. Maybe she could rinse away a little of her disappointment, too.

Man, she'd fucked that up. Royally.

Splashing a little cool water on her face was refreshing at least, but the hotel towel felt rough against her cheeks. She figured they made them crappy on purpose so people wouldn't be tempted to steal them.

The babble of a TV in the room next door filtered through the thin walls as she crossed the darkened room to flip on a lamp.

She'd missed a call from Owen while she was out, so after changing into her pajamas, she sent a video chat request. The app blipped and blooped, and then Owen's face appeared on the screen, bowl of cereal in hand.

"How'd it go?" Owen asked, mouth full.

Darger covered her face with her hands.

"Out-fucking-standing."

"What happened?"

She summarized the evening for him, reliving her failure.

"You convinced her to stay with you, though," he said, crunching in between words. "She didn't ditch you for an Uber, I mean. That's something."

"Except when I dropped her off, I asked if we were on for

tomorrow night. She said she had to think about it."

Darger had wanted to push Nicole on it, but she sensed that pleading and getting desperate would only make things worse.

Owen pointed a spoon laden with Froot Loops at her. "But she didn't say no."

"Stop being such an optimist. I suck, OK? End of story."

A frown invaded Owen's face. It wasn't an expression she was used to seeing on him. Smirking like a devil, yes. Mischievous glint in the eye, sure. But frowning?

"What?"

He blinked a few times, shaking the dour look from his face, and took another bite of cereal.

"Nothing."

"You're being shady again."

The focus of his gaze fixed on the camera, which had the effect of him looking into her eyes on the screen.

"I just… want you to be careful. I worry about you."

"I appreciate that. But I'm fine. I mean, aside from screwing everything up tonight. Peachy."

"Promise me you won't do anything I wouldn't do."

Darger snorted. "I'm not sure that's the best advice considering I haven't figured out anything you wouldn't do yet. Speaking of which, how's your stint as Ace Ventura, Pet Detective going?"

"I wouldn't dangle my bare ass above a shark tank," he said, ignoring her teasing.

"Good to know. And while I have yet to find myself in that particular situation, I think I could safely say I wouldn't either."

Owen slurped the last of the milk from his cereal bowl and set it aside. It clanked against the table.

"You sure you're not doing that right now?"

Darger made a show of glancing around the room, paying special attention to her own rear end.

"Well, I'm definitely not bare-assed. I don't see any sharks either, so…"

For the second time that evening, Darger's joke fell flat. Owen was being uncharacteristically serious again.

"I'm not kidding around, Violet. And neither is Leonard Stump. That letter was a baited hook."

"I'm confused… am I the shark in this scenario now?"

"You'll be the chum if you don't watch yourself."

Darger ground her molars together.

"He sent that letter to get under my skin. To scare me. So far it seems to have worked on everyone but me."

"That's exactly my point. If you're not scared, you're an idiot."

"So now I'm an idiot."

"You're a stubborn, impossible mule of a woman who won't listen when the entire world is trying to tell her there's danger ahead." He stopped, squeezing his eyelids shut. "What I'm trying to say is that maybe it wouldn't be so bad if you were off the ride-along detail."

Darger scoffed.

"This is my job, Owen. You should understand that as well as anyone. Everyone keeps acting like I'm a delicate piece of china that needs to be put on some out-of-the-way shelf. I won't do that. And I won't let anyone tell me to do that."

She sighed, the air rushing out of her lungs like a punctured party balloon.

"It's late. I should go."

"Violet, wait…"

"Maybe we'll talk tomorrow."

She broke the connection and tossed her phone to the foot of the bed.

CHAPTER 31

Emily's fingers work at the screws that attach the leg to the desk. Stinging. Bleeding. Flesh torn. Shredded and pink like hamburger.

So far she has made no progress. The screw feels like it will move, like it could move, but so far nothing.

She opens her eyes. Her fingers are fine, of course. No hamburger to be seen. Not one drop of blood.

But the pain is real. It jolts down the length of the bones in her hand, radiates in her wrist, tendrils surging into the meat of her forearm.

It makes her want to quit.

Every time she thinks the hurt can't get worse, it gets worse. A bottomless hole of agony. Like a wasp's stinger jabbing deeper and deeper into her fingertips. Injecting more and more of its venom.

It reminds her of getting her blood drawn as a kid. A nursing student had wielded the needle like a pickaxe, digging at the soft flesh inside of her elbow like the veins were some precious metal that had to be mined out of her.

Images flutter into her head then. Dream pictures that open like flowers and lurch into motion.

She sees a beach. Sand puckered with endless footprints, but there is no one here now. No one but her.

Choppy waves lurch out near the horizon. White crests rolling atop the rest of the blue.

And closer, the water laps up onto the banking earth. Here the sand is darker. Wetter where all the footprints have been

171

washed away.

She walks toward the water, and the wind blows in. Cold and dry and salty. She holds her arms out to her sides and feels the air everywhere.

A bead of sweat trails past the corner of her eye, and the wet itchiness of it brings her back to reality, back to the room in the cabin. Back to the blistered feeling in the tips of her digits.

It feels like the skin must be gone. Stringy muscle tissue must be touching this screw. The piece of metal jamming sharp edges into the yellowed wad of nerve endings. But there's still no blood to corroborate this line of thinking. She can see a little redness, a little irritation, but the skin is otherwise unmarked.

The ebb and flow of the sting makes her lips move, makes them widen out to the sides, going flat and exposing her teeth during the worst of it. She tries to imagine what this expression looks like and can only picture a pug dog in a bewildered moment.

New pictures arrive to take her away. Her breath hitches in her throat, and the images flood her head, projecting themselves over the top of reality, blocking it out.

This time it's her son, Austin. He's on the rickety swing set behind their apartment building in Palo Alto.

His tiny, mittened hands wrap around rusty chains. Arms and torso flexing, his body sprawling and contracting to propel himself forward and back, like a pendulum gaining momentum. Going higher, higher, higher.

It's cold, at least by California standards. She can see the steam of his breath. Little clouds that spiral from his mouth and nostrils, congeal into swirls of vapor, and vanish almost at once.

She watches him from the little cement slab patio. A charcoal grill sits at her left elbow. The sliding glass doors into their apartment shimmer reflections to her right.

Now Austin swings high enough that the chains buckle a little at the height of the arc. The tension is momentarily broken, he seems to float for a beat, and there's a stiff jerk as he falls back under the purview of the rusted metal links, back into the steady tempo of forward and back.

She knows by the slate gray winter coat swaddling his torso that he is four years old in this memory. Neither of them know that this will be their last year in Palo Alto, that everything is about to go wrong. Fall apart.

He smiles at her. Little red beanie pulled down over his eyebrows, encroaching on his actual eyes in such a way that he has to lean his head back to see her, his chin all jutted out.

The wooden support beam squawks like a seagull on every backswing. A throaty sound.

And now the grill to her left is gone, and it's Sadie instead. The little two-year-old girl with the lips and brow that curl into a resting serious face. Like she's always weighing something existential rather than what kind of cookies she wants for her snack.

But this isn't right. She shouldn't be there. Not with Austin at this age. She should be an infant still.

And the weight of the illusion diminishes. It can no longer breathe the way it did. She can longer believe in it.

These are distracting pictures, she realizes. A defense mechanism. Her imagination conjuring anything to take her away from the awful truth, the pain and despair and utter hopelessness of a reality that finds her trapped in a kill room.

"Focus," Gabby says. "Focus on what needs to be done."

The pictures fade, the children's faces turn translucent and wispy, and reality appears there before her again.

The desk. The metal leg. That little screw pinched between her thumb and index finger. She grips it and spins it the best she can. Over and over.

And the room is quiet. The whole world is quiet. Still. Empty. Nothing is real except for that image before her.

The screw.

Her fingers.

The feel of the rounded steel. Hard. Totally unforgiving. She squeezes and twists, but it will not budge. No matter how many times she changes her grip. No matter which hand she uses.

The metal has gone warm. Its cold long ago vanquished by her body heat and the friction. It's a little tacky from the oil of her flesh.

The sharp edge of the Phillips indentation cuts at her. Tiny little stabs and slashes carved into the whorls of her fingerprints.

And she breathes. The air gliding in and out. Cold and dry. She feels it on some barely conscious level. Filling her and emptying her over and over.

Her fingers rotate. Adjust. Rotate. Adjust. The attempts fall into a throb of a rhythm. Hypnotic.

And the screw moves. Twists. A tiny fraction of a rotation. She feels it give. Relent.

At first the movement is so infinitesimal that she thinks it's her imagination. Her mind breaking away from reality to create what she wants to happen. What she needs to happen.

But she keeps working, and it keeps spinning. It fights her for a while yet. Makes her work for each degree of rotation.

And then the grip releases. Gives up. The screw spins without hesitation. Wobbling like a loose tooth.

Her heart thunders in her chest, and the adrenaline rush is more euphoric than fearful this time. A tingle roiling over her scalp in pulses. All of her skin going sensitive. Tight. Every pore slicked with sweat. Every nerve ending feeling giddy, light, pleasant.

There is a noise — almost a sucking sound — as the screw finally exits the hole. The warm nugget of metal squirts out of her fingers. Clatters to the floor.

She hesitates for a second. Watches that empty socket where the threads spiral into the dark screw hole. Her fingers pinch air in little convulsive twitches like crab claws.

And then she gets back to work.

The second screw comes easier. Faster, she thinks. Maybe it's the confidence of having done it. Maybe she has entered some kind of zone. Achieved a Zen-like state of transcendent focus and concentration.

Time stretches out into something almost meaningless to her. She exists in her head. In the dream part of her brain that allows her to function without fully accepting the physical reality she finds herself in.

All the world whittles down to this second screw slowly loosening between her fingers like it's a game. Turn the screw to win. It's the only thing that matters.

And it's free. The leg is free.

The metal rod tilts away from the desk. Pulls away from the tabletop. Clatters to the tile floor and clangs around a while. Quivering there like some newborn creature.

The heat flushes Emily's face, her scalp, her neck and chest. It must have been there the whole time. The temperature building in her blood. The result of her effort, of her focus. But she blocked it out. Blocked everything out until she had what she needed, so it hits her all at once.

And she swoons. Head dipping. Arms and legs going weak.

The heat is too much. Filling her skull. Melting thoughts together into something tangled and sticky.

She's alert enough to get her hands between her and the floor. Her arms fold up as she descends, perhaps absorbing some of the blow.

She lifts her head, and in the blur she sees a shape. A human form. One that she thinks must be her friend. A smudged blob on the other side of the room. But when she blinks, the sweat and tears roll away, and it's gone.

She is alone.

CHAPTER 32

The first Pabst Blue Ribbon tasted like moldy bread. It always did. It went down fast and easy, though. He could pour half a tall boy down his gullet on the first drink, hesitate a few seconds to let the foam settle in his gut, and then kill the rest of the can on drink number two.

And after the first one? Well, it tasted pretty goddamn good from there on out. Less mold. More bread.

Mark Morgan sucked 'em down after work, standing at the kitchen counter with his head tipped back, his body already angled halfway toward the refrigerator door, poised to grab the next one. Usually it was just three or five, but tonight there were twelve tall cans in the fridge, and he planned to kiss every one of them full on the mouth.

It'd been a weird time for him and Claire. All of this Leonard Stump talk. The grisly stories on TV. Law enforcement parading through his kitchen, lounging on his furniture, invading his space. They showed Claire pictures of crisped bodies and everything. Gave her nightmares.

So yeah. He deserved this. A good, clean drunk. No moderation tonight, thank you very much.

He cracked the second can, the high-pitched metallic click echoing funny off the linoleum. The sound brought the house's emptiness — its stillness — into sharp focus. He liked it. An almost religious quietude.

His lips parted, snuffled like a vacuum hose at the little bit of runoff and suds caught in the lip of the can. Then he opened his throat and poured most of it down.

He closed his eyes as he guzzled. The empty kitchen around him disappearing, even the absolute stillness of the house falling away until the only thing that was real was the golden fluid cascading over his gorge like a waterfall.

Claire wouldn't be home for a bit yet, so he could bask in it without interruption for the moment — an experience he savored over most anything else in life.

Pabst had an acidity to it that the other cheap beers didn't have. He thought that and the price were what made it his go-to beverage, that little chemical zing he felt on his tongue and the lining of his cheeks.

He paced down the hall and back, can number two hovering before him, poised in his hand for the next round of chugging.

Claire didn't like it when he drank this much. In fact, she hated it. She had her reasons, he knew.

Well, maybe she should have thought of that before she got a little mouthy with him that morning. She should have known better.

He'd put his hand on her back. That was all. And she'd bit his head off for it. Jerked away from him. Recoiling from his touch. Nose all wrinkled up. Words spitting out through clenched teeth. From there, she gave him the stink-eye silent treatment until he left for work.

Why'd she have to do that? Put his balls through the wringer with all of this other stuff going on. All of this stress and strain and tension that kept him — kept both of them — up at night.

By the time Mark pulled the tab on his fourth can, a goodly amount of alcohol had seeped into his bloodstream. When he drank this fast, especially on an empty stomach, it hit him quickly. The booze soaked in through the walls of his stomach almost immediately, a euphoric rush that only built as he guzzled down more. It was a different brand of drunkenness entirely, almost the equivalent of injecting the stuff intravenously. His favorite buzz of all.

He'd take it slow after the first handful or so, though. Savor 'em. Drink 'em deep into the evening, into the night.

When he was younger, he never limited himself. He'd drink until he couldn't remember, until he passed out, until he found himself puking in the backyard of his parents' house before he snuck in through the garage window. Four or five nights a week. Those were good times, aside from the puking. Fun times. Times when anything felt possible. Not like now.

The memories flared and faded rapidly, and his thoughts circled back to the topic of the day: These cops that kept poking their noses into their business. Clomping around his fucking house.

This Fed, Loshak, was a particular pain in the nads. Talking to Claire. His woman. Getting her all riled up about things best forgotten. Ancient history, as far as he was concerned. The two of them looking at each other with sad eyes like a pair of abandoned puppies.

He stopped gritting his teeth long enough to finish off another beer. Burped.

Why'd she have to bring all of this on them? All of her baggage, years and years of it, cluttering his home, their relationship. Like his life was just supposed to stop and start at the whims of her problems.

He just wanted to relax. Kick back on the couch. Watch some TV. Pursue happiness one 16-ounce can at a time. But he couldn't. Not with this black cloud hanging over them. Goddamn law enforcement dropping in whenever to play twenty questions — the 1993 edition — for the millionth time.

Claire did this to them. It was her fault. Anyone with eyes could see that. She did it, and she welcomed more of the same, didn't she? She accommodated this Loshak prick more than her own man.

All Mark got for his trouble was yelled at, a few dirty looks, made to feel like he was some monster for putting his hand on his girl's back.

It would never end, if things were left up to her. It'd drag on and on.

Well, fuck that.

The tab of the next can sang its song, the crack and pop filling the kitchen.

By the time Claire got home, Mark was ready to fight.

CHAPTER 33

Darger almost couldn't believe it when her phone tittered the next day, and she found a text from Nicole asking to be picked up. Her fingers folded into a fist and punched the air. So she hadn't completely fucked things up after all.

Still, she didn't get her hopes up for much friendly conversation. That was fine, though. She'd just focus on her task. Her job was to be vigilant, to keep a trained eye on the surroundings. Other than that, she would keep her mouth shut and stay in the damn car.

But there was an extra surprise when Nicole slid into the back seat that evening. A little white box in the girl's hand. She leaned forward, extending the box within Darger's reach. The clear plastic window on top revealed a cluster of small brown orbs. Chocolate, it looked like.

"What's this?"

"Truffles," Nicole said, thrusting the box at her. "I made them for you."

Darger was so taken aback, she didn't make a move to take them. A flicker of doubt clouded Nicole's green eyes.

"You're not like… diabetic, are you? Or on some freakish diet?"

The box retracted an inch, and Darger grabbed it before it could disappear into the back seat.

"Hell no."

She popped open the box and sniffed. Each sphere was smothered with a layer of dark chocolate and sprinkled with sea salt. It smelled like heaven.

181

"I can't believe you made these for me. Thank you."

Nicole waved her hand impatiently.

"Try one."

Darger lifted one of the chocolates to her mouth. The outer layer cracked as she bit through it, a hard contrast to the silky smooth interior. It was rich and sweet and bitter, with an extra tang at the end.

"What is that? Coffee and something else…"

"It's espresso and cognac."

Darger closed her eyes and popped the rest of the bite into her mouth.

"Sweet Jesus. They're delicious."

Nicole's smile was 90% gums and 10% teeth. It made her seem like a little kid.

"I'm glad you like them."

The urge to eat more was strong, but Darger resisted. She closed the box and set it on the passenger seat.

"I better pace myself. And if I don't save at least one for my partner, he might never speak to me again."

That got a chuckle out of Nicole. Maybe Darger hadn't screwed up as bad as she thought.

She found Nicole's eyes in the rearview mirror as she started the engine.

"You should be a pastry chef. For real. Open a bakery or a candy shop or something."

Nicole shrugged.

"Maybe someday, but…." She shook her head.

Darger drove on. A blue light lit up the back seat where Nicole fiddled with her phone.

Suddenly her head poked between the seats.

"Do you mind if I turn on the stereo?"

"Be my guest."

Nicole fiddled with her phone and the touchscreen on the dash for a moment. A low hum poured out of the speakers.

At first Darger thought it was just background noise from the speakers being on, but then she detected a shift in tone, followed by a rattle and soft chimes.

"What is this?" she asked.

"Oh, it's my mood cleansing music. It's like a specific frequency that's supposed to wipe out negative energy."

Darger smiled with half her mouth.

"Are you a hippie?"

"No," Nicole scoffed.

"You sure?" Darger teased. "Because this sounds an awful lot like hippie music."

The girl rolled her eyes, fighting a smile. "I'm not a hippie."

"OK, let me ask you a few questions then. Do you enjoy the smell of patchouli?"

"Not particularly."

Darger pretended to ponder this. "Hm. Have you ever had dreadlocks?"

"No."

"Have you ever sewn patchwork panels into your jeans to turn them into bell bottoms?"

"I don't even know how to sew."

"So far you're doing well. But how many Grateful Dead albums do you own?"

Nicole laughed. "None."

"Have you ever played hacky-sack?"

"Once, and I was really bad at it."

"Final question," Darger said. "How often do you eat granola, and there are five bonus points if you've ever made

183

your own."

"That's not fair! You know that I bake."

Darger prodded the air with a finger.

"I don't make the rules."

Nicole sighed.

"I suppose I've been known to burn a little sage now and then."

They were stuck at a long red light near the Strip. People poured out of a movie theater on the corner, a sudden rush of bodies and voices crowding the crosswalk.

Darger's phone vibrated. It was a text from Owen.

I'm sorry. Please call me.

Darger stared at the black letters on the glowing white screen for a beat before she tucked the phone away again.

"Boyfriend trouble?"

"Why do you say that?"

Nicole shrugged. "Or girlfriend. And I know you're not married, because you don't have a ring. Either way, I know that look."

"Boyfriend. And I guess it must be a face I make often, then," Darger said with a sigh. "Sometimes I think I'm just not meant for relationships. Maybe I'm supposed to trade men for some weird hobby. Going to bird shows. Or dumpster diving. Maybe pickling."

The light finally turned green, and they left the bustling intersection behind.

"How about you?"

"Me, what?"

"Do you have a boyfriend?"

Nicole flung herself back against the seat and crossed her arms.

"Kinda hard to date for fun when you date for a living."

Her head lolled against the leather upholstery.

"Some days I don't want to be touched at all when I'm done with work. My son being on the spectrum... he's not always the most physically affectionate. And those nights, the nights where even a hug would set my teeth on edge, I'm almost glad. That probably sounds horrible. But I would feel worse if he craved that physical affection, and I couldn't give it to him."

The tires bumped over the lip between the road and the parking lot as Darger steered the car into the motel parking lot. She found an empty spot and cut the engine.

"Can I ask you another personal question?" Darger asked.

A slight nod indicated she should continue.

"Aren't you afraid you'll get caught?"

"I mean, yeah," Nicole said, blowing a strand of hair out of her eyes. "But I have a pretty good system."

Darger's curiosity got the better of her, and she blurted out, "What is it?"

Nicole's face pinched into a frown.

Damn. Maybe Loshak was right about her being too tenacious. She put her hands up, surrendering.

"Nevermind. You don't have to tell me."

The girl was already halfway out of the car.

"See you in an hour."

The steady click of her heels faded as she moved off to one of the numbered doors.

The car seemed extra quiet now that Nicole's music was gone. Darger turned on the radio, but abandoned it almost immediately. All the music sucked, and the ads were worse.

After twenty minutes, the gun was bothering her again. She'd completely forgotten about the thigh holster, like an idiot.

She scooted forward and back, trying to find a comfortable position, but there was something about the design of the seats that was just unbearable in combination with the bulk of her gun pressing against her ribs. It felt like the Glock 22 was trying to burrow itself into her body like a parasitic insect.

Fuck it, she thought. She slid the gun from the holster and set it on the passenger seat. She stretched out against the seat, arching her spine. So much better.

Well, mostly. The seats were still hell on her lower back, but at least she wouldn't have an imprint of the grip on her torso at the end of the night.

Her eyes wandered the interior of the car and then fell on the box of bonbons. Might as well, she thought. One more wouldn't kill her.

It was salty and sweet and boozy and bitter. A nearly overwhelming combination of flavors that made her eyes water.

Through the windshield, she could see a little of the Strip. The bright colored lights in the distance looked like some kind of 365-day-a-year Christmas display.

Such a strange city. Darger was used to the tree-lined streets of Virginia and Denver. Not that there weren't trees in Vegas, if you counted all the palms. But overall it was a flat, desolate-looking place, despite being surrounded by mountains. It really did look like some kind of oasis or mirage that had sprung out of nowhere in the middle of the Mojave.

Voices approached. An elderly couple sidling up to the car next to Darger's. She nudged the candy box over her pistol and smiled at the old woman. A lot of people got weirded out seeing firearms out in the open like that, and Darger didn't want to have to get out her badge to explain. Nicole would be done soon, and the last thing she wanted was to be caught outside of the car again.

Darger went back to scanning the parking lot and absently drumming her fingers against the steering wheel.

There were still ten minutes left on the hour when Nicole returned. She tossed her red leather bag in first and then climbed in after it.

"You're done early."

"He fell asleep."

Darger turned in her seat and peered back at the girl. "During?"

Nicole threw her head back and cackled.

"No! After. It happens sometimes. Especially with the older guys."

The engine started with a mechanical rumble, and Darger headed for the next call.

They were at another red light when Nicole's voice piped up behind her.

"OK. I do tarot readings."

Darger glanced into the rearview, almost doubting that Nicole had been talking to her.

"Pardon?"

"That's my system. The guy pays me for a tarot reading. That's when the money changes hands. Anything that happens after that is a casual encounter between two consenting adults."

Traffic moved. Darger accelerated, thinking it over.

"That's pretty slick."

"In theory, anyway. I'm sure if the cops wanted to bust me, they could."

The blinker ticked out a steady rhythm.

"Well, your secret is safe with me."

"That wasn't what I was worried about, really," Nicole said.

"It wasn't?"

"No," she said, holding back a smile. "I was worried that being a tarot reader would add more points to my hippie score."

Darger laughed.

"I wasn't going to say anything, but yeah. That puts you way over the line."

CHAPTER 34

Mark picked at the bubbled spot on the laminate countertop, thumbnail chewing at the peeling layer of shiny plastic, pressing into the spongy particle board underneath. The scraping sound his work produced was somehow satisfying. A symphony of crinkles and multi-textured scratches.

He knew Claire could hear it, too, even if she was in the next room. She hated it when he messed with the flawed spot like this. Maybe that was why he did it so often.

Yeah, well, we've all got shit to deal with. We've all got our cross to bear, right? That's the way he figured it.

"What's for dinner?" he said, his voice loud and sharp so she could hear through the wall.

There was a pause before she answered.

"I'm not hungry. You should have whatever you want."

The heel of his hand thumped the counter, and a breath hissed out of him.

Of course this was how she'd play things. It was typical, really. She did shit like this. Sulked away into a corner. Closed herself off from everyone. Left him on his own. Abandoned him.

He took another slurp of beer, and the brew and a small pocket air caught in his throat. Gagged him a little. The muscles in his neck got tight as the swallow descended, and it felt wrong every step of the way down, finally arriving at his stomach and depositing the orb of discomfort there to linger.

He hitched in a breath, diaphragm flexing to try to coax the burp out. When that didn't work, he hovered a hand in front of his belly, clenching and unclenching his fist, twisting a little like he manually could loosen up some valve in his belly.

Stupid Claire. She got him so worked up like that, and he couldn't think straight, couldn't even walk or talk or swallow correctly. One of these days, he'd wind up choking thanks to something she did. What was the word? Asphyxiating.

He burped, the air vibrating out of him, catapulted from his stomach with some oomph. It came with great relief and a burning feeling in his throat that felt a little like acid reflux.

Enough of this. He wasn't going to stand around in his kitchen feeling like this. Wasn't going to be held hostage in his own home for Christ's sake.

He stalked around the corner to confront her, head tipped way back to kill off his last beer as he proceeded.

The bedroom door blocked his path. A panel of wood erected between them.

Mark hadn't expected this, and it stopped him in his tracks. She rarely closed it. Even during the worst of their fights, the door stayed open.

He stared at the grain of the wood, but it offered no answers. His shadow laid a dark shape over the veneer, blocking out some of its glimmer.

His fingers closed around the empty beer can in his mitt, cinching tighter and tighter. The aluminum crumpled in his grip, and there was something satisfying about that. He liked the feel of it bending and distorting and breaking at his whim.

He looked down at it, the can pinched in the middle as though he'd given it a woman's waist.

A breath sucked into him. A deep inhale. Cool wind gathering in his lungs. Somehow it made his insides feel like wet flaps. Weird moist walls at odds with the air.

The Girl in the Sand

And some clarity came upon him. Some sense that he had a choice. He could let this go. He could walk away, and it would all be over.

He could walk back into the kitchen, toss the empty can in the recycling bin. Maybe pour himself a glass of water. Then he could head into the living room and watch TV, and the whole thing would blow over. It would be forgotten by this evening. Perhaps never thought of again for as long as either of them lived.

Instead he cracked his right forearm into the door. It shivered open in slow motion, shaking like a struck gong, humming out a vibrato note.

And where the door slid out of the frame, Claire took shape. Lips parted. Eyes open wide. The fear made her look younger. More innocent.

She lay on the bed, blanket pulled up so high it concealed most of her chin and jaw, and he couldn't even see her scar. She seemed to be frozen in a partially upright position — perhaps about a quarter of the way up, propped on her elbows.

He hovered in the doorway, waited a moment for her to speak, but she said nothing. Just blinked a few times, her eyes meeting his and darting away over and over.

"What's for dinner?" he said. His voice sounded small and oddly soft, even to himself.

After another flurry of blinks, she answered.

"I said you just eat whatever you want. I'm not hungry."

He smashed the can against the door jamb, one thrust of his arm, driving it home with the heel of his hand. The immediate violence of it surprised him. He pulled his hand back, the wilted piece of aluminum clenched in his fist. Flattened.

It didn't seem like her eyes could get any bigger, but they

did. The slightest tremble overtook her bottom lip.

He strode forward, moved three steps closer to her on the bed, legs solid underneath him despite his drunkenness. He didn't think anymore. Didn't analyze anything. Didn't intellectualize. He just acted, as though the orders came from somewhere else, came from above.

And he stood over her now, and once more his shadow darkened that which lay before him. Last time it was the door. This time it was her body.

The long shadow fell over her legs, then torso, then face, and finally it pulled up to a stop. Twitching a little as he brought himself upright. He could see the pride in it somehow — that slight curve to the spine — and he liked that.

"I'm going to ask you one more time, and I want you to think real hard before you answer," he said. "What are you making for my dinner?"

His voice came out slow and controlled. The truth was that he only felt this confident in these moments of conflict, these moments when the possibility of violence became real. She had the upper hand in every other facet of life, didn't she? But here she couldn't match him. He had the power.

Her quivering lip picked up speed, and soon her top lip joined the shaking dance. The skin on her chin puckered into about twelve distinct divots.

The words spilled out of her all at once.

"I don't know."

And her eyes went up another size, cartoon level shock in them now, as though she was surprised by what came out of her mouth.

Somehow, it was what he expected to hear, what he wanted to hear. She'd walked into it. Accepted what was coming for her.

The Girl in the Sand

He watched her now. Small and pathetic. She trembled before him.

His fingers relented, letting the crushed beer can drop to the floor, but her eyes didn't track its fall.

She stared out at nothing, watched him out of the corner of her eye, something she always did in these dramatic moments.

"Wrong answer," he said, at last.

He lurched toward her, his fist drawing back behind his ear to deliver the blow she'd asked for.

But just as he went to let his hand go, went to unleash the overhand right, she cowered. Twisted. Brought her hands up to defend herself, and the blanket slipped away from her face.

The jagged scar appeared there near her chin. Revealed itself like the end of a magician's trick. A tattered slash of pink flesh all mottled. Rough in texture.

And he froze. Stopped himself. Balled hand still raised over his shoulder. Face all clenched up. Nose wrinkled. Teeth exposed.

His chest heaved, and the breath huffed in and out of his nostrils, whistling and ragged and strange. But he didn't move.

And her fingers parted, and they looked at each other, eyes seeking one another out, fastening, and staying there. Some wordless significance passing between them.

Mark pivoted, his arm dropping as he turned. He didn't say a word, didn't so much as think one. He just stormed out through the garage and climbed into his Jeep.

Even as drunk as he was, starting it and backing out of the driveway happened all at once. A reflex more than a conscious course of action.

He sped away.

CHAPTER 35

The metal bar lifts high over Emily's shoulder. Waggles a few times. Descends.

It's an overhand delivery. A clean stroke. The desk leg plunging like an axe splitting wood on a block.

The flat end with the screw plate clobbers one of the boards nailed over the window. The sharp edge gouges at the wood. Chips at it. A flake of lumber the size of a crooked toothpick removed. Fluttering away.

And the reverberation of the force explodes in her hands and wrists. Jostles her arms up to the shoulders. All of that momentum cutting off at once knocks her back a step.

The pain of the impact flares and recedes. Makes her grit her teeth.

It's useless, of course, and she knows this. Knew it before she took the swing.

She may have grooved a little indentation into the wood, but that's all she can muster. Surface damage. The equivalent of a flesh wound. Nothing more.

There's no angle to pry at the boards. No use in bludgeoning the cylinder of the deadbolt, though she gave that a few swings as well, mostly missing it and peppering the door with dents.

There's no way out of here.

All she can do is vent frustration. Swing her weapon with wild abandon. Know the pain of clubbing immovable objects.

She hefts the bar in front of her. Fingers probing the length of the metal.

The screw plate wobbles some at her touch. Pivots at the

194

seam of the weld. It's coming loose.

Damn it. That's her sharp edge. Her blade, more or less. The spiked ball at the end of her mace. It's the part that might gash Stump's head when the time comes.

And she's weakened it for no good reason. Dulled it.

Hot tears flush her eyes, the wetness somehow intensifying the sharp sting of them. Little grains of sand that cut like glass every time she blinks.

And the heat overtakes her again. Swirls confusion into her skull. Opens up that pit of black noise to swallow her.

Her legs buckle, all of their strength sucked away. The whole world careens.

And she's falling. Falling.

She lands on her knees, the desk leg tumbling away from her, jarred free when she hits the floor.

She thinks the worst is over, but her balance still betrays her and she tips forward. Flailing. Weightless.

Gravity doesn't make much sense in this moment. It seems strange and cruel. Somewhat arbitrary.

Her hands move in front of her out of reflex. Fingers splayed. Bracing for impact.

Her arms are too weak to catch her, to bear her weight, so she can only soften the blow.

She folds up into something small when she hits, the rounded dome of her forehead clunking the tile pretty good.

And now reality retreats a little more. Distances itself from her.

Everything gets farther away.

Goes darker. Darker. Not quite reaching black.

She lies there. Full body pressed against the cool ceramic. Face resting on her hands.

Her eyelids flutter several times. She fights them. Gets them opened to tiny slits.

And she pushes herself up onto hands and knees. Not quite sure why she's doing this, why she continues to put up a fight.

She hovers in that position. Poised to crawl. Huffing and puffing all the while. Hissing and spitting and choking. Something strange happening.

Gabby speaks from somewhere behind her.

"Breathe, Em."

It occurs to her that her friend only appears in moments like these. Always fluttering at the edge of things. Always just out of view.

And now the salt of Emily's tears reaches her mouth. Coats her lips. The tang of it reminds her of the ocean, and she sees that beach scene again from when she was small. The dark place in the sand where the tide had washed all the footprints away.

"Just breathe."

But she can't. She can't.

Her diaphragm hitches. Her chest spasms. Little clicks and gasps scraping out of her. Some detached part of her grasps after what this sounds like and finds it: a vomiting cat.

"Listen to me, Emily. You're hyperventilating. You have to take a deep breath."

She obeys. Concentrates. Sucks in.

There's a little snap at the back of her throat like a bubble popping, and then the cool wind rushes into her lungs. Bloats her chest cavity. Lifts her up.

She breathes. Inhales. Exhales. Repeats.

"You have to be smart now. You're one step ahead of him, but only if you're smart about it."

Emily nods. She talks to Gabby, even if she can't see her.

"I have a weapon, and I'm not chained to the desk. That's something."

"That's right, and now you need a plan."

CHAPTER 36

Nothing like a nice, drunk drive to clear the mind, Mark thought. He chuckled a little at this, but in some ways it was true.

He tossed the empty can out the window of his Jeep. The can hovered next to him for a beat and then dropped out of sight, falling behind the speeding Jeep. He watched it tumble in the rearview, the yellow tube of aluminum somersaulting and bouncing before finally disappearing into the dust and scraggly plants.

Out here, he could forget about her for a little while. He could focus on the road.

With the dancing object gone, the desert landscape went back to the still, beige emptiness it usually was. Oppressive in both its monotone and its flat expanse that stretched out to the horizon.

Mark didn't know why anyone would choose to live in a place like this — all brown and dead. He and Claire lived there because they couldn't afford to move, couldn't escape the jobs they had and start over somewhere else. They were trapped here. Stranded in the suburbs in the desert. Surrounded by a sea of asphalt and sand with massive casinos towering over everything, the gaudy lights blinking all night every night.

His eyes flicked from the mirror back to the road — an empty stretch of blacktop cut through the level swath of sand. Cacti and desert scrub poking up from the plains.

Out here, he was alone. No other cars on the highway. No gas stations or fast food joints. No signs of any life at all, in fact.

The Girl in the Sand

He could open the throttle up. Push his little Jeep as hard as he wanted. The vehicle rode higher when he jammed the pedal to the floor. It stood up taller on the wheels, and he liked the feel of it. It topped out within a few mph of 100, the fenders beginning to shake and shimmy. He backed off, let the speedometer hover closer to 88.

He kept one eye on the road as he fished a hand into the box on the passenger seat. Cold cylinders met his fingertips there. He secured one and plucked it free.

The fresh can cracked like a gun when he opened it, the metallic sound somehow louder and more percussive out here on the road, out here in the emptiness.

He'd grabbed a twelve-pack of Coors Banquet at the party store. They were out of Pabst. These cold yellow dogs were his second favorite, so it wasn't so bad, though they did cost a little more.

He took a drink, long and deep. It was cleaner tasting than the PBR, just a touch heavier, too.

Without warning, the image popped into his head, made him cringe. He saw Claire cowering on the bed, the blanket falling away to reveal her scar. His fist hovered there next to his head, ready to strike.

Damn. He'd tried to avoid that memory and had mostly done so up to this point. Apparently fourteen beers weren't enough to keep it away. Not quite enough to kill the proper brain cells, even if they'd turned in a valiant effort.

He took another drink, gulped three times, licked his lips. He felt the beer foam and spiral in his throat, all of it sucked down into his belly like the water swirling in a bathroom drain, vanishing slowly but surely.

He wished the image — his shaking fist — would disappear

199

like that, would drain from both his head and Claire's, but it wouldn't. She'd never let it go. Never. Even though he hadn't touched her, she'd hold onto it, hold onto the negativity and let it fester between them.

Of course, he had hit Claire in the past, but that was just what it was. The past. It was over.

He hadn't laid a hand on her at all in three months, and the last time was just a little slap. What do they call it? A love tap. Three months for Christ's sake, and it felt like even longer. It really did.

And it hurt both of them when he did it. He let that rage inside of him out, let it express itself in physical violence, and he felt guilty as hell afterward.

He cried after the first time. She'd been needling him all afternoon, finally made some comment he couldn't take. He'd backhanded her in the kitchen — another one of those violent bursts that caught both of them entirely surprised. She bled right away. Gummy red pouring out of her, collecting in thick pockets in the crevices between her teeth, seeping down her chin. His knuckles had mashed her bottom lip into her teeth. Gashed it pretty good. And she had a fat lip for almost a week after that.

He had stormed out right when it happened. Got in his Jeep. Drove out here to the desert just like today. The empty highway.

And once he was alone amongst the sand, he sobbed like a little child. He blubbered. Had watched the road through the blur of tears.

Now the heat swelled in his face and neck and chest. A pulsing warmth that rippled through him.

And he could hear the sound from that memory over and over again. The wet slap of his hand busting her lip against her teeth. He caught her clean. It snapped her head back, tipped her chin up just like a stiff jab.

He changed his grip on the steering wheel, toe fidgeting against the gas pedal, and he could feel the beer buzz thrumming in the tiniest bones of his hands and feet, some strange electricity. Pleasant. Almost euphoric, but not quite.

He ducked his head under the dash to take another drink before he remembered that it wasn't necessary now that he was out in the middle of nowhere. It made him laugh, the way he'd bowed out of view like he was sitting at a stoplight downtown. Those little drunk driving habits can be hard to break.

And he saw himself standing over her again, but it was different this time. He didn't cringe. He licked his lips. God, it would feel pretty goddamn good to let his hand go. No. Hands. Both of them. That would feel good, wouldn't it? And she always shut her trap after. That was the hardest thing to accept in a way. The thing that drew him back to this headspace over and over, maybe. She always learned her lesson. She did. For a while, anyway.

The desert all around him seemed to dim now. Seemed to recede, to pull back from the edges of the road, like it wasn't real anymore. Not all the way. He was real. His mind. His imagination. The canvas of his dreamscape grew, the pictures in his head gaining intensity until they reduced reality to a soft focus, mostly drowned the physical world out.

And his thoughts grew clearer, grew nuanced and intricate, every idea somehow amplified out here alone on the road. An incredible sensitivity occupied his head, a religious lucidity — a feeling he'd known perhaps a handful of times in his life, always when drunk, sleeping, or in that flash of adrenaline during a dangerous event. Strange states that gave him a fleeting glimpse into the subliminal.

And he understood it now, had words for what lay at the heart of his conflict with Claire.

What hurt was the way she kept things from him. Hid them. The good and the bad both. She blocked him out of the things that pained her, and the things that made her happy. All of her history was locked away from him, trapped somewhere in that skull of hers.

She kept him at arm's length. Apart. Alone.

And something about it jammed a blade into his guts and twisted. She made him worthless. Made him bleed.

There were topics in every relationship, he supposed, that couldn't be talked about. Things both partners knew that could never be pulled up from the murky depths, could never be discussed out loud. Secrets that must be taken to the grave.

This hurt she caused was one of those things. The wound would never heal, so it festered. Got worse and worse and worse until he couldn't take it anymore. Until he had to express the agony in the real world.

He told her in bruises. In black eyes. In busted lips. His hands scrawled it on her body in a language of cruelty, etched it in marks all over her skin.

And his breath would get hot in these moments. He could feel its heat on his tongue, pushing out in spitty bursts between his teeth.

All of the outside world would go quiet, and he could hear only those muffled sloshing sounds inside of his head like when he was a kid at the public pool holding his breath underwater. The blood beating in his ears. The wind whistling in his sinus cavity as he blew a flurry of bubbles out of his nose.

He felt powerful when he stood over her. He felt whole. A

terrible oneness that was only real in those moments of violence when his heart hammered in his chest and ice water flooded his veins.

And once it was done, that feeling faded out all at once. The heat fled his face, and he felt awful. Nauseous.

This was the cycle. Intense cruelty followed by guilt. A dramatic tonal shift that felt important. Almost sacred.

In the quiet after it was done, the tidal wave of guilt and shame washed over the two of them, uprooted them from their lives, from their ideas of themselves, threatened to swallow them up for good. An overwhelming surge of suffering that was somehow shared, somehow belonged to both of them, even if he was the one who'd wronged her.

And from there they acted out the guilt ritual like they always did. The ceremony.

He told her he'd change. Told himself the same. The words came out solemn. Serious. With a somber rhythm like a prayer. He swore up and down that he'd never do it again. Sometimes one of them cried. Sometimes both.

But the awful truth crept into the blank spaces where neither of them dared to look. It was always there. Always all around them. Because, like he'd already reminded himself, every time it happened, she learned her lesson. For a little while, she learned her lesson. For a little while, the wound was healed. For a little while, they felt closer. Bonded by chaos, by the sheer intensity of the act itself, of the emotional shift. It was, after all, an experience that only they shared.

And now? Now it was worse than before, wasn't it? Now it wasn't just her blocking him out. She had a whole team of law enforcement professionals helping her. All of them conspiring to hurt him, to make him worthless. This Loshak fuck leading the charge.

Well, it couldn't stand. No fucking way. He was going to do something about it. Something big. Something permanent. He had to. It was the only way.

He would show them.

He would take care of it.

He blinked a few times, and the sand and rock along the road seemed to return from the dreamscape, all of reality congealing back into solidity.

The desert didn't move outside. If it was aware of his existence, it showed no sign of it at all.

CHAPTER 37

Darger watched Nicole through the windshield like it was a TV screen. The girl clomped across the lot, weaving between parked cars, the streetlights shining through her hair so it almost glowed.

She moved slow on her stilettos, a methodical back and forth strut, and the shoes were loud. Clicking away at the emptiness, each footstep sending out a call that pinged back a clapping echo as a response. Darger could hear the knocking plainly through the closed doors and windows of the rental car, which seemed amusing.

They were well off the Strip tonight, parked off to the side of a third-rate hotel so Nicole had easier access to the side door — apparently the preferred entry for some calls. And even if the parking lot was damn near full, there was no traffic out this way, making the clack of the shoes all the more prominent, all the more obnoxious.

Flaring light in the cup holder drew Darger's eyes away from the rhythmic totter of Nicole's back. Her phone lit up there, rumbled a beat later. She checked it.

Spam. Of course.

She sighed. Swiped the cash advance text away. And just then the clicking footsteps cut out.

Her gaze returned to the windshield. Scanned from left to right. Nothing. No movement.

Nicole couldn't have reached the door yet — she still had a few more rows of cars and an alley to cross. So where was she? She couldn't just vanish.

205

Darger swallowed, eyes swiveling everywhere, heart thundering in her chest.

She waited a few seconds for Nicole to emerge, to pop out from behind a row of cars, futzing with a broken heel, some simple explanation like that. The girl could be lighting a cigarette. Texting. Checking her phone.

But she wasn't. Darger knew she wasn't. She felt it.

Nicole didn't appear. The clicking of her heels did not resume.

She was gone.

Wait. Wait. Darger caught herself before the panic took hold. She couldn't leap to the worst case scenario. She'd done that last night and made a fool of herself. Really pissed Nicole off, too. If she blew this, the girl would never forgive her. They might lose her for good. Darger had to stay calm. Reasonable.

Think.

OK.

Maybe the john wanted to conduct business in his vehicle? Could that make sense?

No. Nicole was definitely headed inside. She'd mentioned entering the side door specifically.

Darger's eyes still scanned the lot. No Nicole. Nothing.

Then she saw it. Movement to her left.

She snapped her head that way. Squinted.

Someone stood in the lot. A man wearing a baseball cap. He was moving, leaning against the passenger door of a pickup truck with his back to her, but she couldn't tell what he was doing.

This wasn't right. Something wasn't right.

A truck.

The truck? The one from the gas station security video?

The Girl in the Sand

The man squatted to the ground, and she could just see his head and shoulders. He was moving something. Something heavy.

Darger moved without thought, her hand finding the door handle. She pulled it, careful to avoid making noise. Slid the door open a crack.

The dome light clicked on — lit up everything — and she panicked for a moment. Worried he'd see.

Now her hand flailed at the light. Found the switch. Turned it off.

Shaky breaths entered and exited her nostrils. She could hear the blood squishing in her ears.

He hadn't turned. Hadn't seen. Though he seemed to be frozen for the moment. Spooked, maybe.

Good. She didn't want him wary, of course, but his pause was buying her time.

Time to get close.

She eased out of the car, crouching beside the door, closing it with a soft touch.

Now she shuffled forward. Staying quiet. Staying low.

She skittered between cars, sneaking glances across the way.

A red glow flared, lighting up the hotel lot. Brake lights from the truck. The engine whirred to life.

This was it. He was leaving. She was going to lose him if she didn't hurry.

She sprinted to the back of the pickup. Stopped just shy of it, staying low to keep out of the rearview the best she could.

She stared through the back windshield.

Nicole was there. Lit up green from the dashboard lights.

The girl's head slumped over on one shoulder. Limp.

And the man leaned over her as Darger watched. Wound

something around the girl's wrists.

Darger couldn't see, but she knew what it was: a plastic zip tie.

Ice water coursed through Darger's body, the cold rush of adrenaline.

It was him. It was Stump.

She reached for her gun.

Nothing.

It wasn't there. Her holster was empty. Then she remembered taking the gun out. Setting it on the passenger seat. Covering it with the box of chocolates when that old couple had passed by the car. Jesus Christ.

But there was no time to go back for it. She barely had time to think.

If she lost him now, she'd never find these girls. Not alive, anyway.

And she realized it wasn't even a choice. Even if she'd had the gun, there was no choice — because of Emily.

If she arrested Stump here and now, they'd never find the other girl. He'd never tell.

There was only one way.

The manual transmission whined as he popped the clutch. The truck rolled backward, inching just a little closer to Darger.

It almost seemed like an invitation.

She didn't think twice. She climbed into the bed of the truck, sliding forward on her belly.

When the truck lurched, her weight shifted with it. It felt like it was pulling her in, welcoming her.

She went with it, rolling her body under the crumpled blue tarp that was now flapping in the wind.

She watched the hotel lights grow smaller and smaller as

they cruised down the street.

The wind whipped her hard as the truck picked up speed. Cold. Slapping the tarp at her.

But it was OK.

This truck would take her to Stump's lair, would take her to Emily Kessler, would help her save Nicole.

It was the only way.

CHAPTER 38

Loshak sat at a red light, arms draped over the steering wheel. His eyelids were heavy, and a frustration headache pounded at his temples. Too much time in the rental car. This long behind the wheel gave him a headache every time.

But his ride-along shift was mercifully over, and as soon as he dropped the girl off, he could get back to the hotel and stretch his legs out. Get some sleep. At last.

His eyes drifted up to the mirror, gazed on the strange creature in the rearview.

The girl, Misty, hunched in the back of the rental. She was frail. Small. All bony elbows and long neck. Makeup smudged raccoon blackness around her eyes.

Her thumbs danced atop her phone's screen, and little typing sound effects and notification chirps accompanied her furious texting. She blinked a few times, and he thought perhaps she felt him watching her, but she didn't look up. She never did. Not once during all of the hours they'd now spent together in this car had she made any kind of eye contact with him — in the mirror or otherwise.

The light turned green, and Loshak's foot slid from the brake to the accelerator. The car coasted out of its stillness and got up to speed, the lights and buildings along the streetside turning back into that incessant flicker rushing past the windows.

His lips parted, but he didn't speak. The mundane question he'd been forming there died somewhere in the back of his throat. What would the point of pestering her be? She didn't trust him — not even a little — and he didn't blame her. It was understandable for a girl in her position to be guarded. He was well aware of the way most prostitutes characterized their treatment at the hands of law enforcement. Trust would never be possible for many of them. In any case, she'd made it plain — absolutely obvious — that she didn't want to talk to him, and that was OK. He could let it be.

Even when the car pulled into a parking spot outside of her building, the silence between them seemed reluctant to let up. Loshak waited a beat — hoping, he supposed, that she'd realize where they were and exit the vehicle without words passing between them.

Instead, her face remained tilted toward the glowing screen in her hands, expression all blank and slack, thumbs pistoning away.

He lifted a finger for reasons unclear to him. Perhaps he hoped the movement would catch her eye, but it didn't.

No. Of course not.

He licked his lips, felt his breath hesitate in his nostrils. It took a real effort to get his mouth to obey the command to talk.

"We're here," he said, finally.

Her shoulders jerked a little. He'd startled her. Ripped her out of the phone's abstract reality.

Still, she said nothing. She gathered her things, shoved the glowing phone into her bag, and stepped out into the night.

Loshak's eyes stayed fixed on the mirror. He watched the empty spot where she'd been, the parallel lines stitched into the upholstery. He thought she might have made a little noise — more a vocalized syllable than an actual word — just as the door slammed behind her, but he wasn't sure. Either way, he took it as a goodbye.

He turned his head. Watched her pass through the doors of her apartment complex. Her silhouette flitted on the other side of the glass, just faintly visible through the glare. Her shape disappeared about halfway up a flight of steps, finally moving out of the window's view.

His hands assumed their position on the wheel and gearshift, but they held steady there. He sensed a reluctance in them, in himself. Something, somewhere told him to wait. Nothing more. Just to wait.

So he waited.

His eyes flicked back to the door, half expecting Misty to reappear there, but the glass remained occupied by drywall and carpeted steps, empty of humanity. Still, he watched. He couldn't shake the feeling that there was something he was missing.

The stillness grew awkward around him, made his shoulders twitch just a little.

Christ. What was he doing? He must be more tired than he'd realized.

And then he saw it. His phone caught his eye, resting in the cup holder. He'd turned it off some hours ago. He always turned it off when he got a headache. That was what he'd been missing. He needed to check his messages. See how Darger and the others were faring.

He fired the phone up, the once blank screen now shining bright white in his face. He waited for it to load, fingered the appropriate button.

And now the robotic voice spoke in his ear. He had one voicemail message. From Claire.

As soon as the girl's voice exited the tiny speaker, Loshak sat forward in his seat.

"Hey, um. Hi. It's Claire. I just.... There's a situation I thought you should know about."

She sounded distraught, like maybe she'd been crying or still was. And she sounded scared.

"Things are getting a little weird tonight is all. I guess I was thinking.... I don't know."

Loshak's off hand returned to the shifter, ready to roll out. Despite the hemming and hawing in Claire's words, he heard trouble in the tone of her voice. He heard danger. He heard someone asking for help. Didn't he?

"You know what? I'm being a little over the top. This is nothing to worry about, OK? I was hoping to talk to you, but I know you're busy, and I'll try you again later tonight. So. Yeah. Talk to you later on."

Loshak's brow furrowed. Now he wasn't sure what to think. Had he been hearing things?

He played the message again, listened to that note of fear exit her voice all at once halfway through her call. When the message was done, he sat there, listened to the long beat of silence transmitted over the line, and now the robot voice squawked in his ear again.

"End of messages."

He hung up the phone, slowly peeled his hand away from the gearshift. Maybe he'd been wrong. Maybe what he'd heard wasn't danger after all. Nothing serious. Nothing immediate.

He dropped the phone into the cup holder where it rattled around the rim before settling down.

Stump's return had stirred up a lot of emotions for everyone connected to the case, Claire more than anyone else. Maybe she just needed someone to talk to about that kind of thing.

He grabbed the phone. Swiped. Hovered his finger over her

name.

Maybe. Maybe not.

She said she'd call back. Would it be better to let her proceed on her own terms? Yeah. Probably. She did emphasize that she was fine and everything.

Again the phone dropped from his hand, danced in a spiral around the perimeter of the cup holder, fell into a leaning rest.

Finally, his hands took their place on the wheel and gearshift in earnest, and this time, he followed through.

The car lurched forward, merged with the sparse flow of traffic here. The evening had hit that point of dusk when the first signs of grayscale crept into all things, and about half the cars had flipped their headlights on.

Something about it gave him a chill. Somewhere out there in the city tonight, Leonard Stump was probably driving around in one of those vehicles. Was he one of the people with his headlights on, or one of those yet to fully embrace the night?

He drove a meandering route to his hotel, careful to wind his way around the Strip. His headache was bad enough without dealing with the droves of tourist traffic and lights.

Claire's message replayed in his head as he drove, the most dramatic fragments echoing around in his skull.

He didn't know if he'd made the right choice in not calling her back, had no feel for it one way or the other. Even so, he found some relief now that he was in motion. Rocketing forward to something else, whether it was the right thing or the wrong thing.

Another stoplight halted his progress toward slumber, the car's engine changing its pitch to a low rumble as it idled.

Stump. God, they were close to him, weren't they? One step ahead of him for the first time in twenty years. If they got lucky with the ride-along detail, they might well have him in custody within a day or two. It was a big *if*, but it felt real. It felt possible. For the first time in so long he couldn't remember, it felt possible. Like he could actually breathe again.

The light turned green, and he pressed on.

The bigger buildings of the downtown area died out, and smaller brick structures lined the streets in their place. Seedy strip joints and 24-hour wedding chapels, and right in the middle of it, his hotel, with his little box of a room that gave him that picture postcard view of a barren desert landscape. Hellish, really.

The phone vibrated against the plastic wall of the cup holder, the brittle rattle of it catching him off guard, making his skin crawl. He grabbed it once it was done trembling and clattering, the screen still bright.

He knew what the sound meant. A text. He checked it. From Claire.

The body of the message featured one word:

Help.

CHAPTER 39

The truck hummed beneath her, the steady thrum of a purring cat, only catching now and then when Stump changed gears.

Well, Darger thought to herself, *this might just be the most ridiculous stunt you've pulled yet. Hopping into a moving vehicle with a serial killer. And don't forget the part where you left your gun behind. Good one, dummy.*

She sighed, knowing she'd had no choice. If she hadn't jumped aboard, Stump would have ridden out of sight before she'd even reached her car. Nicole and Emily would have been abandoned to certain torture and death.

Darger couldn't live with that. No way.

Emily's sad Twitter picture flashed in her head. *Please let her still be alive.*

She pressed her eyes closed, willing herself to stay calm and to keep her wits about her. One step at a time.

Her nose filled with the industrial smell of rust and exhaust as she took stock of her surroundings. Bumping against her hip was a 5-gallon gas can, one of the heavy-duty metal deals in army green.

On her other side, pressed against her back, there was a large Rubbermaid tub filled with tools and strapped in place beneath the tarp. It was taller than the sides of the bed, so it gave the tarp a gentle curve, like a tent.

She gazed down toward her feet, which pointed at the open end of the truck bed. She could see the ball head of the hitch from here. Was that how he did it? He towed the cars to an isolated place, perhaps with the girls already secured in the trunk, and then when he found a nice, desolate stretch of asphalt, he stopped, unhitched the car, and doused it with gasoline?

Overhead, the tarp flapped in the wind, creating a shuddering sound that drowned out almost everything but the chugging of the engine.

Despite the noise, Darger was glad for the tarp. Aside from the fact that it was the only thing concealing her from view, it also offered some protection from the cold. Night had fallen and brought with it icy fingers that prickled over her bare skin.

A shiver ran through her then, and she wondered if the tarp was truly keeping her all that warm. It shielded her from the wind, at least. That was something. But wherever her body pressed against the cold steel of the truck bed, she could feel the body heat leaching out.

She rolled from her side onto her belly, wriggling a little closer to the cab to risk a peek up front. Through the sliver of window visible from her position, she could see the black outline of Stump's form. Just a shadow of a man.

Her fingers felt for the rectangular outline of her phone where it nestled in her pocket. She couldn't stop checking for it — reassuring herself it was still there — even though she couldn't use it. Now that they were out in the desert, there were no streetlights around. No illumination aside from the occasional passing car. In this dark, even the small amount of illumination from the screen could be enough to get Stump's attention in the rearview mirror. The tarp would make things worse, she thought, acting like a huge diffuser.

No, she had to wait. They'd come to a stop eventually, and she'd find a safe place to make the call. After that, she'd have to play it by ear. Loshak would tell her to stay put, to wait for backup. But if Stump went after the girls, if he tried to hurt them, Darger wouldn't be able to wait.

She took a breath. Better to not look too far ahead. Better to take it slow, take it step by step.

All of the rest would come in time. For now her only job was to wait and try to keep from freezing to death.

A car passed going the opposite direction, and by the time she felt the whoosh of air as it went by, the taillights were already disappearing around the last bend in the road. The brief, red-tinted glimpse of the surrounding landscape told her nothing. All she could really tell was that they were on one of the curving mountain roads.

The truck swayed and shimmied through the many twists and turns. It struck her suddenly that it felt more like she was in a boat than a vehicle. Above her, the tarp flapped like a sail as the vehicle hurtled on through the darkness. Darger huddled in her hiding place, a weaponless stowaway. Lost at sea, set adrift with no say in her destination. Left to the whims of the shark at the helm.

Thoughts of sharks reminded her of that last conversation with Owen. She'd never responded to his messages or texts after that, like a bratty, pouting child.

Her hand caressed her phone again, and she imagined what the conversation might be like if she were able to tell Owen where she was right now.

She remembered then something he'd said to her after the mess in Atlanta, where they'd first met.

"You know," he'd said, "when the shit hits the fan, most people duck for cover."

She'd waited for him to go on, but Owen liked audience participation when he was doing a bit.

"And?" she'd asked finally.

"And you're the kind of person that runs face first into the blades."

She gazed out through the open back end again and saw the first glimmer of stars. A nursery rhyme from childhood echoed in her mind at the sight.

Star light, star bright.

First star I see tonight.

I wish I may, I wish I might.

Have this wish I wish tonight.

What was her wish, then? For courage? For strength?

In the end, she begged the stars for luck. Just enough to last her through the night.

CHAPTER 40

Mark paced the kitchen like an animal in a cage, the soles of his shoes thumping out a rhythm on the linoleum. Keeping time.

Claire's whimpers laid a sad melody over that beat. Feminine mews that stopped and started and broke off into choked sobs and silent shivers.

God, he wished she'd stop that. Just for a little while. It'd all be done soon, and then… Well, he didn't know what happened then. He'd find out when he got there.

He could feel the tension physically now, manifesting itself in his body, in his posture, in the tightness along his neck and shoulders.

What was going to happen was what had to happen. Had to. There was no choice. This was the refrain in his head. The idea he looped back to over and over, trying to etch order onto the chaos swirling inside of him. And he could almost make it work, could almost hold all of the black spiral in his head and be OK with it.

He just wished Claire would stop crying.

"You gotta be quiet now," he said, trying to keep the hard edge out of his voice and not quite pulling it off.

She sat on the floor in the corner, nearly all of her body, it seemed, leaned up against a cupboard door. Pressed into the green paint like it might morph into some means of escape, like that little door could lead out of this room after all, out of this place.

She kept her face mostly tilted away from him, weeping softly.

The Girl in the Sand

But even at an odd angle, he could tell, somehow, that she was trying to stop crying and couldn't. Some tightness in her cheeks communicated this, an extra set of wrinkles pulling at the sides of her mouth. He'd seen the expression before.

Nevertheless, her eyes stayed fastened to him in their way, watching him out of their corners, swiveling along with his every motion. She didn't look him in the face, though, didn't dare meet his eyes.

He glanced down at himself, his stride coming to a stop. He squinted. Concentrated. Huh. What was it that she was looking at, exactly? He tried to follow the trajectory of her vision, but this was easier said than done with all the beers he'd guzzled down. She was all fuzzy, flicking in and out of double.

Wait. Maybe it was the gun.

Again, he dipped his head for a look.

The slim piece of black polymer dangled at the end of his arm. The M&P Shield 9mm from good ol' Smith & Wesson. It was about as compact as a piece could get while maintaining full-size power — a touch over six inches long and, incredibly, not even an inch wide.

He'd always maintained a pride about the gun, about what its purchase said about him — other people went out and bought big ass cannons — Magnums, Desert Eagles, etc. Almost like they were compensating for something. Well, this little gun was easily concealed, practical, and it could still poke holes all through someone's guts or brains if and when necessary.

Anyhow, that was probably why she wouldn't stop crying. The gun. It upset her. Well, that made sense. Shit.

"Hush now, baby. It's… This is something I have to do. That's all."

His words didn't help. At all. If anything, Claire's sobs came

221

harder and faster.

Goddamn. He opened the cupboard above the fridge, looked in at the couple bottles of vinegar, the big plastic jug of olive oil.

He brought the gun up to eye level, his arm slowing as it extended toward the cupboard. The weapon's progress stopped, so it hung there above the fridge. He licked his front teeth, worked his jaw a few times.

His arm retracted, brought the gun back to dangle at his side. With the opposite hand, he closed the cupboard.

He couldn't do it. He couldn't put the gun away. Not now. Not even for a little while to calm her down. It wasn't worth it. He wanted her to stop crying, but not at this price. No way. He needed the gun in his hand. Needed to feel it.

He went back to pacing the length of the room. Down and back and down and back.

The sink dripped every once in a while. Drops of water ticking away the seconds until the agent arrived, until it all went down.

He couldn't wait to see the look on Loshak's face, that telltale flash when he saw what Mark had for him.

CHAPTER 41

After what felt like hours — though she doubted it could have been that long — Darger sensed the forward pull of the truck slowing and heard the downshift. How long had they been on the road? She wasn't certain. Time had grown strange in the dark. Murky. Hard to measure.

The truck took a sharp right, and Darger's weight pressed up against the plastic tub. The smooth hum of asphalt under the tires was replaced by the crunch of gravel. Gas sloshed against the metal sides of the jerry can as they bumped over ruts and potholes. A dirt road, she thought, or maybe a driveway. From her narrow view out the back, all she could tell was that it was a slender lane, hugged on both sides by Ponderosa pines and quaking aspen.

As they wound around a tight bend, gravity signaled that they were heading uphill, a steady rate of ascent tugging at Darger's body. Dust swirled in the red glow of the taillights. She scanned the dark landscape for anything she might use: a fork in the lane that could signify a driveway, lights that might indicate a house in the distance. She saw nothing but the silhouettes of trees and rocks and scrubby undergrowth rising out of the dirt.

The land leveled out, and with a whispering hiss, the tires came to a stop in the sand. The truck continued to idle. Darger held her breath in anticipation of the silence that would come when he cut the engine. Seconds ticked by.

Adrenaline flooded her veins and her pulse swished in her ears so loud she was certain he'd hear. Her lungs felt like they were about to explode, but she didn't dare let herself breathe.

What was taking so long? Darger dug her fingernails into her palms, but eventually she couldn't help it. She released the lungful of air she'd been holding, slow and steady, like a leaky tire. Her head swam with relief on the inhale. She let herself breathe regularly after that, though she was sure to be quiet.

The air was different here, clean and scented with cedar. How far from the city were they? She wasn't sure, and she still hadn't been able to look at her phone to figure out how much time had passed.

The stillness when the engine finally cut out was sudden and absolute. Eerie. Unnerving.

A latch clicked and hinges moaned as the driver's side door opened. There was a patter of what sounded like heavy boots striking the ground, one after the other.

The whole truck listed to the port side as Stump climbed out, shimmying and lifting higher on the shocks from the change in weight. The door slammed shut with a metallic thunk, followed by rasping footsteps through the gravel drive.

It took her several seconds to identify the next sounds, but she was able to piece it together: the screech of an old-fashioned screen door, the scrape of a key in a lock, the clunk of the deadbolt sliding free.

Darger had her eyes closed as she listened, but now they popped open as a thought struck her.

Had he left Nicole in the truck?

Of course, he'd want to get the door open before he dragged Nicole inside. It made sense.

She should grab Nicole while he was inside, get her away from the house, away from Stump. But Darger had no idea how far into the house he'd gone, how soon he'd be back. If he surprised her in the middle of her rescue maneuver, she was still unarmed.

Something plucked at her mind, wanting to be acknowledged, but she couldn't get the thought to solidify.

Her heart thudded with the indecision.

And then she heard the shrill squawk and slam of the screen door again. Footsteps.

It struck her then that he might come around to the back of the truck for some reason. To get his tools or the gas can. Or to check for hitchhiking FBI agents.

Shit.

She should have rolled out of the back as soon as they'd come to a stop.

Panic welled in her belly, face flushed, the palms of her hands writhing with pins and needles.

Too late now. If he came around back, she'd have to ambush him. The impulse to search the truck bed for a weapon struck her, but her instinct to keep absolutely still and silent won out. If she heard his footsteps coming this way, she'd reach into the Rubbermaid bin and go with the first thing she found.

She lay in the truck bed, as taut as a mountain cat waiting for a jackrabbit to hop into sight. Her muscles quivered with the tension, starting to ache, and again she found herself wishing for her gun.

The stun gun. That was what her brain had been trying to tell her before. The stun gun in Nicole's purse. If the purse was in the cab, she could have gotten the jump on him. But it was too late now. Always too fucking late.

She tried to remember what the purse looked like. A little shoulder bag, she thought. Red or maybe brown. Leather.

Darger followed the sound of his footsteps as he moved around the truck, her body almost aching with the tension, every muscle coiled tight. Her eyes started to water from not blinking, staring into the rectangle of darkness beyond the truck bed.

The footsteps came right up to the truck and stopped. There was an agonizing pause before she heard the passenger side door open.

Darger squeezed her eyes shut at last.

The truck swayed again. She could hear him breathing now with the effort of dealing with Nicole's unconscious body, the dead weight. He grunted as he pulled the girl's bulk from the truck and shut the door.

The footsteps back to the house were slower, dragging a little with the extra load.

It wasn't until the door closed that she released the tension in her muscles. Her head thudded softly against the truck bed as her body went slack, and her lungs sucked in greedy lungfuls of air.

She strained her ears and heard nothing, no further sign of him, but her instincts told her to wait, told her not to move. Some part of her wanted to hide, wanted to stay concealed in the truck cab until morning. Until help arrived.

But no. She *was* the help. Hiding wasn't an option.

Her tongue prodded at the inside of her cheek, and her eyes blinked rapid-fire.

OK. She'd obey those fearful instincts, she decided, but only for one minute, and then she'd move out.

She forced herself to count to sixty, like she was playing hide and seek as a kid.

While she counted, she prayed that Nicole's purse — and the stun gun — were in the cab.

The minute passed. It was time.

The Girl in the Sand

Ready or not, here I come.

CHAPTER 42

Moving what felt like one muscle at a time, Darger sat up and slid down to the rear bumper. She settled one foot onto the ground and then the other, taking care to jostle the gravel as little as possible. Then she crept around to the side of the truck, keeping her body tucked low.

When she reached the door, her hand snaked up to the handle and hovered there. She scanned the front of the house for movement. Curtains shrouded the windows, prevented her from seeing much, but at least that meant she was concealed from this angle as well.

Slowly, she pressed her thumb into the button on the door. With the smallest click, the latch released. It seemed loud in the quiet, made a lump form in Darger's throat. She hesitated for a moment, eyes locked on the house. When no movement showed there, she swung the door just wide enough to peek through, praying under her breath that the dome light wouldn't blink on. It didn't.

The bag was there, on the floor, so close she didn't even have to pull the door any wider. She snatched it by the handle and eased the door shut again.

She shuffled away from the truck, feeling instantly vulnerable now that she was in the open. As soon as her feet were off the noisy gravel, she quickened her pace. With a final glance back at the house, she ducked behind a thicket of some kind of prickly shrub.

She knew she should call Loshak immediately, but she couldn't resist getting her hands on the stun gun. Fumbling with the zipper, Darger reached inside and felt around among Nicole's things until she found it. Her thumb found the button on the side but stopped short of pressing it. The sizzling blue light could reveal her. She'd have to trust that it would work when she needed it.

A shaky breath rattled out of her chest. She moved on to the next task.

Swiping a thumb at the screen of her phone, she had to squint to keep her eyes on it. After so long in the dark, the glow from the screen was piercing, almost violent.

Nine letters hunched in the top corner where the bars should be.

No Service.

Fuck.

She lifted the phone in the air, tried different angles and stood on her toes in a desperate attempt to get even a single bar to show up.

"Come on," she whispered to no one. The words came out as puffs of steam in the cold night air, hanging there for a moment before vanishing.

When a bar finally blipped on, she almost shouted in celebration.

She froze in position, the phone held over her head, and carefully moved her thumb to Loshak's name on her list of contacts. She waited for the call to connect, but she could tell already something was wrong. The phone wasn't ringing.

The bar vanished, and the *No Service* message reappeared.

No, no, no.

She glanced back at the house. This was taking too long.

Nicole's phone wasn't getting a signal either. She tried dialing 911 in the hopes that she'd at least be able to get emergency service, but nothing happened.

Her gaze fell on the stun gun. This was it. She'd have to go in alone.

She tried one last time to get a signal. When she found the fickle bar again, she sent Loshak a text. A red exclamation point popped up with the error message: *Not Delivered.*

She'd been on a camping trip in West Virginia once. Cell phone service was unreliable at best, all of her outgoing texts marked as *Not Delivered.* About half got through, anyway, though they were delayed by up to an hour. There was hope.

She sent the SOS text to Loshak nine more times, hoping that at least one went through.

Her fingers flailed around inside Nicole's bag, taking stock of the rest of its contents: a lighter, cigarettes, a small vial of perfume, condoms, breath mints. Nothing of use. She replaced Nicole's phone and hid the purse in the undergrowth beneath a pinyon tree, then had second thoughts. What if Stump went back for it and found it missing? He would get suspicious.

But no, it didn't matter, she decided. Stump wouldn't have enough time to get suspicious.

She was coming for him. Now.

CHAPTER 43

Emily sits at the desk again, everything back the way it was. Or so she hopes it will appear.

The tabletop rests on the unscrewed leg. The whole thing propped up. Balancing. Maybe a touch wobbly, but she did her best to keep still.

Knowing the screws aren't there makes it feel precarious to her, like perhaps the breeze of Stump walking through the door will knock the thing over.

So she aids the loose piece of metal with her legs, making sure both thighs stay in contact with the underside of the desktop at all times. Her lap a failsafe.

And now she waits. Watches the steel door. Wonders when he'll be back. Who or what he might have with him when he arrives.

He would be bringing a girl, wouldn't he? He practically said as much before he left, even if he was slightly indirect about it.

Two girls. One and then the other. That was how he worked. His modus operandi.

Emily licks her lips. Tastes the salty remnants of dried tears there. A little dried blood.

She tries not to imagine the other girl, tries not to picture a face, a shape, a tone of skin, but she can't help herself. Can't stop the pictures from forming in her head, mutating into endless variations.

She closes her eyes. Tries to clear her mind. But it's no good.

The shape of the girl in her imagination shifts. Morphs. Changes faces over and over.

And soon enough she will be real. The picture in her head will be that of a real live human being. A girl. A girl who will likely bleed to death in a bathtub at the hands of Leonard Stump.

These thoughts help the imagined pictures clear away at last. The grim reality. It brings her back to the horror of the situation before her. Sharpens her focus. Steels her will.

She clenches her jaw. Goes back to watching the steel door where he will appear. Soon.

But the stillness remains, and her mind drifts for a time. Floats out into the big nothing. She is not sleeping, though she closes her eyes and achieves some distance from the here and now.

Drifting. Drifting.

A slamming door elsewhere in the building shakes her awake. Tips off his return.

This is it.

She sits up a little straighter. Rolls her neck from shoulder to shoulder. Takes a deep breath.

Emotions well up from deep inside her. Rage. Hatred. A yearning for violence she has never experienced before. A genuine bloodlust.

But her face stays blank. She checks it with her hand. Feels her brow undisturbed, the flesh of her cheeks all slack and smooth.

Good. Her face must stay that way. Must show no emotion at all. And when he arrives, she will not look at him. Not directly. Her eyes must stare into nothing. Pierce the empty space. Let him think she's still in some kind of drugged stupor.

She listens. It's hard to place the sound of the door relative to the room she's in. She has no feel for how big the cabin is.

Silence rings out for a long time. Too long. It reminds her of listening to someone sleep when she was a kid — that extended pause between breaths that sometimes made her wonder if the person sleeping next to her just died, growing more and more certain that the pause would turn endless, that the next breath would never come.

The key rattles at the deadbolt. Scrapes a little before it finds the hole and slides home.

Her heart flails in her chest, thrashes against her ribcage.

Hatred sloshes its heat all through her body. She is ready to pounce. Ready to kill.

The key retreats, and the door jerks free of its frame. Swings into the room in slow motion.

She holds her breath. Stares into the wedge of empty space that separates this room from the next.

Nothing.

There's no one there.

She hesitates. Should she run for it now? Dash free of her cell while she can? Take her chances from there?

Yes.

She rips the leg out from under the desk. Brings it to her shoulder like a baseball bat.

The tabletop wobbles, but it stays upright. Balanced on the remaining three legs. Good.

She strides for the open doorway. Soundless. Stalking forward like a cat.

The other side of the doorway slides into view a little more with every step. An empty hallway. She can't believe it.

He unlocked the door, pushed it open, and left? Was he testing her? Laying a trap of her own?

But then it occurs to her. He is going to retrieve his cargo now. The second girl. Tied up. Possibly unconscious. He'd unlocked the door ahead of time to avoid having to fumble with it while transporting her. To clear his path.

Something about this notion shoots a fresh round of ice water through her veins. The chilly adrenaline rush turns the palms of her hands frigid. Makes her pulse pound in her ears. Spurs her forward.

She hurries her pace as she nears the door itself, feet skittering from tile to tile, hell-bent on crossing the threshold as quickly as possible.

The doorway frames her for a fraction of a second. Boxing her into a tighter rectangle of white wood. Somehow claustrophobic.

And then she's through. Into the open. Into the hall.

Carpeted floor touches the soles of her feet now. Tightly woven. Warm compared to the ceramic.

The walls out here are plain and white. No rough wooden beams like her room.

Overhead fixtures spill light everywhere. LED bulbs. It must be night.

The hallway widens to her left. Forms a little cranny there with a potted plant resting on an end table, tucked into the corner. The sight of this stops her in her tracks.

A plant. English ivy from the looks of it. In good shape.

The idea that this man would cultivate a plant is somehow difficult for her to absorb. He cuts throats. Makes people watch him do it. And in his downtime, he cares for houseplants. Nurtures them. She tries to picture him carrying a watering can. Tilting it here.

But she can't dwell on it. Can't linger. She presses on.

She shuffles past the plant. Moves to the place where the

hallway opens up into a real room.

It's a modern kitchen. Clean. Attractive.

Stainless steel appliances huddle in strategic locations around the perimeter of the room. Fridge. Oven. Dishwasher. All top of the line from what she can tell.

In the middle of the room, gas burners and a cast iron griddle jut out of the granite countertop of the island.

What the hell? None of this is right. This is not the ramshackle cabin she had anticipated. No rustic details. No dated decor. No signs of neglect or disrepair.

A car door slams somewhere off to her right, and she ducks out of instinct. Huddles behind the cover of the kitchen island.

Her grip tightens on the metal bar until it quivers in her hands.

She looks down at herself. No. It's not the bar shaking, she realizes. Her whole body trembles. Knees. Elbows. Even her head and neck seem to have taken on a palsy for the moment.

She holds her breath. Listens.

Footsteps pound toward her, the gait choppy and heavy-footed. Strained, she thinks. He must be carrying the new girl, perhaps struggling to finagle her through doorways and around corners.

Emily sidles along the island. Reaches the corner. Peeks her head around the side where movement catches her eye.

Looking through the dining room into the hallway beyond, a shadow dances on the far wall. A darkness that undulates like something underwater, something that usually remains in the black depths of the sea.

She knows she should tuck her head back behind cover, but she can't do it. Can't look away. Wants only to see it. To know for certain what stalks the hall.

But the shadow is shrinking, not growing. Moving away. The footsteps confirm this, going ever so slightly softer.

He must be rounding the corner now. Heading for the room. The cell. The wooden beams on the walls. The empty desk where she's supposed to be.

The footsteps cut off, stopping with an abrupt final thump, thicker than the rest.

Her whole body tingles. Skin alive with an abundance of prickles.

An angry grunt that sounds more animal than man rings out over the silence.

He knows.

Now he's running. Thudding back toward her.

She scrambles to her feet. Rounds the island. Jukes to avoid hip-checking the dinette set.

She hits the hallway going so fast that she skids into the wall attempting the sharp left, shoulder banging into the drywall, jostling a couple of hung paintings of abstract art, but the collision is OK, maybe. It keeps her upright.

The volume of his steps increases, battering the floorboards like croquet mallets. Close.

Fuck. He's behind her. Right behind her.

She weaves to the right. Into a foyer. The floor switching back to tile underfoot. Another potted plant manning the far wall. Some type of fern.

And she can see the door. Can see the narrow window running along the side of it, revealing a tiny strip of the night outside. A circle of light interrupts the blackness out there. The moon.

She grabs the handle. Turns. Peels the door open part of the way.

The Girl in the Sand

And freedom is just there in that opening. So close.

A sliver of the night spills into this awful place. Touches her skin.

But she knows it's too late.

And he's on her. Crashing into her. Their collective weight bashing the door closed.

He bounces off. Both of them stumbling.

She wheels. Swings the desk leg like a baseball bat. Catches him in the shoulder.

He dives for her. He's off balance, and the force bashes him into the wall, but his forward momentum is too much to overcome. He caroms off the drywall still rocketing ahead, falling toward her.

She lowers her shoulder. Tries to push off into the oncoming human missile, to deliver the blow rather than absorb it. Some distant part of her mind remembers overhearing middle school football players repeat this adage: be the hammer, not the nail.

She coils up and unloads, launches herself. Everything goes into slow motion.

The bodies collide in the air. The crown of her head spears him under the chin with a crack like shattering concrete, and she stands him straight up. Kills all of his momentum.

The two of them seem to float in empty space. Speeding bodies that have pummeled each other into inertia.

His head flings back on his neck like some floppy child's toy. She seeks out his eyes and finds them glazed and distant.

She has dazed him, though she is only vaguely aware of this through the fog of her own stupor. Her mass isn't quite enough to put his lights out, even if she got close.

The bodies crash back to the floor like satellites re-entering the Earth's orbit.

On impact, the desk leg is torn from her grip, and she bites her tongue. The metallic taste of blood flooding her mouth again. It takes a second for the pain to hit, but when it does, it kills. An ice pick stab of agony so huge and raw that she feels the pain deep in her eye sockets.

The second phase of her landing jars her arms. The force sends a jolt through the heels of her hands and all the way up into her back, wrenching her shoulder blades, the muscles there straining like rope about to break.

His fall is more of a belly flop. He bashes an elbow into the potted plant on his way down. Fern leaves and black potting soil flung everywhere, still raining down like confetti long after everything else has settled. The hiss of it bleeding all over the would-be silence.

They both struggle to their feet. Clumsy. Woozy. Her hands pat around for the desk leg as she goes to rise, but it has skittered across the tile of the foyer. Out of sight and out of reach.

And Stump changes before her eyes. Transforms. Morphs. He becomes something new.

She sees it in his posture first. A change in the carriage of his back and shoulders, in the way his arms splay at his sides. Something powerful in his core that wasn't there before. Something menacing. Threatening.

It reminds her of those mutation set pieces in werewolf movies. The claws busting through the fingertips. The teeth lengthening into fangs. Musculature stretching out into something lupine in the legs and along the abdomen.

She backpedals. Wanting to scramble after her weapon but unable to turn her back on him. Her legs wobble beneath her, and she veers until her shoulder grazes along the wall, the vertical surface once more offering its support.

He stalks closer. His face hovering just next to hers. He growls at her.

"You want to do it your way, we'll do it your way."

All of that wry intelligence she could read in his face before has vanished. All of those thoughtful expressions and mannerisms replaced by animal aggression. Hostility. For the first time he wholly and fully seems capable of the things she knows he's done, the things he's talked about as though they were intellectual constructs.

He grins as he pulls back from her. Tongue flicking out to glide over his teeth.

She swings at him with her chained fists, but there's no strength behind it.

He bobs his head, dodges.

She doesn't see the counterpunch coming until it snaps her head back. Drizzles drool and blood out of the corners of her mouth. Shuffles her a few stutter-steps to the left.

That *thock* noise fills her skull again, reverberating, all other sounds now strangely distant.

Something cranks the dimmer switch in her head down a quarter of a turn, too — the dark somehow growing closer, encroaching.

She grabs at him, struggling to stay upright, no longer thinking about anything but surviving until the next second.

His hands clasp around her shoulders, incredible strength in his grip, thumbs and fingers digging into her flesh like it's as soft as Velveeta.

He lifts and flings her to the ground in one motion. A vicious heave like she's nothing.

The floor smacks her hard. Her little stick arms are unable

to shield her, unable to soften the blow.

Everything goes black for a second, and then she's back. His weight presses into her back. Both hands grinding her face into the carpet.

She tries to scuttle forward, to jostle free from his grip.

He rocks up into something closer to a seated position, pulls her up with him by her hair, bending her backward as far as she'll go.

And now he unloads. Driving her head first into the seam where the wall and carpet meet.

Her skull cracks into the corner, glancing off and pounding the floor.

The pain flashes in her head, and then everything is far away again. Cold and quiet and distant. Darker still.

And the strength flees from her body. Her arms all limp. Any tautness that had once occupied her core now easing, softening. She is not unconscious, but she is not really here, either. Not all the way.

She is nowhere. That's what she thinks. She is nowhere.

Still he writhes against her. His body twisting and jerking against hers. Relishing the control he has over her.

Their struggle stimulates him. Arouses him. She can feel it like a wave in the air. Some infrared shimmer forming a cloud that surrounds both of them in animal heat.

And she retreats further into the nowhere. Into the nonsense mess of dream images, memories and creations flitting in her skull, bits of those memories of her children in the backyard, the waves crashing on the beach.

Her mind tries to spare her from the worst of the trauma, tries to save her the only way it knows how. It takes her to another place and time. Transports her to dreams of somewhere else. Anywhere else.

But she can't. She can't run away from it.

She blinks a few times. Tries to concentrate. Tries to pull herself into the here and now, out of the mindscape and into the concrete world.

His body no longer thrashes against her, his bulk removed from her back.

Everything hurts, and at first that's the only thing that cuts through the grogginess.

She is alone. Still crumpled on the floor. Time has passed. Minutes? Hours?

She tries to sit up, but the ache of moving feels like it splits her brain down the middle. Worse than before, as impossible as that seemed back then.

Did she take another blow to the head while she was out? She's not sure.

She blinks a few more times. Tries to take in her surroundings. To focus.

Shadows spread around this place. Black shrouds all color here, blocks it out. It's darker than before — darker, even, than her cell had been.

And yes. The room has changed. Grown. Even if she can't make out much detail in the dark, she can see that the walls spread farther and wider here. A great expanse of a room compared to the tiny foyer.

No more door and window nearby. No more remnants of a potted plant explosion strewn about.

He moved her while she was out. Of course.

Her fingers dab at the floor, half expecting to find the familiar ceramic tiles but finding carpet instead.

That cements it. Not the foyer. Not the cell. It's a new room altogether.

CHAPTER 44

Loshak chewed on an aspirin, waiting at another red light. He caught his expression in the rearview, nose and brow all wrinkled up from the bitterness. Nasty shit.

He'd managed to dig the headache medicine out of the first aid kit in the glove compartment, little paper sleeves of the stuff to be torn open. Bright yellow and glossy. Travel packages, he supposed. They made him think about fun size candy bars on Halloween.

He finished one tablet and popped the next into his mouth. It tasted even worse than usual. The normal bitter flavor was accented with a vinegar note — almost a booziness. They were probably past date. Oh well. Too late to worry about it now. This over the counter crap almost never worked for him, but what the hell? His head hurt like it was coming apart. Anything was worth a shot.

The traffic lurched into motion again, all of those impatient machines jostling about, their antsy little movements giving way to real forward momentum. Tension relieved. Loshak barely noticed these things. His eyes watched them automatically, and he adjusted his driving as necessary, but his thoughts were elsewhere.

Claire's house was only a few blocks off now, and he had no idea what to expect. He'd tried calling her back en route, but she didn't answer. Something about all of it felt off. Wrong in a way he could find no words for.

He needed to wake himself up, needed to get his head straight before going into a situation like this. An unknown.

Without taking his eyes off the road, he reached for his thermos in the passenger seat, placed it between his knees and screwed the lid off with the fumbling fingers of his left hand. Vapor puffed out of the thing as soon as it was open, and the coffee smelled tired — a little acrid — but it wasn't all the way cold at least.

He didn't dick around with the little mug, bringing the metal lip of the thermos itself straight to his face. His mouth and throat opened up. Welcomed the sludgy fluid. He sucked down a long slug of lukewarm coffee. Not terrible. Tasted better than it smelled. But the bitter aspirin flavor rose to the surface of the aftertaste, still lingering on his tongue, coating the roof of his mouth, and that sullied the experience some.

Stupid aspirin.

The caffeine soaked into him quickly, and he could feel the tiredness relent a little within a few seconds, mostly in his eyes. The sting didn't leave them, but it receded a notch or two. Better than nothing.

Dirty buildings slid by on the sides of the street now, aluminum and cinder block structures all smeared with black streaks. He was in an industrial neighborhood, and he could smell the soot and chemical stench of it.

The factory windows burned bright, and thick black smoke climbed the stacks of bricks and spiraled into the heavens. He could see it twirling past the streetlights, partially blocking out the stars.

Claire lived not far from this grungy part of town. This didn't seem right to Loshak — didn't seem good enough for her — but who was he to judge?

Over the final two blocks, he seemed to gain focus. His thoughts tightening themselves, finding greater clarity and purpose after wandering at random — daydreaming most of the day — as he killed hour after hour waiting in the car. He was thankful for the renewed efficiency, for the sense that his actions had meaning.

Claire was what mattered here. She needed his help, one way or another, and he would deliver for her.

The factories faded away, and small houses emerged in their place. He gazed at the rows of tightly packed brown boxes that sat close to the street, knowing he had to try to remember which one belonged to Claire. With everything rendered in shades of brown, it was a little like looking into a mouth full of bad teeth and trying to pick one of 'em to pull. The lucky winner.

He slowed when he got onto her street. Craned his neck to get a closer look, to scan the faces of these homes. It was damn near impossible to tell the difference. All stucco boxy things in beige, umber, and khaki.

The cars in the driveways were easier to tell apart than the damn houses, all those distinct colors and shapes. He couldn't remember what make or model Claire drove — didn't even have a rough guess at it — but he thought maybe he would know it when he saw it, like the sight might jar something loose in his memory, recognition dawning on him.

But then the gold numbers on house 6206 shimmered in the headlights, a glittering spot just next to the screen door. It seemed right. He could dig through the texts in his phone to verify the house number, but his gut was pretty sure.

So screw it. Just get on with it.

He parked. Got out. Moved to the side door off the driveway he knew they used and rang the doorbell. He could hear a muffled version of the electronic bell ding-donging a couple times.

He took a step back, watched the kitchen windows.

Movement flitted on the other side of the glass, shadows faintly visible through the gauzy curtains there.

It felt good to stretch his legs, and he'd relished the walk up the cement path that dead-ended at the doorstep. The step itself had been a goddamn delight to take. It was a little too tall, a little awkward, and the strain it put on his leg muscles made them ache with pleasure, so thrilled to elongate, to exert themselves. Even now, standing here before the screen door, his calves and quads sang songs of bliss and contentment.

So why did he feel like he was walking into a disaster?

CHAPTER 45

Emily feels his presence before she hears him creeping up behind her. Some disturbance in the atmosphere. A darkening.

The patter of footsteps fades into her consciousness, scuffing some as he draws near.

His shadow falls over her. Darkens her. Splits her just below the waist.

And the blackest shape rises out of that shade. Towers over her. Indistinct.

She wants to run. Wants to scream. Wants to pounce and latch on and claw out his eyes.

But she can't. She's frozen. Powerless. Lost.

He lifts her then, hands scooping under her arms, plucking her from the ground with little trouble.

She feels so small in his grip. A little thing. Helpless. Totally subject to his whims.

She watches the carpet pull back, the camera zooming out from the floor. The shadow swallows the carpet up as she drifts away. Cloaks it in a dark haze. Totally without shape or texture.

Her arms and legs dangle from the trunk of her body. Floppy sticks that sway and wobble. As limp as Lo Mein noodles.

Her head is too heavy on her neck, so it flops against her chest. Slack and useless.

He doesn't draw her into a bear hug like she expects. Instead, he reaches his arms out. Extends her in front of him.

And she hovers in the emptiness of this dark room. The faintest tremor in his outstretched arms shaking through the

247

meat of her.

He lowers her in slow motion, working with great care.

What lies beneath comes clear to her in stages.

A box.

A box made of wood.

A box made of dark wood the exact shade of those beams embedded in the walls of her cell.

It's just bigger than a coffin — a touch taller and wider. More angular, too. This lacks the rounded contours of a commercial casket. The corners are all squared off.

The lid hangs wide, attached by hinges. The top opens like a mouth, and she can just make out that there's something inside through the gauzy gray of the shadows. A rough texture coating the box's bottom.

Sand.

The box is full of sand, a trench roughly her size gouged out of the middle. Uneven. Dipping into a point in the middle so the sides form a letter V.

Her eyes go wide and breath rushes into her. She pieces these concepts together.

He is going to put her into the box, shove her right down into the sand, and he is going to close the lid.

She squirms. Flails. Ignores the pain stabbing deep into her frontal lobe, the level of hurt blinding her, making her breath seize and sputter in her throat.

But it's no use.

He nestles her into this vacancy, this shadowed place, this wedge carved into the dirt.

She feels the wooden walls close around her. A darkness. A black nothing that encases her. Holds her in its hollow.

And it's cold. So cold inside the box. The sand pressing its chill into the flesh of her face, chest, arms, legs.

He presses her head down into the sand. Tremendous weight. Tremendous pressure.

And shackles close around wrists. Snap into place. One then the other. She hadn't even realized he'd removed the cuffs from earlier, but he must have, when she was unconscious.

The weight lets up, and she squirms. Her movements are clumsy, but she rights herself. Bucks up onto her hands and knees.

But it's already too late.

The lid crashes into her back, and her hands slide out from under her, the heels skidding through the dirt, and the weight of the lid presses, presses. Knocks her flat on her chest.

The blow to her torso sucks the breath out of her lungs. Paralyzes the middle of her.

And then the dark closes in the rest of the way, and it is everything. Everywhere. The only thing.

She panics. Twitches like an idiot animal. Pushes herself up too fast. Bangs the back of her head on the lid.

Anyway, it's too late. It's closed now. Bolted. There's no way to open it from this side.

She hears the metallic scrape of a padlock threading the hasp. The snap of it locking her in.

She focuses. Works to slide her belly along the dirt. Hands and knees carefully attempting to turn her over.

With her shoulder dipped into the deepest part of the trench, there's just enough room to roll onto her back. And then she sees it.

A slit in the lid. Maybe a foot long. About the width of a finger.

She gazes through it. Sees only the shadowy ceiling above

from this angle. White paint on drywall. Nothing else.

What the hell is this for? A line slashed in the lid? And then it hits her.

It's a breathing hole. So he can keep her here — keep her conscious — for as long as he wants. Trapped in a little box.

The lack of noise out there puts a new fright in her: Is she alone?

She presses her eye to the hole again. Swivels it around in its socket for no good reason.

Her view of the ceiling remains unchanged.

Jesus. Is he gone?

On cue, his voice rasps on the other side of the wood. She is repulsed and relieved at the same time.

"I told you. I told you how it would be, didn't I? I didn't expect this out of you. I don't know. I guess I don't know what to think."

All is still for a beat. He sighs. There's a scratching sound like he's pawing at his chin.

"You'll stay here until I'm ready for you. Half buried in the sand. Not the big sleep yet, though. Just a mini dirt nap, you know. A little taste of what's to come."

He breathes again. Stomps away.

And defeat washes over her. A loneliness like she's never felt.

CHAPTER 46

Darger crept along the house in the darkness, careful not to kick any loose stones. Her heart picked up speed in the quiet, in the dark. Thudding away like a kick drum in her ribcage.

Stump's house seemed normal enough in the moonlight. A handsome stucco home — certainly nothing like the ramshackle affair he'd been arrested in all those years ago — not boxy like most out here. Curved terracotta tile lined the peaked roof. Arched window tops gave it a Mediterranean look.

She shuddered walking along it, finding the home attractive. How long had he been hiding in this place, creeping out like a spider to claim new victims? How many years? How many girls?

She couldn't dwell on it. Kept moving. Sidling right up against the plaster.

A window interrupted the wall, and she ducked under it. Waited.

She checked her phone. Still no signal. No notifications that any of her texts to Loshak had gone through. No surprise there.

The white nub of the window sill jutted out over her head. Darger stared up at it, licking her lips.

She hadn't peeked in any windows up close yet. She'd scanned them on her way up to the house, of course, but now that she was close enough to stick her nose to the glass, she found herself hesitant.

No. Beyond hesitant. Scared.

Some part of her was convinced that he would be there, that she'd press her face to a window and find Leonard Stump staring back at her.

It was silly, of course. A girlish, horror movie fear.

She needed to get a handle on the layout of the house, figure out where the girls were being kept, pin down and track Stump's location, if she could. And she would look through the windows to accomplish these tasks. She had to.

OK. No more dallying.

She tucked her phone in her pocket and counted herself down.

5…

4…

3…

2…

1…

Her knees wobbled on the way up, her calves already tired from squatting.

The window slid into the frame of her vision little by little, white grille lines dividing it up into twelve tiny boxes.

And she peered through the glass.

The kitchen stared back at her. Empty. Fluorescent bulbs gleamed on stainless steel appliances. Kitchen implements hung on the wall: ladles, spatulas, whisks. No knives that she could see, and the pans looked flimsy. None of the skull-cracking cast iron variety. Too bad. The stun gun was her best option right now, but she couldn't help but look for a backup weapon.

Like the outside of the house, the kitchen struck her as attractive. Unexpectedly modern.

She looked through the doorway into the next room where a dining table and chairs filled much of the space. That made sense. A kitchen and a dining room.

OK. Rooms one and two down. She had done it — had looked through a window without Stump popping up like some horror movie villain. She could do this. *Would* do this.

She held her breath. Waited.

The wind whistled over the hills.

She looked at the kitchen one more time. Did Stump cook for the girls before he killed them? Homemade omelets and spaghetti? She could imagine that, in a sick way. Playing house with his pets before he finished with them.

This thought focused Darger's resolve. She didn't have time to observe in such detail. She had two girls to save.

She scrunched back down into a squat and moved on, keeping right up against the side of the house. The next room she peeped into was a small bedroom equipped with a dresser, nightstand, and double bed draped with a southwestern style wool blanket. Something about it struck her as unused. A spare room, she figured.

No clues about Stump or the girls, so she kept moving to the last window on this side of the house.

Cold fear seemed to creep over her more and more now. That long ride in the back of the truck, the sneaking, the dark — all of it contributed to her jumpiness. It felt like she was playing Russian roulette. Sooner or later, she'd reach a chamber that wasn't empty.

She swallowed, her throat clicking, and rose to survey the next room.

Darger's brow furrowed in confusion as she gazed through the panes of the window. It was roughly the same size and shape as the small bedroom she'd seen moments before, but this room had no bed, no dresser, no nightstand. No furniture at all, unless she counted the strange box pushed up against one wall. It was oblong, roughly the size of a coffin, but maybe a little taller. Aside from the box, the only other distinguishing feature in the room was a mirror hanging on one wall. Storage, she supposed.

Beyond the empty room, she could make out a hallway with a steel door set into one wall. The door instantly drew her eye. It was definitely out of place — the thick kind of door you'd expect to find on a garage or industrial building, not inside a nice house like this. She figured she knew what that meant, and she dropped back down to a crouch.

A spindly, half-dead juniper bush stood between Darger and the far end of the house. She got even lower and skirted around its scraggly fingers.

This part of the house was older and more rustic than the rest, with rough log and chink walls. Probably this was the original cabin, and the rest of the home had been added on later. There was another window, but it was boarded up.

Yes. That fit with her developing theory. The steel door led to this back room with the boarded window. This was probably where he kept the girls. It almost had to be.

A small barn-style shed sat behind the house. The door was unlocked, and Darger poked her head inside. It held a jumble of the standard shed ephemera: a wheelbarrow, several tangled extension cords, an old rusty push mower, a kettle-style charcoal grill. Nothing she deemed useful or notable.

She skulked back to the house, passing another window secured with wooden planks. The uneasy sloshing in her gut only seemed to reiterate what she already suspected about this part of the house. She had to hurry.

The first window on the far side of the house was smaller and higher than the rest. Standing on her tiptoes, Darger caught a glimpse of a mirrored medicine cabinet and a shower stall. A bathroom.

The pictures from the Stump file flashed in her head —

bathtubs stained with red spatters. He'd committed at least his first few murders in bathrooms. Icy prickles overtook the flesh along Darger's arms. How many women had bled out here, just beyond that pane of glass?

A muted thud startled her. She threw herself to her knees and huddled in the shadow for a moment. The silence stretched out, long enough that she started to doubt herself. Had she really heard something, or was she imagining things?

Just as she reached for the bathroom window again, she heard a muffled shout from inside. This time, she had no uncertainty. It was real.

She moved, scrambled toward the sound.

More yelling and thumping erupted, louder this time. Clearly the sounds of a scuffle. Something clanged and then a noise like bags of kitty litter being dropped on the floor.

She scuttled to the next window. It was the living room that spanned the front of the house, half-lit from the light spilling in from the kitchen.

Movement in the darkened hallway beyond drew her eye, and she instinctively ducked away from the window, then slowly rose again to peer inside.

A dark figure took shape in the hall. Hunched over. Working at something.

Her heart fluttered in her chest at the sight of him again. Leonard Stump, in the flesh.

He sat on his haunches, bent over a crumpled form on the floor. Was it Nicole? And was she alive? Darger couldn't tell.

Stump grabbed the girl by an arm and a leg and dragged her closer, lifting her limp body up and over his shoulder. He stood, and Darger got a better look at her.

The hair wasn't right. It wasn't Nicole. The other girl then.

Emily Kessler.

That confirmed it. He had his two girls.

He plodded down the hall now, toward the back of the house. Darger aimed to follow his progress, wanted to know where he was keeping them for certain, though she was sure she already knew.

She quickened her pace, not wanting to lose him. Passing by the windows, she caught the movement of his shadow at times, stretched out and distorted on the wall of the long hallway that ran through the center of the house.

She lost sight of him as she sprinted around the windowless stretch at the back of the house, crunching over a dried out pine cone with her boot, but no longer caring.

At the window of the box room, she snuck a glance into the hall, chest heaving now with exertion. Nothing. No movement beyond the door.

Where the fuck was he?

Darkness spread into the open crack of the doorway. He was coming this way. Darger stooped a little lower, still watching.

But he passed up the steel door. Kept coming straight at her. He pushed the door aside with his bulk, carried the girl inside the weird little empty room.

Darger's breath caught in her throat. He was so close. If she had a gun, she could shoot him from here, a clean shot through the glass.

With no effort to be gentle, he dumped the girl on the ground. Was she dead? No, Darger didn't think so. Despite his roughness, he was still taking too much care with her. If she were dead, his game would be over. He'd have to go find another girl to complete the ritual.

So what the hell was he doing with her?

The Girl in the Sand

The answer dawned on her as she watched him slither to the oblong box. He moved a latch aside, lifted the lid.

Darger reached out and pressed a hand to the side of the house, suddenly feeling dizzy.

Stump pulled the girl into his arms, picked her up, and dropped her into the box, like a child returning a doll to his toy bin. The movement seemed to rouse the girl. She squirmed in his grip, but it was too late. He was already shackling her inside.

The lid shut with a hard thud that caused Darger to flinch.

As he set to fastening the various latches and locks on the outside of the box, a new thought broke through the horror of knowing that he would keep this girl inside a box.

This was it.

She knew where he was.

While he was occupied here, she had her chance to get inside the house.

Go.

CHAPTER 47

The door swung open, and Claire stood in the threshold for a second before stepping aside so Loshak could enter. He noted that she spoke no greeting, so he piped up with one of his own.

"Good to see you, Claire. I'd say it's a nice night, but it'd be a lie. I'm running on caffeine fumes at this point."

She seemed to choke on her response, her lips sputtering some before she finally got it out.

"Come on in."

She was quiet, which he was used to. He often compensated in their conversations, particularly early on, by talking a little more — hence the verbose greeting. But her hesitation in this case seemed off. Strange. It felt wrong in his gut.

She stayed angled away, her body language not so inviting as her words had been. Her back was mostly to him, and her posture and arm positioning seemed defensive, hands and forearms crossing her body in front of her chest and closing herself off from him. Guarded. A little stiff.

He hesitated short of the door for another beat. His instincts read bad news in everything he saw in her, but she had called him here for help, so maybe that made sense. Needing help made you vulnerable — pretty much by definition — and that could be what he was seeing.

He sought her eyes as he stepped up and into the house. He thought he would know what to think if he could look into her eyes, read her that way. When she wouldn't return his gaze, blinking and looking at the floor instead, Loshak knew in his heart that everything was about to go terribly wrong.

A man's voice spoke up from behind her and to the left, some grit to it. Perhaps a slight slur.

"Make a move for your weapon, and I'll blow your fuckin' head off."

Loshak stopped there, two steps into the kitchen, and the man revealed himself from just around the corner. Actually, the gun revealed itself first.

A pistol extended from the man's arm. Some part of Loshak knew this was a small handgun — about as small as they come — but it looked rather big just now. Funny how that worked.

He had to concentrate to pry his eyes away from the weapon and direct them at the face of the one wielding it.

Haggard stubble and bloodshot eyes stared back at him. A drunk? For a split second, he thought it was a vagrant, that he'd walked in on some kind of home invasion, but squinting a little, he began to recognize the face.

It was Claire's man — what was his name? Matt? Mitch? It was definitely an M name. Maybe. Loshak couldn't remember, but it would come to him.

Whatever his name was, he looked like shit, and this situation was much more complicated than a home invasion.

The man gestured with the gun as he spoke, ticking the barrel up twice.

"Hands up, big shot."

He staggered forward a step. Wobbly on his feet.

OK. Not just drunk, Loshak thought. Utterly shit-faced.

He stepped close to the agent and weaved his off hand inside Loshak's jacket, unbuttoned the shoulder holster, fumbled at the Glock for a moment before he pulled it out of the leather sheath and tucked it in his own belt. He never broke eye contact with Loshak as he worked, glaring at him with those bloodshot eyes all the while.

Claire's man laughed a little, a hissing cackle, spit squirting between his teeth, and the smell of beer rolled out of his mouth.

Loshak knew what the expression on his face said: He had caught his mouse, and now he wanted to play with it a while.

The drunk took a sidestep, lost his balance and almost tripped. Lurching forward, he caught himself on the edge of the counter with both hands, the gun clattering against the laminate surface. For a second he remained in that position, hand and gun propping him up, and he laughed a sheepish laugh, face going red.

Now he backpedaled a few paces, and the gun wavered a little at the end of his arm. A tremor. Adrenaline. Probably spiked due to the moment of fear when he almost fell on his face.

Good Christ.

Loshak's internal monologue stated the facts of the case, frank and deadpan: *This guy is so wasted he can barely stand. He has a gun. He is pointing the gun at your face. And he is as frightened as a house cat. Not good.*

Mark. His name was Mark. Loshak knew it would come to him. He thought he should use that knowledge to his advantage, lean on the familiarity and see if it got him anywhere.

"Mark, I don't know what's going on here, but I know there must be some kind of misunderstanding."

The glee drained from Mark's face, the smile shifting to pursed lips.

"That right?" the drunk said.

"You're not yourself. Had a few drinks. I get that. Happens to the best of us. But we can get this all cleared up, if you want."

Mark stared at Loshak, his expression seeming to go blanker

by the second. The gun arm seemed to slacken just a touch, too.

What did this guy want? Loshak wasn't sure. To get anywhere in the conversation, he either needed to ask or take a guess at it.

"Why don't you tell me what you want? You can put down the gun, and we can talk."

All those angry folds and wrinkles resurfaced on Mark's face. The arm holding the gun grew taut again. In one motion, he pointed the piece at the ceiling and squeezed the trigger.

The crack of the gunfire filled the kitchen, impossibly loud, bouncing off every hard surface to create a ringing resonance that almost seemed to gain volume before it receded. Loshak felt like he'd been hit with the noise, a great whoosh of sound rushing at his face and chest.

The slug punched a neat hole in the popcorn ceiling, and after a second, a fine dusting of white powder spilled out of the plaster wound. It rained down, pattering the floor audibly like grains of sprinkled sand.

Loshak hopped back out of instinct, and Mark eyed him. Laughing.

"Jesus Christ! Look at him dance. Ol' big shot's a bit of a scaredy cat, ain't he? If only he had one of his books here with him, eh? He could look up the right answers to this little problem."

Loshak shrugged, tried to play up the idea that he was embarrassed.

"Oh, and I'll pass. Your offer to talk? That's a hard no from me," Mark said. "I appreciate it, but I think we've had quite enough *talk* with law enforcement in this house. Quite e-fucking-nough."

Loshak detected movement out of the corner of his eye.

Glanced that way.

It was Claire, her eyes gone huge and wet, one hand cupped over her mouth. She cowered, leaned up against the place where the countertop met the wall.

Holy shit. Claire.

He'd been so occupied with Mark and his gun, he'd almost forgotten she was there in the room with them, tucked away in a corner.

That was one of the troubles with dangerous situations like this, Loshak thought. It was so easy to get tunnel vision, easy to lose track of your surroundings — things as simple as who else was in the room.

That's how the brain functioned in moments of great stress. It filtered harder, all of reality whittling down to just those few immediate things creating the tension. All of one's attention got sucked into that tunnel of staring at the gun, the seconds stretching out until time lost all meaning. He couldn't let that happen here.

Loshak forced himself to take a deep breath, in and out, slow and deliberate. He could feel his nerves steadying before he was even done exhaling.

He blinked. Looked around. Really looked. Took in the room for the first time.

Cabinets the color of an avocado stared back at him, the paint chipped and peeling in a few places, little black lines etched into the corners like spider webs. The appliances likewise looked like they were probably original to when the place was built. Maybe 40 years old.

And he scanned for possible weapons. Alternative solutions to their problem here. His eyes darted everywhere, sought blunt objects and the like, cataloging them all the while. Fire extinguisher. Plates. Any knives were tucked away in shelves or drawers somewhere, out of sight and out of reach. Nothing viable stood out. It was never the best idea to bring a fire extinguisher to a gunfight. Even a knife wouldn't help much there.

Still, noting these details helped him get his mind right, helped root him back in the present moment.

And it made his immediate quandary clearer: He didn't know what lay at the heart of this scene. What was motivating Mark? Why was he doing this? What did he want?

That was the first stage of any hostage negotiation, right? Figuring out what the guy with the gun wants. When he'd asked, however, it only seemed to result in fresh rage.

He didn't want the usual — money. That wouldn't make any sense.

He was angry, but to what purpose? Loshak didn't have any guesses for the moment.

Mark paced the room, now staring at nothing. That look of exaggerated glee had returned to his face, stuck there like an expression baked into a Halloween mask. Though he didn't speak, he gestured with the gun often, wagging and tipping the barrel, turning the gun sideways and shaking it. Loshak thought he must be accenting his thoughts with flicks of the wrist and various firearm flourishes.

Pleasure. He was enjoying this. In the short term, that must be what he wanted — to lord his power over his hostages. Loshak still didn't know what the long-term goal was, but that might be something to work with. A starting point.

With the gunman distracted, Loshak snuck a longer glance at Claire.

Her hand still covered her mouth, and the sleeve had rolled

away to expose her wrist. She slid her palm slowly up from her lips to cover her eyes, and that was when he noticed it.

The bruise. No. Two of them. Deep purple splotches on her wrist, loosely connected with a thin line of a lighter, almost translucent violet shade. It looked like she'd been grabbed. Pulled.

Loshak's eyes traced the outline of the bruise, snapped to Mark's hand and traced a similar shape there — the curve of his thumb and forefinger.

Yep. That'd do it.

Now he looked at Mark's face and saw it anew. Saw the red lines crisscrossing the whites of his eyes like stitches, the purple pouches of flesh puckering beneath each of them.

A drunk — that he knew already. A drunk *and* a batterer. Yes.

That was the piece that had been missing before. Mark was an abuser. A wife beater.

This scene Loshak had walked into was starting to make sense. Finally.

CHAPTER 48

The panic constricts Emily's breath. Grabs her by the shoulders and shakes her.

No. No. No.

This can't be happening, but it is. Can't be real, but it is.

Her whole life led to this. Winding her along a circuitous path — all the ups and downs, all the rises and falls, all the forks in the road — to place her in this moment.

To put her here. To leave her here.

A box. Trapped in a box. Wooden walls encasing her. Closing the darkness around her.

Leonard Stump. The universe put her in the hands of Leonard Stump. This is her fate. Her life story. It all led to this.

And perhaps for the first time it occurs to her that all of those victims on TV and in the newspaper are real people. All the way real. Fully formed personalities. Unique. Individual. Lost souls who had dreams and flaws and families and friends. They had loved and lost, broken their hearts and mended them.

All of that suffering. All of that agony. It's all real. As real as this.

These thoughts flit through her head. Racing. Fleeting.

A rush of shifting feelings. The panic surges to swallow them. To take them away. To shove her forward to the next awful moment.

Her hands fumble at the underside of the lid. Slide over the grain of the wood. Fingers wriggling at the slitted hole like insect legs. Nails catching on the hard edge over and over.

The wood remains impervious. Unmovable. Uncaring.

There is no way out. None. She knows this. Understands it. But all she can do is look for one anyway. Search with her hands. Pat and scratch and dig at the walls to prod for any weakness, any means of escape. She feels for some tiny chink in the wall that she knows isn't there.

And the panic only grows. The darkness spirals its black noise into her head. A tangle of sounds pounding in her skull. A deep rumble that won't let up.

Her head goes hot and swimmy. Thoughts fevered. Frenzied. Bordering on nonsensical.

And the tears gush from her eyes. Spill down the tops of her cheekbones. Trail into the seashell folds of her ears.

She can feel her lips pull back into a grimace. Teeth exposed.

Hot breath heaves in and out of her. Lungs sucking in oxygen in great gasps. Greedy. Manic.

The air in the box is already moist from her breathing. Heavy with the wet.

Her insides feel gooey and hot.

And she chokes a little now. Throat cinching and clicking and sputtering. Spit flying out of her mouth.

All the way confused. All the way lost.

She isn't doing it right. She knows that. But she can't remember what it is. Can't think straight. Can't think.

Breathing.

She isn't breathing properly. She is hyperventilating.

And Gabby is there. She can feel that she is right there with her in the dark, and she is talking, but Emily can't make out the words. Can't understand.

Her hands slow. No longer thrashing about on the underside of the lid so much as brushing it with fingertips. Caressing it. Smearing at it. Losing speed all the while.

The Girl in the Sand

Slower. Slower. Slower.

And now her hands descend. Sinking. Retracting to her torso. Folding against her like the stalks of a wilting plant.

She knows that Gabby's lips are moving. That something important is being transmitted to her, but she cannot comprehend it. Not even a little.

Instead feelings slosh in her head. Hysteria. Horror. Disorientation. They roll in and out like waves. Lurching and swaying and spitting.

The blackness comes over her in splotches. Smudges. Pressing its darkness over her vision bit by bit. Taking her consciousness in little pieces.

Her hearing flutters out. That ambient sense of the space around her closing up into nothingness. Beyond silence. The negation of sound.

She still feels herself breathing. Chest rising and falling over and over. Air rushing to fill her and empty her, fill her and empty her. But she no longer hears it.

And now the black smudge closes in. Finally ready to finish its job.

She twitches a little as the lack of oxygen blinds her. The final movements she can muster — meaningless flexes and thrusts, spittle bubbling between her lips.

And when the panic wins, and she finally passes out, it almost comes as a relief.

☾

Emily wakes. Wiggles her legs. The sand grits in every joint now. In every orifice.

It feels like she rides lower in the sand now, whether or not that makes any sense. Sinking. Slowly digging herself in. Like some sea turtle threshing its flippers on the beach to craft a hole.

She finds herself calm. That roiling, flooded feeling has drained from her skull. The worst of the panic has mostly left her. The memory of it all jumbled in her head.

She breathes. A deep inhale. Holds it. Lets it go.

Good.

Lifting her head to the hole, she stares at her one slice of ceiling.

A strip of white paint the texture of an egg. It looks gray in the half-light. The lifeless color ground beef goes after it sits in the fridge for a month, when something essential has been sucked out of it.

She blinks, and it all disappears. The universe shut out completely. All of reality stained black. But when she opens her eyes, it's back. The gray stripe that represents the outside world.

Something moves next to her, the sand shifting there in the dark.

It's Gabriela. Yes. She remembers now. Gabby has been there all the while.

Her friend speaks from the shadows.

"Remember when we used to eat at the Carnival World buffet?"

Emily blinks in the dark.

"I remember," she says.

"We ate there every day for a month when they had that lunch special going. Sat in the corner and watched all of the tourists shoveling prime rib and crab legs into their faces. Hawaiian shirts. Fanny packs. Baseball hats with the brims all straight and stiff."

The girls are quiet for a beat before Gabby starts up again.

The Girl in the Sand

"Remember the shrimp guy?"

"I remember."

They both know the shrimp guy story well enough that it doesn't need to be spoken aloud. Not anymore.

She sees the little old man sporting dark denim overalls. She and Gabby watched from across the room as he ate shrimp cocktail — shells, tails and all. He just kept piling the things into his mouth, using the little curved shrimp like spoons to scoop in as much cocktail sauce as possible.

"I couldn't stop laughing," Emily says.

She doesn't realize she is smiling until she hears it in her voice.

"Christ. I thought you were going to die, you were laughing so hard," Gabby says. "Face all red and puffy. Tears streaming down your cheeks. I wanted to get some ice cream, but I had to get you out of there."

A puff of air exits Emily's nostrils, and it takes her a second to recognize the sound. Laughter. She almost can't believe it. Silent or not, this didn't seem possible just minutes ago. Not here. Not now.

"You should try to sleep if you can," Gabby says. "Conserve your energy, you know. It's not over yet."

Emily's breath is shaky from laughing. It catches in her chest like a hiccup.

"I know."

"You can handle this. Being here, I mean. Being in this box. You can handle it. You know that? It's going to get worse, but it's OK. You've been through a lot, and you've survived. Don't ever forget that."

Emily nods, sand gritting at the back of her head. She watches the unmoving gray stripe of ceiling out there while

Gabby continues.

"I'm not going to lie to you. Not going to sugarcoat it. This man might kill you. It's possible, you know. But whatever he might think, he won't break you. Not your mind. And so long as that's true, you have a chance. A chance to get out of here. A chance to fight. A chance to save yourself."

They're quiet for a while. As Emily begins to drift, Gabby starts up again.

"Remember when that guy tried to mug you in that alley off Fremont street?"

"I remember."

"What did you do?"

"I fought."

"You kneed him in the balls, and his face turned as red as a Skittles bag. He wound up being the one running away from the scene, running away from you. Well, he kind of waddled away, but still…. That's what you have to do now. You have to fight. Whatever it takes."

"That's what you keep telling me."

"Well, it's important."

"I know."

"OK."

The quiet settles again. Holds strong. It seems to Emily the conversation is over, but Gabby isn't quite done.

"What I'm saying is that you can do this. If you can get over the fear, you can do this. I'm not saying you won't be scared. You will be. You will be fucking terrified, OK? But the fear will make you want to quit. It will make you want to freeze. To curl up in a little ball and be done with it. And you can't do that. Not even for a second. You have to keep fighting no matter how scared you are. OK?"

They're quiet, but Emily only lets the silence linger for a few seconds this time.

"Look, if there are any other memories you'd like to go over, might as well get them out of your system here and now, right? No point waiting until I almost fall asleep."

She hears a little smile in Gabby's voice.

"OK. Remember when we rode the High Roller?"

"I remember."

"That must have been the first week you got here. You were all excited, still had the tourist look in your eyes and everything. I tried to deflect, but you weren't having it. You insisted we ride the stupid thing. I told you it was just a big Ferris wheel, but you wouldn't listen."

"It was fun. I thought it was fun."

"Maybe."

"The view from the top was cool. 360 degrees. What's it called? Panoramic. Looking down on all the big buildings and everything. All the lights."

"If you say so. Remember when we took Austin and Sadie to Disneyland?"

"I remember."

"The kids loved it, but you were paranoid the whole time. Fidgeting. Head swiveling around so you could watch the swarms of people, scan all of the faces in the crowd, and even when you could steady that skull on your shoulders, your eyes were glancing everywhere."

Emily blinks a few times. Her lips move but no words come out, so Gabby keeps going.

"I knew you were scared. I didn't say anything. At the time, I mean. I didn't say anything, but I knew. I knew you were scared that he would find you there. Scared to death. Maybe it was crossing the state line that triggered it for you. Being back in California. The state that belonged to him, belonged to his family."

Emily licks the back of her teeth. She grasps for something to say — wants to change the subject — but nothing comes to her. Thankfully, Gabby has another memory locked and loaded.

"Remember when you stepped in gum?"

"I remember."

"A pink wad of goo stuck to your heel. All stretched out and gross. Stringy. Like some strands of it were so thin they looked like pink hair. You insisted on squatting right there on the sidewalk — the streams of people rushing all around you — and picking it off with your fingers. Grossed me out. Still does, I guess. Touching it like that. Getting that juice or whatever all over your fingers. Jesus. I'd need to wash my hands for about six months after that. Scalding hot water."

Emily considers pointing out that their profession was having sex with strangers — probably grosser than touching chewed gum — but she stops herself. Why let reality ruin the moment?

"Remember the butter lady?"

"Of course I remember the butter lady."

On another buffet excursion, they'd watched a tourist eating lobster, an older woman with dyed red hair going to town, dipping the chunks of crustacean in a little cup of melted butter, slurping at every bite before she chewed and swallowed. And when all the seafood was gone, she downed the butter like it was a shot of Jägermeister.

"What goes through someone's mind as they make that choice? That's what I want to know," Gabby says.

"Probably wondering what it feels like to clog an artery in

record time, looking forward to the rush of it all.”

“Can you imagine what drinking butter would feel like? Grease drizzling down your throat?”

“The way she slammed it, I don’t know if there was any drizzling involved. Straight to the gullet.”

She feels Gabby shudder next to her.

“Coating your insides with butter. It would be all warm, too, you know? Maybe just warmer than body temp.”

Another shudder.

“Do you remember when we first met?”

“I remember.”

“I saw you on the street. Fidgeting. Antsy. Glancing all around like a stray cat.

“Your skin glowed in alternating red and yellow under the lights downtown. And you were so scared. So obvious about what you were trying to do. Even dressed casual like you were, your body language screamed what you were selling, and how scared you were about it. The slope in your upper back. The way your head always angled at the ground, and you looked up at people like that, eyes half obscured by your bangs hanging in the way, with your chin all tucked against your chest. I wanted to tell you to run away from here and never come back.”

“You did. That was the first thing you did. You told me to leave. Offered to buy me a bus ticket to the city of my choice.”

“Yeah. Yeah, but then I took you out to eat. Got you set up, didn’t I? I pulled you in off the street where you’d work for practically no money and get popped by the cops sooner than later, for sure. Took you back to my place. Took a couple pictures. Set up a couple listings for you. And then it was calls all night, every night.”

“Two hundred roses.”

"What about 'em?"

"I remember when you put that in the first ad. On the website, I mean. I didn't understand at first. Roses instead of dollars."

"Right. You know, I doubt that's any kind of legal protection, using that euphemism. If they're gonna bust you, they'll find a way. But I guess that's the custom. Roses, I mean. Who am I to buck fifteen years of internet prostitute tradition?"

"Two hundred roses an hour. I never thought I'd make that much, to be honest. In an hour? No way. I guess I don't know what I expected, really. I didn't know how any of it worked."

"You don't have to tell me that. I was there. It was written all over you."

Gabby pauses for a beat, and Emily hears her swallow.

"Everything in Vegas is a mirage. An illusion. There's the facade, and then there's the real motivation lying somewhere beneath that. The lights. The sounds. Even the smells. It's all some great creation, some great seduction."

"The smells?"

"Yeah. The smell of the casinos. Each of 'em manufactures a signature scent and pumps it through their ducts. Didn't I ever tell you about that?"

"Maybe. It sounds vaguely familiar, but I don't remember it very well."

"Every casino has its own scent, special made by experts, tailored to their specific tastes. They have these metal devices attached to the ventilation systems — they're about the size of a breadbox. The devices vaporize aromatic oil and distribute the smell throughout their resorts. Every vent, every register. You go to one of these places? This box affects you. Gets under your skin — into your bloodstream — without you ever realizing it. It blows this cloud of emotions at you, and you breathe it in. Every single breath, you breathe it in."

"So it's like the real estate agent baking cookies the morning before an open house, right? To kind of create a positive atmosphere or whatever? I remember the Mirage smelling like cologne. Reminded me of my grandfather on my dad's side, actually. Once he got old, he wore too much of the stuff."

"See? There you go. The scent triggered a memory for you. That's how powerful this stuff can be. I mean, smells are a funny thing. They're wired right into the emotional part of your brain. Tied to your memories. They can get really specific with different blends as far as what they're trying to evoke in their customers. It's fairly sophisticated. They can trigger people to feel how they want them to feel, which is relaxed, mostly. But they mix in sensuality, a sense of strength, a longing."

They're quiet for a long moment.

"How did you find out about all of this?"

"I read about it on the internet."

This time, it's Emily who keeps the conversation going.

"How did we wind up here? In this place?"

She hears Gabby take a deep breath as she ponders a response.

"Has to happen to someone, you know? They always say, *It could happen to anyone,* but in a way, I think it's better said, *It* actually *happens to someone.* Every awful thing, every tragedy, every nightmare — it happens to someone. A person. A real live human being."

Gabby pauses and then adds, "This time, it's us."

CHAPTER 49

With a twist of the doorknob, Darger moved out of the clear black night and into the stuffy interior of the house. She held her breath for that first step over the threshold, moving through the doorway into the foyer, the smooth feel of the ceramic tile underfoot.

Inside the house smelled like cedar and ash. Rugged smells. Exotic in some way that only made sense in the desert.

She kept low as she moved. Crouched. Her feet stayed light, nimble and noiseless as she crept onto the carpet and into the living room.

There was a rug behind the velour sofa, an additional layer of fabric to muffle the sound of her boots. She paused there a beat to catch her breath, gather herself.

The adrenaline seemed to hit on some kind of delay, flooding her all at once. Making her chest shake with each breath in and out. Jesus. She'd done it. She'd gotten inside. The screen door out front had been the most nerve-wracking part, she thought. It was like a built-in anti-theft device. Every movement yielded a creak or a moan or a clack that threatened to give her away.

Thinking back on these initial steps of entering Stump's lair, part of her almost detached from reality, wondered if any of this could really be happening. Was she having a surreal nightmare? Should she pinch herself?

She took a breath. Willed her heart to slow in her chest. Waited. Listened.

She adjusted her grip on the stun gun, thankful to have a

weapon, to feel it in her hand. But it still felt wrong to be here, to be approaching this darkness on her own.

And yet she had no choice. She'd watched Stump secure Emily in a box. He could — probably would — begin his ritual soon. Waiting was not an option.

She moved out. Stayed low. Glided into a little dining room area.

A floorboard creaked, and Darger froze, lungs half-filled with breath.

A sharp bang nearby shot ice water through her veins.

She wanted to scream but stopped herself, flinching instead, shoulders shimmying.

By the scraping, chafing sound that followed the more percussive noise, Darger put together that it was a door. One that stuck in its frame, the jamb warped from the years of dry desert air. It was the steel door to the sealed back room, she was sure of it. And it was a good thing to know since she was headed that way sooner or later. Stump would have to be incapacitated or out of the house when she went into the room, or he was liable to hear.

She skittered forward to take cover behind the kitchen island, turning so her back pressed into the wood. She listened.

A metallic clatter told her he was locking the room. Securing the deadbolt in the hallway through the kitchen. He'd have his back to her, then. Should she risk a peek?

Her heart hammered. Shook her ribcage.

She eased her way to the corner of the island. Held her breath. One quick glance and then she pulled back to her hiding spot.

She saw him. A hulking thing. Not bulky but strong somehow. Powerful. Menacing and wiry.

Again she shook a little with jittery energy. Looked down at the stun gun. Soon. Soon.

His keys jangled. Heavy footsteps pounding along with the metallic sound. She could tell by the way the sound went muffled that he'd turned into one of the side rooms.

While she kept track of his movements, she tried to formulate a plan. She'd considered trying to get the girls out before confronting him, but that seemed unlikely now. First, because of the keys. Both girls were locked up — one padlocked into a box, the other deadbolted into a room. But even if she had managed to sneak the keys from him, it sounded like the squawking door would give her away. Beyond that, the girls might not be in condition to move. Emily had been out cold when Stump put her in the box. She might still be unconscious. Nicole, likewise, had been dead to the world when Darger last saw her. If even one of the girls couldn't walk, they'd be in trouble.

That settled it, then. She had to go for Stump.

She grew aware of the phone shoved into her hip pocket. Fuck, she wished one of those texts had gone through, wished she had backup en route or at least looking for her.

The urge to act now made her arms and legs feel itchy, restless, but it was in her best interest to wait. Wait for him to come to her. Wait for him to go to sleep. Wait for him to make a mistake, to telegraph a moment of vulnerability. Otherwise, she was walking in blind. Not good.

She stayed tight against the island, the countertop of a breakfast nook stretched over her, helping conceal her if only a little.

Minutes ticked by in agony. Stump was doing some kind of clean-up down the hall, from the sound of it. Shuffling things around.

Her eyes scanned the walls. Too bad there wasn't an old hunting rifle or a shotgun hung up somewhere. She could picture something like that in a place like this, out in the boonies. Even if there were, he wouldn't keep it loaded. Too dangerous in the event that one of his captives got loose or fought back, like Emily had earlier.

Footsteps. He was on the move again. Darger's chest grew tight. She pressed herself against the island, as flat as possible.

The footsteps moved further off. Away from her. Away from the rooms where the girls were held.

There were noises she couldn't quite identify. The jangle of something, possibly the keys. And then a series of soft, scuffing sounds.

And then something she did recognize.

Running water.

He was back in the bathroom. Taking a shower.

A wide grin spread over her face. She couldn't believe it. The piece of shit was taking a shower. It was perfect. She could get the keys and zap the daylights out of him before he'd even know what was happening.

She had to bite down on her cheek to keep from giggling maniacally.

Get control of yourself, Violet. Time to focus.

She waited until she heard the slippery sounds of the shower curtain being pulled aside, the slight change in the rhythm of the water falling from the showerhead.

She counted to fifteen, and then she took a step toward the hall.

Her first few paces were slow, tentative. She paused and exhaled, still listening to the water.

Emboldened, she quickened her pace. The hallway was dim and unlit, but from the crack of light emanating from the partially-open bathroom door, she could see something hanging on the wall.

The keys. He'd hung the keys on a hook right next to the door to the locked room. He must have set them there before he went into the bathroom.

Again an odd-placed sense of glee swelled in her chest. She was going to do it. She was going to get the girls out alive. The end of this nightmare was right there in front of her, maybe minutes away.

Her eyes locked onto the keys, ears focused on the patter of water hissing off to her left. She moved slowly, with care, waiting for any tiny shift in that watery sound, anything at all.

It felt like a dangerous game of musical chairs. If the water stopped, it was time to fight.

The keys seemed to glitter on their hook. Was that real? Her imagination?

A few paces from the door, she paused again. This was it. With the way the door was open a crack, Darger was visible from the bathroom. She had to be quick.

She could see a thin coil of steam through the small gap where the bathroom door lay open. And she knew Stump was right there. He must be. Just inside that room, the shower curtain forming a thin barrier of vinyl between them.

She turned to the locked room, and her hand reached for the keyring.

Her fingers closed around the jagged pieces of metal, pulled them from the hook. She half-expected them to still feel warm from his touch, but the keys were cool. She glanced down at them, flicked through the nine keys on the ring.

The Girl in the Sand

And then there was movement. But not from where she expected, not from the bathroom. From the right and behind, in the darkened threshold of another doorway.

Sensing his presence, she pivoted on the ball of her foot, brought her arm up, pointed the stun gun, squeezed the trigger button on the side.

Blue light arced between the metal prongs on the stun gun and the air filled with an electric crackle.

He slammed into her, his full weight hitting the wrist of the hand holding the stun gun, knocking it from her hand, sending it spinning through the air and out of sight.

She hit the ground. Flat on her back, wind knocked from her lungs. It all happened so fast, she had no chance to try to break her fall. He collapsed as well, belly smacking like a felled tree.

The stun gun was gone. Lost. Too dark to look for.

Forget it. Fight. Fight now.

He sat up. *Shit.* If the electricity had hit him, it was a glancing blow. He was still conscious, still awake.

She wheeled. Kicked him in the face. Drove the heel of her boot into the side of his head.

He grabbed at her. Hands snaking around her leg and twisting, trying to roll her face down.

No way, motherfucker.

He lunged at her. Bent over her. Tried to pin her down.

She bucked. Stayed on her back. Curled in on herself. Going toward him instead of trying to get away, scrabbling at him like a wolverine, all teeth and claws and rage and hate.

Her legs wrapped around him. Her arms found purchase. She thought of the way a bee latches onto someone it's about to sting.

And her head leaned in. She bit him. In the web of muscle

281

between the neck and shoulder. Bit him with the full strength of her jaw.

She wanted him to scream. Wanted him to howl.

But he only grunted and reached for her. Grabbed a handful of her hair at the top of her head and slammed the back of her skull into the floor.

Bright white flashed in her head. She blinked. Opened her eyes as he dashed her head against the hard plank floor again.

She had one thought before everything went black.

It was a trap.

CHAPTER 50

Emily brushes at the underside of the lid again. Presses it with the palm of her hand. Some part of her half expects it to yield to her touch — to open — but it doesn't.

When Gabby speaks again, her voice sounds different. Softer. More serious.

"You remember when you told me about Dan?"

Emily chews at her lip. She remembers, but she wishes she didn't.

"I remember," she says after a beat.

"New Year's Eve. We were in the back of my Impala. When we finished our shift, we celebrated with a bottle of Glenlivet. You'd never had scotch before. Is that right?"

Emily nods.

"It was the only time we ever drank together."

"Yeah, I'm not much for the stuff, but New Year's Eve is New Year's Eve," Gabby says. "I'm not an animal. But yeah, I remember it was real late and just cold enough that the windows built up a layer of frost from our breath after a while. Maybe it was just where we were parked, but the city felt so empty that night. It's weird to feel alone like that in Vegas. On New Year's Eve of all nights.

"And maybe we'd told all of our regular stories. The amusing anecdotes. Embarrassing moments. Slips and falls. All the light stuff you'd tell anybody. We'd told all of that stuff, so you told me about Dan. About how he turned everything in your life into a nightmare."

Emily swallows, feels a strange lump bob in her throat.

"You two had gotten married young, right?"

"I was nineteen. About to finish my freshman year in college. He was a year older."

"And he was the perfect guy. The man of your dreams. Smart. Funny. Good looking. From a well-to-do family in the—what line of business was it? Something in technology."

"Data security."

"That's right. So yeah, everything is a goddamn dream come true for a while. Newlyweds going to school together, their future wide open in front of them. Living in a nice apartment off campus in a building his parents owned. You guys have a son a year later. A daughter a few years after that. Somewhere in there you graduate college and he goes to work in his family's firm. Would that be appropriate? To call it a firm?"

"Yeah."

"Things with you and him had been on the decline for a long time. Not terrible. Just not the ideal version you'd imagined. But it still blindsided you when it happened. You'd been fighting all afternoon. Over dumb stuff. Over practically nothing. The little annoying things that always seemed big in the moment. The ones you can't even remember two hours later."

While Gabby talks, Emily's breath rasps in and out of her chest. A steady beat.

"But maybe the fight was always about something else. Some subtext that underlay the relationship in the long term. Some tension that persisted. Let's just say he had issues."

Emily's hand is still pressed against the lid of the box, and she imagines the wood grain leaving an impression on her palm. Whorls and knots and wiggly lines.

"He burst into the bathroom out of nowhere. Hit you. Not

so much a punch as he clubbed you with his fist. The way a toddler hits. A weird looping of his arm, semi-overhand, hitting you on the downward stroke. Anyway, it knocked you down. Knocked you flat on your ass. You pulled a couple of hand towels down with you, grabbing them to try to keep your feet and ripping them off the wooden dowel they hung on."

It plays in Emily's head like a movie. It feels like something that happened to someone else. She is merely an observer.

"And you were confused. You were frozen there on the bathroom floor. You'd seen flashes of his temper, but he'd never gotten physical before that. Never put his hands on you that way."

Emily turns her head away, knowing what comes next. Trying to avoid it.

"And then he pissed on you. Before you had a clue what was happening, he had it out, standing over you, and he pissed in your face. With your kids in the next room eating hot dogs and macaroni and cheese for lunch. Hitting you wasn't enough, see. The humiliation needed to go further. Needed to cross some line of decency. A hurt worse than physical pain. That was his intent."

There is a hard edge in Gabby's voice. Anger seeping through to color the words red.

"For weeks after, you sleepwalked through your days. In a daze. Eyes out of focus. Mumbling when you spoke. You couldn't process it. Couldn't accept that it really happened. Couldn't fit this awful, jagged piece into the mosaic in your head that comprised his personality.

"How could he be all of those characteristics you'd always known — smart, funny, attractive, generous — and also be the person who did this to you, did this to his wife, to the mother of his children? How could you bridge that psychological gap? Find a way to make peace with it in your psyche and figure out how to deal with it? You couldn't."

Gabby pauses just long enough for Emily to blink twice and then continues.

"Until it happened again. The same as before."

The silence is a nothingness all around them. A sucking vacuum of blackness. Impossibly huge and empty. There is no noise at all for miles and miles.

"Except this time, after he pissed on you, he raped you."

Emily retracts into the mindscape some, her consciousness retreating to the deeper spaces inside. Anything to get away from these words Gabby is speaking.

"Emily," Gabby says, her voice all soft and smooth, speaking right next to Emily's ear.

Emily opens her eyes. Tries to focus on the eggshell strip of white ceiling up there. It's the only thing that's real.

"Emily, talk to me."

"You're dead. You're not even real. Gabby is dead."

"Is that what you think?"

"Yes. I don't know. Maybe."

A little swallowing sound fills the box. Emily can't decide if it was her or Gabby.

She adjusts a little. Stretches. The sand gritting at her back.

"You tried to tell people. About Dan, I mean. Friends. Family. But everyone had a way of shutting you down. Like they could sense where you were going, what you were going to tell them, and they didn't want to hear it, wouldn't hear it."

Her eyelids flutter, and the little slit in the lid of the box flashes in and out of existence.

"His family had roots running all underneath that town.

The Girl in the Sand

Wealth going back generations. They had ties to everyone and everything. Control over everything without even trying. Like what they wanted just mattered more than what everyone else did, you know? People catered to it automatically. They didn't even have to ask."

Emily swallows.

"And you knew you had to leave. Had to get away from him. And you knew he'd never allow that. Because you were his possession. But also because you were a threat to him. What you knew made your very existence a threat to him. When the private investigators started following you, you knew you had to go. You had to get out. So you took the kids and you ran. You ran to Las Vegas, where the girls go to disappear."

Emily's mind wanders back to these old places, these old dreams, these old versions of herself. To all the old wounds reopened. And in a way, it's not so bad to confront them from this strange vantage point. To see with great clarity that she never had a choice. That none of it was her fault.

She acted to survive, to protect herself and her children. That was all.

She closes her eyes. Lets go of the tension in her neck and shoulders.

Drifts away.

A sound brings her back to the moment — a grind and then a click.

She flutters her eyelids. Checks on the eggshell ceiling. It's still there, hung way up above her, above the box.

There are no other signs of life or movement outside, at least not in the little slice of the world she can view.

And then she sees it. The source of the noise.

The cherry of Gabby's cigarette burns bright orange to her

left. Beyond the wall of the box. In the dark. In the nowhere.

It flares when she inhales. Glows brighter. And then it dims. Collects a dark spot of ash on the tip until Gabby flicks it away.

It's nice to have some company, Emily thinks, even if she's not really there.

CHAPTER 51

Loshak shifted his weight from foot to foot, felt the linoleum sag with his movements.

Instead of confused, he now felt determined. He knew all about guys like Mark, knew them inside and out.

All batterers were the same. They felt powerless. Deeply, deeply insecure. They desired not just control of their situation but a sick, fetishized version of control. Domination expressed through exaltations of violence.

For some of these guys, the wife could submit entirely, give in, give the batterer everything he wanted, and it wouldn't be enough to sate him. The beating itself became the ritual. The violence almost religious — the only way a man so small could feel good about himself, feel like he's worth anything at all.

Loshak recognized all the signs and symptoms in Mark's behavior, and now he had ideas for how to proceed. Above all, he needed to make Mark feel in control.

The gunman grinned like a jackal. He'd taken to babbling off and on, seemingly stuck in some loop of pacing the kitchen and puffing himself up.

"Think you can just trample people. Stomp around their houses. Like the whole world stops and starts when you tell it to. No fuckin' way, Jack. Not today."

How long had they been in this kitchen? Minutes? An hour? Longer? Loshak couldn't say. He supposed it didn't matter.

It occurred to him that Mark had mentioned *his house* a bunch of times. Defensively. The Stump investigation was a violation of space — his space, his home. That was how he saw it.

When the agent spoke now, he did so in a quiet, even tone, the words trickling out slowly. A little sleepy sounding, perhaps. Bringing the volume of the conversation down was the first step.

"You think no one is listening?" Loshak said. "Well, I'm listening. I understand where you're coming from."

"You don't understand shit," Mark said.

"You make some interesting points is all I'm trying to say. Us folks working in law enforcement, we sometimes get tunnel vision, sometimes get so focused on catching the bad guy, we don't realize how we're disrespecting innocent people in the process."

"Goddamn right you are."

Mark stopped pacing, his eyes wide. Loshak had his attention, and a hush had fallen over the room. No more pounding footsteps. No more ranting and raving. Mark had to be quiet now. Had to listen.

"I get it, OK?" Loshak said. "There's all this Leonard Stump shit swirling around — a tsunami's worth — and a heaping pile of it gets dumped on your doorstep."

"Through no fault of my own," Mark said.

He nodded as he spoke, an exaggerated gesture that reminded Loshak of a toddler. The gun now dangled at his side, no longer gesticulating along with his every word and thought. For the first time in this conversation, the pistol was not Mark's primary form of expression.

"That's right. Through no fault of your own. You're innocent in this thing. The victim," Loshak said. "I can understand — we can all understand — how something like that would get under a guy's skin. Hell, you wouldn't be much of a man if this kind of thing didn't stick in your craw a little bit.

Truth is, we see stuff like this all the time, and it's not a big deal. We see you. We understand. So why don't you put down the gun, and-"

The gun snapped back to attention. Muzzle leveled at Loshak's head.

And those wide eyes narrowed on Mark's face, squinted to slits with angry puckers all around them.

"Don't you walk into my house and fucking profile me, you piece of shit. Don't try to get in my head and twist me around. I'm not some textbook case study bullshit. I'm just the guy with the gun, OK? The fucking *guy* with the fucking *gun*."

Mark resumed pacing, and the atmosphere in the room shifted from something bordering on nap time back to that tension of being near a hostile creature, locked inside the beast's cage.

Loshak blinked a few times. He replayed the words in his head — *the fucking* guy *with the fucking* gun. Yes, of course. The gun was what gave Mark power here, the thing that put him in control, and someone had asked him to give it up. A direct threat. Loshak had practically issued a command, the way Mark saw it, and he was almost saying as much out loud, reassuring himself that he was the one with the gun.

Loshak realized that he'd already made this mistake once already. Asking him to give up the gun was what set him off the first time, when he'd fired a round into the ceiling.

If Mark was going to part with the weapon, he'd need to feel like it was his idea, not Loshak's.

OK. Time to pivot.

Again, Loshak lowered his voice, hitting that hushed volume just above a mumble, striving for a matter of fact tone.

"Look at this thing from my point of view, Mark. I'm in a

bad spot. I'm up to my ass in Leonard Stump paperwork as it is, and now I've got this situation here with you. I get where you're coming from. Totally understand it. But on paper, it could look like a whole different deal, you know? Guy waving a gun around, threatening an FBI agent. That's what it'll read like on the page when all of this is over. That's how the FBI does all of its business, you know? The written reports — the paperwork — that becomes the permanent record, and I'm worried people could get the wrong idea. They could think all of this was your fault, when you and I know it's not."

"That's bullshit."

"That's exactly what I'm saying. It won't be the truth, but imagine how it will look. I'm not sure how we get around that, unless you have any ideas."

Mark's eyebrows tilted up in the middle. It looked, Loshak thought, like he wanted to be angry, wanted to dismiss this, but was having a hard time following through on it.

Every desperate act was driven by fatalism, and fatalism made a person live in the moment. To counteract that, Loshak needed to make the gunman look ahead, to think about consequences, to consider the days, weeks, months, and years that would unfold after this moment had passed. The life that would go on.

Loshak pressed him a little harder.

"Look, this Stump thing is a pain in the balls for everyone involved. You think I want to be driving out to your place to play twenty questions a couple times a week? No fuckin' way. I could be home right now, feet up on the coffee table, smoking a cigar, sucking down a six-pack of Miller High Life. There's probably a bowl game on right this minute. One of the early, crappy games with two teams no one's ever heard of. But still."

The Girl in the Sand

Mark's tongue flicked out twice, wetting the corners of his mouth. He looked more tired than fierce now. Eyes a little glazed over from listening to Loshak talk.

"Look, the real problem here is the gun, OK? I come over here and we get in a disagreement? No one bats an eyelash at something like that in a report. Just two guys arguing a little bit. Happens all the time, man. Typical stuff. But you add a gun to that picture, and the whole thing just looks bad. Real bad. That's all I'm trying to say."

Mark's eyelids wanted to close. Loshak could see that standing across the room from him. They looked heavy. Folded puffs of flesh.

"So you're saying…" Mark said. His voice sounded thick, his cadence slowed to a confused crawl as he sought after words. He'd lowered his voice to match Loshak's muted tones.

Loshak suspected the man holding him hostage was hitting that critical backstretch in a drunken evening where he would either need to drink more to catch a second wind, or he was going to pass out, and it looked for all the world like he was headed toward the latter.

"I mean, what you're saying is… if it weren't for the gun…."

The room fell to silence whenever Mark trailed off. A peaceful kind of quiet that would have seemed impossible just a few minutes earlier. The dripping sink provided the only noise, that *tick-tock* of water in the background.

Loshak felt all the follicles on his head tingling as he anticipated Mark's next words. He was so close. So close.

Mark's lips parted, twitched, just on the edge of speaking.

Loshak's phone chirped from his inside jacket pocket, vibrating against his chest. A text message notification.

It came at the worst possible moment.

Everyone in the room jumped a little when the phone went off. Startled. Throttled back into motion after the extended lull.

Claire sucked in an audible breath, clutched at her chest with both hands. She hunched her back in a way that made Loshak think of a raccoon.

Loshak's shoulders jerked hard enough to knock him off balance, and he staggered back a step. The soles of his shoes slid around as he fought to regain his footing, skimming over the linoleum with little scuffing noises. When he steadied himself at last, he wound up in something close to a karate stance.

And Mark woke right up, his face tightening into a mess of hateful wrinkles. His lip curled, and he snorted twice like an angry dog, his posture going rigid all at once. He didn't hesitate.

He charged.

Lunged at Loshak.

Swung the butt of the gun at him in an awkward right hook.

Loshak dodged the blow, bobbing and weaving away from Mark's advance. Staying just out of the flailing arm's reach. He couldn't tell if the lunatic was trying to pistol whip him or punch him, but he didn't intend to let either happen.

"More bullshit," Mark said through clenched teeth. "Put your fucking hands up."

Now he stopped chasing after the agent and trained the gun on him again. His ribcage heaved, and he bared his teeth.

Loshak complied, hands drifting up in slow motion. What choice did he have?

Mark crept close. Pressed the muzzle against Loshak's forehead.

"You think you're pretty slick. All this goddamn talk that never ends. Running your mouth like some kind of fucking shrink or something."

The Girl in the Sand

Loshak listened to his pulse pattering away in his ears, eyes drifting closed. He pictured the black hole where the gun pressed into his skin, the one the bullet would come from, if it did.

And every breath felt strange. Too long. Too smooth.

Hot air from Mark's nostrils spiraled into Loshak's face. He was right there. A drunken, wife-beating fiend. Sober, he probably wouldn't have the balls to pull the trigger, even if he really wanted to. But this drunk? He was unpredictable. Not just an unknown variable in the equation Loshak had been trying to solve — an unknowable one.

Maybe he'd had him, too, if that text hadn't come. Maybe he was just about to set the gun down, let this go, whatever it was. It had sure seemed that way.

In any case, Loshak thought it best to say nothing in his current situation. To listen for a while.

Mark went on.

"You think I don't know what you're doing? Setting me up. Fucking with my head."

The barrel of the gun pressed harder at Loshak's forehead, the pressure increasing until it stung a little bit, until he was certain it was leaving a mark — a pink circle indented just beneath his hairline, marking the place where the hole in his skull would be. A bull's-eye.

And now he felt something at his side. Mark's hand reaching into his jacket, removing the phone. The fabric tugged a little, making Mark work for it, and then the phone was gone. He felt the absence like an ache, the lack of weight, the little rectangular emptiness where the phone had been.

When the barrel of the gun peeled away from his skull, Loshak opened his eyes. Blinked at the kitchen lights which seemed so much brighter than before.

Mark stared into the glowing screen of Loshak's phone, white light cast on his shiny face.

"Looks like you got a text message from, uh, Darger," Mark said. He pronounced her name incorrectly, said it with a hard *G* like *burger*. "Could be important. Could be official FBI business, huh, big guy? Well, my God. I better file it in the special filing cabinet right away."

He tossed the phone into the stainless steel sink and cranked on the faucet. The water gushed out, doused the glowing screen, aerated liquid slapping at the surface and puddling over it with a hiss.

Loshak could see the little blue box in the center of the screen, the one that he knew must say Darger's name. He had just enough time to wonder if she was OK before the screen's light guttered to a white point and went out.

CHAPTER 52

Darger woke to hissing sounds, fevered little whispers that made no sense, gibberish spoken in an endless raspy breath. The stream of syllables ebbed and flowed and stuttered, but their babble never ceased. Not all the way.

She peeled open her eyes, found herself face down on a high school desk, cheek plastered to the smooth plastic of the tabletop. Her wrists were cuffed to the desk, and the metal rings cinched tightly enough to pinch her skin, make it sting a little.

Trapped. Of course.

She sat up, blinked a few times. Her eyes spun around the room. Dizziness. Motion sickness. She pinched them closed to keep from throwing up, but the glimpse was enough.

She wasn't in a classroom. She was in the room with the thick log walls. Stump's torture room.

She stayed that way for a beat — eyes closed, chin up. Oxygen surged into her lungs. Deep breaths revealed the sour smell of this place — stale sweat and smoke.

The stabbing pain in her skull brought back blurry memories of the fight, but she couldn't dwell on them. Not now. She opened her eyes and scanned the room instead, fought through the wooziness.

A fire raged in a cast iron stove on the far wall, flickering its orange glow everywhere — so there lay the source of the hissing.

Inky darkness smudged the rest of the room to various degrees, the black thickest at the corners. She squinted to look through the shadows, to discern the shapes the dark obscured.

297

The size of the room struck her first — it had to be close to 25 feet to that stove on the opposite wall. The length of the room and the ceramic tiles lining the floor lent a strange echoing ambiance to the fire's cracks and pops.

Thick boards lay over the windows, and she could just make out the steel door off to her right.

But if this was the room, the girl should be here. Shouldn't she?

Darger swiveled her head again.

There. Behind and to her left. Nicole took shape in the shadows, chained to a desk of her own.

What the fuck with the desks? She remembered playing pretend games of school as a kid, making up fake homework assignments, handing out made-up grades. But this was the nightmare version. Psycho 101, Intro to Murder.

Nicole looked to be asleep sitting up. Neck limp, chin tucked and resting against her chest. Black eyeliner smeared all around her eyes, trailing down at the corners where the tears had spilled.

"Nicole," Darger said, her voice just louder than a whisper.

Apart from the rise and fall of her chest, the girl didn't move. She was out.

Darger gritted her teeth. She went to wipe a hand at her brow, but the cuffs yanked at her arm, stopped her hand short of its destination.

And this moment somehow snapped Darger back to reality. Awareness cut through the fog in her head — she had become one of Stump's pets. One of his captive girls. One of his victims. The thought sent an electric prickle of fear over her flesh, made all of the hair stand on end.

The panic rippled outward in her mind, swirled everything

together into a sludgy mess of feelings and fractured thoughts, but no. She couldn't let that happen.

She took a deep breath, let it out in slow motion. She had to think. Now more than ever, she had to think.

Based on the Stump profile, they at least had time, and that was something huge in their favor. Time to plan. Time to act. He always kept the girls for a few days, doing God knows what to them, but that left an opening, however small. It left a reason to hope.

"Nicole," Darger said again, lifting her voice to normal volume.

Still no response.

She looked down at the metal fastening her in place and noted that Stump had used two sets of cuffs on her — each one attaching a wrist to the steel bar under the desktop. He'd only used one set on Nicole, cuffing both wrists and looping the chain around the bar.

He was being more careful with Darger. He feared her. That made sense. The FBI agent was a bigger threat, of course. Could she use that to her advantage in some way? Try to get in his head? Maybe.

A log shifted in the stove, and the fiery reflections danced on the walls, orange shapes writhing all around her.

He would move them eventually, wouldn't he? He would move them to the bathtub where he'd bleed the first girl out for his audience. That was her chance. He'd unlock them at that point. Unlock the door and the cuffs both. And they had to be ready to pounce when the time came, to risk everything in that one moment.

Now she had to wake Nicole up. Get her on the same page. If they worked together, they might have a chance.

"Nicole." Her voice was loud. Piercing.

And still, Nicole didn't stir, the point of her chin still jabbing into her sternum.

That settled it. Talking wasn't going to work. Darger needed to get closer.

She wound her fingers around the steel bar and braced herself. Took a few breaths.

She bounced her legs and sort of bucked her hips at the same time. The desk legs screeched something awful against the tile floor, a multi-throated sound like a flock of wounded birds, but the thing scooted a few inches in the right direction.

OK. This would work. It would take a few minutes and make a lot of noise, but it would work.

She repeated the hip slide — a pair of rapid reps — but the dizziness invaded her head again, so she had to stop and close her eyes for a bit. She took it slower after that. Worked at it little by little. Patient. Methodical.

A giddy feeling welled in her chest as she got closer to Nicole, a crazy optimism she hadn't felt in a long time. It tingled outward from her core, surged into her arms and legs. Made her cheeks go warm.

Just as quickly, the fear overtook that feeling. Something between a sob and a laugh coughed out of her lungs. What an idiot she was. Sitting here pretending this would work. Pretending two unarmed women could take out Leonard Stump so long as they worked together. It was preposterous.

And some part of her told her that she would die here, in this house, at the hands of Leonard Stump like so many others. All those girls dumped out in the desert. All those shallow graves in the sand.

But no. She couldn't think like that. Not yet. They had time.

The Girl in the Sand

They just had to work out a plan. Had to blindside him somehow. Maybe one of her texts had gone through. Maybe the cavalry was on their way even now. She couldn't give up hope. Not ever. She would fight, would fight until the end.

Her left foot looped out, a circular kicking motion probing for Nicole. She suspected she was a few inches shy still, but her big toe caught the girl's ankle.

The contact jolted through Nicole's body and wobbled her head. On the second kick, her eyelashes fluttered.

"Nicole," Darger said, that warmth coming over her again. Hope.

The girl's chin lifted in slow motion, eyelids parting. She was awake, but dazed.

"Why are you here?"

Now Darger lowered her voice.

"Listen to me. We're in danger, but I need you to stay sharp, OK? We have time, and we'll have our chances to get out of this, if we work together. Follow my lead. Keep your mind clear. And be ready to fight."

"It's him?"

"It's him."

But the alarmed look in Nicole's eyes told Darger that she'd misunderstood. She followed the girl's gaze to that steel door.

It was him. At the door. She could hear the rattle of the keys at the latch, the snick of the deadbolt sliding out of the way.

Without thought, Darger slid herself backward, some instinct to hide her actions taking over.

She managed to scrape perhaps halfway back to her original position when the swollen door popped out from the frame and Leonard Stump stepped into the room.

He was a dark spot, the blackest shade among the shadows.

He stopped three paces inside the doorway and stood, his body language hard to read in the dark.

The air from the other side of the door was cooler, fresher. It spiraled against Darger's cheeks and the bridge of her nose. A light draft.

Like a child murmuring in the midst of a nightmare, Nicole shifted and twitched. Darger perked up as if someone had slapped her across the face. The fear was contagious. Intoxicating and strange.

She traced the path of Nicole's gaze, and then she saw it. The hard lines of the metal so striking in the blackness. The silhouette of the gun in his hand.

She gasped, breath creaking into her. That wasn't right. Stump didn't use guns.

The clinical words that occurred to her sounded weak in her head, powerless and small: *This doesn't fit the profile.*

"Violet."

He sounded intelligent. Younger than his age.

"You know, I never dreamed it would go like this. Our meeting, I mean."

He lifted the gun some, and Darger jumped in her seat, the cuffs gouging at her wrists, but he was just adjusting his grip.

"I mean, this is probably where I'm supposed to give my big speech or whatever. Lay everything out. Give you your chance to say or do something heroic."

She wanted to answer, wanted to play this little game with him, but her mind was blank. Empty.

"It's a bad time, I guess. I've given it a lot of thought. Wish it could go some other way. My plate is full for the moment, and you're too dangerous to keep around, so…."

He stepped forward, the details coming clearer as he moved.

The Girl in the Sand

His face showed no great aggression like she might have expected. Instead, his features portrayed a somber expression. Perhaps thoughtful.

The gun lifted at the end of his arm. A Glock much like her own, if only she'd brought it.

She stared into the depths of the barrel, the black hole that seemed endless. Looked for something there, though she knew not what.

He did not delay.

His forearm flexed. He squeezed the trigger.

The metal bucked in his hand. The muzzle blazed and popped.

And the bullet sheared off the top of Violet Darger's head.

CHAPTER 53

Choppy breaths sucked in and out of Nicole's mouth and nostrils. Little choked sounds that seemed muffled in the aftermath of the splitting crack of gunfire.

Still, she could hear the gasps from inside her head. A closed off sound with her hearing blown out. Muted and moist. Wind rushing through a throat and sinus cavity wet with saliva.

Shock. She was in shock.

She watched Darger slump forward, head and shoulders flopping onto the desktop. The agent looked limp. Lifeless. Dead.

Nicole couldn't move. Couldn't think. Couldn't slow those stuttering breaths. She could only stare at the wounded being before her, the red puddle spreading outward from the broken head, shiny and dark, creeping closer and closer to the edges of the desktop.

A ribbon of blood fluttered out of the head wound, a red stream about the width of a pencil — one burst and then it seemed to slow. To stop? She couldn't be sure. The puddle still advanced, but the spurt from the head subsided.

Movement finally tugged her eyes away from the gore.

Stump shifted his weight from foot to foot. He stood over his latest victim — a shadow hovering there, the gun dangling at his side — but Nicole realized that his shoulders weren't squared at Darger anymore.

He was facing her. Looking at her. Staring straight at her.

She hiccupped a few times in panic. Squirmed in her seat until the cuffs gnawed at her wrists. She squinted to see him better.

His face took shape in the charcoal smears of shade, and at last she could read his expression.

A disappointed frown jutted his lips out, and his eyes looked dead. Disinterested. Bored.

Now Stump turned back to Darger and stepped forward, a slow pace in the agent's direction, raising the gun again partially. His tongue flicked out, wet his lips, and there was a quirk in his chest and shoulders — the slightest hitch in his breath.

He shuffled another step and a half. Careful. Cautious. Nicole read no fear in his body language, but the vigilance was obvious.

He kicked at Darger's ankle. Twice. The muscles in his arms coiled as he leveled the gun at her skull again, and he hesitated, waited for any sign of movement.

But the agent was still. Inert. No response at all.

He crept closer. Pushed her shoulder with the barrel of the gun. Waited a beat. Still nothing.

His tongue brushed over his lips again, and the tension in his shoulders seemed to sag a little. A deep breath rushing in and removing some of the stiffness on its way out.

He stooped, leaned over the bloody woman, began to work at her cuffs.

Now the blood spilled over the lip of the desk. Thick droplets gathering at the precipice and raining down in fits and starts. The spatter sounded different than rain. The pitch was wrong, somehow — the viscosity and temperature making it wholly distinct from the sound of falling water.

Metal scraped against metal as the cuffs came loose, and the dead weight of her arms pulled away from the steel bar all at once.

Stump stood, getting a little off balance, bumping her on the way up.

The slack figure spilled from the desk like liquid, tumbled to the floor, arms and legs and torso so flimsy, so malleable.

She landed face down in the puddle of her own blood, and the impact of her cheek hitting the tile echoed its wet slap around the room, a shrill sound.

Stump took a step back at this, and both he and Nicole held their breath, the room going silent as they watched the fallen figure.

Crumpled. That was how she looked on the floor. A lifeless thing. So small.

And still some part of Nicole expected her to get up. To move an arm or leg. To do something. Anything.

But Darger lay silent and motionless, her arms pinned under her torso, an awkward resting place.

Jesus, she looked dead. She looked dead, dead, dead. That wasn't supposed to happen, was it?

Stump snorted once and turned, his shadow trailing away for the door, his silhouette growing darker with every step. He disappeared through the doorway, leaving it open behind him.

Nicole's eyes snapped back to the broken girl on the floor. She was alone with her now. Alone with a dead body.

Again, she held her breath, the quiet rising up to fill the emptiness in this place, in this room.

Darger didn't move. No rise and fall of the chest. No quiver from laying on the cold floor.

And that pool of blood surrounding her had ceased its advance over the tile, going static at last.

Dead.

The Girl in the Sand

Nicole's heart picked up speed. She had never seen a dead body before — not in person — and it was a terrifying thing.

No.

Beyond terrifying.

Meaningless.

Seeing it up close, she saw how meaningless it was. A massive gaping hole where any purpose or reason should be. A vacancy at the center of the universe. A void where the heart was supposed to lay.

Nicole's breathing grew loud again. Ragged. Spasming in and out of her. Her gasps were the only sound in the nothingness, in the darkness.

Stump's shadow took shape in the doorway then. Something clutched in his arms.

He advanced toward the girls, the details of what he held filling in little by little.

A tarp. A blue vinyl tarp.

He spread it partially on the floor, careful to avoid the blood, and flopped Darger onto it, rolling her so she lay on her back.

Loose folds of vinyl bunched around her shoulders. Nicole's eyes sought the agent's face but a flap of blue descended to obscure her view.

Stump gathered two fists full of tarp and began dragging Darger away. The vinyl crinkled and rasped over the floor, a sound that grew smaller, trailed away, as they moved.

As they neared the doorway, Stump adjusted his grip. The tarp shifted. Billowed and collapsed. Closed around the body so it disappeared like a child hiding under a blanket.

He grabbed and mashed two more handfuls of tarp in his mitts, and the agent's face appeared again. Bobbed to the surface. Tilted into a semi-upright position as the slant of the tarp lifted her top half like a hospital bed.

Just before she passed through the doorway, Nicole got a look at her face.

Darger's eyes were open but blank. No more light in them. Nothing at all.

CHAPTER 54

Footsteps clatter into the room. Thumps trailing toward her, growing closer with each impact.

Between the beats, the floorboards squeal out little whisper sounds. Muted whimpers that seem to hold their notes. Stretch them and bend them. Tiny screeches. A straining of the wood.

Emily feels these whines almost as much as she hears them. A shifting. A vibration in the floor beneath the box.

At last there's a final step — a thump that is louder and closer than the rest — and both noises cut out.

Silence.

She holds her breath. Tries to listen over the thunder of her pounding heart.

Nothing.

So much of her wants to scream, to call out to anyone who might be there standing over her, but she stops herself. Bites her lip. She doesn't know why. The impulse to remain silent fires in her, and she obeys.

If it's him, maybe it's best to lie low for a while. To avoid his notice for as long as she can. Like maybe she can disappear. Hide in this box until he goes away. Hope that someone — anyone — eventually comes along and finds her. It's not a likely scenario, she knows, but what does one hope for when locked in a wooden crate?

She thinks back on the sound of the footsteps, replays the memory in her head. The thuds. The squeals. The sudden stop once they got close.

From inside the box, it's hard to get a read on noises, to

discern the nuance, to place them into any kind of context. Was it a conflict of some type? A fight? Was it someone moving on light feet, attempting to keep quiet? Someone storming in, perhaps some anger in their movements? These are distinctly different sounds, but she wouldn't be able to distinguish them. Not from in here.

Being in the box warps all of her senses, all of her thoughts. For all she knows, the footsteps were a dream. An auditory hallucination. Or maybe she was sleeping and just woke up. It's hard to tell the difference in here, she thinks.

She stares up at the eggshell ceiling, but it remains indifferent. Unchanging. Offers no clues one way or the other. No guidance.

When her heartbeat slows — quieting, at last — she hears it. Heavy breathing.

It's close. So close. They are probably looking down at the box right now, whoever it might be.

A man, she thinks, though it's hard to be certain.

No. She can't think that way. Can't let the doubt paralyze her.

There is no certainty to be had in a situation like this. She has to trust herself, trust her senses, trust her instincts. It's all she can do.

Through the filter of the box, the breathing is very quiet, but her gut tells her it's a man. A man in an agitated state, in fact.

The footsteps resume. Somehow indistinct at first — more sounds she cannot place — but soon it comes clear that they trail away from her.

The thuds soften until they disappear.

CHAPTER 55

Mark directed Claire and Loshak down the hall, conducting them like a maestro with waves of his gun. He'd grabbed two beers out of the fridge and pinned them to his chest with his free arm.

The floorboards creaked underfoot, long squeals that filled the narrow corridor where the three of them walked in single file. It gave the procession an eerie feel.

But then they turned right through an arched doorway, and the confined space opened up into a cozy living room.

A sage green couch sat in the center of the pale wood floor, big puffed up pillows forming the back cushions. Looked comfortable, Loshak thought. A paler green love seat angled off its left corner, not quite a matching shade but close.

The walls were the color of cream, conveying just that faint tint of yellow to the white that was somehow softer — less harsh — than a plain white wall.

All told, it was a neat space, Loshak thought. Even though he had been in this room before — had spent a total of maybe two or three hours interviewing Claire there over three visits — nothing about it seemed familiar now. He remembered her well, of course, remembered the things she said about Stump, even remembered the expression on her face as she said some of them, the way she angled her eyes up and to the right as she tried to pull fresh details from those awful memories, but the room itself he remembered not at all. Funny how the brain could hold onto every morsel of the things it thinks it will need and discard the rest.

Mark waved the two of them toward the couch, and they sat. The gunman milled in the doorway a moment longer, fiddling with how to set down his beer.

The living room. Well, it could be worse.

Marching to the orders of your would-be killer could be unnerving, but Loshak thought the living room would be OK. That was the most public area of the house. If he planned to kill one or both of them, he might take them someplace private — a bedroom, basement, or closet perhaps — a place where he felt alone, where it felt like no one might see.

With his beer sorted, Mark plopped on the loveseat and propped his feet up on the coffee table. He cracked open a pale yellow can of Coors, sucked on the mouth of it for a beat. When he detached his face from the aluminum tube, he gave a satisfied gasp, shook his head a little.

"Best part of waking up," he said, as much to himself as them.

As soon as they sat down, Loshak's headache came roaring back. He'd forgotten about it for a while. Too distracted by the drama, the strategy, the barrel of the gun pressed to his skull. But now intense throbs of pain bludgeoned his brain over and over.

He pinched a thumb and forefinger at the bridge of his nose, pushed upward on the pressure point there, but it was no help. No relief.

Worse than the headache was the dejection currently settling over him. He felt it in the gritty sting in his eyes, in the ache of exhaustion in his feet and ankles. He'd squandered so much progress in his negotiation with Mark, was back where he started, maybe worse off. For the first time, he thought this situation might get away from him, that it might end on a sour note after all.

And in a strange way none of this came as any surprise. He'd always thought the Stump case was the one that threatened him directly — for twenty years now he'd felt it in his guts. Never did he think it would come this way, and yet the inevitable danger surrounding Stump had found him nonetheless. After all these years, it had found him, had beaten him down.

Mark's lips looked juicy, dripping wet with Rocky Mountain Kool-Aid. The fact that he was drinking again was another blow, another strike against Loshak's plans.

He'd gotten his hopes up for a while, but there was no way around it. Things looked bleak.

The indications of progress flashed through Loshak's head, those moments when Mark had lowered his gun, when the hatred had left his face, his features melting back into plain shapes, into a placid surface. He'd talked the gunman down, gotten almost all the way there, only for his efforts to come undone when that little chirp rang out of the phone. A goddamn text message.

Now Loshak had no gun, no phone, and Mark was drinking again. He immediately updated his mental list: No gun. No phone. *No hope.*

But no. That wasn't true. He couldn't think like that.

Mark glugged down the rest of his first can and popped the top on the second. A perpetual smile curled the corners of his mouth, even as he drank, and that manic energy seemed to well in him once more, fresh alcohol flooding into his bloodstream, killing a new round of brain cells, bringing on a new wave of euphoria, of energy.

He was refueling, Loshak thought. Not only refueling his

beer buzz, but refueling his hatred, his aggression, his animosity, hostility, and fatalism. Liquid courage. Bottled violence.

Not good.

"Did I ever tell you about the time I got into it with Mick Ferns?" Mark said.

Was he talking to Claire? To Loshak? Neither? He went on.

"We'd been partying out in the desert, and we were on our way back home in Mick's truck. Middle of the goddamn night, you know. So we was coming up on the city proper, but we weren't there yet, and I had to piss like crazy. Bladder full up to my fuckin' lungs. Wasn't gonna make it another two minutes, OK? So he pulled over, and I got out on the shoulder and pissed in the sand."

Loshak squirmed in his seat, eyes glancing around everywhere. He tried to think of any way out of here, but his eyes kept drifting back to the gun bobbing along with Mark's words.

"Mick, though, he had a reputation for being a crazy motherfucker. He was this huge guy. 6'8", like, Undertaker lookin' son of a bitch, always gettin' in fights. A brawler. A cutthroat, right, but fucking shady as hell on top of it. He ripped people off is what I mean — especially when he was real fucked up, which he was that night."

He slurped his beer, punctuating the story's preface with a dramatic pause.

"So just as I shake those last few drops free and put my dick back in my pants, I turn, and he's there. Mick. And he has a knife on me. I'm talkin' one of those, like, Crocodile Dundee hunting knives. Gigantic. Serrated on one side. Must have had it under the seat in the truck. Christ knows where he got it.

The Girl in the Sand

"So I'm not even zipped up, and Mick just says, *Wallet*. That's it."

Another dramatic pause to take a drink and burp.

"See, I had this factory job at the time, an automotive deal, runnin' steel exhaust pipes through benders, makin' $18 an hour back when that was more money than it is now. So I typically had $500 or $600 cash on me, the bulk of my most recent paycheck. Sometimes closer to two paychecks' worth. I didn't advertise it or nothin', but people like Mick have some kind of radar for these things or something. They just know when there's a wad of cash nearby, and they're like raccoons spotting something shiny and getting all lustful for it, getting all greedy, groping after it with their grabby little hands.

"Anyhow, like I said, I've turned, and I'm facing Mick, but I'm not lookin' right at him. I've got my head all hanging down, eyes facing the ground, got my hands raised palms up. I'm looking as non-threatening as possible, you know. I mean, I don't want to upset the guy with the huge knife, right? I'm talking all soft, and even though I'm lookin' at the ground, I'm watching him. I'm watching him. And as soon as I see that little bit of tension release in his shoulders, I crack him right in the throat as hard as I can.

"He goes down to his knees. Knife goes flying. He's gagging, got both hands on his neck. I think I, like, jammed his Adam's apple way in there or something. Got it stuck. What's the word? Lodged it. Lodged it back in his pipes. So he's massaging at it, trying to pop it back out."

Mark eyed Loshak and Claire on the couch, perhaps realizing that the story had reached its abrupt ending.

"I don't know. It was fuckin' hilarious. I grabbed the knife and threw it as far as I could, way out in the scruff. Mick got to

315

where he could breathe again, and we drove home like nothing happened. I tell you what, though. He never tried to fuck with me again. Not ever."

He took another big drink.

Of course. Of course the insecure male would tell a story that painted him as the tough guy, as the brave one, as proving his masculinity through violence. Once more Mark reveled in his control over a situation, just like he was doing now, holding them at gunpoint.

Loshak bit his bottom lip, pain flaring there for a second. He knew what he needed to do now, though he didn't know why.

He stretched a little, straightened up in his seat.

He didn't always understand the impulses that flowed out of his mind, but he'd learned to trust them.

The agent broke into applause, his heavy claps echoing funny off the walls, creating a thin fluttering that sounded like a bird's wings. The smile faded from Mark's mouth, and a series of parallel creases took shape on his forehead.

"I have to say, I'm really impressed, Mark," Loshak said. "Really impressed and a little surprised, frankly. I didn't figure you had it in you. Didn't think a wife beater like you could ever have that kind of courage in him. To sucker punch someone bigger than you like that? I mean, wow. Truly, truly impressed."

Loshak didn't break eye contact as he said these words. He stared straight at Mark, and he knew his eyes weren't smiling at the gunman the way his lips might be. He knew his eyes offered no mercy at all.

And when Mark didn't say anything, Loshak let the silence linger, let it grow awkward. Mark's clenched mouth moved like he was chewing, looked like he wanted to speak and couldn't bring himself to, couldn't find the words.

The Girl in the Sand

Good. Let him stew in it. If there's one thing a bully doesn't know how to do, it's dealing with someone who's not afraid, not looking the other way.

Loshak cleared his throat.

"You ever brag about that? Hitting Claire? Beating on someone sixty pounds lighter than you? Or is it just sucker punching drunks that warrants the full-blown story treatment? You don't think we'd be quite as impressed with your other efforts?"

Mark stood now, and he pointed the gun. He gestured for Loshak to stand, but when the agent leaned back in his seat instead, Mark's face turned bright red and then seemed to quickly darken toward purple. It looked like he wasn't breathing at all, lips pulled back in a grimace, frozen that way.

"A man never stands so tall as when he stoops to strike a woman. Am I right, Mark?"

Now Mark snorted in wild breaths. Lips pulled down at the corners to expose his bottom teeth.

"Stand up," he said, his voice coming out strained, almost Cookie Monster-ish, Loshak thought.

The agent stood.

And the gun extended between them, shaking.

Loshak read the lines in Mark's face. There was anger there, but a softness, too. His vulnerability was showing through the mask at last. His fear. After all that huffing and puffing, he was, of course, too scared to act.

Every batterer is a coward deep down, after all.

Loshak swiveled his stance, angled himself nearly perpendicular to Mark. He took a breath, cool wind rushing to fill him. He felt the thudding of his heart pick up speed.

It was time to finish it. The now or never moment.

Loshak lurched forward with ape-like aggression. Pushing off with an explosive first step.

He launched his chest and arms into the side of the gun as though he were tackling the weapon, driving it straight toward the wall.

The force tipped Mark into a careening stagger. Yanked the gunman's arms like strings. Jerked the top of his torso along with the momentum like some stretchy child's toy.

They crashed into the dead end of the drywall. The impact rocked both men back a step. Bounced them off the wall gun first.

As they struggled, Loshak hugged the side of the gun tightly to his chest. He snaked both arms around it and ripped at it with his mitts, trying to strip it from Mark's hands like a strong safety forcing a fumble.

And the gun jerked to life between them. The muzzle blazed and cracked, the weapon bucking like an angry fish in all four of their wriggling hands. Something wild trying to escape their clutches.

The shot went wide.

Glass exploded around them. An eruption of sound. Violent. The front window dropping all at once, raining forth a cacophony of high pitched tones as the shards piled on top of each other.

Claire screamed, her throat wide open. Her voice going ragged and shrill.

And maybe it was these distractions. The gunshot. The glass. The scream. The weapon thrashing like a living, hateful thing in both of their hands.

But Mark let go.

The gun came free. Wrenched into Loshak's fingers. Sole

possession.

He stumbled back two paces, the tug-of-war cutting out abruptly and almost costing him his balance.

And as soon as he hit that second backward step, he launched himself forward again. Adjusted the weapon in his hands as he moved.

He smashed Mark's nose with the butt of the gun. The cartilage collapsed like a rotten peach. Crushed to the bony pit. He felt the squish of it, the tattered flesh caught between the metal and that snubbed piece of bone.

Blood poured out of Mark's face like a spigot. He cupped both hands at it. Smeared both of them red up to the wrist.

All the fight had drained from Mark's face now. His eyes were wet, the eyelids almost greasy. A toddler's frown pushed his bottom lip out.

Loshak reached for the forgotten Glock in Mark's waistband. Plucked it free. Holstered it.

Mark made no move to stop this. He just dabbed at the mix of blood and tears gushing down his chin, painting a red goatee there.

And still the fire in Loshak's gut could not be squelched. He wanted to bash away at the face before him. To just smash it with the metal in his hand until it wasn't a face at all. A bloody jelly laid over a skull.

He lifted the gun again. Poised it over his shoulder.

But he stopped himself. He took a few breaths. In and out, slow and even.

The hatred's flames still raged, but he could imagine them being over — could imagine them passing at some point — and there was some relief in that.

He turned, at last, to check on Claire.

She cowered in the corner. Folded up against a rocking chair. Bawling.

He went to her. Knelt. Put a hand on her shoulder.

Again, he tried to catch his eyes with hers. To make a non-verbal connection to her just like he'd done on his way in the door.

But she stared into space. A lost girl. Rocking back and forth.

He wanted to tell her that it would be OK. That she would be OK.

He wanted to tell her that she didn't deserve any of this. That it wasn't fair. None of this was fucking fair.

And that he was sorry. Sorry that she ever had to deal with this, endure this. Sorry that the world worked this way.

Above all, he wanted to tell her that people can heal. That souls can heal. With time and peace they can heal.

That it was what made life worth living. That it was what made the entire universe make sense in some small way.

His lips parted, moved, but no words came. A lump bobbed in his throat instead.

She looked at him, finally. Their eyes locked. And he knew that she knew. That they didn't need to talk.

Her hand sought his. Found it. Held it.

And his breath felt wet and heavy coming in now. A soggy blanket between him and the world.

He stood after a while. Stretched. Looked over the scene.

Claire hunched in the corner, head resting against the wooden arm of the chair.

Blood still poured from Mark's nose, though perhaps it came slower now. He looked small. Pathetic. Defeated. A wounded child feeling sorry for himself.

The Girl in the Sand

Even after everything, the awful way he'd treated Claire, Loshak felt a strange sympathy for him. He wanted him locked up, yes. Still wanted to bash his skull in, sure. But he felt a sorrow for the injured creature nonetheless.

He would call it in now — not with his own phone unfortunately. He'd detain Mark until the local police department arrived to cart him off.

And then this night would be over. As much as it ever could be, anyway.

As he cuffed Mark, he wondered what Darger would have to say about all of this, wondered what she was up to tonight. Her evening couldn't be any worse than this. Could it?

CHAPTER 56

The hours passed, and sleep helped ease the fear out of Nicole's body. It didn't calm her so much as sap the feelings from her, draining them, replacing them with that numb warmth of slumber, a pleasant nothingness.

Stump had come back in the room just one time — a few minutes after he'd dragged Agent Darger out on the tarp — to throw a fresh round of wood into the stove and stoke it back into a roaring fury.

The orange light tinted the front half of him, glowed against the side of his chin and jaw. She thought he might look back at her, even just a quick glance, but no. Once the fire was raging, he was gone. The door closed and the deadbolt clicked into place behind him.

Heat surged into the room. A wave of it engulfing her, like the shimmer that rose perpetually from the desert sand. Soon even the metal of the cuffs and their chains had gone warm to the touch, indistinguishable from the temperature of her palms.

The tremor in her arms and legs abated right away. The hitch and hiccup of her breathing likewise steadied. The heat seemed to salve so many things, to lull her away from the panic so exhaustion was all that was left.

Still, she didn't go down easy. Sleep settled over her in tiny increments. She fought it at first. Jerking herself back to an alert state over and over, picturing Darger's body being dragged away, that final blank look in her eyes before she disappeared through the doorway. The agent's fate seemed to help her focus for a while.

The Girl in the Sand

But it didn't last. After a time, each lolling of her neck lasted longer, each drooping of her eyelids progressed further. The anesthetic of sleep spread from her core, out into her limbs, up into her neck and head.

At last, she slept. Long and deep. She didn't know for sure how long, but it had to be an hour or more.

She woke now and then. Blinked a few times. Looked around the empty room. Repeated the process.

The raging fire burned down, receding a little each time she woke. The crackle reduced to whispers. Eventually only coals were left, black hunks that flickered orange at random intervals.

Each time she came around, part of her thought Darger would be back at the desk where she'd been. Hurt, perhaps, but alive. Returned. Talking and breathing and moving.

But no.

The desk was empty. The agent was long gone.

CHAPTER 57

Emily shakes herself out of a half sleep. Startled. Hot breath heaving in and out of her open mouth.

She has to pee. Badly. The sting of it rushing back to her bladder as soon as her consciousness flicks back on. But there's something more pressing happening.

Something stirring outside the box.

Goose bumps pull her skin into weird tingling patterns that creep over her chest, her back, the nape of her neck. Every pore alive and wriggling.

He's here. Or someone is.

Metal clatters just on the other side of the wood panel above her. She recognizes the sound, of course — the padlock rattling against the hasp. Those interlocking loops of steel that trap her, seal her in the dark.

She reaches out a hand. Presses her palm flat to the wood. It's cold against her body heat. Smooth.

The whole world exists beyond this slab of timber. All of the people. All of the best and worst they have to offer. It's right there. About to open itself to her.

The mix of terror and excitement welling just behind her face is overwhelming. A hot, wet swirl of emotions sloshing about in her skull. Human contact is so close now. It is all she wants and all of her worst fears. Both at the same time.

There's a final thump, louder than the rest, and then the wood groans. The hinges squawk a little to her left. The door is loose.

And it's there. The tiniest sliver of light where the lid pulls free of the frame.

So strange.

A beam that runs the length of the box. Slices into the darkness. Spreads over the underside of the lid like a gray puddle.

Somehow light is not how she remembered it. Not quite. All that time in the darkness has warped her memory of it. Distorted her expectations.

And the reality is so unexpected — so striking — that it tears a gasp from her throat. Flutters more warmth into her chest and head until she's almost dizzy with it.

She squirms. Grips two handfuls of her shirt as though bracing herself for some violent impact.

The crease of light grows in fast motion. The lid lifts along the arc of its hinges. Up and over.

And the heavens rip wide open in front of her.

Light.

Everywhere.

Blinding white surrounds her. So bright. Impossible.

Tears flood her eyes. But she holds them open, anyway, if only to slits. And she stares into it. Into the great wide open.

It makes no sense at first. Just a bright blur. Painful.

And then color swells into the world. Fills it. Populates it with shapes and contours. Every line sharpening into focus.

It's still just the ceiling up there — a wider swath of it now — with the dark frame of her box jutting up in the foreground. And yet, in this moment, it is everything. A vast expanse. Overwhelming.

Her breathing has gone ragged. Choppy snorts and snuffles wracking out of her. Choked sobs mixing in for good measure.

And she feels the cool air of the room swirl over her body all at once, over her skin. Dry and soothing after so long trapped in the box with her sticky breath blowing back on her.

She shakes all over. Her eyelids flex and contort. Her arms and legs quiver like branches in the wind.

Gabby's voice speaks from somewhere else. Somewhere far away.

Breathe, Em. Remember to breathe. He is near.

She throws her head back. Opens her throat. Invites that cool air into her lungs in a sucking expansion of her ribcage. And she holds it. Holds it. Lets it out slow.

Yes. Better.

Her thoughts still smear together, wet and hot and messy, but not so bad as they did.

After a second deep breath, it occurs to her for the first time that she should sit up. In all the excitement, she'd almost forgotten this was a possibility.

She wets her lips as she eyes the space beyond the rim of the open box. Reminds herself that the world out there is not merely a fantasy to dream about, a room to watch through the sliver in the lid.

And yet she finds herself hesitant to actually follow through on the impulse.

A shadow flits over her then. A passing darkness.

Her eyelids flutter, flushing the tears away.

She glances everywhere. Seeks that dark shape. The blackened smudge against the ceiling's eggshell white.

He bobs back into view.

It is him.

Something round in his hands. Something she can't see.

His voice trills soft and deep. Detached. Almost bored with all of this.

The Girl in the Sand

"You can sit up, but if you try anything beyond that, you'll only cut your wrists up. The chains will keep you where you are."

Her abdominals contract. Bend her at the waist. Lift her top half.

Her field of vision scans her ascent of that wooden wall which contains her. Slides up it at an angle like an artful shot in a movie.

And then she's past it. Over it. Looking out at the world outside the box.

Vaguely she recalls this room. This space. Her struggle with Stump here. Fragments of memory rolling over her in waves, not quite sequencing themselves into a coherent narrative.

Her eyes dart over the room. Swiveling. Taking in everything.

Beige carpet. Closely woven. Cropped tight to the floor like short hair.

White walls surround her on all four sides, matching the matte finish of the ceiling.

A single mirror hangs on one wall. A circle of reflective glass encased by a woven wicker border. Angled perpendicular to her so she can't see herself.

Apart from that, it's a plain room. Not much to look at.

And he bends. Lowers himself toward her. Not quite looking at her. Extends the rounded object in his hands.

A stainless steel bedpan is placed in the box. Just beyond her feet.

He turns his back, walks a few paces away, and without hesitation, she moves to it. Squats over it to use it.

The release is euphoric. A rapture. She falls into a total surrender to the needs of her bodily function. It is alleviation on a profound level.

Thankful.

Just like that, she is thankful. Not angry. Not rebellious or strident or viciously trying to bite off the hand of her captor. She is thankful. Deeply so. It almost makes her nauseous when she thinks about it.

Their last encounter, she'd tried to bludgeon him. Harbored homicidal rage toward him.

And yet this close to him again, she finds no anger. No violent urges. Her body fills only with fright, watching this dark figure out of the corner of her eye.

She is a scared child when he is near. Scared of him, scared of not knowing what to do, how to get out of here, how to fight him or even stand up to him at all.

When she had the desk leg, it felt like she knew what to do, felt like the physical presence of a weapon — a hard rod of steel — centered all of her hopes, gave her courage. But he took that away. Looking back, it felt like there was little doubt that he'd get the better of their conflict, the outcome always inevitable.

Her lips twitch, twice, three times. She wants to talk, wants to say something to him to defy this feeling in some small way, but her mouth won't quite obey the command. She is frozen.

What he wants is so much bigger than what she wants. He bulldozes forward no matter what, and it's hard to make the commitment to stand in his way, even in the smallest sense.

He removes the pan when she's done and tosses some moist towelette packets into the box, which she tears open and uses.

They smell so clean. The medicinal tang that typically might remind her of a public bathroom or a hospital is now incredibly refreshing. So different from the earthy smell of the sand. Almost miraculous.

The Girl in the Sand

She swipes the wet over the skin of her hands in great, greedy strokes, and it almost feels like the flesh absorbs the moisture, soaks it up like a sponge. Thirsty for it.

Then she tears open another packet and rubs a fresh wipe over her face and neck, dislodging grit which sprinkles down around her. All those little shards of sand falling away from her.

The relief of using the bedpan seems to unblock a lot of sensory perceptions — how tired she is comes into focus first.

The sting in her eyes intensifies, as does the sleepy ache that has taken hold in those muscles along her spine, running up and down the fibers of her limbs, the stabbing shards of pain near her temple where she'd now taken a number of blows. She could worry about these things now that soiling herself was no longer a concern, could long for sleep again.

But the smell of the food quickly trumps all of that. The vapor entering her sinuses and taking hold of her there. It smells like meat, she thinks. A little sweet, though. All she can think of is the Mongolian barbecue place her dad used to take her to back in California. It seems like it was decades ago.

"Drink," he says, the lilt of a tiny smile in his voice.

He hands over a mason jar of water — a quart-sized monster of a jar — and suddenly the food can wait. Forgotten almost at once.

The fluid's surface lurches and sways as she takes the glass from him, brings it to her lips. And she sees nothing else in the world but that careening liquid, that collection of moisture she needs so badly.

She drinks, long and deep. A bead of water dribbles down her chin.

It's sweet. Water has never tasted so sweet, so pure, so delicious. It makes her scalp tingle in waves moving from front to back and repeating.

She glugs three-quarters of the jar down in one drink. Feels it tumbling over her gullet to cool her belly.

She stops. Gasps for a few breaths. Finishes it.

Now comes the food.

She hands the empty jar to him, and he exchanges it for a plate that is hot to the touch. Piled with odd shapes that take a moment to make any sense at all.

Chicken nuggets. French fries. A generous dollop of barbecue sauce.

The smell of meat is almost sensual here. A little pungent, yes, but the pleasant notes override the questionable ones.

Again, she doesn't hesitate. She eats. Dunks anything and everything in the sauce. Smears the caramelized substance over and around the rim of the plate. Wipes at it with her fingers to get every molecule.

The flavor blossoms on her palate. Salty and sweet and savory and tangy. All of these at once. Divine. Immaculate.

The food is all straight from the freezer, she knows. Doesn't matter. This is the best meal she has ever eaten.

Heavy on protein. Maybe that's what a hungry person craves most. Maybe that boosts her enjoyment. Enhances it.

When the food is gone, she licks the plate. Leaves it looking clean.

Again, she experiences that blend of gratitude and disgust.

The dark figure responsible for all of this angles away from her. She can make out the silhouette of his square chin in profile, but the rest of his features remain obscure.

He has abducted her, taken her away from her life, from her kids, and yet he could have killed her and hasn't. Instead he has given her some small version of comfort. Sustenance. He has given her life.

The energy from the food courses through her. An elated post-meal feeling bolstered by a sense of returned strength.

Stump takes the plate. Begins to gather things up. She knows he will leave soon. That she will be sealed once more in the darkness. Alone.

Her eyes dance over his back, over that muscular neck connecting his head and torso.

He is many men, it seems to her. Several different personalities entirely in her imagination. Distinct. All of them at once. All of them unknowable, shrouded in shadows.

He is a shape that never stops shifting, never stops morphing like an image in a dream. His essence always just out of reach.

She chews her bottom lip. She wants to engage him. Wants to speak, but considering it sends a tremor through her chest and arms.

He stands. Holding the plate and bedpan.

"When?" she says, her voice so small.

He stops moving. Body going rigid. She thinks he will turn to look at her before he speaks, but he doesn't.

"What?"

"When will you do it?"

He takes a breath, in slow and out slower.

"Soon."

He strides out of the room. Disappears into the hall. The sound of his footsteps trails off into nothing.

She listens to the quiet. To the emptiness of this awful place.

Too tired to sit up any longer, she lies back. Nestles into the cold sand. Feels all of the tension release in her spine. A glorious relief.

And just as the back of her cranium settles to the dirt floor of her enclosure, the words pop into her head:

Stockholm syndrome.

The imprisoned person slowly identifying with their captors, slowly humanizing them and developing something like affection for them.

Is that happening to her? Maybe it would explain the gratitude she feels. This strange psychological phenomenon. Some impulse to project humanity onto the inhuman.

Guys like Stump may feel no empathy for other beings, but she wasn't like him. She couldn't turn it off. Even face to face with a murderous monster, she couldn't turn it off. She looks for humanity in him, and given time, her imagination finds what isn't there, starts to believe.

When he comes back, they make eye contact for the first time since she went into the box.

She detects something different in the way he looks at her. His eyes open wider than before. The disinterested look has been replaced by an inquisitive one. Perhaps she's imagining it, but she thinks she sees the faintest glimpse of warmth there.

A curl occupies his lips. Something perfectly between a smile and a blank expression.

He squats next to the box again. Close now. The quiet between them grows intense.

"I knew you were different," he says at last. "I knew it."

The detachment has left his voice, some hushed reverence taking its place.

"They never talk. The girls who go in the box. Apart from begging, they never talk. Can't bring themselves to engage with me, I think. They just cry and cry."

Emily's eyes flick to the ceiling. A fluttering lightness enters her skull.

It takes her a moment to process her emotional reaction to what he is saying.

She is proud. It makes no sense, but she is proud to be different. Proud that he sees something in her.

He goes on.

"This was what had to happen. I know it's true. My whole life, I've been on the path to find you. We're looking into the darkness now. Staring straight into it. And we have to decide, you know. Is there something there? Some glimmer of light, however faint. Some blip. Some flash. Some reason to wonder."

She continues to stare at the eggshell surface above them.

"Is there anything at all? Or is it only the dark? The big nothing that stretches out forever and ever."

She wants to cry. Wants to scream. Wants to thrash at the chains binding her to the box, but she does none of these things. She blinks. Looks at him.

"Need anything?" he says. "More water, maybe?"

She hesitates a moment.

"Yes, please."

He fetches it, and she drinks. Chugging down another quart in three passes.

Again that almost smile quirks his mouth as he takes the empty jar from her.

"When you're in the box, those bodily functions become everything, don't they?" he says. "Eating, drinking, pissing, shitting. They occupy more and more of your thoughts, more and more of your time is spent worrying over them. And yet, those needs are so easily met. I've brought you food and water. Brought you the bedpan. Despite all that worry, in just a few minutes the body is sorted out. Easily satisfied. It's your soul

333

that really suffers, confined like that, but that's harder to worry over, harder to comprehend. Your body is fine. Your heart pumps, your lungs breathe. The meat lives on and on, not even knowing the difference. But the soul gets twisted up from too much time in the dark. It changes, doesn't it?"

Some strange relief washes over her as he talks. He is identifying with her, isn't he? He understands, to some degree, what she is experiencing.

Even if she knows her fight will resume in time, she can see the glimmer of humanity in him again. A warped version of it. A madness having seeped into his thoughts, into his soul, if he has one. But the faintest bit of humanity nonetheless.

"But it's like I said: That's what we're here for. To look into the dark. And that's why I need to put this on you."

He ducks. Disappears behind the wall of the box. Fiddles with something there. She listens for identifying details.

When he reappears, he has a plywood contraption in his hands. Homemade. Metal hinges. About the size of a hatbox until he unfolds it. The bottom of the square opens like a mouth, and she sees that it has double walls, that the interior of the box is carpeted.

"Hold still now," he says, his tone soft. Almost tender. "I've had this for years, but I've never used it but once before. It never felt quite right, I guess. But this is the time. I know it is."

She doesn't understand what's happening until he props her up in a seated position and begins to lower that open plywood structure over her head.

Now she sees. There's a semi-circle cut out on each piece of that wooden mouth, and the pieces of this puzzle click into a place of understanding for her.

This will become the neck hole.

The Girl in the Sand

She bucks. Tries to rock down and forward to avoid the head box, but it's too late.

He drives an elbow into her chest. Pushes her back and pins her. Speaks through clenched teeth.

"I said hold still."

And the carpet closes in. Cinches around her on all sides. Encases her in another level of darkness. Imprisons her in a tighter space still.

Tighter, tighter.

It snaps when he closes it around her head. The edge of the neck hole rough against her skin.

The outside world deadens immediately. All ambient noise cut to nothingness by the barrier, by the nappy floor covering hung up around her skull.

She scrabbles in a panic. Arms and legs flailing. Pushing her deeper into the corner of the coffin box. Jamming her shoulders into that wall over and over.

Disorientation blossoms until nothing makes sense. Until everything outside of the head box barely seems real at all.

And even in the dark, she can feel how close the carpet is to her face. The way it mutes everything. The chemical smell of the textile. Somehow nauseating.

And this is just like being dead, she thinks. Just like being dead except that she is experiencing it. The infinite dark. The quiet. The total isolation from anyone or anything outside. She is getting a sneak preview.

Her breathing goes choppy again. Gasping. Choking.

Little sounds escape her lips. High pitched. Involuntary.

But the carpet muffles her whimpers.

Closes her inside.

CHAPTER 58

This time when Nicole woke the fire was out, and the room was cold. No flutter of orange coals animated the stove's chamber, just the matte black of ash and shadow.

The tile floor stretched out in front of her, the room at its darkest since she'd arrived. A cold, dark chamber. Some monster's dungeon.

She shifted in her seat, and a fresh wave of goose bumps prickled over her arms. The air nipped at her skin, dry and harsh, and the tingle of stirring flesh ached in places, especially her neck.

Her head rolled from shoulder to shoulder out of habit, tendons popping, muscles straining. She missed the warmth, the numb of sleep, wanted only to crawl back into unconsciousness for a while, but she knew, somehow, it wouldn't happen that way. Not anymore. The end was near. The feel of it was everywhere.

She tested the cuffs, pulled her chains taut — still secure as expected, though the metal had gone cool to the touch.

She wanted to hold her breath, to listen, but she was too keyed up to do it. Her chest kept heaving, kept sucking in breath, whether she wanted it or not.

She didn't realize Stump was in the room until he moved, the soles of his shoes scuffing the floor, the shifting hulk in the darkness revealing his position to her. He'd been standing against the wall in the far corner, but he moved toward her now.

The rush of air entering her throat was mercifully silent, not that it really mattered. A gasp would have been embarrassing somehow, cementing her powerlessness with a weak sound. She didn't know why saving face meant anything to her now, but it did.

He took a few steps — slow, almost careful movements. His lip and brow curled, an expression she read as disgust.

Her heart continued to pick up speed as he drew near, pulse banging away in her ears. She could only maintain eye contact with him for a fraction of a second at a time, their eyes connecting and pulling apart over and over in rapid succession.

What the fuck did he want? She couldn't tell, which seemed wrong. She could always tell what a man wanted, could read it in the set of his posture, in the folds around his eyes and lips. It was what she did for a living. Stump clearly wanted something from her. There seemed a strange curiosity in his manner, a tentative quality that struck her as at odds with the disgust she also read.

He pulled up to a stop a few paces shy of where she sat. Waiting, she thought. Waiting for what? His eyes flicked back and forth from her eyes to her lips. It almost looked like he was waiting for her to say something, waiting for her to weigh in on the proceedings.

And she wanted to oblige him and defy him, to scream in his face, but her mind was blank. Devoid of complex thoughts, of words. In the end, all she could muster was a whisper.

A little whistle formed in her mouth. Not a word. Not even a real syllable. Just the sibilance of an "s" sound.

That curiosity drained from his face all at once, his eyes going dead.

"Quiet now. It'll be over soon," he said.

CHAPTER 59

Emily's eyes are open, but she does not see. Doesn't blink. Doesn't exist on this plane.

In this terrified moment after the head box goes on, her consciousness pulls back into the abstract, into the mindscape.

A drain opens where her skull gives way to the neck, deep within her head. A drain that sucks all of her down into the hole, away from this place.

Away from reality.

Into the nowhere.

But a voice persists there in her head. Her companion. Her only friend. The voice that's been there since all of this started.

She cannot see her. Cannot even feel her presence. But her voice pierces the empty space. Disembodied.

Gabby watches for her. Narrates for her. Keeps her tethered to reality in some small way.

Emily. Are you there?

You need to come back. It's almost over now — almost the end — and you need to come back.

I saw him. Looking through the hole, I saw him standing over the box. Just for a second. Checking on you, I think. Listening.

I don't know what he expected to see. You're lying in a box with another box on your head. A box within a box? Not much to look at.

His face was all screwed up like he was thinking, though. Concentrating. Wrinkled forehead. Lines around his eyes. Mouth all puckered.

The Girl in the Sand

There's nothing up there now. Just that eggshell ceiling. It's more white than gray at this point, though. Daylight, maybe?

Anyhow, I think he's going to do it soon. One way or the other. I think he's going to go through with it.

And you need to be ready by then, OK?

I know you're tired. Know you need a little time away. I can understand it.

Your soul has retreated. Retracted. Disappeared within itself. It's the only way it can rest, maybe.

I know it's only for a while. I know he can't break you like that. No one could. Physically, maybe. Any body can be broken, but not your mind. Not your soul.

So get your rest. Or whatever this is. Just be ready to roll soon, OK? That's all I'm sayin'.

It's lonely here without you. Empty and boring and strange.

I guess it'll be lonely forever where I'm going. I think sometimes that's why I'm here. To make sure you don't go where I'm going. Or to try my best to help prevent it, in any case. If so, I like that. Hope it works.

The inside of the box smells like puke now. That acidic bite to it. The stench of sweetness. Is that new? Did it always smell this way? I don't remember it, but maybe it did.

Maybe someone puked in it at some point. You've got to figure you're not the first to get stuck in this thing, right? He had it all ready to go, you know? Already fitted with a lock. Already loaded with sand for no good reason, this little trench dug into it.

Hell, he even said he'd strapped that head box on somebody before. Their breath all steaming up the carpet for God knows how long.

Emily, you don't know where these boxes have been. You're probably going to want to wash your hands once you get out. Just sayin'.

I kid.

In all seriousness, I think you should stab Leonard Stump in the face as soon as you get out of here. A lot. Like a whole bunch of times.

Bite. Claw. Kick. Bludgeon. Whatever you can do.

Focus on his eyes, maybe. That's arguably the weakest spot on the human body. A single fingernail can incapacitate a man of any size if you jam it into his fucking eyeball hard enough.

Remember the time we— Wait.

I can hear them now. Voices.

Talking. Fighting, maybe?

In the room, I think. It's hard to tell with the way the sounds echo down the hall. Reverberating everywhere.

I don't know who. I mean, it's him, but I don't know who the other is.

He's coming.

Emily, it's time.

CHAPTER 60

She had to open her eyes. The words repeated in her head, an endless, mixed up cycle: *I have to open my eyes have to open them my eyes open open open.*

It might have been seconds or minutes or hours later that they finally obeyed.

Darger's head lolled to one side. Blackness all around her. The air felt close and thick, and the thoughts in her head had the viscosity of pea soup.

And then the dark closed in on her again. Lost in the abyss.

Awake.

Sort of.

Struggling to gain consciousness.

Open.

Again, her thoughts were slow. Had to open her eyes. Not sure why, but had to. Needed to. Something important to do. Time. Time was limited. No time for sleep or whatever this was.

Where was she? Maybe that would help.

It was a moment before she could determine whether her eyes were actually opened or closed. Her eyelids fluttered, blinked. Everything looked the same either way. Black. But there was a discomfort to having her eyes open. She wanted to close them again. To go back to sleep. But no.

Stay awake.

Eyes open.

She had the same sense of closeness on all sides, and it was then that she was able to get her thoughts in order enough to wonder if she was inside the box. The one Stump had put Emily

341

in.

Wet, hot panic flushed into her skull, a tea kettle of boiling water dumped in with her brain. Instinctively, her arms flailed out at her sides. Only her right moved, and then just barely. But even so, something changed. The light.

In one place, the pure blackness had been replaced by a little bit of light. Blue.

Blue?

Not the box.

It was familiar, this vaguely translucent blueness. And something else. The sound when she moved.

Crinkle. That was the sound it made. Plastic or vinyl or...

The tarp.

In the back of the truck.

This realization jolted her a little further awake, though she was still groggy and confused.

She was cold, she realized. Shivering. The air was icy and raw in her nostrils and throat and mouth. It almost burned with cold. Filling her lungs and touching her insides.

How did she get back to her hiding place? Had she crawled here?

She tried to move again, shifting from her back to her side. With the movement came more swishy tarp noises, and then her senses seemed to snap on, like someone flipping a switch.

Pain.

Pain, somehow hot and cold at once. The heat of fresh blood and the cold of air touching the wet places.

Head wound. Those were the words that came to her.

The pain was everywhere. Shooting down from her skull, blinding bolts of agony that she somehow felt in her mouth, in her teeth. And the left side of her body was on fire. Beyond fire.

A searing chemical burn. But then she wriggled, an involuntary movement in reaction to the pain, and it changed. Not fire. Worse.

Numb. Dead from the neck down. She felt nothing on the left side of her body now.

And then she remembered what happened. Why she was in the back of the truck, wrapped in a tarp.

She was dead.

☾

In the fleeting moment when she'd looked down that gun barrel in Leonard Stump's hand, Violet Darger had finally realized her own mortality. It seemed silly now, to have been so blind to it. Even back in Ohio, with James Clegg, when she knew she had to fight or die trying… she never really believed she'd lose. Part of her knew that she'd get through it.

She'd been lying to herself. The big lie everyone tells. She *could* have died. She could have made a wrong move or never gotten her hands on the pistol and drowned face down in the river that night.

She saw now how lucky she'd gotten with Clegg. And that was the real problem. No one got that lucky twice.

With blood crusted over one eye, she lifted the tarp with her good hand, looked at the left. She willed it to move. Concentrated on just the fingers, urging them to make even the slightest twitch.

By the end she was shaking, tears welling and spilling from her good eye. She couldn't do it. Couldn't move the fingers on her left hand. Not even a little. It was only by some miraculous turn of fate that she wasn't dead yet, she realized. But she would be soon. She could feel it the way you felt a coming storm. A certain charge in the air.

For the first time, she imagined what would happen if she died. *When* she died. Would they even find her? Or would Stump make her disappear like he had all those other girls in the desert? Hide her away in the sand until she was only bones and a few scraps of clothing.

It was hard to fathom. That she would just cease to exist. And the world would go on spinning the way it always did when someone took their last breath.

There was an arrogance to life. A feeling that, yes, death happened, and sometimes it was unexpected and perhaps even unfair, but that won't happen to *me.*

But the veil of denial had lifted. Just now, Darger knew she was actually going to die.

She wanted to close her eyes. To stop fighting. To let it happen already.

She thought of the people she'd leave behind. Owen, who'd already lost his twin brother only a few months ago. She hated to think of him suffering another loss so soon. Her mother, who'd never stopped worrying about the risks of Darger's job. And now she'd be proven right. Lastly there was Loshak. Her mentor and partner, and in many ways, the father she'd never had.

And then she snapped back to the reality of the whole scene — the big picture. She was going to die. So what? That would have happened anyway, eventually.

But this wasn't just about her anymore. Stump had two other girls he planned to kill tonight.

Maybe that was why she was still here.

She wasn't sure she believed in fate and destiny and all that.

The Girl in the Sand

A big wheel with your predestined life turning as you lived through your days. Screeching to a halt when your time came. But she was sure of one thing.

She had an edge now.

She was still alive, and Stump didn't know it.

He'd placed her in the bed of the truck until he was ready to dispose of her. She wondered if he'd planned to burn her first. To lock her in a trunk and light her up. A little gift for his old friend, Victor Loshak.

Whatever his intent had been, that wasn't important. What mattered now was getting the jump on him when he wasn't expecting it. It was the opportunity she'd been looking for when she'd still been chained to the chair. Of course, it would have been nice if the advantage wasn't being shot and wounded so badly you were mistaken for dead, but hey. Sometimes you had to take what you could get.

She half-smiled but was sure it came off as more of a grimace.

OK, then. She had to move. Now. She didn't know how long she'd have before Stump came back to finish the job, and she had to finish him while she was still breathing.

She squirmed free of the tarp, slithering like some primordial creature. She had no clue how she was going to do this, confront Stump like this, defeat him. But she would. There was no choice. Shaking, she dragged her bloodied body from the back of the truck.

She was a sorry-looking savior, she was sure of that. Hell, if she was being honest with herself, there was a pretty good chance that this plan would fail. That she would hobble into the house, and Stump would kill her. For keeps this time.

Strangely, the fatalism that had frozen her blood earlier

didn't bother her so much now.

She was half-dead anyway. What did she have to lose?

Leaning too heavily on her left side sent her stumbling forward. Reaching with her good arm, she steadied herself against the side of the truck, then caught a glimpse of herself in the side mirror. She looked like Carrie White, after her shower in pig's blood.

It wasn't just her one eye, but her whole face that was covered in it. In the night, the blood shone black on her skin. Like oil or the thick, black mud from the bottom of a lake. The blackness made the whites of her eyes glow with a manic intensity.

Her hair was matted to her head, damp ropes of clotting blood. She thought she could see a place where a flap of her scalp hung open, skull exposed, possibly fractured, and her hand reached for it. She stopped herself. Looked away. Nothing to be done now. No good would come from poking at it. Best to leave it.

She focused again on her eyes, huge and glittering in the mirror.

I look like death, she thought to herself.

No.

I am death.

She thought of Kali the destroyer, with her open mouth and lolling tongue. Eyes red with rage. Around her neck, a garland of men's heads. In one story, she took vengeance on a band of thieves by decapitating them and drinking their blood.

And yet despite appearances, Kali was not the embodiment of evil. She was considered the kindest of the Hindu goddesses. The mother of the universe. A great protector.

Very slowly, Darger let her tongue loll out of her mouth.

The Girl in the Sand

Death was coming for Leonard Stump. Maybe.

CHAPTER 61

A bang coaxes Emily to the surface of consciousness. A slammed door she thinks, though she isn't certain. The head box makes it almost impossible to tell.

She is alone again. In the quiet. In the dark.

After a while, she closes her eyes. Drifts a little. Sinks away from the surface. Not sleeping so much as floating out into those black seas which are thankfully placid for the moment.

There are other noises, but they're far away — scrapes, a slamming door, a distant thump. She no longer notices. Not all the way. She follows the momentum of the dream currents, lets them pull her further and further out to sea.

It's not until the lock rattles outside her box that she perks up.

The clicking clicks. The clacking clacks.

There's a sense of intense suction from her neck down, which she realizes must be the whooshing air of the outer lid opening.

The chill of the air swishes against her, little eddies of it snaking against her body, ringlets that writhe and flutter on her skin.

He's there. Above her. She swears she can feel his shadow creeping over her body.

Cold hands grip her by the shoulders, coax her into a seated position.

The wooden frame surrounding her skull is heavy, disorienting, awkward now that she's upright. It tilts her to its whim, tries its best to tip her over. She lurches forward and to

348

the left, bashing into the wall of the box. And when she lifts herself, she overcorrects, careening back to the right, but the box butts up against something solid there and the swaying stops.

It's him. She knows it is. The box leans up against him even now. She can feel the warmth pulsing off his body so close to hers.

Great pressure mashes at her shoulders. His forearms press the muscles along her neck, sharp arm bones biting at her flesh. His elbows twitch and fidget as he works at the contraption attached to her head, the effort nudging her skull this way and that, bending her neck around like she's a pliable doll.

At last, the head box snaps and peels open, those carpeted walls pulling apart, the black space about her head rushing outward like a universe expanding.

And shards of light spill into the black nothing. Strange shafts of illumination blossoming upward from the box's mouth. Another puddle of gray spreads over the carpet, over her face.

The box lifts at last, its weight releasing from her neck and spine. The carpeted walls slide upward out of frame.

A tingle prickles on her scalp. Slides lower to flush excitement into her cheeks, neck, and shoulders. The pangs of giddiness shoot up and down her arms and legs.

And it's too bright. Blinding. Everywhere. She closes her eyes, but the sting cuts right through her eyelids.

Cool air swirls around her cheeks and brow. Air that is alive. Fresh. Pleasant.

Her heart beats joy all through her, a wild vibration surging through her body.

He offers the bed pan again, placing it at her feet and

turning away. Her chains jangle as she moves to it. Uses it.

When she's done she trades the pan for another mason jar of water. Her fingers brushing his as the glass changes hands.

She drinks. That sweet water rushing down the drain at the back of her mouth. Spiraling into her. The moisture soothes her mouth yet again, wets all the dry places. Revitalizes them. It's the end of a long drought for her lips and throat.

He faces her now, though he doesn't look at her, shoulders angled slightly away. Likewise, she doesn't direct her gaze at him, not straight on. She watches him out of the corner of her eye.

He seems more distant than ever before. His cheeks sallow. His eyes vacant. Looking through everything around him. Piercing empty space.

There's something gaunt about him now. Morose. His complexion almost gray.

She expected him to be jubilant as he worked his way toward this climax, but if he is, there are no signs of it for the moment. Only those grave lines of his lips and brow.

At last their eyes meet, fastening to each other and holding on for a long moment. She thinks he won't say a word, not anything, but he does speak after a moment.

"It's almost over now. But you know that, don't you?"

She considers this. Nods.

He moves near again. Leans the top half of his body into the box. Begins to unlock her chains.

She sees the gun now. A piece of steel resting on the floor just next to him. So close, in a way. Just close enough to be maddening in its distance.

The chains go slack, her wrists finally free to fall to her sides, slack entirely.

The Girl in the Sand

His torso retracts from the box. He gathers the gun and stands. He points it at her, ticking the barrel up as he speaks.

"Up."

She hesitates for a moment, then obeys.

Her legs wobble under her on the way up, but he holds out a hand to help her step out of the box.

She plants one foot on the lip and hops down on the other side. Her knees buckle and then catch, taking a moment to right her as though she's spent the last month on a boat and finds the stillness of walking on dry land foreign.

She can't ignore it. Her legs are mostly dead. A little cramped from being cooped up in the box, sure, but exhausted beyond that. Drained. Not a good setup in a situation where fight or flight are the only ways to survive.

He gestures with the gun, a rotation of the wrist that indicates he wants her to step in front of him, facing the doorway.

Now he presses the gun into the small of her back, the cold of the metal bleeding through her t-shirt to chill her flesh. Goose bumps ripple out from that spot, crawl over most of her back, swelling to a peak and then slowly releasing.

The gun pushes harder, the muzzle jabbing the muscles along her spine. It urges her forward, and she obeys, glides across the room.

The frame of the doorway swallows her, oversees her transition into the hallway.

And his footsteps sound uneven behind her. Little shuffles and half steps that emit an offbeat pitter-patter, struggling to match the rhythm and length of her shorter stride.

The hall stretches out before her. Long and narrow. At the far end, she sees the carpet give way to that tile floor of the foyer where they fought. Earlier? Yesterday? She's not sure how long she was locked in the boxes.

Bars of the first morning light slant through the window to reflect off the tiles. Elongated shafts of glare that change shape if she squints and releases her eyelids.

And she remembers the tactile impressions of her near escape, can still feel the cool of the tile on her bare feet, the smooth metal of the doorknob twisting in her fingers, that sense of release when the door popped out of the jamb, peeled a quarter of the way open at her touch.

The outside world had been right there, inches away, ready to take her away.

But then he'd tackled her. Throttled her. Wrestled her to the ground and confined her. Locked her away. Strapped a box on her head.

She licks her lips. Considers the notion of running, sprinting toward that point of exit, but no. She's too weak now, too worn down to beat him in a footrace.

If she has any hope of surviving this, she'll need to find another way. She'll need to wait and watch. To pounce only when the time is just right.

Still, she scans that tile floor, hoping for no good reason that she might find her piece of metal there — the desk leg turned melee weapon that she'd lost in the scuffle. Her eyes dance back and forth and find nothing more than the ceramic grid seamed with grout lines, but just as she's about to give up, she spots it.

The little flat foot of the thing sticks out from under the closet door, though most of it is tucked into the shadows. Hidden. Forgotten.

Her lips curl at the sight of it, not quite reaching an actual smile but something close. Funny. It does her no good, but she's somehow glad it's still there, somehow glad to see it.

"Turn left here," Stump says, prodding the gun in her back twice for emphasis.

His voice shakes her up, rips her away from that daydream space at the end of the hall.

She blinks. Turns to face the open doorway coming up on the left.

It's the bathroom.

From her angle, she sees the lights glowing over the vanity, a little wedge of the seafoam wall, glossy paint. Most of the room remains blocked from her view.

But she knows what waits beyond.

When she reaches the doorway, she finds what she expected.

A girl waits inside, eyes wide like a frightened animal's, eyelids fluttering in fast motion. She is positioned on hands and knees in the clawfooted bathtub, handcuffs adorning her wrists and chains fastening her ankles.

This is her. This is the other girl.

Emily's heart accelerates.

She studies the girl. Locks eyes with her.

Black eyeshadow smears down from her eyelids. Dark trails that roll over her cheekbones and cascade down to the jaw, showing where the tears must have trailed.

Emily freezes. Stops in the doorway.

She can't help but think it: The room seems pleasant enough — the antique vanity with the ornate woodwork and black marble countertop, the linoleum floor that looks like black and white tile, the aforementioned seafoam walls and clawfoot tub.

Stump jabs the gun into her spine again, and she steps onto the linoleum.

She doesn't look back, but she can hear the excitement in his voice — that enthusiasm she'd anticipated arriving at last. He whispers from just behind her right ear.

"It's what I said, isn't it? It's just how I told you it would be."

CHAPTER 62

Her left leg dragged a little as she shuffled along the side of the truck. Clumsy, but functional. Her left arm on the other hand… it dangled like a limp noodle at her side. Idle and useless. Not so much as a finger twitch on that dumb hand. For a moment she wondered if it might be permanent, but then remembered it didn't matter. *She* wasn't permanent.

OK. A plan.

Think.

She peered under the tarp for something to use as a weapon. The heaviest item in the back was a shovel. Darger considered her good-for-nothing left arm and decided the shovel was too long and too heavy for one-handed swinging. She wished for a pickaxe, or even a regular axe, but no such tool was found in the bed of the truck.

She slid around to the cab and climbed inside.

On a hunch, Darger flipped open the sun visor, and out spilled the keys.

Well, well. What an arrogant bastard.

There was a temptation to take the truck now, make a run for help, but she knew that if she left, the girls would die. For all she knew, they were already dead. But she'd be damned if she abandoned them to Stump now.

No. She needed to go after him.

She wondered… if Stump was ballsy enough to leave the keys in the truck, might he also leave a weapon of some sort?

The glove box popped open with a thunk. Inside, she found a pair of sunglasses, napkins from a fast food joint, a small flashlight, and a screwdriver. No gun.

Damn.

She removed the screwdriver, gripped it with her fingers.

Not exactly the kind of firepower she'd been imagining, but it was the most promising thing she'd found yet.

As she lowered herself back to the ground, finished with the search, her gaze fell on the cigarette lighter. Too bad she couldn't use that somehow, couldn't burn him like he did the bodies.

Something fluttered in the back of her mind. An idea she couldn't wrangle. Her mind felt goopy. Slow and thick.

It struck her that her normal cognitive processes were all fucked up.

Darger could almost hear Loshak's response to that epiphany. *You mean a bullet to the head does brain damage? Imagine that.*

But Stump had left her will intact, so she pressed on. Her body was damaged, perhaps beyond repair, but he couldn't touch what was inside.

OK, Darger. What about the cigarette lighter?

Surely she didn't think that was an appropriate weapon?

The answer came then in a slow drip, like the words were made of thick syrup.

Not a weapon…

A contingency plan.

She left the truck, dragged herself down the drive a ways, and then moved off toward the wild brush.

Darger stared at the cluster of trees and bushes, trying to decide which one held the prize. The sky to the east was just beginning to lighten, but the tall pines surrounding the yard kept everything in shadow for now.

The Girl in the Sand

Was it one of the low creeping junipers or the taller pinyons?

She couldn't remember.

She should have taken more care in hiding Nicole's purse. She'd never find it now.

Darger limped to the first clump of greenery and kicked out her right foot, feeling for it in the darkness under the branches.

Nothing.

She moved onto the next and came up empty again.

But beneath the feathery foliage of one of the trees, her toe connected with something oblong and not altogether organic.

She had to take care as she stooped to pick up the handbag. It threw off her center of balance, which was already shaky at best.

But that didn't matter. She'd found it. She could go ahead with her plan.

She almost smiled again and imagined what a horror she must look with the blood drying on her face. She could feel the drips and smears starting to crust over.

Darger unzipped the bag, checked that the lighter was still inside, and started back to the truck.

It was only a hundred yards to the shed, but the gas can was heavy, and she struggled with the weight of it. If she could just take a break to set her load down and rest her aching forearm. The muscles felt on the verge of cramping, but she didn't have time to stop.

When she finally reached the shed, she practically dropped the can to the ground. Luckily the grass behind the house was longer and muffled the metallic clang. Darger shook her arm out, rotating the elbow joint in an effort to loosen the muscles.

The door of the shed still stood open a crack, from when

she'd peeked inside before. Had there been anything useful? She hadn't really been looking since she had the stun gun. Maybe she'd find that pickaxe she'd been hankering for.

She pushed inside and squinted at the now familiar but disappointing array of standard lawn equipment. Leaned against one wall was another shovel, a garden hoe, and a long pole with a hooked saw on the end that she was pretty sure was for trimming tree limbs. Again, too cumbersome for her on this night.

Abandoning the shed, she got back to the real reason she'd hauled her ass back here. She took a minute to consider the best way to do the job.

When she'd first remembered the cigarettes, her idea had been to use one or two as an almost timed fuse — time for her slow ass to get away before the big *whoomp*. But somewhere on her long, slow trek to the shed, she had a moment of clarity in which she recalled learning that the cherry of a cigarette will not ignite gasoline. She was frustrated now. It had seemed like such a good plan.

She frowned down at the jerry can. Glanced back at the house.

When the solution finally hit her, it was so simple she almost let out a groan.

She reached for the gas. It was show time.

Darger swung the can, dousing the side of the shed, letting gas spatter onto the woodpile below. The liquid sloshed and splashed, and it wasn't until then that Darger realized her right ear was ringing. She couldn't hear anything out of her left ear. Another heartening sign.

All about her, the fumes hung in a noxious vapor, causing the skin on her arms to prickle, like her body knew she was standing in a toxic cloud. She tried to angle her face away as she poured, not wanting to inhale the fumes. But the stench surrounded her, invaded her nostrils and her mouth and throat. Tears collected along her eyelashes and eventually she gagged on the caustic smell.

She stumbled away in search of a few breaths of fresh air. It took several seconds for the sick, dizzy feeling to pass, and then she stepped back into the haze, resuming her efforts. When there was roughly a gallon left in the can, she stopped. Gas dripped down the siding and pattered off the edges of the stacked wood, forming dark pools in the sand.

Darger shook the can and listened to the remainder of the gas slop around inside. She hoped she'd left enough. She was almost finished.

Slowly, starting at the end of the woodpile, she dribbled a trail of gas through the yard, following along the side of the house, making her way to the front door.

When she reached the driveway, she let the last dregs of the gas pour out into a puddle. She set the can down, careful this time to be quiet about it. And then she pulled the lighter from her pocket.

She held her thumb over the flint wheel, nervous to make the first spark. She hoped she hadn't gotten any gas on herself.

She tried to trace the trail she'd made in the grass with her eyes, but it was too dim still. She'd just have to light it and pray it worked. Pray the fire would create enough smoke for someone to see. She remembered Corby talking about the dry desert air. About how clear it is, and how you can see the smoke for miles.

Someone would come. Even if she failed again. Eventually someone would come.

And now it was time.

Darger flicked the lighter and a flame sprang to life. She dipped down and touched it to the wet circle in the sand. It burst into flame with a small *whoosh*.

It was tempting to stand there and watch, to follow the flickering trail as it wound around the house to the shed, but she didn't have time.

As quickly as her broken body could manage, she hobbled up to the front door.

CHAPTER 63

Stump approaches the girl in the bathtub and stops. A muscular thing towering over her.

He bends. Unlocks her cuffs. Grunts something Emily can't quite make out.

The girl scoots into the back corner of the tub and massages her wrists, fingers squeezing at the pink creases where her cuffs had been. Her eyelids flutter again. Smeared black eyelashes flapping like spastic butterfly wings.

Emily checks the towel rack she is now handcuffed to. Watches the nearest screw plate wiggle a little when she gives it a yank, the painted wall around it bulging like a flexed muscle.

She's pretty sure she could rip the whole thing free from the wall if and when the need arrived. Of course, he said he'd put a bullet in her brain without hesitation if she tried anything. She's in no particular hurry to test him.

Now he kneels at the side of the tub. Reaches for a coil of rope at his feet. Lifts it.

His voice comes out a growl.

"Put your hands together."

She doesn't seem to hear him. Staring at the floor. Shoulders hunched. Not quite present in the moment.

"Nicole. Put your hands together."

Nicole. He called her Nicole.

Those black butterflies flutter again, and she listens.

He clutches at Nicole's clasped hands, yanks them out away from her body, and Emily sees fresh hostility in his movements. Hateful aggression. A little glint of glee that reminds her of their first encounter, those vicious punches to the back of the skull that filled her head with that *thock* sound, knocked her out.

He begins winding the rope around Nicole's wrists. Works the line with care, wrapping it neatly. But periodically he interrupts this to give her arms another yank, to jerk her into a new pose at his whim. His big body arching over her.

Emily focuses on that spiraling cord.

White nylon rope. She remembers watching a mountain climber sing its praises on TV. Strong. Durable. Resistant to UV damage and rot. More tightly woven than manila. Better for heavy duty use than polyester.

Rope. Rope? Why was she getting stuck on the rope?

He leans back to tighten the coil at Nicole's wrists. He strains with the effort, the thick musculature at the top of his back quivering a bit.

The girl squeals as the cord cinches tighter, sounding more frightened than pained. And Emily swears she sees his body quake in ecstasy, an almost orgasmic gesture.

Pleasure.

Rope.

Yes. Now she gets it.

He had taken great care in binding them along the way, hadn't he? He'd changed the method over and over. Zip ties. Cuffs. Chains. The boxes. Now rope.

He enjoys this part of it. Enjoys constricting their limbs. Obsesses over it. Like a fetish.

Even now he fusses over the rope, fingers working delicately, meticulously. Removing the slack. Tying the knot. He gives her arms another violent tug before reaching for a second rope on the floor.

"Ankles together."

The Girl in the Sand

Nicole slides her ankles together, and he starts another coil.

He already has her at his mercy, but he can't fully enjoy it unless he revels in the control, unless he makes a little show out of it.

Emily can't resist the urge to speak up.

"You enjoy this."

That hypnotic coiling of the rope halts. Frozen mid-wrap.

His shoulders rise a little, drifting up so slowly she almost misses it. Surprised? Irritated? She's not sure how to read his reaction.

"What?" he says, half-glancing back.

"The ropes. The chains. The box. You talk all this philosophy, but I don't see a philosopher in you. I see a lonely pervert with delusions of grandeur."

He's quiet for a beat.

She holds her breath.

Finally, he laughs. Little sniffles exiting his nostrils, an almost silent chuckle.

"Of course I enjoy it. Why else do it?"

He pivots now, letting the rope go to face her. His smile is a savage slit peeling open his face. Intense. His teeth all sharp and gleaming.

He goes on.

"Cruelty is the source of much human joy, isn't it? The purest expression of power, and, as such, the purest expression of pleasure. Even children love watching cartoon violence. Home videos of people getting kicked in the balls."

He stares straight through her. Pale eyes that pierce her.

She wants to look away, but she can't. Can't give him the satisfaction of letting him stare her down. So she watches his face, those eyes somehow glittering with both hatred and joy.

And more words come spilling out of him.

"Dominating. Degrading. That's part of the appeal. Anyway, enjoying one's work hardly diminishes its meaning. If anything, the truth is closer to the opposite, I'd say."

Emily grits her teeth, but she keeps the fury from registering on her face, or so she thinks. She focuses. Fights to keep her face blank. Emotionless. Perhaps vaguely assertive but nothing beyond that.

"Keep telling yourself that," she says, her voice sounding detached.

His eyes flick over her again. Measuring her response. Weighing it.

After a moment, he turns back to Nicole. His hands plunge for the rope, find it, return to winding it around her calves again.

At least she'd slowed him down. Distracted him. Got in his head a little bit.

She'd bought them some time. Just a little.

She didn't know if that was worth anything now, but she didn't know what else to do.

CHAPTER 64

Darger pecked at the front door with her good hand. Ran her fingers along the surface.

Her hand found the knob. Twisted. Pushed.

She held her breath, focused on keeping her movements light. Quiet. Careful.

It slid inward without sound, parted from her path.

She hesitated there, perhaps scared of the deeper shade inside, but the fear only held her still for a second. She didn't have time to waste.

She crossed the threshold. Moved inside, into that final darkness. Waited a beat for her eyes to adjust, for her pupils to catch up.

Her fingers dug at her pocket, found the screwdriver there, armed herself. It wasn't much of a weapon, certainly wasn't ideal, but it was better than nothing.

As shapes and textures began to take form in the blackness around her, she shuffled forward, taking little half-steps. Gliding on the balls of her feet.

Light spilled out of an open doorway down the hall.

And now voices tumbled out of that opening. Strained speech. A woman and a man. Arguing, she thought, but she couldn't make out the words.

She recognized Stump's growl, but the girl didn't sound like Nicole. It must be the other. Must be Emily.

And by the tinny echo of the voices, they were in the bathroom. This was it. It was happening now.

She tightened her fist around the screwdriver's handle, and

breath heaved into her chest. She was ready.

But something caught in the corner of her eye, the tiniest glitter of light along the floor to her right.

She turned. Saw the foyer closet door there. She scanned the seam of darkness running under the sliding door, but whatever the glimmer had been, it didn't reveal itself now.

Still, she knelt. Hating herself for taking the two seconds to do so. Ran her fingers along the gap, even if she didn't know why.

A sharp edge pricked at her knuckles. Cold metal.

It scraped out a little whisper on the tile as she pulled it free.

Even lifting the thing in front of her, it took her a second to sort out what it was, this long, tapered cylinder of polished steel. A leg from one of the school desks. She remembered the scuffle she'd witnessed before. Emily's escape attempt. This must have been her makeshift weapon, the piece that helped her get all the way to the door before Stump pulled her back, locked her up.

And now it was along to finish its job.

Upgrade time.

Darger tucked the screwdriver into her sock and stood, testing the weight of the bar in her hand. It was light enough to swing one-handed. Could do some damage, too, if she got lucky.

Down the hall she crept, that glowing rectangle of the bathroom doorway growing bigger and brighter as she closed on it.

The voices had fallen quiet, and she knew time was almost up now. Stump's ritual was about to begin.

And something changed in her over those last few steps.

Animal heat flooded her face. Puffed her chest and shoulders. Whittled her thoughts down to pointy, hateful things. All sharp and simple and frenzied.

The Girl in the Sand

Kill you. Kill you. Fucking kill you.

She saw Stump's face in her head even before she rounded the final corner. It made her grit her teeth.

Kill you. Kill you. Fucking kill you.

And she was there. Turning. Gazing through the threshold and into the kill room.

Stump towered over Nicole in the bathtub, white rope wound around the girl's wrists and ankles. He adjusted his footing, knife poised in his hand.

Emily huddled against one wall, positioned to view the carnage, cuffed to a towel rod.

Stump's forearm twitched, and the blade jerked forward, its metal glinting.

He bent over Nicole then. Brought the knife to her neck. Pressed its edge against the jugular there.

Her flesh quivered. Pulsated with the beat of her blood.

And he turned, and his eyes sought those of his audience, of Emily. Tongue flicking out over his lips and teeth.

Darger lurched into the room, planting and lunging off her good leg. The metal rod rose over her head, all of her body going into the strike.

Stump tried to scramble away, but there was no place to go.

The screw plate bashed him on a downward stroke. Sliced him open right at the hairline. The red sluiced out right away.

Even with one arm, Darger felt incredible force unload. All of it driven into his skull.

He tipped forward, and she cracked him again, this time on the back of his head. The recoil reverberated up the length of the metal rod and yanked at Darger's shoulder, jolted her pretty good, but she held on and swung again. Not as big of a windup this time, but not bad.

The little square screw panel raked over the cupped occipital bone and gashed his scalp. Blood wept down the back of his head, a sheet of red that slid down his neck, soaked the collar of his shirt.

Stump toppled into the tub, past Nicole, smearing red on the smooth enamel surface. The knife tumbled from his grip, clattered near the drain.

Nicole screamed. Emily fumbled at the cuffs chaining her to the towel rod. They needed to run. To take the truck and go now. Darger wanted to tell them this, but her mind was a red pulsing thing incapable of words.

Stump tried to lift himself, push himself up onto arms and legs, but he wobbled and crashed back down.

Nicole wriggled over the lip of the tub, sobbing, finally finding the will to move. She squirmed over the floor as the struggle continued, still bound by the rope, working her way toward the door.

Darger circled around the girl and went to swing again, but her bad knee buckled, and she missed.

The effort spun her off her axis, twisted her around and sent her stumbling into the wall. She steadied herself against it, but Stump had recovered from the blows.

He stood, reached an arm behind himself, and she realized what he was doing even before she saw it.

The gun.

She'd almost forgotten the gun.

He plucked it from his waist at the small of his back, raised and leveled it, and her mind flashed to the last time he'd done so. Boom. Lights out.

Darger dove at him.

The gun bucked, the crack deafening. Her eyes cinched

closed out of instinct.

She felt it — the shock wave passed just over her head like a puff of wind. Inches.

And their bodies collided.

She struck him chin first, her arm wrapping around him a fraction of a second after.

Momentum flung them into the wall, and she felt the desk leg fly from her fingers on impact. Together they landed in a tangle of limbs at the bottom of the bathtub.

The gun. She had to get the gun.

She opened her eyes.

Stump's hands were empty, he'd lost it. Darger threw herself onto her belly, fumbling her hand along the porcelain surface. Trying to feel what wasn't there. The gun was gone.

But the knife still lay there, resting on the drain.

She lunged for it, but Stump's hand snaked out ahead of her, grabbing it.

Panic.

She jerked away, legs kicking out a doggy paddle without thought. Flopped out of the bathtub and onto the floor, squirming. Not quite able to concentrate long enough to sit up, to get up. A turtle trapped on its back.

And he was there. Hovering over her.

Light danced along the edge of the knife as it sliced through the air, a horizontal slash meant to open Darger's belly. She rolled to dodge the blade.

And she was up. On her feet.

When he came at her again, she caught his arm with her good hand, gripping it and slamming it down on the sink. His fist unclenched, an involuntary movement of the muscles.

The knife slipped from his hand and disappeared under the

sink.

Darger couldn't see the knife, but she went for it anyway, dropping to her belly, scooting closer to the wedge of shadow beneath the sink cabinet. The gleam of hard steel caught her eye.

The tips of her fingers brushed against the handle, and then something snaked around her neck, yanked her back before she retrieved the weapon.

Stump dragged her upright and arched his back, lifting her off her feet in a headlock. His forearm cut into her larynx. She wheezed once as he pinched off her oxygen supply.

And now she was off the ground. Powerless. The bony edge of his arm cutting deeper and deeper into her throat.

Darger tucked her knees to her chest and kicked off from the bathroom counter, driving Stump back into the wall. She heard the air rush out of his lungs. His grip loosened, and she wriggled free, hammering her right elbow into his ribs for good measure.

He grunted.

She wheeled and went for another blow, swung her right fist at his temple, but he caught her arm and flung her away from him.

She careened across the bathroom, a small, limp thing, slamming into a mirror, sliding to the floor, glass tinkling around her.

Darger crouched on all fours, trying to catch her breath. Her vision ebbed, growing hazy then clearing. Shards from the mirror crunched under her knees.

Movement caught her eye. Emily was huddled just outside the bathroom door, arms wrapped around her knees like a frightened child. Why? Why didn't she run?

Clutching the windowsill, Darger rose to her feet. Stump

had the desk leg now, and he advanced on her.

Darger's eyes swung down to the floor, searching for the gun. Where the fuck was it?

He raised the leg over his head like a club, and Darger could only lift her arm and turn her head to try to steel herself against the blow.

And then Nicole was there, the ropes gone from her limbs. She ducked low and drove her shoulders into Stump's legs. He wobbled but did not fall, adjusting his swing at the last moment, bringing the table leg down across Nicole's back.

She collapsed, cracking her chin against the edge of the bathtub, crying out in pain. Stump grabbed her by the hair and heaved her against the wall. Her head hit the tile with a dull thud, and Nicole's body folded up on itself like a dead spider.

Howling as she attacked, Darger kicked out at the back of Stump's knee. His hands whispered against the shower curtain in an effort to stop his fall. *Pop! Pop! Pop!* The rings ripped away from the curtain rod.

At the last moment, he spun away from the tub, using his momentum to take Darger down with him. The curtain twisted around both of them, a slippery film that made the struggle even more awkward.

Darger aimed her knees and elbows for his balls, her fingernails for his eyes, but he was wily and strong and bucked away from her each time.

His hand shot out, reaching for something behind her. The gun? The desk leg? With one vicious tug, he yanked the vinyl shower curtain over her head, looped it all the way around. Layers of white plastic blotted out her vision. She scratched and flailed, but she couldn't see.

His arms were clumsy but strong, pinning her thrashing

limbs to her chest, turning her so she was face down. Posed like an unwilling doll. The weight of his big body crushing her small one.

And then she felt the plastic sheeting cinch tight around her head, around her neck. He was suffocating her.

Darger clawed at the thick vinyl, but her fingernails couldn't break through.

She bucked and writhed, but he was too strong. Too strong. Holding her down. Grinding against her to maintain his grip, to quell her movements.

Confusion. Swirling feelings in the dark. Trapped. Out of control. Lost.

Everything hot and wet from the humidity of her own breath. Her final breaths.

The incredible pressure of the vinyl pressed into her face and throat, taking her life.

His body was taut, muscles rigid and straining. And then all at once they loosened. Went slack. His weight shifted off her back.

Darger ripped the curtain away from her face. The cool air rushing to fill her lungs in quick, greedy breaths.

Pink and purple splotches clouded her vision as she peered over her shoulder. Stump's eyes were wide. Shocked. He gasped a little, and a strand of saliva flew out of his mouth and dribbled down his lip. It was red.

She rolled away from him, and he oozed onto the tile, not seeming altogether solid. A blob of flesh and bone.

And Emily now filled the frame of Darger's vision. Standing over both of them. A bloody knife in her hand.

The girl's face was expressionless. Dead-eyed.

She held still, and the room went so quiet. So empty after all that fighting and crashing about.

Stump sprawled face up. His chest still moved, still went up and down with each breath. But his teeth and lips were stained red with blood.

And Emily moved at last. Squatted over him. Her knees sliding up over his shoulders to straddle him at the neck. Knife poised.

The blade disappeared into an eye socket, pierced the bridge of his nose, carved red gouges into his cheeks and lips and chin.

Her face remained blank as she worked the knife up and down. Stabbed him in the face again and again.

It sounded wet. Her fist slapping at his open wound of a face as she drove the knife in to the hilt.

Each outward thrust flung flecks of blood everywhere, spattered it all around the bathroom like an abstract painting rendered only in red.

Darger could only watch this unfold. Somehow frozen. Her lips parted in shock. Her mind not quite able to process it.

Stump's chest trembled and a pink bubble of bloody spittle formed over his mouth. Popped.

The girl still straddled him at the neck, but her knife lay still, hanging lifeless at the end of her arm.

She stared into Stump's ruined face, a strange look on her own. Curious, Darger thought. She looked curious.

"Well?" Emily whispered, talking to the barely living body between her legs. "Anything?"

And Darger couldn't breathe. Couldn't blink. Couldn't look away.

"Yeah. I didn't think so," Emily said.

The girl's chest heaved in and out, her eyes still locked on the ruined face, on the blood trickling out of it everywhere.

Nicole pulled Emily off then, scooping her under the armpits, hugging and lifting.

"Come on," she said in a small voice. "It's done."

Darger closed her eyes for a little while. And everything went quiet.

She and Stump lay bleeding together. Dying together.

A tiny mewl came out of Leonard Stump at the end. A feminine sound. Almost feline.

And then, at last, he was still.

CHAPTER 65

By the time Loshak arrived at the scene, the sun was up, casting its piercing yellow brilliance over everything. He tried to block the harshness out with a pair of sunglasses and a baseball cap pulled down low on his brow, but they offered little help.

The driveway was unmarked, an unpaved gash in the landscape. No mailbox. No house number. On most days he would have driven past without noticing it at all. But today the narrow lane was choked with vehicles. Law enforcement. Media people. Even pedestrians out to gawk, filming it all on their phones.

News vans sat at the bottom of the hill, antennas protruding from their roofs. A mess of cameramen pointed their lenses at reporters wearing channel specific windbreakers, all gesturing to the area beyond the police tape.

Further up he found police cruisers and a few unmarked units he knew to belong to detectives and local Feds. Quite a turnout. And understandably so. Everyone wanted a piece with a case this big, wanted to experience it, to celebrate it, to see it up close with their own two eyes.

He pulled past the media and parked the rental off to one side of the drive, keeping his head down until he got out of sight of the cameras, thankful he'd worn the cap and Ray-Bans.

Loshak flashed his badge before ducking under the police tape, getting a nod from the officer guarding the perimeter. He walked the driveway, mounting the slope.

The blackened husk of a shed seemed to rise from the ground as he crested the hill. Steam still fluttered out of the structure, evidence that the fire department had doused it.

It was the smoke that led them here — that black coil snaking into the sky. The full magnitude of the scene had only come clear when the girls approached the firefighters, frantic and covered in blood.

The house itself looked normal enough in the daylight, Loshak thought. Nice, even. He wondered if it had seemed more sinister the night before. He tried to picture it — Darger storming the place in the dark without her gun. The violent pictures that came made him uneasy, a little nauseous, so he let it go.

Investigators swarmed the property. Latex-gloved crime scene techs snapped photos, logged and bagged various pieces of evidence. Three detectives huddled just outside the front door, discussing, heads bobbing, arms and fingers pointing to parts of the house, parts of the property.

The atmosphere was entirely different from the earlier scenes — the burned cars in the desert, the mass grave. Back when the killer was still at large, the tension vibrated in the air, kept everyone on edge. But nobody had to worry about that this time around, and he could read it in the body language, in the tones of the chatter. The scene maintained a certain level of professionalism — the stoic disposition of people doing detail-oriented work — but there was a jubilation to be felt here. Subtle but present.

Loshak slipped past the detectives without drawing their notice, and once again he was thankful. He didn't care to partake in the small talk today. Not with all that had happened. He wanted — needed — to see it for himself, and then he could get out of here. Be done with it.

He passed through the doorway, entered the shade of the

house. He thought about taking the sunglasses off, but a pang of anxiety told him not to, told him to stay covered up, and he obeyed.

Potting soil crunched underfoot in the foyer, an upturned fern explaining the mess. Loshak pictured Emily fighting Stump here, swinging a blunt object into his jaw, grappling with him in this dirt. Again a queasiness welled in him. He swallowed and moved on.

The hallway stretched out. Led the way to the bathroom.

And he was there. Standing in the doorway. Looking in on where it all happened.

The room was empty. Quiet. A reverent feel occupied this space, a stillness totally at odds with all those swarming busybodies outside.

Light spilled in through a single window, clouded by the frosted glass. And Loshak's gaze danced over all the surfaces here, filling in some of the missing pieces that had already been collected as evidence.

Jagged shards of mirror on the floor, a few still clinging to the frame, cracks running all through the glass like veins.

The shower curtain ripped away from the rod, exposing the seafoam tiles that lined the tub.

Gummy blood pooled on the linoleum. Red puddles and smears slowly congealing as time passed, growing thick and opaque, almost cloudy.

He squatted. Looked under the clawfoot tub. The gap was empty now — a piece of linoleum tucked in the shade. That was where they'd found the gun. It had skittered between the wall and the tub during the skirmish, out of reach. If that hadn't happened…

Loshak stood. Pursed his lips. Hesitated for a moment.

He walked back down the hall, crunched through the foyer, and exited through the open doorway. He'd seen quite enough.

☾

When Loshak stepped into Darger's hospital room, he found her nestled in a mess of small white blankets. Various monitors blinked and fidgeted over her left shoulder, keeping track of her vitals, and bandages swaddled her head, gauze wound all the way around so she looked like a mummy from the eyebrows up.

She didn't see him come in, flexing and unflexing her left hand on the bed before her, totally focused on that routine movement.

"Knock knock," Loshak said.

Her head turned to him, at last, and a medicated look occupied her gaze. Spacey. Far away. But awake, nonetheless. As alert as could be hoped for someone doped to the gills on opioids.

"Who's there?" Darger said, mustering a trace of a smile.

He puffed a courtesy chuckle from his nostrils.

Darger's face morphed then, her eyes going huge like something in a cartoon.

"Are the girls OK?" she said, dropping her voice to a lower register.

He hesitated for a moment, caught a little off guard by not only her question but her demeanor.

"Yeah, yeah. Everyone's fine."

Her face softened some, eyes squinting at him. She was sizing him up, he could tell. Trying to see if he was telling the truth.

"They're fine, Violet. Fine as someone could be after something like that. I met both of their kids this morning, when we got everyone reunited."

The squinting intensified for a beat and then let up.

"OK," she said. "Good."

"I talked to one of them — Emily — for a little bit when the LVMPD was going over stuff with them. She was nice and everything. Smart, but... I don't know. I got the feeling there was something more she wanted to tell me, something that trickled to the tip of her tongue, and then she backed off. I don't know. Maybe it wasn't the right time."

Darger had zoned out. Looking at her flexing hand again. Loshak figured that was the strong meds at work.

He watched for a moment, her fingers folding into her palm and unfolding. Again his eyes moved to the tiny white blankets piled about her shoulders.

"Can I ask you something?" he said.

She turned to him, nodded like a toddler.

"What's with the blankets?"

"Hm?"

"Why so small?"

"I don't know. That's what they gave me. The nurse kept saying I looked cold and wrapping another one around my shoulders. I was shivering, maybe."

"Weird. Must be some new hospital thing. Little blankets."

"I guess."

"I mean, what the hell was wrong with full-sized blankets?"

"I'm fine, by the way. Just to get it out of the way so you can continue with your blanket rant. The surgery was a success and everything. I mean, apart from the traumatic head wound, I'm fine."

Loshak laughed.

"Your sense of humor appears to be intact. I'll give you that," he said. He blinked a few times before he went on. "I talked to the doc. He said you were lucky. Said only about 10% of people who take head shots survive, but everything went just right for you. I guess I don't know what else to say. I could give a speech about how you can't keep putting yourself in danger like this, but it wouldn't do any good, would it?"

Darger's smile was a beat late — must be the pain pills, he figured. She shook her head.

"Uh-huh," he said. "I guess if a bullet to the skull can't get through to that brain of yours, mere words have no hope at all."

Now she was the one providing the courtesy laugh.

"I just went," Loshak said. "Checked out the crime scene. I wanted to see it, you know?"

"Nice place, right?"

"Yeah. Bathroom was a little bloody for my taste, but yeah. It was nice enough."

He took off his jacket before he went on.

"Look, I'm sure you've gone over the details enough times for one lifetime, but I have one question. You were shot earlier on, right? That's primarily Stump's blood all over the linoleum in the bathroom?"

She nodded.

"Most of it, anyway."

Loshak sucked his teeth.

"I assume they told you that Stump is alive."

Her head bobbed almost imperceptibly.

"Yeah. I made Corby swear they'd keep him double-cuffed to the bed for the duration of his hospital stay. In addition to the armed deputies standing guard outside of his room."

The Girl in the Sand

"Eighteen stab wounds." He shook his head. "I guess some of your luck must have rubbed off on the piece of shit."

Darger looked at him for a moment, blinking. She looked far away. Somewhere else in her head. Maybe it was the drugs, but he thought she was remembering something, reliving something. And then the corners of her mouth curled upward.

"He lost an eye, though."

EPILOGUE

Darger slept most of the first few days in the hospital, groggy from the drugs and her wounds. During visiting hours, Loshak rarely left her bedside. She'd turn her head, half-awake, to find him perusing the newspaper, reading glasses perched on the tip of his nose.

A nurse woke her at eight for her morning cocktail of meds. Some she swallowed, others were pumped directly into her veins. Next came the nursing assistant, who emptied Darger's catheter and helped her with a sponge bath.

"When can I take a real shower?" Darger asked, hating the way her skin felt sticky and clammy even after scrubbing vigorously with the washcloth.

"Doctor doesn't want you out of bed, yet. It'll be a few days more, at least."

"Delightful."

After she left, Darger reached for the little packet of toiletries on the bedside table. Lotion, lip balm, a disposable razor, and a small mirror. She tore the plastic wrapper free from the mirror and held it up to her face.

The hand clutching the mirror started to shake. She'd never thought herself all that vain, but with the combination of shaved head, swelling, and bruising, she looked like a potato. A fuzzy, half-rotten potato.

A breathy sob escaped from her mouth, and she tossed the mirror in the trash can next to her bed. The doctors had warned her she may never walk without a cane, may never regain full use of her left arm and hand, but here she was crying because she was ugly.

Reaching for a tissue, she dabbed the tears from her eyes and blew her nose.

Someone knocked at the door. Darger's eyes went to the clock on the bedside table, figuring this was usually the time Loshak showed up. The door opened, revealing a familiar face, but it wasn't Loshak.

"You're awake," Owen said, smiling. "They said you're still in and out."

He came around the side of the bed to kiss her, and to his credit, Darger didn't see a flicker of disgust cross his face at the sight of her misshapen head. But she was sure it was there. Owen had always had a good poker face.

She shouldn't think that way, she knew. Not when he was only trying to comfort her.

"Bullet to the head," he said. "Way I figure it, you finally got yourself a little street cred."

"Yeah, my album drops next month. It's going to be huge."

She tried to focus on the joke, to forget what she'd seen in the mirror, but it was a struggle.

He studied her face, got a glimpse of what she was thinking perhaps, and frowned.

"What's wrong?"

Darger turned her head. Fiddled with the tape on her IV tubing.

"Nothing."

"Horse shit. Come on, Violet. Tell me."

Without looking over at him, she muttered, "You don't have to do this."

"Do what?"

"Stay. I know this isn't what you signed up for."

Owen leaned back in his chair, crossing his arms.

"What are you going on about?"

"Oh come on, Owen. I look like fucking Quasimodo."

"And?"

"Well first of all, you're supposed to tell me it's not that bad."

He cocked his head to one side.

"So which is it? I'm supposed to sugarcoat it for you, or I'm supposed to be so shallow that I scream at the sight of you and run for the hills?"

Darger picked at a nubby spot on one of the flannel blankets.

"Technically, you could do both."

Owen let out a dismissive scoff and wrapped one hand around her wrist.

"You got shot in the head. Of course you look like hell. I don't think I looked so fresh after my liver transplant. The swelling will go down. Your hair will grow back."

He shrugged.

"And if it doesn't… well, then I'm definitely out."

Darger clamped her lips shut but couldn't keep the smile off her face. Owen grinned back at her. She let him entwine his fingers in hers.

"You didn't think I'd scare away that easy, did you?"

Tears prickled at the corners of Darger's eyes. She wiped them away, her throat feeling thick.

"Sorry. I think the morphine is making me weepy."

He took her hand again and squeezed it.

The Girl in the Sand

"Almost forgot. Loshak wanted me to let you know he's taken care of everything. He's picking your mom up at the airport now."

Darger almost choked on her own tongue.

"My mother? Who called my mother?"

Owen put his hands up defensively.

"Don't look at me. That's all on your partner."

"Fuck me. She's going to flip when she sees my big ugly potato head."

They talked a little more, but eventually the morning round of narcotics started to kick in, and Darger started to fade.

"Trying to stay awake," she said, eyelids fluttering.

"Go ahead and sleep."

She felt Owen's lips brush the little scar near her eyebrow.

"I'll be here."

☽

When Darger woke again, Loshak was back in his chair, paper in hand. Her mother was there too, flitting around the room, fussing over her, over everything. She was too tired to make out the particulars of what her mom was saying, still fading in and out of consciousness for most of it. She was thankful for that.

Some time later, Owen came in, and that roused her some. She introduced him to her mother.

"I can't remember the last time I got to meet one of Violet's boyfriends."

Darger rolled her eyes.

"Oh Jesus. I thought maybe getting half my head blown off would get me some respite from the motherly nagging, but no."

Pursing her lips, Darger's mother turned and gave her a pointed look.

"I don't like that kind of talk."

"When did you get so devout?"

"Not that," her mother said, eyes starting to water. "That nastiness about your head getting blown off. It's not funny."

Owen, a southern gentleman all the way, guided her to a chair and helped her sit.

"I was so worried. And I couldn't get a flight! They kept putting me on standby, but all the planes were full. I finally had to fly all the way down to Dallas, but we were late, so I missed the connecting flight. It was a nightmare. And the whole time, I kept thinking about what if something happened, and I wasn't here."

Darger glanced at Loshak, trying to tell him with her eyes that he should get her mother out of here before she went into full hysterics. But he either didn't understand or was choosing to ignore her pleading looks.

"It's OK, mom. I'm OK."

"No, you're not!" she wailed. "Please tell me you're through with this, Violet. You promised me after Ohio that nothing like that would ever happen again, but since then your life has been one disaster after the next. You can't continue on like this. There are plenty of jobs at the FBI that don't put you in the... the line of fire like this."

Darger closed her eyes. She could explain to her mother that she might not have a choice. That if the doctors were right, if her left arm was lame or she needed a cane to walk, she wouldn't be allowed back in the field.

But her mother's talk only made her realize how committed

she was to her job. Not to the FBI, but to the victims. Fuck what the doctors said. She was going to do every damn thing she had to do to get back out there. It would take more than a bullet to the head to stop Violet Darger from hunting the Leonard Stumps of the world.

"Mom, can we not talk about this right now?"

Her mother swiveled in her seat, fixing her gaze on Loshak.

"You're her partner. Tell her. She never listens to me."

Loshak sighed.

"Ma'am, I hate to be the bearer of bad news, but she doesn't listen to anybody."

COME PARTY WITH US

We're loners. Rebels. But much to our surprise, the most kickass part of writing has been connecting with our readers. From time to time, we send out newsletters with giveaways, special offers, and juicy details on new releases.

Sign up for our mailing list at:
http://ltvargus.com/mailing-list

SPREAD THE WORD

Thank you for reading! We'd be very grateful if you could take a few minutes to review it on Amazon.com.

How grateful? Eternally. Even when we are old and dead and have turned into ghosts, we will be thinking fondly of you and your kind words. The most powerful way to bring our books to the attention of other people is through the honest reviews from readers like you.

ABOUT THE AUTHORS

Tim McBain writes because life is short, and he wants to make something awesome before he dies. Additionally, he likes to move it, move it.

You can connect with Tim via email at tim@timmcbain.com.

L.T. Vargus grew up in Hell, Michigan, which is a lot smaller, quieter, and less fiery than one might imagine. When not click-clacking away at the keyboard, she can be found sewing, fantasizing about food, and rotting her brain in front of the TV.

If you want to wax poetic about pizza or cats, you can contact L.T. (the L is for Lex) at ltvargus9@gmail.com or on Twitter @ltvargus.

LTVargus.com

Made in the USA
Coppell, TX
06 March 2020